CRCFELLOWSHIP
BURNABY
604 527 7200

PRAISE FOR *BILLY GOAT HILL*

"*Billy Goat Hill* is a poignant tale of a little boy's loss of innocence and his longing for redemption. It is a boy's search for God—and God's search for a little boy. Ultimately, *Billy Goat Hill* is a story about all of us. Mark Stanleigh Morris is a master storyteller who brilliantly displays the freedom that comes from forgiveness—forgiveness received and given. This is some of the truest Christian fiction I've ever read."

KYLE LIEDTKE, CHRISTIAN MEDIA CONSULTANT,
MEDIATALK COMMUNICATIONS

"Mark Stanleigh Morris has written a feel-good, make-you-cry, hope-and-tragedy, dramatic mystery adventure that packs an unexpected redemptive punch before letting you go. The fate and lives of *Billy Goat Hill*'s characters really hit home, from being skillfully crafted around the real-life events of the author's world. From start to finish *Billy Goat Hill* teases our minds and reaches deep into the good and evil realities of our human experience. I found it to be both very satisfying and well worth the time to discover the treasures of *Billy Goat Hill*."

CRAIG S. PREST, COFOUNDER OF UNREACHED NATIONS, INC.

"A remarkable tale that dives to the depths of utter hopelessness and despair and rises to the highest callings of human aspiration which lie at the heart of the word *forgiveness*. In a world full of hurting people, my prayer is that every single one would be blessed by this message of hope and inspiration."

DAVE ROGERS, SENIOR PASTOR,
FELLOWSHIP BIBLE CHURCH, BEND, OREGON

"*Billy Goat Hill* is a genuine and gripping slice of life. With God's grace and guidance, Mark Stanleigh Morris brings to light the key question for anyone challenged with past betrayal and loss. Can years of being harmed or harming others really be undone by a simple act of faith? The answer is not that harm can be undone, but that harm can be both redeemed and redeeming. A must-read for those of us seeking truth about God's plan for our lives regardless of the past."

SHELLEY MAURICE-MAIER, AUTHOR OF
THE SAMPLER: 10 LIFE ENHANCING CONCEPTS AT YOUR FINGERTIPS

"Possibly the greatest challenge God's people face is breaking down the wall that helps you to forgive and hinders you from being forgiven. Mark Stanleigh Morris clearly articulates through his nostalgic and descriptive writing style that, 'We must find a way to forgive, or we only end up blaming ourselves.' *Billy Goat Hill* is filled with real-life experiences that we all can relate to. This is one of those 'once you pick it up you won't put it down' books. It will literally change your life!"

DR. GARY L. PINION,
FOUNDER/PRESIDENT OF ENCOURAGEMENT DYNAMICS

"Mark Stanleigh Morris hasn't just created fascinating characters. He's given us authentic soul-searchers very much like those of us reading this book: honest and hopeful, yet sometimes wondering if inner peace in real life may be just outside our reach. Truly a remarkable story!"

DR. TED W. PAMPEYAN, LEADERSHIP RENEWAL CENTER

"*Billy Goat Hill* is an incredible story of the healing power of forgiveness, the great redeeming mercy of God, and the strengthening hope that accompanies salvation. No matter what life may have thrown your way, through this story you'll find encouragement and comfort that God truly does work in all things, even the deepest, darkest moments of life, for the good of those that love Him."

REVEREND JONATHAN HAYASHI, YOUTH PASTOR, CHRISTIAN
EDUCATION DIRECTOR—PLYMOUTH CONGREGATIONAL CHURCH

"Mark Stanleigh Morris's writing is very expressive and creative as he draws pictures for the reader's imagination and brings alive emotions for the soul to feast upon. By the time this heartfelt adventure concludes, one may likely discover new depths of God's love and forgiveness."

JERI PREST, COFOUNDER OF UNREACHED NATIONS, INC.

billy goat hill

A NOVEL

mark stanleigh morris

Multnomah® Publishers *Sisters, Oregon*

BILLY GOAT HILL
Published by Multnomah Publishers, Inc.

Published in association with Van Diest Literary Agency
© 2004 by Mark Stanleigh Morris
International Standard Book Number: 1-59052-406-3

Background cover image by American Stock Photography

Multnomah is a trademark of Multnomah Publishers, Inc.,
and is registered in the U.S. Patent and Trademark Office.
The colophon is a trademark of Multnomah Publishers, Inc.

Printed in the United States of America

For information:
MULTNOMAH PUBLISHERS, INC.
POST OFFICE BOX 1720
SISTERS, OREGON 97759

Library of Congress Cataloging-in-Publication Data

Stanleigh, Mark.
    Billy Goat Hill : a novel / Mark Stanleigh Morris.
        p. cm.
    "Published in association with Van Diest Literary Agency"—T.p. verso.
    ISBN 1-59052-406-3
    1. Boys—Fiction. 2. Brothers—Fiction. 3. Forgiveness—Fiction.
4. Los Angeles (Calif)—Fiction. I. Title.
PS3569.T33196B55 2005
813'.54—dc22

                                    2004028494

05 06 07 08 09 10—10 9 8 7 6 5 4 3 2 1

For my wife, Karen

ACKNOWLEDGMENTS

It is said novel writing is a solitary endeavor. It is also said no man is an island. Writing is solitary in nature, but no writer is an island. We collaborate on many levels. From the collective influences of environment and personal experience, to the support and encouragement of family and friends, to the technical review and advice of editors and publishers—we are helped with what we do. It is through this grand collaboration that *Billy Goat Hill* found its place in the sun, and I am thankful to many for their kind and generous help. Most of all, I thank my Lord Jesus.

Special thanks to those who were there for me in the early years, members of the Lake Tahoe Writer's Group and Silver State Fiction Writers; to Paul and Kim Morris for support and encouragement; to my agent David Van Diest for suggesting the rewrite and envisioning the perfect fit at Multnomah Publishers; to Don Jacobson and Doug Gabbert at Multnomah for seizing the moment and saying yes with conviction and enthusiasm; to my editors Julee Schwarzburg and Lisa Bowden for helping me reach higher than I ever could have without them; and to the rest of the wonderful staff at Multnomah who work so hard to keep your trust...one book at a time. God bless you one and all.

prologue

I never thought I'd live to see my fortieth birthday. I consider it a miracle that I survived past the age of ten, much less that I am here now, about to tell you my story. My memories of my childhood, vivid and detailed as they are, rise up from a deep and well-guarded place where innocence once dwelled. The thing is, innocence is like a hard shell surrounding a vulnerable yolk—eventually the shell must break. I don't mean to second-guess God, but some shells seem to break early, before we are prepared to deal with things profound and complex.

I have learned a thing or two, most important that we are born into this troubled world to learn about forgiveness—how to receive it and how to give it. I think this is the great opportunity of life.

I have come to know this, in part, because of a man I once knew. He was a Los Angeles city cop who gave me the best and the worst of all that he was. For a long time I tried to forget him, but he wouldn't let me. Something about falling face first into the open eyes of a dead man stays with you, no matter how hard you try to forget. Some things cannot be forgotten, but they can be forgiven. This is the hope of my heart. It is the reason I tell my story.

My name is Wade Parker, and I come from a place called Billy Goat Hill.

one

He's not breathing! Mom! Dad! Help! Matthew's not breathing! I scoop my baby brother up from his crib, his cold cheek pressing against my neck, and I run, and I run, and I run…tumbling headfirst into the treacherous deep of the Crippler.

Whee-e-e-e-chug-chug…Varoom!

I awake in a startle as the distinct ignition signature of Carl's 1955 Chevy Bel Air pummels the night calm. I gasp for air, my heart pounding, as the cracked windowpane next to my bed rattles like a snare drum from the percussion of badly corroded mufflers. I wipe away tears and whisper in the darkness, "I'm sorry, Matthew. Please forgive me."

Trembling, I sit up in bed and peer out the window as Carl puts the poor Chevy in gear. The transmission clanks and the car lumbers away from the curb. A trail of smoke lags behind the sickly sloth. The window by my bed hums louder, then gradually falls silent as I track the red glow of one working taillight until it fades into the night. This is the way it is, Carl rescuing me nearly every night.

The firing up of the Chevy means it is midnight, plus or minus one minute. Our next door neighbor, Carl, is a baker married to the night shift and the most punctual alcoholic I'll ever know. He isn't very keen on the virtues of preventive maintenance. His Chevy is not yet three years off the assembly line, and it already looks and sounds as decrepit as Betsy, our embarrassing-to-be-seen-in '40 Ford.

In the bed next to mine, my brother Luke sleeps on, snoring softly under his blanket. He is oblivious to the commotion of Carl's routine departure. Through the narrow dimness that separates our beds, I can just make out the top of Luke's red fuzzy head poking out from under his blanket.

Luke is something else, able to fall asleep at the snap of a finger and remain there in peaceful slumber until it's time to get up. He's like a light switch—off or on, awake or asleep, nothing in-between. I envy him. He doesn't lie awake worrying about things like I do.

I shiver, visualizing the Crippler as I listen to Carl drive off down the hill. Absently, I anticipate the screech of brake pad rivets scraping against pitted and scarred metal drums. I hear fingernails on a chalkboard and feel it in my teeth when Carl halts for the stop sign at the bottom of the hill.

Luke stirs not, and except for his rhythmic wheezing, the night reclaims its calm, which ushers the return of my worried state of mind. Irritated, lonely, I flip my pillow over to the cool side and lay my head back down. I close my eyes knowing there isn't enough time left to go back to sleep. Tossing and turning, listening to the quiet, I struggle in vain not to think about the Crippler. My mind swirls, searching for options that do not exist. I have to go through with it. I have to be a man and not back down.

But a larger dread, one bigger and far heavier than my immediate dilemma, has left me as weakened and tired as a fish slowly being starved of oxygen. *Keep swimming or you'll sink to the bottom and never come up. Things will get better*, I keep telling myself. But I feel like I am being tricked or duped by something I can't see, a dark and dangerous foe—one who follows no rules, observes no code, intends me great harm, and takes pleasure in my suffering. Playing upon my fears, the invisible darkness is slowly sapping my essence. It is a bad way to live, looking over your shoulder all the time.

I wish I had someone to talk to. I have questions, lots of questions…

Who am I?

Why am I here?

Can you hear me?

Please, I need answers.

I can't stand it any longer. Distracted, I get up and dress as quietly as possible, not daring to wake our mother, Lucinda, whom we regard with careful unease even when she is awake on account of her being sad or angry ever since our baby brother, Matthew, died.

Some nights I awaken to hear Lucinda crying in her room. I lie there and listen until my heart hurts so bad for her I tiptoe down the hall to her room and tap on her door. She never lets me in. "Go back to bed," is all she ever says, and I feel my dangerous foe pull me a little farther into the darkness.

Fully dressed, I am ready, but it is still too early to head out. For a while I just sit on my bed and watch Luke sleep. I do that a lot, just watch him sleep; hearing him breathing comforts me. Over and over I tell myself…*he won't stop breathing.*

The waiting gets to me, and I reach over and gently shake Luke's arm. "I'm already awake, you big donkey," he says grinning, and I feel a thousand percent better.

"Come on, Luke, hurry up!"

"Keep your shirt on. I can't find my other tennis shoe."

With one leg already hanging out of the bedroom window, I wave for him to follow. "Mac probably got your shoe again. Come on. I bet we'll find it in the garage."

Mac is asleep at the foot of my bed. His ears twitch at the mention of his name, and he lifts his head. He's mildly annoyed that we are once again stealing out into the night. It's two o'clock in the morning. Mac knows better than to bark, though. We do this kind of stealthy night crawling all the time.

Depending on his mood, Mac sometimes joins us on our nocturnal adventures. On this particular night, he opts to break the triad. Mac is very smart—he understands the concepts of culpability, accessory, and accomplice better than I do. I think he knows when we are up to no good. Besides, he manages to get himself into plenty of trouble without tagging along with us.

Luke complains while he hops across the dew covered lawn on one shoe. "Darn grass is wet."

I love him and all, in fact he is my best friend, but sometimes Luke can be a royal pain in the rump. I tell myself all little brothers are annoying sometimes.

Opening the side door to the garage, I pull up as hard as I can on the doorknob to silence the squeaky hinges. Garage smells wafting in the blackness—grease and turpentine mixed with the fragrance of fermenting grass on the old push mower—fill my nose as I step through the doorway.

I flick on my Flash Gordon flashlight and scan the oil-stained floor, then smile when I spot Luke's shoe lying next to Betsy's front wheel. "Like I told you, Red, there it is."

Luke balks, begrudging my intuitive powers. "You think you're so darn smart, Wade; how come you're not on *Ed Sullivan*?"

I am convinced Luke must be half myna bird. The way he mimics Lucinda can sometimes drive me up the wall.

"Maybe I'll be on TV someday." I jerk his brand-new Los Angeles Dodgers cap down over his eyes, and he swings at me in the dark, missing as usual. I pick up his errant sneaker, pooch out my mouth, plant my free hand on my hip, and try my best to sound like Ed Sullivan. "Tonight, ladies and gentlemen—we have a really, really, really big shoe."

"You don't even sound like him."

I toss him his sneaker. "Put your darn shoe on and let's get going. They're probably already waiting for us."

Luke methodically makes a bow with an over-long lace as I train the flashlight beam on his foot. He is only six years old and has yet to fully master the art of shoe tying. I wait patiently for him to finish. I have learned not to rush or bad-mouth his handiwork unless I am up for contending with his prickly temper. The opposite of me (the blond, blue-eyed, reserved older brother), Luke isn't the least bit shy about expressing himself. He is a redheaded firecracker and making him mad is not a good idea at this moment. If he makes a ruckus, we're sure to be discovered.

Back in the yard, we both jump when Mac materializes in front of us. He whines a little, as if to warn us not to go, then disappears into the inky black behind the garage.

"Darn dog! He's just going to do his duty."

"Shush, Luke. You wake up Lucinda and I'll tan you good, right after she tans the both of us."

He swings at me again.

Luke is quick to make judgmental or disparaging remarks about Mac. It is his way of clarifying his own position in the pecking order. I understand. But the fact is Mac, being the beneficiary of the best genes of the German shepherd and Doberman pinscher breeds, can make a snack out of little Luke anytime he cares to. Fortunately for Luke and me, Mac loves us more than…well, more than almost anything.

We're risking the skin off our behinds this night because I ran my mouth off, an unusual behavior for me.

I suppose it's not a bad thing to make bold and daring statements to an audience of admiring fellow daredevils, but it's not a good idea to do it in the middle of a crowded schoolyard when Guerrmo Francisco Torres Smith, Gooey for short, is standing right in front of you. Gooey is nine, a year older than me, and does not like the fact that I am a better cardboard slider than he is. He also carries a grudge against me for letting him take the blame for the green dye that mysteriously ended up in the Highland Park public pool last summer.

It wasn't enough for me to be the humble champion cardboard slider of Billy Goat Hill. No, I had to be prideful and brag that I could take the Crippler from top to bottom—IN THE DARK!

"Is that so?" Gooey had chided, challenging my outlandish claim.

Instantly I knew that I had messed up. Clamps of unease gripped my shoulders and I cleared my throat. "Yes, that is so, Gooey."

He grinned. "Well now—let me get this straight. You are actually claiming you can run the Crippler in the dark?"

"You heard me." I gave him a look that implored him not to push it any further. That was all he needed to drop the hammer.

He flashed a meaner grin. "So, for all these witnesses to hear...you are promising to run the Crippler in the dark. Is that right?"

"Yep."

"Well then, Wade Parker, Mr. Big Shot fancy pants champion cardboard slider—how about tonight then, say at about 2:15 or so? It should be quite a show. Maybe we can sell some tickets."

Sensing the brewing of something big, more kids had quickly gathered around us. Some of them were Billy Goat Hill regulars. And just like that, the cards were on the table. It was not possible for me to back down.

"My old man's out of town again..." I said with a measure of thespian couth. "...2:15 shouldn't be any problem at all."

"You are poco loco, man."

My own words had pricked at a raw corner of my heart. Despite his many faults, I sorely miss Earl, our antisocial, often drunk father. Soon it will be my birthday, and I know all the luck in the world won't help him remember it. The thought makes me angry. My eyes lock on Gooey and I spend an overdraft of gratuitous nonchalance.

"See you tonight then." I feel a new pain in my gut.

Like old west townsmen roused by talk of a showdown, the crowd stirs and murmurs with excitement. With controlled desperation, I scan the onlookers' faces, seeking their devotion, their genu-flection in the presence of their champion. But I find no loyalty in their eyes, only the lust to be entertained, to be thrilled. I have some-how created a circus and they want to see the lions eat the trainer, the fall of the trapeze artist, the fatal crash of the champion of Billy Goat Hill. Their aggrandized hero has learned a painful lesson—*Life is tough at the top.*

I do however spot one friendly soul in the shifting crowd. Luke, his freckly face beaming with adoration, his chest swollen with pride, gives me the strength I need to endure Gooey's relentless grin.

Cardboard sliding is a poor kid's version of bobsledding. Our modest bobsleds are nothing more than sturdy chunks of cardboard cut from the large boxes used for shipping new appliances, and our snow is the thick dry weeds and grasses native to the hilly surround-ings of Los Angeles.

Unlike real bobsleds, our cardboard bobsleds have no runners, no brakes and no steering mechanism. Directional control is mini-mal. You can shift the weight of your body by leaning left or right, or you can alternately drag your left or right foot, using them as rudimentary rudders—but only if you wear boots or at least hi-tops, lest you lose the meat off your ankles. Neither procedure does much to help steer. Mostly there is only one direction—down. And once you start down, with no brakes, there is no stopping. The most important objective is to stay on the cardboard while keeping the cardboard on the run. I have developed and perfected my tech-nique, but the truth is, cardboard sliding is far more art than science.

The Crippler is the longest, steepest, most dangerous run on Billy Goat Hill. Many of the kids refuse to try it at all. It got its name when an out of town boy foolishly made a headfirst run and ended up on a permanent wheelchair ride. The Crippler runs a course of about 350 feet with a total vertical drop of nearly 200 feet. What makes it dangerous are the jagged rocks, century plants, prickly pear cactus, tree stumps, rusted-out car bodies and assorted other debris that have been dumped down the incline by people too lazy or too cheap to haul their discards to the city dump. It's a sharply tilted minefield of natural and man-made hazards, any one of which holds disaster for the slider unfortunate enough to veer off course. The Crippler is the best of the myriad runs that mark the variant slopes of Billy Goat Hill. You couldn't design a better ride if you tried—the perfect dare for young boys bucking for manhood.

It is almost 2:30 when Luke and I make it to the top of Billy Goat Hill. Luke plops down on a rock next to me, catching his breath. "We should have brought Mac with us to help tow the box up the hill."

Luke often comes up with good ideas after the fact. I don't say anything.

With a razor knife I have indefinitely borrowed from Sal's, our neighborhood liquor store, I trim up the water heater box to form a bottom, two sides, and a front. It looks like a square-nosed canoe with its back end cut off. I am not planning to use my feet as rudders, if I can help it.

Luke and I drag the canoe over to the top of the Crippler and find a good spot to sit and wait for the other kids to show up. I am surprised that none of them are here yet, especially Gooey, although it is common knowledge that his mom often has to throw cold water on him to wake him up for school. I try not to think about the reckless stunt awaiting me.

The low clouds hanging over the City of Angels this night are a disappointment—no stars to tickle my imagination, no Dippers to trace, no moon to make faces at. It is almost cool enough for long sleeves, but we are sweating after lugging the water heater box up the hill. We take our jackets off and let the night air cool us down. I look at Luke in his sneakers, blue jeans, and horizontal striped T-shirt, and realize that except for his red hair and my blond hair, he is the spitting image of me. We are a couple of matching goslings astray from the goose. I tug his Dodgers cap down over his eyes again. He swings and misses again.

We are still buzzing from the excitement of seeing our first big league baseball game, the first game of the Los Angeles, by way of Brooklyn, Dodgers. Seeing the game hadn't been easy. Without Lucinda's permission and with no tickets in hand, Luke and I, a pair of pikers with a plan, ventured across Los Angeles by city bus and stole like rats up a gangplank into the Coliseum. *Rattis Gangplankis.* It has a nice ring to it. That or something like it is probably what my teacher, Mrs. Barr, would call us. She aspires to be a Professor of Latin at UCLA and often practices her gobbledygook on our class. Even the Catholic kids who are used to hearing Latin at mass think she is weird. I like her, though.

Luke has been jabbering about the game all day. "Man, I've never seen so many people in one place before. That Coliseum is huge, huh?"

"Yeah, it's colossal. It sure was lucky Davenport forgot to touch third base, because when Mays knocked in Kirkland the game would have been tied up."

Luke rolls his eyes. "What a pity for the Giants."

"Yeah, the Dodgers rule."

Luke nods and yawns. "I used to like the Chicago Cubs best, but now we have our own team. Who's your favorite player?"

"Come on, Luke, you know the answer to that one—the one and only Duke Snider, the greatest player in the game today."

"I like Charlie Neal the best. When I grow up I want to play second base just like Charlie Neal."

The conversation is helping keep my mind off the Crippler.

I look at Luke and chuckle a little to myself. He's thinking about being as good as Charlie Neal, and he can't even catch or throw well enough to play catch with me yet. Actually, I'm not much better than he is, and before too long he'll probably be a better ball player than me. I doubt he'll ever be as good a cardboard slider, though.

I love talking baseball with Luke, although sometimes it leads to arguments.

"You know what's weird, Luke?"

"Nuh uh." His eyes droop as he pulls his coat over himself like a blanket.

"Hank Sauer hit two home runs for the Giants and he only lives a couple of miles from the Coliseum. Sauer should be playing for the Dodgers."

Luke nods again, but I doubt that he is listening. A minute later his eyelids slip shut and his mouth falls open. His chest slowly expands and contracts with the well-paced rhythm of sleep. My faithful understudy is officially off duty. I pull his cap down softly over his eyes. He doesn't swing at me.

My Howdy Doody watch reads 2:45 as I lean back against the same rock Luke is nuzzling. He is snoring in his typical cat purring way. I rest my head on the rock and gaze up at the clouded charcoal sky. Deep and dark, the expanse appears to swell like the ocean. I watch from my weed-covered crow's-nest, alert for whales, or the welcoming twinkle of a lighthouse, or maybe even pirates. Off to the southwest, a billow of low-hanging clouds radiates like a giant efflorescent night flower enchanted with the nocturnal glow of downtown Los Angeles.

I sit unafraid in the dark, watching over Luke and partnering with the sky for a while. Luke's snoring seems to call the crickets to song, and soon a soothing chorus of nature's music surrounds me. *He's breathing.*

As I often do, I begin to think about poor Matthew again—he only lived fifty-five days. The memory makes my eyes water. I wish again that I had heard him cough or choke, something, anything that might have brought me running. A big brother is supposed to protect his little brothers.

How can a happy, healthy baby just stop breathing in the middle of an innocent nap? I don't get it. I don't think I ever will.

We are all badly wounded, but no one more deeply than Lucinda. Overcome by the anguish of losing her baby, she has taken refuge in a long, sad silence. Earl is messed up pretty bad, too. He took off not long after Matthew died. In a way, Lucinda is also gone, except her kind of gone is worse. It's right there for you to see.

I do understand one thing, though—Lucinda's pain. Now she works all of the time, and when she is home she cleans. All the time cleaning. I think she does it to keep her mind off of Matthew, and maybe to keep her mind off of hating God so much. I heard her tell Earl she hated God. Earl just grunted and didn't say anything back to her.

I don't hate God for anything. How can I hate someone I don't even know? I give the sky a longing glance.

Things didn't start out all that bad for Luke and me. We don't have much, more than some. But it isn't material things we miss. Sometimes I think it would be better if there had been no love at all. To have it and lose it is worse than never having it in the first place.

Before the bad things happened, there was some good. Our parents were together and happy, so I believed; though Earl drank too much and Lucinda would never be nominated for mother of the year. But we were a family, and in that family is where I belonged. I felt safe. When Matthew died the family seemed to die with him. I wish I could feel safe again.

My father will come back some day. He knows the way home. Lucinda is the lost one, and I have to try to help her the only way I can, by seeing to it that Luke and I look out for each other. I must take better care of Luke than I did Matthew.

Sitting here next to Luke, I close my eyes and see myself standing at the trailhead to a vast wilderness, the netherworld of my remaining childhood. The path leads straight into that tricky darkness, but I see no other route. I am scared, but I must go forward into the unknown and take whatever comes. They say what doesn't kill you makes you stronger. Well, I sure hope things don't get worse.

Loneliness sets me adrift on thoughts of my father. *Where are you, Earl?* For a second my spirit seems pulled skyward, and I vaguely sense something stir within me, a small comforting sent from afar, perhaps. But it's not enough. I want more. My arms wrap around me in a self-consoling hug, and remembering the last time I saw him, I begin to smile inside.

He said I was shooting up faster than July corn. We wrestled on the grass in front of the house, Mac barking and playfully nipping at my feet. Earl tickled my ribs and tossed me up in the air so high I could see all kinds of stuff scattered on the porch roof. And I couldn't stop laughing because everything was so great, even with his whisky breath blowing right in my face. I miss him more than I ever let on to Luke.

Why did he leave us, God? An ache in my chest closes the door on those thoughts. I guess some things can't be comforted.

Gooey's goading me to run the Crippler in the dark, to put my cardboard where my mouth is, has coiled my nerves up tight. As I look toward the night heavens, the tension slowly dissolves in a wash of fantasy—me and Duke Snider taking batting practice, shooting the breeze, slowly gearing up to rip the hide off of anything dumb enough to be low and away.

What would it be like to be Duke Snider's son?

A small break in the clouds appears directly overhead just in time for me to see a shooting star through the opening. Shooting stars are wondrous things. Hey, maybe it's Sputnik? After a moment I reject the notion. No satellite would be big enough for me to see without a telescope.

I lie here next to Luke feeling oddly content for the moment. A red flashing light wanders across the opening in the clouds. Nothing more than a common airplane. Or could it be—a Russian spy plane?

I think about our next-door neighbor, Carl the baker. Carl is famous for sitting on his front porch drinking beer and warning the neighbors about the dangers of communism. He calls them rotten Ruskies, cowardly commies, or just plain dirty reds, and he claims they are out to take over America. Sometimes he curses out loud and mutters that the only good thing about the commies is that they make decent rye bread. His mournful complaining grows louder and louder with each bottle of beer. Finally, after ten or twelve empties—which he calls dead soldiers—are lined up in a row on his porch rail, he launches into a medley of his favorite flag-waving songs. His deep, baritone voice, reminiscent of Tennessee Ernie Ford, booms throughout the neighborhood.

Eventually, his wife convinces him to come inside and go to bed, after which she hastily makes the sign of the cross, collects up the beer bottles, and closes the drapes in her front window.

We think old Carl is terrific entertainment, but his behavior must embarrass his poor wife. There is something different about her. I don't even know her name, but I do know she is patient with Carl and very kind-hearted. When she heard about Matthew, she left flowers and a sympathy card with a picture of Jesus on it on our front porch. The only time I ever saw Earl break down and cry was when he brought the flowers and the Jesus card in the house and gave them to Lucinda. I sat next to him on the couch, and he let me hold his hand for a while.

The hole in the clouds suddenly gets bigger, and I begin to play connect the dots with the stars. Luke continues harmonizing with the cricket choir while Duke Snider comforts my heart with whispers of baseball inside my head.

The cardboard canoe sits poised at the top of the Crippler thirty feet from where Luke and I nestle together in the dark. I can just make out its shape. My watch now says 3 a.m., and I allow myself to believe Gooey and his friends aren't going to show up. I did show up though, and that's all that matters to me.

Baloney! I am glad they didn't show up!

It's funny though, as I sit here with my thoughts, I start to wonder if I really have the guts to make the slide in the gloom of night. But if I do it now, no one will see. Nobody will believe me. Even if I wake Luke up to watch, he doesn't qualify as a reliable witness on account of his being my brother.

Gosh...do I really want to go down the Crippler in the dark? It's nutty! So this is why Gooey calls me *poco loco:* a little bit crazy. He's right. I seriously contemplate getting in the canoe and shoving off, until a picture of me stretched out on top of a cactus patch like an Indian guru painfully prostrated on a bed of nails flashes through my mind.

How about them Dodgers.

Wow! Another shooting star descends into nothingness. The next time I see Carl I'm going to tell him I saw the Russian's Sputnik over Billy Goat Hill. That ought to make him sing. I smile and chuckle to myself. Could I get Carl to sing "Take Me Out to the Ball Game"? I picture myself sitting side by side with Duke Snider in the Dodgers' dugout.

I am a dreamer. I love to dream. Dreaming is like delicious medicine, it's tasty and good for you. Some people claim they can go back to sleep and finish a dream if they wake up in the middle of it. Well, I can do something even better than that. I can actually decide about what I want to dream and then dream it, almost like picking out a movie before going to the theater. Sometimes my dreams don't turn out exactly the way I plan, though. For example, if I intend to take flight on a magic carpet, I might find myself soaring above the clouds on a braided throw rug with floppy pelican wings. It is a matter of concentration.

Before Earl left, I rarely had nightmares—even my monsters would crack jokes. But I don't seem to have good dreams as much anymore. Sometimes I wonder if something is broken inside of me.

When I do have a good dream, it's often about playing ball with my teammate Duke Snider. I am always the youngest professional baseball player in history, and I always play for the Dodgers. Any position I feel like playing is always fine with the team, and we always win the game in the ninth inning with me on base and Duke smashing an awesome game winning homer.

I concentrate on making a picture of a ballpark in my mind. I can hear the announcer reading the starting line up. As I walk out of the dugout onto the field, I look up to see Earl in the stands, drunk, but clapping enthusiastically. Luke and the crickets drone on as soothing as a cradlesong and soon, I too am fast asleep—dreaming.

I have no idea how much my life is about to change.

two

Seals Stadium, San Francisco. It's windy and colder than a well digger's behind. We're in the top of the ninth with two outs, and we are down by one run. I'm pumped up, ready to explode toward second base, but holding a cautious lead off first. Duke Snider is at the plate with a count of two and one. His confidence is enough for both of us. I scan for the sign…Duke is swinging away. I visualize a hanging curveball and wonder if Duke is thinking the same. The pitcher stares in to the catcher, nods, and grinds his back foot hard on the rubber. He goes into his stretch, gives me a look, and then fires the ball…

From somewhere deep within my dull slumber a jarring rumble begins. My neck muscles tense and jerk, banging my head against the rock backrest that Luke and I have been sharing. Confusion reigns as a cloud of choking dust blows over me. For a dizzy second I think I've been picked off, caught leaning the wrong way, dust flying in a desperate lunge back to first base. What the heck? That's not supposed to happen! Stop the dream!

Lights lambaste my face, overwhelming my sleepy eyes. One arm goes up to ward off the brightness while the other slaps futilely at the smothering dust. My ears itch and my entire body vibrates from a bombarding roar. Luke is awake too, his fingernails like talons digging hard into my thigh. I know I am screaming, but the sound is swallowed up in a terrible thunder.

Dust billows away as a jet-black tire wrapped around a gleaming silver wheel stabs out at me on a long chrome fork no doubt belonging to the devil himself. The tire stops about an inch from the toes of my well-worn sneakers, which now appear like the witch's feet did sticking out from under the house that fell on her in *The Wizard of Oz*. And she was dead!

Luke's feet snap back under his thighs in a flash. Defenseless against this unimaginable intrusion, we huddle together quivering. Playing possum except for my eyes, I scan the periphery and count sixteen choppers belonging to a gang of murderous gargoyles known to us locals as Satan's Slaves. I have a powerful urge to pee as Custer's ghost, thorny with arrows, smiling sympathetically, looms out of the thickening background.

The last Harley quits dieseling and chokes itself mute. The chorus of crickets is already halfway to San Bernardino County. Now the silence is deafening.

"Well, well, well…this here is what you call an unexpected complication. It appears we've got ourselves a couple of party crashers!" the gang's leader barks.

He reminds me of the drawings of Stone Age cavemen that I studied last year in second grade. Except this brute wears classic biker togs—black engineer boots, greasy blue jeans, no shirt, a silver-studded black leather belt with a matching scabbard sheathing a Buck knife as long as my arm, and a black leather jacket. A red bandanna tied around his head somehow fails to keep his oily black hair out of his eyes.

I catch myself staring at the ugliest scar I've ever seen. A puffy groove of recent origin slashes from above his left eye, across the bridge of his nose, under his right eye, and down his cheek where it finally hooks under his right earlobe. The scar makes his beard part in a funny way. No, not funny, scary. I am trembling.

"My name's Scar!"

I blink uncontrollably. "Uh huh."

"What's yours?"

His dark hooded eyes bore deep into my soul, and I have to look away. I am about a mile short on nerve, an inch away from tears, and my throat has turned to sandpaper. "Uh…my name—is Wade—sir." Minnie Mouse sounds like a baritone compared to me. I feel Luke trying to squeeze himself between me and the rock.

Scar snickers in a way that I take as scorn. "Wade, you say?"

"Uh huh—" *gulp*—"Wade Parker, sir." I dare to look at him. Scar's eyes never leave mine as he bites off the end of a new cigar and spits it to the ground. I take it he could just as easily do the same with my head. My stomach squirms.

Slowly shifting his gaze, he scrutinizes Luke's exposed hindquarter like a vulture ogling carrion before the feast. "What's that hiding behind you?"

His deep voice rattles me up and down with chills, and when I don't immediately answer, he flicks his eyes back on me, the more appealing hunk of sustenance, and angrily jams the cigar in his mouth.

Magically, a Zippo lighter appears already aflame, a living creature anticipating its master's every wish. Trembling, I watch as Scar puffs hard, engulfing his head in a glowing fog of pungent amber smoke. The luminous cloud queerly pulses in the capricious licking fire of the lighter. My heart trips in sympathy with the hypnotic flame as the fissure dominating Scar's face catches and spills the light, casting an evil liquid shadow across his face. He brandishes his disfigurement like a weapon, a sign of absolute invincibility. I see Frankenstein's monster in the flesh, and intimidation stabs me with a syringe full of paralyzing fear, making me inert, and incapable of further speech.

A woman straddling the banana seat behind Scar looks over his shoulder at me. Her face captures some of the flickering light, startling me. I hadn't noticed her before due to the harsh glare of the motorcycle headlights. I squint to get a better look, and she immediately acknowledges me with a scintillating smile.

Gosh, she is pretty. No, more than pretty—lovely. I begin to thaw, to relax. I can't help myself. I smile back at her for a second or two until a spurt of instinct or just plain providence makes my eyes dart away. It can't possibly be prudent to smile at Scar's woman.

Scar grunts at me, a sovereign wild boar barking a dismissive command to an inferior male. "What's the matter, cat got your tongue?"

The woman distracts me, causing my comprehension to lag a couple of beats behind my hearing. "Beg your pardon, sir?"

Scar grins, the expression making him look almost handsome. I wish he'd keep the smile permanently because he doesn't look nearly so dangerous that way.

"Pardon you for what? We haven't tried and convicted you for anything yet. I asked you who that is hiding behind you there." He cocks his head slightly to get a better visual angle on Luke.

The presence of the woman somehow makes me feel safer, less threatened. "Oh. Sorry, sir. That's my brother, Luke. He's scared. He's only six."

"Look at them sitting there—oh, aren't they just the picture of innocence," the lovely lady gushes, further diluting the oppressive tension surrounding me.

With a burst of enthusiasm, she swings her long legs to the ground and lithely slips herself off Scar's Hog. Now I can see her completely awash in the motorcycle lights. *Wow!* She is stunning. Her hair, thick and golden blond, flows nearly to her waist. She's wearing brown leather boots that run up to her knees where white riding pants take over and cover her up to her waist. Draping from her shoulders, a pale blue gypsy blouse plunges to a snug fit around her waist, which seems tiny behind a big glimmering belt buckle. Her silky mane glows in an amorphous circle surrounding her angelic face. A beauty queen she is, and for a moment she seems to pose in front of the motorcycle lights like an actress dramatically lingering in the focus of stage lights.

Somehow I scrounge up the courage to smile at her again. I feel a little woozy, spellbound.

She starts toward us, but Scar grabs her arm. "You best be careful, Miss Cherry." He playfully pats her behind. "You never can be too sure. Even this sorry looking pair of squatters could be dangerous."

The gang enjoys a hearty laugh while several more women riders dismount and come toward us. I dare to stand up as she approaches, Luke rising up with me like my shadow. Gosh, she is even prettier up close.

"How old are you, honey?"

Miss Cherry posed the question to me, but in my starstruck state Luke gets the jump on me. "He's eight. He thinks he's some kind of big shot."

The gang laughs again. I give Luke a discreet elbow in the ribs.

"What are you guys doing up here at four o'clock in the morning?"

She steps closer and I notice her perfume, inhale a little deeper. Unlike the male members of the gang, Miss Cherry is clean and—lovely.

Luke allows me to answer this time. "We got up at two, ma'am. We were supposed to meet some of our friends here."

"What on earth for?" She casts a quizzical smile back to Scar.

Scar chimes in. "Yeah, what are you guys planning?"

"Nothing much, really."

Loud-mouthed little Luke steps on my words again. "He was gonna run the Crippler in the dark." He blurts it out before I can get my hand over his mouth. He shoves my arm away and glares at me.

Miss Cherry smiles sweetly at Luke. "What's the Crippler?"

"It's over there." Luke points past me toward the cardboard canoe.

Scar gets off his chopper and strolls over to the cardboard box, his heavy biker boots kicking up puffs of dust. He looks over the ledge and squints into the black.

Miss Cherry walks over next to him and peers down the slope. "Oh my gosh!" She eases back from the ledge and stares at me.

My cocky smile shows up unannounced, the same one that got

me into this predicament when I mouthed off to Gooey. Miss Cherry starts giggling, and again I can't help noticing her unusual beauty in the headlights as she walks back toward me.

Her thickly painted eyebrows arch up into upside down V's. "Were you really going to slide off that cliff in the dark?"

"Well, ma'am, yes I was. But Gooey, the kid who challenged me, hasn't shown up yet."

Several in the gang chuckle suggesting I lack nerve. One of them says, "He's afraid," but Miss Cherry spins around and hushes him.

"I'm not afraid to go down that hill."

Luke is a little miffed, too. "Wade isn't afraid of the Crippler. He's the champion of Billy Goat Hill."

With that the whole gang roars. Luke snarls at them, not understanding what is so funny.

Scar seems riled. "The heck you say? I thought I was the boss of this hill."

"This boy is claiming your turf, Scar!"

"Yeah. What are you gonna do about it, Scar?" chimes a big fat biker wearing a chrome Nazi helmet with a spearhead on top.

The gang passes around assorted snickers and guffaws, and even Miss Cherry can't resist another giggle as she turns to look at Scar. He tries to be serious and play along, but when he looks over at me, the sight is more than he can take. My failure to appreciate their humor apparently has my face looking as stern as a consti-pated preacher, and he lets go and laughs out loud.

Although still very frightened, I begin to feel that we probably aren't in any serious danger. Each one of these marauders looks like he would slit his own mother's throat for a cold beer, but in my gut I don't feel they intend to harm us.

Scar finally gets the laugh out of his system. "Hey, kid, come over here. I want to ask you a serious question." He sucks hard to restart the cigar that almost extinguished during his fit of laughter.

I move only a couple of hesitant shuffles in his direction.

"Go on." Miss Cherry gives me a gentle push. "He won't hurt you."

Reluctantly, I ease myself over next to him. Luke, no longer my twin shadow, opts to stay by Miss Cherry, and she promptly puts her arm over his shoulders.

I decide it can't hurt to be respectful. "Yes, sir?" I can tell he likes being called *sir*, so I say it again. "Yes, sir?"

"That's one heck of a drop down there." He looks at me and gulps for dramatic effect, cigar smoke puffing from his nostrils, and then resumes looking down the pitch-black slope.

"It is pretty steep, sir."

"No telling what you might run into."

"The trick is to stay on the cardboard."

He flips me an admiring glance and then quietly, so the others can't hear, he asks, "Do you really think you can run the Crippler in the dark?"

"If I can't, nobody can. I'm the champion of Billy Goat Hill."

He smiles, and with his eyes growing big, he adopts a melodramatic tone. "You could get hurt real bad. Maybe even kilt."

I giggle when he says *kilt*. It reminds me of the actor Fess Parker speaking in the voice of Davy Crockett. "I've been hurt before."

He leans closer and whispers, "Or even worse—you could get paralyzed."

"Paralyzed?"

In an explosive change of direction, he yells over my head, making me jump so I darn near go down the Crippler without the cardboard canoe right then. "Hey, Cherry! What's that called that happened to Moose Bachman when he crashed his Hog up on the Angeles Crest last summer, para-something?"

Geez. My ears are ringing.

"The word is *paraplegic*, baby."

Scar shakes his head. "Moose is a real sad case now, Wade. Poor guy can't even use the restroom without some help." He sighs, and his face shifts to a pained expression that makes the ghastly gash fold in a zigzag across his cheek.

Curiously, now I feel good. Mr. Scar is talking to me as if I were one of his gang members and not just a rambunctious eight-year-old daredevil out on a moonlight run. "Poor Moose," I solemnly concur.

"There won't be any more manly business for Moose either. Myself, I'd rather be dead." He shakes his head some more.

His directness catches me a little off guard, but I notice that Miss Cherry doesn't seem to mind. As a denizen of the wrong side of the tracks, I am familiar with most of the slang terms for sex. And I have learned better than to make inappropriate utterances in the presence of a grown woman. A year ago, Lucinda overheard me saying the "F" word, and being a disciplinarian inclined to proverbial remedies, she helped me experience how long it takes to get the foul flavor of soap out of your mouth.

"I don't know anything about manly business, sir."

Scar chokes on a puff of cigar smoke and laughs. He playfully slugs my shoulder. "No, I don't imagine you do."

Just then, one of the bikers hollers from the back of the pack. "Hey, Scar! The cops are coming!"

Everybody turns to look.

In the dark-filled distance, a red emergency light crawls along a rutted firebreak that runs up the knobby north side of Billy Goat Hill. Several of the bikers grumble their displeasure over the impending visit with LA's men in blue; a few laugh. However, none make any effort to leave. My gut tells me this is not a good sign. Scar shows no reaction at all, which in itself is a disturbing reaction.

He turns his powerful gaze back on me. "You guys better make yourselves scarce. The cops won't take kindly to finding you two out here with us, especially in the middle of the night like this." He nudges me to get moving.

"Come on, Luke."

I am not interested in the cops finding us out here, period. Our nocturnal habits have thus far gone undetected by our most immediate form of authority, namely Lucinda Parker. If she ever finds out we are sneaking out at night, there will be serious consequences.

There is a small outcropping of rock about thirty feet down

from the top of the Crippler, a nook custom made for hiding two young boys. I heave the cardboard canoe over the edge and motion to Luke to go ahead of me.

Scar watches while we slide down to the rocks and secrete ourselves behind a jagged boulder. I look up the slope and he pats his lips with his forefinger. I wave to him, acknowledging the universal sign of silence, and lower my head like an Indian brave preparing to ambush a paleface cavalry scout.

Luke's head bobs up like a curious prairie dog sniffing the wind, and I have to yank him down behind the rock with me. He is hypnotized by the flashing red light, which now washes over the hill in surreal waves the color of blood.

This moment, a mere wink in time, burns deeply into my psyche. A fantasia of impressions and emotions crystal clear in every detail is locked into my memory forever. The smell of the weeds, the gritty dust in my mouth, the break in the low hanging clouds directly overhead, the shattering red bursts of the police cruiser's emergency flasher igniting across Scar's muscular torso—all will be relived time and time again.

Oh my gosh! What have I gotten us into?

A black-and-white 1956 Ford police cruiser pulls to a dusty stop among the enclave of two-wheeled rebels. I can just see over the top of the rise above me and observe the upper bodies of the bikers and the top half of the police car. The crickets have returned, adding a dramatic whirring meter to the scene. The air feels hot and charged with electricity, as if the potential for violence is packing the oxygen molecules tighter and tighter, creating the heat of friction. Current skitters over my dampened skin, giving me chills, while my breathing squeezes down into shallow, rapid pants. My terrified heart drums loud in my ears, a frenzied drum…a drum of war.

I am as scared as I have ever been in my entire life. But at the same time I am consumed by an intoxicating fascination for the show. A libertine grin beams forth revealing my jangled emotions…

I want to leave. I want to stay. But this time the theater has been locked from the outside. Man oh man…this is better than a John Wayne double feature at a drive-in theater. Even popcorn, bonbons, and a ten-cent Butterfinger couldn't make it better!

Everything stands still as though the forces of nature have converged on this historic site to impose a pax, to hold the fiasco back, to force reconsideration before untold tragedy lays waste to this no-man's-land.

The group trance breaks when two uniformed officers burst from the patrol car. They do not look happy, particularly the one who slams his door and stomps toward Miss Cherry. His rigid comportment and piercing glare warn of vested anger aching for release.

"Lieutenant Theodore Shunkman," Miss Cherry spews. "How nice it is to see you out and about on this lovely evening."

Her sarcasm is venomous as she defiantly throws her head back, tossing her long blond hair over her shoulders like a high-strung filly whipping its tail. Some of the bikers chuckle in a way that is clearly intended to needle the cops.

Scar stays at the top of the Crippler directly above where Luke and I cower in the dark. I hope his plan is to guard us and make sure we remain safe. Glancing nervously from the center of the action to Scar and back, I am thankful he has chosen to stay close by.

Without warning, Lieutenant Shunkman grabs Miss Cherry by the arm and drags her over near Scar. I duck, and for a second I fear the irate cop has seen me. But he is blinded by his anger, oblivious to everything except Miss Cherry and Scar, who is standing completely unperturbed with his arms casually folded across his chest. The back of my neck bristles, and my cheeks are hot. I do not like this cop one bit.

"How's it going, Shunkman?" Scar inquires dispassionately, outwardly not offended in the slightest by the cop's rough treatment of his girlfriend. I am dead certain he is ready to kill, though.

"Let go of me!" Miss Cherry struggles for a moment, then manages to break free of the cop's humiliating grip.

I am astounded when she doesn't move away from him. Instead, she leans right in and swears at him, something long and vile that makes me cringe, and then she plasters him with a haughty, defiant glare.

The other cop, a baby-faced rookie, positions himself at the open door of the squad car. The motor is idling, and occasional unintelligible squawks blare out from the police radio. Everything about the young cop—uniform, shoes, leather, even his haircut—appears new and clean-cut in a fresh-out-of-the-academy textbook sort of way. At the moment, however, the rookie appears as nervous as a mouse surrounded by a pride of pugnacious alley cats.

His stance is tentative, and his collegial face is gaunt with fear as he obviously struggles to find the poise that has so recently been drilled into him. His eyes blink and twitch as they dart around the group of bikers, all of whom remain steadfast upon their imposing chrome mounts. One of the bikers hawks up a wad of phlegm and spits it onto the hood of the police car.

I imagine the rookie cursing himself for not calling for backup when they first spotted the motorcycle gang. Even from this distance, I can see rivulets of sweat trickling down his forehead as he repeatedly brushes his arm against his side, double-, triple-, quadruple-checking that his service revolver is where it is supposed to be. He reminds me of Mac during a thunderstorm—desperate for something to crawl under.

Lieutenant Shunkman ignores Miss Cherry's invective and reels around to face down Scar. His malignant profile throbs crimson with each slapping pass of the whirling emergency beacon. His eyes are death daggers, eminently threatening. On the brink of detonation, he clenches his fists and steps within punching distance.

Unbelievably, Scar just stands there twiddling his thumbs like a bored third cousin at a family reunion. He remains completely cool, apparently not worried in the slightest by the policeman's menacing approach. I am dumbfounded, exasperated.

Like the poisonous spit of a viper, saliva sprays from Shunkman's mouth as he rails at Scar. "I told you before, loser! I don't want my sister hanging around with the pathetic likes of you!"

Sister?

A chilly silence closes in.

Scar doesn't move a muscle. Impalpably at first, his face blossoms into a tantalizing smirk. "Cherry does what she pleases—and she does *it* very well. Ain't that right, boys!"

The gang hoots and hollers their agreement, and Scar's smirk ripens into an all-knowing grin that is so specific even I resent the salacious implication.

Lieutenant Shunkman's face flashes a gangrenous purple, and he lunges at Scar. Miss Cherry screams, and several of the bikers dismount in blurs of motion, all of them instantly ready to take action. With the speed of a mongoose anticipating the serpent's strike, Scar shifts his weight and effortlessly pins Shunkman's left arm behind his back. A look of shock quickly turns into a grimace as Scar forcefully restrains him.

I bite down on my lip, squelching a cheer that nearly bursts from my mouth. I taste blood, and I am transformed into one of the old west townsmen delirious with the thrill of violence.

A heartbeat passes.

O God, please stop this!

The young rookie panics and reaches for his gun, then instantly checks himself when he sees two sawed-off shotguns already set to blast him in half.

"That's the funny thing about fear!" Scar yells to the rookie. "It seizes you like some kind of two-part poison! A frigid-hot fever makes you shiver and sweat and makes your brain skip between conflicting impulses to hide or jettison all cargo and flee!"

The rookie, whose jaw has dropped to the ground, is stunned beyond belief. So am I. Now I'm squeezing Luke's leg, making him whimper. Realizing I am hurting him, I relax my quivering hand and fight back the urge to jettison the contents of my stomach. I want to run from this place. I do not want to witness the cataclysmic conclusion of the big-league conflict rising only a few yards from where I hide shivering in the dark.

But the tears welling up in Luke's little frightened eyes and my keen awareness of the ominous hazards of the only escape route possible force me to hunker down, close my eyes, and wish that we were back home safe and sound in our cozy little beds.

Please, God, stop this madness before it's too late!

Then miraculously, the entire temper changes. It's as if we've been watching a Boris Karloff horror classic and in the blink of an eye Bugs Bunny appears and sticks carrots into both barrels of Elmer Fudd's shotgun. Some creative film splicing has reversed the action and thrown us into another dimension where absolutely nothing makes any sense whatsoever.

Suddenly, Scar is smiling, Lieutenant Shunkman is grinning, and Miss Cherry is doubled over with laughter. In fact, everyone is in stitches except the rookie cop, Luke, and me. The next thing I know, Luke and I are standing at the top of the Crippler, and from the look of incredulity on Lieutenant Shunkman's face, we must appear to him like matching pint-sized apparitions materializing out of thin air.

"What in the heck are they doing here?"

I am dumbstruck, though amazingly Luke seems to warm to the festivities.

"Meet the Parker brothers," Miss Cherry says. "That's Luke there with the Dodgers cap, and next to him is Wade, aka the champion of Billy Goat Hill."

"Hellfire, Cavendish! These boys are gonna have to forget all about what they saw up here tonight. Our unit is under enough scrutiny these days. The last thing I need is a couple of nosey street urchins gettin' an eyeful of things not meant to be seen." Shunkman grumbles, shaking his head.

Scar steps over by me. "Don't worry, Ted. The Parker brothers are stand-up guys. Ain't that right, boys?"

"Yes, sir," I reply, completely bewildered but certain that yes is the only viable response.

Lieutenant Shunkman gives me a long skeptical dead-in-the-eye stare and then plods back to the patrol car, slapping a few high-fives with the leather-clad heathens in his path. He gets in behind the wheel and then stares back at me again until I have to look away.

He kills the flashing light overhead and testily addresses the nerve-wracked rookie now slumped in the passenger seat. "In case you're missing them, here's your bullets, rook. Now, if you think you can handle it, let's go find some coffee and talk about what we learned tonight."

Glancing out the window at me one last time, Lieutenant Shunkman turns the patrol car around. The bikers slap its hood and fenders to further taunt the chagrined young cop, who has slipped even farther down in his seat.

Slowly, the cruiser jostles back down the same rutted slope it ascended earlier. I watch it slither off into the darkness and struggle to restart my heart and make sense of the nonsensical. One thing I'm sure of…something about that Lieutenant Shunkman doesn't sit right with me. He's left me shivering inside.

Miss Cherry sidles over and scoops Luke up in her arms. I rarely feel jealous of Luke, but at this moment I do. I want her to pick me up, too.

Scar puts his arm around my shoulders. "You okay, kid?"

"Yes, sir."

I do my best to keep a stiff upper lip, but he can tell I am upset. Miss Cherry carries Luke over by the other bikers. One of them gives him a fistful of licorice, and they all include him in the celebration that ensues.

A few minutes pass, allowing my feelings to settle and my thoughts to kindle. I gaze listlessly at the distant twinkles of downtown Los Angeles, thinking, wondering, still utterly confused by what has happened.

As we stand there together, not talking, sharing the closeness of the dark, I begin to feel a worrisome affinity for Scar. Something ricochets inside my head, and I get an eerie feeling, as though I might have met him somewhere before this night. Not as a biker though, or a cop. The sense of familiarity makes me feel both safe and unsettled. We are obviously from different worlds, maybe even different galaxies. Yet, something about him, something strange and mysterious, speaks to me in a way that defies explanation.

As I look up into his face and into his dark unfathomable eyes, he reveals no hint of the past or the future, nor can I discern the slightest clue about what he might do from one minute to the next. He is a man of many surprises, the next of which he is about to spring. Boris Karloff couldn't have done it better.

"Hey, Wade, watch this." With the marvelous ease of a professional magician, he deftly peels the scar off of his face.

"Whoa!" I choke and back away in astonishment.

He laughs at himself as stringy strips of ductile latex stretch and then snap free of his forehead, nose, and cheeks. A large part of the scar peels away in one piece, and he hands it to me. Stunned, I accept it reluctantly.

The initial shock passes quickly and I begin to laugh too, which pleases him and makes him laugh even more. He picks the remaining pieces of theatrical adhesive from his nose and forehead and then pulls off the fake beard and wig. A good-looking face emerges as he transforms from a wild and woolly caterpillar to a handsome butterfly in a matter of seconds.

I put the piece of rubber scar in my pocket. "Who are you, really?"

He throws a suspicious glance to his left and to his right. "Can you be trusted to keep something top secret?"

"Scout's honor, sir." I place my hand over my heart.

He reaches into his back pocket and pulls out a black leather wallet, which he opens to reveal a badge. "I'm Sergeant Lyle Cavendish, Organized Crime Investigation Unit, Los Angeles Police Department."

"Cool," is all I can think to say.

At first I don't know what to believe.

Is that a real badge?

Is any of this night real?

Then it strikes me…Scar, or rather Lyle, is a policeman and so is everyone else on Billy Goat Hill, except Luke and me.

Cops dressed up as bikers?

But what they did to that poor young officer was out-and-out cruel.

He seems to read my mind. "What you and Luke saw tonight is called a hazing. It's something we often do to rookie police officers. We consider it part of their training. The police department doesn't officially approve of hazing, and technically we could get in hot water for doing it. Hazing is an old tradition that has been in practice for many, many years. I was hazed when I was a rookie. Do you understand, Wade?"

There is no doubt about what he wants to hear. "Yes, sir. Luke and I won't tell anybody." I know I can keep the secret, but whether Luke can keep his trap shut is something else. I have my concerns.

Dawn lies shimmering on the dewy grass as Luke and I climb back through our bedroom window. Mac is stretched out on the floor between our beds. He ignores us as we strip down and slip back under the sheets. I pull up my blanket and listen to the crickets fade in inverse proportion to the sunlight slowly peeking into the room.

My mind is still tingling, still numb, quarreling over whether or not any of it had been real. One thing I know for sure, I have never before returned from a dream with a piece of latex scar in my pocket.

Luke's Dodgers cap hangs from the bedpost above his head. He is already snoring softly, a smile on his face. I imagine he is dreaming about Miss Cherry.

"You should have come with us, Mac," I whisper. "This time it was great." Mac thumps his tail once on the floor and opens a tolerant eye.

I pat the bed. "Come here."

He obediently jumps up on my bed and drops his head next to mine on the pillow. We lie there nose to nose. "I'm gonna be a motorcycle cop when I grow up, Mac." He sighs and licks my chin.

I hold out the piece of latex scar, and he gives it a series of thorough sniffs, his wagging tail rocking the bed with somnolent motion. I close my eyes and concentrate my thoughts. What an adventure.

I lay my arm over Mac and begin to replay the night. I leave the house knowing there is a chance I may not survive the night. But I have to go. I can't back down. In the dark, I wait, ready to face my destiny. The call comes not, and the world spins backwards. A horrendous roar, smothering dust, a horde of imposters, a beauty, a beast…and then out of the refining fire comes something far more than a champion's vindication. I have slain a dragon and I savor the victory, for I fear it will not last.

Sleep pours over me and I do not resist…

Guarded by a trustworthy and powerful friend, I am safe. I am a great champion sailing up and down the Crippler on a cardboard magic carpet, the beautiful Miss Cherry riding behind me with her arms wrapped tightly about my waist. It's the best I have felt since Matthew died and Earl deserted us.

three

$\mathcal{I}$ have been listening to Luke grumble all morning.

"Ah pooh! They should have done better. I expected them to at least win the pennant."

We are sitting cross-legged on top of a towering weather-beaten promontory known as Eagle Rock. Luke and I often climb up here to chew the cud on issues of family, school, neighborhood, and of course our beloved Dodgers. Unfortunately for me, the serenity of this high-up place is often interrupted by my concern for Luke's safety. More than once he has forgotten where we are and nearly slipped over the ledge.

"Yeah, me too."

Mac stays a cautious ten feet or so behind us. Once when he was a pup, he followed us up the rock and nearly fell. It was quite a scare, but he learned. Since then, he has not gone near the edge. He sits on his haunches, content to watch us from his position of safety, his moist black nose pointing and sniffing incessantly toward the cloudless sky.

"Darn dog...he doesn't care one diddly about the Dodgers."

The October wind swirls, stirring up dust and leaves on the valley floor below us. A newspaper lying in the gutter down on Figueroa Street flaps in the wind. I watch it come apart, the pages streaming across the pavement like darting little phantoms playing tag with the traffic zooming by in both directions. The vision is pleasant, hypnotic, and lulls me toward the fringe of drowsiness.

A notable landmark, Eagle Rock juts dramatically from the side of a steep hill above the northeast corner of Colorado Boulevard and Figueroa Street. It is said to have been a sacred place of Indian worship. Its name derives from a curious eagle-shaped shadow that appears at midday on the western face of the rock and gradually disappears as the sun arcs overhead. Like the Indians before us, we are fascinated with Eagle Rock and hike to its top as often as we can get away with it. It is a dangerous trek, and kids have been known to take a plunge now and then. Fly like eagles they do not.

This ever-present potential for danger adds to the mystical allure of Eagle Rock. No doubt, if the rock had been a man-made object, it would have been declared an "attractive nuisance" and ordered torn down long ago.

"Don't worry, Luke. Mr. Alston will see to it they do better next year."

I've been infected with Brooklyn optimism since the day my team, the Los Angeles Dodgers, arrived. Luke does not share my positive outlook. He continues grumbling as I lay myself back on the hard surface and delight in the glorious Dodger blue sky. My legs in a pretzel, I clasp my fingers behind my head and stretch out my spine to get comfortable, just like Mac often does. Mac looks at me looking up, licks his nose with a long pink slosh, and hooks his snout skyward again. He doesn't mind sharing the Dodger welkin with me.

Luke responds begrudgingly. "Yeah, Walter Alston is a good manager." His attention is drawn to the same stream of newspapers I was watching. "But don't you wish he'd get mad at those darn umpires sometimes?"

"Nah." I grab the opportunity to get in a dig. "I'm glad he's not a hothead like you."

Luke makes a gremlin face at me, acknowledging he has a temper.

We do not talk for a while, pretending we are Indians paying respect to the sacred rock of the great and wise eagle. Luke gets bored before I do and starts prying off pieces of weathered granite with his peewee pocketknife and tossing odd-size nuggets over the edge.

As happens often since our encounter with Sergeant Cavendish and Miss Cherry, I begin to think about that crazy unbelievable night on Billy Goat Hill. Many times I have thought about trying to contact them, but I don't have the confidence to do such a thing. I let myself off the hook by reasoning that they probably wouldn't remember me anyway.

Still, I think of them nearly every day...especially when I feel sad about Matthew, or think about Earl, or worry about Lucinda. I want more of the Sergeant's strength and camaraderie. And Miss Cherry's sympathy and tenderness have seasoned my dreams ever since we met. Thinking of them now somehow makes me feel better. I felt everything except sadness that night.

Mac watches with great interest as Luke sits with his legs crossed and picks and pries at the rock. He timidly inches closer to Luke, clicking and scraping his nails on the brittle rock, but coming only so close to the edge and then promptly back-pedaling to his original position. Forward and back he goes, over and over again.

"Dumb dog," Luke mutters.

The picking and prying of the knife both fascinates and annoys Mac. He wants what he doesn't have the courage to obtain. This is not lost on me.

Luke tosses another piece of stone and counts. "One thousand, two thousand..."

He listens for the rock to hit the ground. Sometimes the rocks make a thud and sometimes the impact sounds more like a ping. We try to guess which noise each piece of rock will make, inevitably arguing over whether it was a thud or a ping. I shut my eyes and listen to the soothing repetitive cadence of Luke's voice as he times each stone's descent.

"One thousand, two thousand…"

The newspaper phantoms and my brother's verbal metronome soon conspire against me. Just before the moment of surrender my inner voice dispatches a final warning: *This is not a good place to take a nap, Wade.* I ignore the warning, the house lights dim, and a larger-than-life image of the lovely Miss Cherry lights up the theater of my unconscious mind…

Luke is pinging and thudding, pinging and thudding, when all of the sudden his brilliant red crown comes under attack. He has carelessly forgotten to put on his Dodgers cap, and like bloodthirsty Zeros diving on Pearl Harbor, a pair of mockingbirds make a daring high-speed pass at his delectable bright-red hair. They come from behind to avoid detection, swinging low at a cowardly ignoble angle, thus preventing poor Luke from initiating evasive action. The sinister whoosh of slicked-back wings comes a fraction of a second before the birds screech and peck.

Luke yowls like a scalded dog and leaps to his feet, slapping and flailing his arms at the attacking birds. Caught in a whirlwind of flapping feathers, squawking beaks, and clutching claws, Luke wildly hops from one foot to the other. He looks like an Indian medicine man gone mad. It's as if the great, winged spirit of Eagle Rock has been conjured forth to rid the ancient sanctuary of the impious palefaces whose vulgar presence is a blasphemous desecration of this hallowed place.

The birds squawk furiously as they swoop and dive, clawing and pecking at Luke's vulnerable head. They are not dissuaded by the flailing arms and terrified yelps coming from the boy below the enticing red hair. Nor are they concerned with the half-breed Doberman that barks and growls but comes no closer.

"Help! Ahgh! Help me!"

I am aghast. I don't know whether to laugh or scream myself. Then I see blood trickling down from the hairline on the left side of

Luke's forehead. The birds might hurt him badly if they hit his eyes.

Luke is in a panic and rapidly becoming hysterical. Tears stream down his cheeks, mixing with the bright red blood that now runs down to his chin. Mac is all snarls and fangs, but doesn't dare come any closer to the edge. The birds aren't letting up at all.

I scan the barren rock for something to use as a weapon, knowing there isn't a twig to be found. Luke is completely out of control, spinning, ducking, screaming, and slipping dangerously close to the point of no return. The birds are no longer the most immediate threat. Luke is about to go over the ledge.

I dive on my belly and grab Luke's pant leg just as his feet slip out from under him. He's so frightened by the birds I don't think he even realizes he's falling. I get both of my hands around his left ankle and hold on with all of my strength, my heart a locomotive chugging against the impossible load. Gorged with adrenaline, I fight not to let go or be pulled to certain death. I frantically search from side to side, desperate to sight something, anything to grab on to, knowing all the while that there is no hope for a lifeline. Nausea, vicious as a crosscut saw, slashes at my gut.

At most, I weigh ten pounds more than Luke…not enough to keep gravity and friction in equilibrium. Anchoring the toes of my sneakers against the gritty slope, I try to calm myself and think.

"Hold still, Luke! I won't let you fall!"

Luke's reply is barely audible—a faint, wheezy whimper of dread. His leg trembles within my grasp, but a small amount of progress is obtained when he stiffens his body and doesn't squirm.

The direness of our predicament hits me with a massive blast of fear as the unconquerable force of gravity begins to have its way. Ever so slowly we slide forward—like hunks of helpless iron summoned by a giant evil magnet.

Please, God, help me! What can I do?

I think of Reverend Bonner, the pastor of the church we once upon a time regularly attended. I tear through my memory searching for the Sunday school lessons that had gone in one ear and out the other. A fraction of both testaments flare and fade as a refrain of

"Onward Christian Soldiers Marching Off to War" rattles around my skull.

Overcome by hopelessness, I pray:

God and Jesus in heaven, please stop these birds. I am sorry for sticking my gum in the hymnal book. I am sorry for letting Gooey take the blame for putting green dye in the Highland Park public pool last summer. I am sorry for telling our next-door neighbor Carl that eating Russian rye bread means you are a communist.

Please, God, save us!

At that precise instant, we stop sliding and Mac starts tugging on my pant leg. The birds are suddenly gone, too. I seize the moment and clamp my hands even harder around Luke's ankles like Popeye would after a big swallow of power-packed spinach. With Mac's help pulling and tugging at my trousers and using my elbows as a fulcrum, I begin to heave the load backward toward safety.

In my mind, I become a scared but heroic soldier crawling under strafing machine gun fire to rescue my wounded buddy, except I am crawling uphill in reverse. Connected by arms and legs, we undulate caterpillar style making small, painful but steady gains. My long sleeves do little to pad my elbows, and after three or four thrusts of bony skin against rasp-sharp granite, I see red smudges slowly pass in front of me and disappear under Luke's shaking legs. I experience no pain, only dry-mouth fear and a surging desperation to survive. I scream into the rock that is grinding against my sweaty face.

"Pull, Mac—PULL!"

Please, God, we need You!

Then I feel something shaking me, something more than Mac pulling at my trousers, and from somewhere far above me I hear a distant voice call out my name...

"Wade!"

"Pull!"

"Wade!"

"Pull!"

"Shut up, you big donkey!"

"Huh? What? Pull! Crimanee sakes!"

Squinting, I sit up in amazement, expecting to see blood and feathers all over Luke's head. No blood. Not even a tiny scratch. I see splotches of freckles on a face wracked with concern, nothing else.

"What in the heck is the matter with you?"

I wince as a drop of salty sweat stings my left eye. "Why didn't you wear your darn Dodgers hat today?"

"What?"

"Never mind. Did I fall asleep?"

Worry gathers in Luke's eyes. "I don't know. I was tossing rocks, and you started yelling something about a pool. You scared the heck out of me."

"It was—*pull.*" I feel my elbows…no shredded skin. *Oh man.* I rub my eyes.

"Pull what?"

"Never mind that. Are you okay, Luke?"

"Me? Heck, yeah. Why wouldn't I be? But, um, I think we might have a little problem."

"What problem?"

Please, God, no more mockingbirds.

Luke's eyes narrow. He nods in the direction behind me, and Mac starts to growl real low in his throat, like he does when something isn't right.

I look over my shoulder and spot a motorcycle cop clambering up the back side of Eagle Rock. His shiny helmet reflects sunlight like a mirror in my eyes.

"Ah shoot."

There is no place to hide and no way to escape. With nothing to do but stand there and await our fate, I glance back at Luke.

"We're busted," he mouths.

Mac goes on full alert and positions himself at my feet, my command his every wish. He does not bark, though the low growling continues and he shows some teeth. He will attack only on my order or in defense to direct aggression. To lay down his life for ours is his purpose, his heart.

The cop scrambles up to the top of the rock. Pausing fifty feet away, he faces us but says not a word as he lingers catching his breath. Luke and I stand transfixed, like passive creatures relying on highly evolved camouflage to fool an approaching predator. But we are as exposed and vulnerable as baby turtles in the sand at low tide. And at this moment a big hungry gull is in our midst.

The stare-down ends when the cop proceeds to remove his helmet and peel off his black leather gloves. We watch as he carefully matches the gloves palm to palm and loops them under his belt. Then he removes his sunglasses, folds them, and slips them inside the breast pocket of his black leather jacket. He is smooth and precise, even elegant, the way he does these things. His eyes never leave Mac as he slowly comes our way. He smiles, and something seems queer for a second. Then my heart nearly jumps from my chest.

Leapin' Lizards! It's the Sergeant!

I am astounded by how different he looks. Not at all the way I remember him from Billy Goat Hill. He's wearing a muscle-tightened police uniform, he's clean shaven, his dark hair is cut military short, and though not menacing or scary like he was that night, he is every bit as formidable as the biker version I'll never forget. When finally he speaks, it's the same voice I have stored in my brain, just softer and more refined than the raspy-throated speech of Scar.

He keeps his eyes on Mac. "I bet your folks don't know you're up here."

Mac returns the Sergeant's stare but has quit growling. Slowly, he folds his ears back and tucks his tail between his legs, as if the Doberman part of him is concerned about his uncropped, unbobbed appearance. Not afraid, more submissive, he sidesteps over and cautiously stretches to sniff the Sergeant's boots.

"Yes, sir, that's right. They don't know we're up here."

It doesn't take Luke long to spout off. "Our father's a drunkard. He doesn't care what we do. But our mom would sure skin us good, if she knew." He flashes a punctuating grin while I wince with embarrassment.

The Sergeant is unfazed. "Do you guys know who I am?"

Mac suddenly plops his rump down on the toe of the Sergeant's boot. He looks up and accepts a caress from the Sergeant's leather smelling hand. This is an amazing development as Mac rarely takes to strangers. Then I recall the piece of latex scar I'd let him sniff. Though it has been six months, Mac recalls the scent and deduces that the Sergeant is not a threat.

Remembering we were supposed to forget about the hazing of the rookie cop and factoring in the potential ramifications of our present circumstances, I decide it's best to play dumb. "No, sir, I don't believe we know you."

Luke on the other hand is true to form. "It's Mister Scar, you big dumb donkey!"

The Sergeant, momentarily taken aback, blurts out a healthy chortle, and Luke reacts with a nervous, squeaky laugh, which he cuts short when he catches the stern set of my jaw. It is clear he doesn't quite get it.

"Well, if it isn't Wade and Luke Parker…my, how you boys do get around town."

I nod. "You look different, sir."

"Yep. This is what I look like when I'm riding motors, my favorite duty. Once in a while I need to work undercover, like that biker get-up you saw on Billy Goat Hill. You keep that just between us friends, okay? And, by the way, I'm glad you remembered you weren't supposed to remember." He gives me a solemn wink.

I warm to the kudos and flash a lofty smile at Luke, which sails right over his head. It wasn't easy to teach him to tie his shoes, either. *Patience.*

Mac gets up and pads over to the only scrap of vegetation on the top of Eagle Rock, a half-dead little shrub clinging to a crack in the granite. He gives it a procedural sniff and then lifts his right hind leg. It is always the right leg, which makes for a lot of U-turns in his life.

"Darn dog," Luke mutters.

The Sergeant watches Mac as he relieves himself. "How come you think your dad doesn't care about you coming up here, Luke?"

"Earl? Why, he doesn't care about us at all. He's never around much anyway."

Luke does not intend it, but I think his harshness toward our father also reflects poorly on me. I try to recoup some dignity. "Earl is a traveling salesman, sir."

"Yeah? So was my old man. What does he sell?"

"You know all the supplies they sell at truck stops?"

"Not really. Like what?"

"You know—trinkets, gadgets, postcards, books, shaving kits— the stuff truckers need when they're on the road."

"Oh. Well, then I can understand why he'd be gone so much."

"He sells those funny balloon things they put in those machines in the men's bathrooms too," Luke adds.

I roll my eyes.

The Sergeant chuckles out of the side of his mouth and scans the valley below. "Yeah, I guess truckers need those, too."

I want very badly to strangle Luke, but I manage to stand there and tolerate him while I wait for the Sergeant's lecture, which I am positive is coming.

Mac finishes his business and does one of those vigorous scrape-the-ground-with-the-hind-paws behaviors that dogs like to do afterward. His nails scratch and click loudly on the hard surface, which I can tell annoys him. There is no dirt or grass to fling in the air.

"Darn dog," Luke mutters.

I grow tired of waiting for the lecture. "Are you mad at us for coming up here?"

"No, but I am worried about you guys. This can be a very dangerous place. A few kids have fallen from here."

Luke perks up. "Did they die?"

"To my knowledge, no one has ever survived a fall from Eagle Rock. I remember a kid named Jakey Blume..." He looks away. "Jakey fell to his death from this very spot about thirty years ago."

"Did you know him?"

"Yes—he was my best friend."

Luke is intrigued. "How did he fall?"

The Sergeant exhales a long breath and sets his gaze on the distant skyline of downtown Los Angeles. He doesn't speak for nearly a minute, and while I can't read his mind, I can tell from the unmistakable slump of his shoulders that he bears a heavy burden. He ends the silence with a sigh and lowers himself to sit on the rock. I feel sorry for him. I know something about death and loss. The wake of pain and sorrow keeps bumping you long after the ship of darkness sails over the horizon.

Mac comes over and nudges the Sergeant's shoulder with his nose. He wants to hear the story as much as we do. Luke and I sit down, one on each side of the Sergeant, while Mac curls up a few feet behind us.

"It's been years since I've thought about Jakey Blume. You boys would have liked him. He was a real character." The Sergeant cheers himself slightly. "We met in first grade at Garvanza Elementary School."

"Hey, that's where me and Wade go to school!"

"Yes, I know. In fact, I've taken the liberty to talk to both of your teachers."

"You have?" Hearing this makes me nervous.

"You boys made quite an impression on Miss Cherry and me. We were worried about you making a habit of late nights at Billy Goat Hill. We work out of the Highland Park police station, and I grew up here, so I know the immediate neighborhood like the back of my hand. I've made a point to check up on you guys, look out for you a little, you might say. It's nothing to worry about, but a good thing all the more—now that I know your dad's not around. You may be pulling the wool over your mom's eyes, but at least I know you're not ditching school or plotting to rob a bank anytime soon. Both of your teachers said very nice things about you, by the way."

Great. Now we have a neighborhood cop keeping tabs on us. "That's good to know. Uh, so, what about this kid Jakey?"

"Jakey Blume. He liked to pull wild stunts in the middle of the night, too. You had to be careful about daring him to do things, because, by golly, he would do it. He was a little crazy, I guess."

Poco loco, I say to myself.

"I liked to hang around with Jakey. He wasn't boring. I remember one time I dared him to do something outrageous at our school May Day festival—"

"I was in the May Day festival!"

I lean forward, catch Luke's eye, and give him the *shut up* look. "What was the dare, sir?"

"I dared him to dress himself up to look like our principal, Mrs. Hackworth." The Sergeant grins. "Giant gazzangas and all."

Luke doesn't get it, and then does get it when the Sergeant positions his hands, arthritic-like fingers curled in front of his chest, to illustrate his point.

"Hundreds of parents had gathered around the edge of the school yard. When the time came for the festival to begin, one of the teachers started playing marching music real loud on one of those great big Victrola machines we used to have in the old days."

Luke and I look at each other, and the Sergeant realizes we haven't a clue what a Victrola is.

"Anyway, first the kindergarten class came marching out smiling and waving. Next, along came the first graders with long paper streamers tied to their wrists, every color you could imagine fluttering and floating in the wind. Then out came the third graders followed by the fourth graders and so on."

Luke, fancying himself a May Day expert, nods enthusiastically, and the Sergeant laughs.

"None of the groups kept any better step to the music than the younger kids in front of them. They all made a big circle around the schoolyard and then were lined up by their teachers and told to sit on the blacktop in front of the cheering audience. In the middle of the schoolyard, there was a small wooden platform where…"

"…the principal stands!" Luke shouts with glee.

"Yes." The Sergeant grins and buffs his knuckles on the top of Luke's head.

"Our principal, Mrs. Hackworth, was smiling and nodding encouragement to the students as they circled around her. Finally, the sixth graders made up the caboose. They were showing off, marching real cool, like they were in the army or something."

Luke blows out a mouthful of disgust. "Those darn sixth graders always think they're big shots."

I am enjoying the story and listen intently while the Sergeant's deep voice works on me like the expert hands of a masseuse.

"Then, when Mrs. Hackworth wasn't looking, out came Jakey, smiling and waving to the crowd like he was a movie star. I was sitting with my third grade class in a fluffy sea of red, white, and blue pom-poms. I wasn't thrilled to be carrying pom-poms around like that. You know, in front of people and all."

I nod, knowing the feeling exactly.

"Anyway, Jakey was all dressed up to look just like our beloved principal, complete with her peculiar pigeon-toed waddle, blue tinted hair, and goofy condescending smile. At first, many of the people over on my side of the schoolyard didn't notice him. But it wasn't long before the laughter started. In seconds, everyone was watching him strut along behind the last group of marchers. That is, everyone except Mrs. Hackworth.

"Jakey was a great actor. He had the specific walk, the hair, the highfalutin smile, and of course, the trademark gazzangas. Well, let's just say it was obvious who he was lampooning."

Luke interrupts again. "What does *lambdoonie* mean?"

"*Lam-poon-ing*," the Sergeant repeats. "It means to make fun of something."

Luke grins. "I thought so."

The Sergeant nudges Luke in the ribs. "Mrs. Hackworth still hadn't turned around, but she was beginning to get this confused look on her face, not understanding why so many people were laughing. Jakey was really getting into it and so was the crowd. He started walking kind of crazy-like, pigeon-toed, except exaggerated. Kind of like Jerry Lewis."

"Yeah! That Jerry Lewis is cool! He really cracks me up!"

Mac is sitting up now, intently listening in, his head cocked to one side.

The Sergeant shakes off a private memory, nostalgia drifting in his eyes. "The thing is, Jakey Blume was the type of kid who just didn't know when to quit."

I think of Gooey and his calling my bluff about riding the Crippler at night.

"He began to lose control of his performance. You might say he was overcome by the awesome forces of femininity."

Luke and I exchange blank looks.

"I mean the gazzangas kind of took off on him, swinging and swaying, get the picture?"

We do, and we grin accordingly.

Luke is giggling but still manages to speak. "I bet the principal didn't like it much when she finally turned around and saw your friend, Jakey, making fun of her like that. What happened?"

"You're not going to believe it." The Sergeant looks up at the sky, big-eyed, as if he still can't accept whatever it was that had happened.

"What, sir?"

"Tell us!" Luke demands.

"Woof!" Mac barks, making us all jump and start laughing again.

"Darn dog!" Luke shoves Mac away. "He thinks he knows what you're talking about."

"Leave him alone, Luke. Please finish the story, sir."

"Be patient," Luke chides. Then he mimics one of my own little catchphrases. "Duke Snider waits for his pitch, you know!"

He loves to aggravate me by repeating my material back to me. "Would you please cork it?" I shoot him my deluxe evil-eye glare, and he sticks his tongue out at me.

The Sergeant ignores us, his mood tide reversing direction again.

"Please, sir, finish the story. What happened next?"

"Well, the gazzangas were actually large rubber balloons filled with water and tied with twine that looped around his neck. The dress he wore had plenty of room for Jakey and the water balloons, and when his performance got out of hand, the balloons started rocking from side to side until they somehow crisscrossed and flung all the way around to his back. He looked like a hideous cross between a badly deformed camel and the Hunchback of Notre Dame."

Luke and I laugh so hard we scream at the sky.

"At about that moment, Mrs. Hackworth turned around to see just what in tarnation all the people are pointing at. By then Jakey's dress had crept up around his waist exposing his naked scrawny legs, and the blue tinted wig had twisted around and dangled sideways off one side of his head. He no longer resembled Mrs. Hackworth at all, and she just stared at him. He was a sight to behold, looking like some tortured little creature not of this world. Thank goodness he was wearing underpants!"

Luke and I yowl, tears streaming down our faces. The Sergeant is hysterical, too.

"Then, one of the teachers ran to Mrs. Hackworth's side and hurriedly explained what was going on. Her expression slowly shifted to horror as she absorbed the information. She watched as the wig slipped off of Jakey's head and fell to the ground. It became a sombrero for his zany Mexican Hat Dance. Around and around he went, prancing, bobbing, weaving, and inadvertently stomping on the wig every other time his foot came down. It was hilarious!

"However, Jakey was no longer trying to be funny, and that was when I began to realize he might be in trouble. The water balloons had swung every which way, and the twine had become twisted and tangled around his neck. The weight of the water-filled balloons kept pulling the noose tighter and tighter until his mouth gaped open. He couldn't get enough air, and he started clawing at his neck.

"The crowd was mesmerized and convinced that Jakey's frantic struggle was all part of his act. They were into it good, hundreds of hands and feet clapping and stomping in unison while Jakey hopped around doing his crazy tormented dance. His face was a smeared mess of lipstick and rouge and was starting to turn a noticeable blue. Then he fell down to his knees, slapped at his neck for a few more seconds, and slowly rolled over on his side, like a groggy wild animal shot with a wildlife biologist's anesthetic dart."

We stop laughing.

"Geez Louise, sir! What the heck?"

"Yeah! Did somebody stomp on the balloons?"

"Come on, Luke!" I yell and laugh at the same time. "Let him tell us!"

The Sergeant first has to catch his breath after cracking up at Luke's remark. "Somebody shouted from the crowd, 'Hey! He's choking to death!' Some of the women started screaming, and people ran over and hovered over him. I couldn't see through the crowd, and a couple of minutes went by while nothing seemed to be happening. Boy, was I worried. But then, all of the sudden, Jakey scrambled out through the forest of legs and took off running for home with nothing but his underpants on."

Luke doesn't know what to think. He stammers and then blurts, "Unbelievable!"

"You're right, sir. Your friend sure wasn't boring."

The Sergeant slides back to that distant place, the one I now take to be grief. We all sit for a few minutes immersed in a reverie of solemn reflection. My eyes keep drifting down. Where had Jakey Blume's body landed?

The afternoon winds have gone, leaving Eagle Rock still and peaceful, save the murmurs of the traffic that forever hums below this ancient place. I feel close to the Sergeant at this moment, the exact feeling I experienced that night on Billy Goat Hill. He opened his heart to us, and it makes me feel good and important and satisfied.

It wasn't a lecture, but the Sergeant made his point. I look at Luke as he cautiously stares over the ledge. I can tell the story has gotten to him, too. He turns around and smiles at me. It is a trusting smile, one that tells me he thinks it's okay to be up here on the rock because he is with his big brother.

Deep in Luke's eyes, I see Matthew. I glance away but cannot abate the stinging constriction of remorse that seizes my throat and swarms across my chest. I flex my hands, then press forefingers to thumbs and rub them together nervously. I strain hard, trying to fight off a pang of sorrow, but a single rebel tear tumbles down my cheek in full view of Luke.

I wrestle with the reason I am upset, and it pins me to the ground. The saga of Jakey Blume has wrapped me up tight in the realization that I have failed at my responsibility to protect my little brother. *Geez. What kind of irresponsible idiot am I?* My recklessness is constantly placing Luke in harm's way, and to make me see that, I conclude, is the purpose of the Sergeant's story.

"What's the matter?" Luke's little pink chin starts to quiver.

It is automatic that Luke will cry if he sees me cry. I am the same about him. Lucinda calls us symbiotic brats because she can't handle it when we both set off like civil defense sirens. We need only to feign a blast of stereo wailing to head off a punishment. If Lucinda ever catches on to the ruse, the jig will be up, and a new technique will require invention.

Luke frowns and tears up, hundreds of freckles bunching in orange blotches where laugh lines had been.

"Nothing's wrong. I just got some dust in my eyes."

Mac knows better, though. He comes over and puts his head in my lap. I hug him around the neck and can tell he is uneasy being this close to the ledge. His nails seek a purchase in the granite, and he leans against me, pushing away from the ledge.

Luke seems to accept my fib, his freckles slowly returning to where they belong. "Yeah, I think I got a little dust in my eyes, too."

The Sergeant shifts his legs and slides a little closer to me. He puts his arm on my shoulders, his leather jacket groaning with the movement. The noise of the leather registers slight interest with Mac. He twitches his ears but does not lift his head from my lap. The Sergeant scratches him behind his ears, and Mac relaxes. We stay like that for a good long while.

Sergeant Cavendish takes his arm off my shoulder, unzips the front of his jacket, and reaches for something in his inner pocket. The tightness in my throat has subsided under the comforting feel of his arm. I am in control again. Mac can tell I'm okay, and he returns to where he was sitting before.

I hear the faint squawking of a police radio and realize the Sergeant has parked his motorcycle somewhere down below. I can't tell from what direction the sound is coming. Has Luke been throwing his pebbles down on the motorcycle?

Would the motorcycle make a ping or a thud?

Luke resumes picking at the rock with his pocketknife. Mac resumes watching Luke with curious interest. The two of them are capable of going on like this indefinitely. All seems back to normal.

We have been sitting here with the Sergeant for well over an hour, and I am surprised, intrigued, that he has been content to stay with us this long. He isn't preparing to leave and has yet to say anything about getting down off Eagle Rock. I think he realizes it would do no good, but he has made his point about the danger. We sit in silence for a moment or two longer, no doubt each of us thinking some more about poor Jakey Blume.

"That's a good dog you have there," the Sergeant says, his hand still in his pocket. He seems to be toying with something, and Mac trains one curious eye on him while still watching Luke.

I glance at Mac and then at the Sergeant. The insightful glint in his eyes suggests he knows Mac would probably kill to protect us, or die trying, and that he finds great honor in that. "Yes sir, Mac takes good care of us."

Luke and I came up to the rock after school let out. We made a routine stop at home first to gobble down peanut butter and jelly sandwiches and to take the telephone off the hook. The standard plan is to blame Mac for knocking the phone over if Lucinda later bawls us out for not answering. There is great honor in being a scapegoat, too.

Lucinda should be home at about six-thirty, and we need to allow at least forty-five minutes for the return trip. The sun is slipping low to meet the horizon, leaving the valley below us in shadow as I start to think about the long walk home.

"Have you guys seen your father lately?"

"He came home for my birthday last month," Luke answers.

Earl's appearance on Luke's birthday happened only by coincidence. I have let Luke think otherwise. The truth is, Earl probably wouldn't know if it was Christmas Day, but he sure knows when to celebrate Jack Daniels' day.

"We haven't seen or heard from our dad since then, sir."

The Sergeant pulls an Abba-Zaba out of his pocket and hands it to Luke. "Happy birthday!"

Luke sits up straight and grins a mile, his freckles stretching so thin they become almost invisible. "Wow! Abba-Zaba's are my favorite!" He has the wrapper off and the candy in his mouth in three seconds.

"Would you like one, too, Wade?" He reaches back inside his jacket.

"No, thank you. I only like Butterfingers."

As clever as a magician, he slides his hand out from his jacket and hands me a Butterfinger. "Here you go."

The sleight of hand amazes me, as much as if he had pulled a live squirrel from his sleeve. My reaction is a catalyst for him, and he laughs out loud, just like Scar did on Billy Goat Hill.

"How did you know?"

"I'm a well-trained detective."

We chomp on our candy bars and laugh until chocolate streaks down our chins. Our confection-painted faces make us look like descendants of the great Shoshone Gabrieleno, who first sat on Eagle Rock and laughed as we are now partaking in the timeless magic of innocence.

Luke speaks as he chews on the last of his Abba-Zaba. "You know what? I heard Lucinda jawing on Earl the last time he was home. I woke up the night of my birthday and went to the bathroom. I didn't turn the light on, so they must not have known I was up."

"What about it?" I offer the last bite of my Butterfinger to Mac. It vanishes.

"Well, have you ever heard of some place called Barstow?"

"Nope."

"It's a little town out in the desert on the way to Las Vegas," the Sergeant volunteers.

"Oh. Well, I heard them say Las Vegas, too." Luke wipes his sticky chin with his shirtsleeve. "What does *da-borse* mean?"

Now he has my full attention. "That's just kind of a funny word grown-ups use sometimes. What did you hear them say, exactly?"

"Hmm," he murmurs, thinking. "Well, I think Lucinda was ticked off at Earl. She was cursing and all. She said, 'I know about the one in Barstow, Earl. Her name's Trudy. Don't even try to deny it.' Then Earl said, 'Okay, if that's the way you want it. We'll get the *da-borse* in Las Vegas.'"

Luke, appearing content, finishes wiping his chin on the other sleeve. I am thinking that little Matthew never wanted any of this to happen. I look at Sergeant Cavendish and read the sympathy in his eyes. He puts his arm across my shoulders again. We are all quiet for a little while longer.

Luke resumes picking at the rock, his question left to die unanswered. The sad inevitable has arrived and Lucinda has apparently opted not to tell me about it. I am old enough. She should talk to me. I squint at the sun, watch it settle lower and lower.

Soon the Sergeant's leather groans as he moves to get up. He takes his time, stretches his legs and does three deep knee bends. "Maybe it's time we thought about heading for home, boys."

I look at my watch, five-thirty. It's time to go anyway. Luke and I stand, following veiled orders. Mac gets up and goes through his stretching routine. Luke looks over the ledge and tosses one last pebble before we head for home.

One thousand, two thousand... "Hey." He turns to face the Sergeant. "How did your friend Jakey fall off this rock anyway?"

"You wouldn't believe me if I told you."

I am a little irritated that Luke brought up the subject of Jakey Blume again. At the same time, I am also interested to know exactly what had happened.

Luke steps closer to the Sergeant. "I'll believe you."

"You'll be the first one, then."

For a second I think the Sergeant is about to cry; he looks so lost and alone in his memories. Down below, half of the cars have their lights on, casting soft glowing arcs on the pavement in front of them. I watch the lights for a second or two and then look back at Luke and the Sergeant. Luke has moved, his back now to the ledge. Their forms are silhouettes centered in the remaining half-round shape of the dwindling sun.

Luke looks up innocently at the Sergeant. "I'll believe you."

The Sergeant's eyes meet Luke's trusting gaze. He slowly places his hands on Luke's shoulders. He smiles and almost in a whisper, says, "To be completely honest with you, some people actually thought maybe...*I*...pushed him."

Mac stiffens and begins to growl, very low, very tentative. Something is wrong, but what? My heart kicks hard and accelerates. My legs suddenly feel rubbery, disconnected from my body. *Oh no!* I can't move. Terror crashes all around me, rendering me helpless to stop the unthinkable thing that is most certainly about to happen. I try to speak but can't form any words.

What words?
What can I say?
Help?
Who will hear?
Who will help?
O God. No!

"I know you couldn't have pushed him," Luke says. "He was your friend. No way would you do that. What really happened? How did he fall?"

I will my legs to step closer. The gap between us begins to close, and I sense movement like I am floating, but I can't feel my legs taking actual steps. My eyes focus on the holstered gun hanging from the Sergeant's hip. *What an impossible thought, but what else can I do? I want that gun!*

"Let's move back from the ledge, Luke, and I'll tell you what really happened."

Mac relaxes and I slump to the ground and take a deep breath. *I can't take this. I don't know what to believe about anything anymore.* I begin massaging my legs, hunting for feeling.

Luke and the Sergeant sit next to me.

"It happened on a day just like this—a little cool, a little windy, so clear you could see all the way downtown. Jakey and I had climbed up on the rock after school. We liked to come up here and sit. We talked about stuff, you know, anything and everything, whatever came to mind. Jakey was excited about going to Catalina Island with his family the next day. It was to be his first visit to Catalina. I had been there twice before, so I told him what I knew about the island. He was especially interested in seeing the buffaloes and wild goats.

"I also told him about the bright red Garibaldi fish I had seen through a glass bottom boat at Emerald Bay. Funny, I remember telling him the Garibaldi fish had been named after a famous Italian general whose soldiers were known for their distinctive bright red shirts and not knowing for sure whether the story was true or not. Huh, isn't that weird? Oh yeah, and Jakey wanted to know all about the glass bottom boat. I think he was nervous about being on a boat with a glass bottom. Jakey didn't like the water much."

The Sergeant's voice chokes to a stop. He takes a deep breath and resumes his story with more emotion in his voice than before.

"Jakey and I had been sitting for an hour or so right about where we're sitting now."

"Right here?" Luke places his palms down on the rock.

"More or less."

"Gosh."

"Anyway, here's the part nobody ever believed. Suddenly, out of nowhere, two mockingbirds swooped down and started attacking Jakey." The Sergeant averts his eyes and looks off toward the sunset like he expects one or both of us to laugh at him.

But what he said hits me like a sledgehammer right between the eyes. A chilly curtain drops around me as the blood drains from my face. I already know the story.

Luke tugs on the Sergeant's shirtsleeve. "What happened? Tell me. I'll believe you."

"At first, I thought it was funny. The birds were after him and weren't bothering me at all." He looks at Luke and fails at an effort to smile. "They swooped and screeched and dove at him, pecking and clawing at the top of his head like something crazy. Jakey scrambled to his feet. I'll never forget the terror in his eyes. He was swinging his arms over his head, and he just took off running...right over the edge. Before I really knew what was happening, he was gone. His scream still haunts me. It just faded away into the sky."

Luke turns pale, close to tears. "I believe you."

The Sergeant finally manages a weak smile. "Thanks, Luke."

The sun retreats below the ridge line leaving a wake of pinkish-purple brush strokes across the western sky. It is so quiet, so still, I can hear my heart pounding hard, deep, deep down in my ears. I lean back and rest my head on Mac, curled up behind me.

"What color hair did Jakey Blume have?" I close my eyes and wait to hear what I already know. Dreams, including daydreams, are strange and powerful things.

I wonder what Duke Snider would say about that?

four

A Saturday in early July, 1960

Luke shakes my pillow at the first expectant pulse of false dawn and insistently repeats in my ear, "Get up—Wade. I want to go to Three Ponds early today."

I am sluggish after a long fitful night, and Luke has to pester me awake. Mac wants to go, too, and lends his tongue and breath to the effort. I drag myself out of bed and mope my way to the bathroom.

My lackluster mood is due in part to the increasing absence of my mother. The house is so empty without her. Wondering if she is home now, I think about peeking into her room. While brushing my teeth, I consider brushing Mac's teeth as well. Not a chance. He won't cooperate. I slog into the kitchen and spot a note left near the sink.

See you guys tonight.

That's it. No, *I love you, Mom*.

With Earl now completely out of our lives and residing in Barstow with someone named Trudy, and Lucinda working more hours than ever, Luke and I are left to entertain ourselves. What we lack in material things we try to make up for with imagination. Still, our devices are limited. Only three weeks into summer vacation and we are trudging through periods of tedium and restlessness, the onset of the devil boredom. The devil's plucky partners—phone pranks, simple trespass, petty theft, and other minor transgressions—whisper in our ears with the zealousness of overstocked drug dealers.

Luke, the master of pluckiness, keeps pestering, and soon, against my rumpled humor, we are on our way to Three Ponds.

From where we live on Ruby Place, a block north and a block west of the intersection of Figueroa Street and Meridian Street, it is quite a trek east to Three Ponds. Neither Luke nor I own a bicycle, so walking is our stock in trade. Hoofing it affords one great freedom to notice and appreciate detail, which in our case fosters a predictable amount of mischief. If we take the most direct route and do not dawdle along the way, we have at least a forty-five minute walk ahead of us.

I notice Luke concealing something in his right hand, and I snap to the task of running herd on him. He can get me into a pickle in the blink of an eye. "What's in your hand?"

"If that darn Molly barks, I'm gonna throw this rock at her."

Molly, a rather pretty but dumb Irish setter, belongs to Mrs. Roberson, who is not dumb. To the contrary, Mrs. Roberson is more than adept at investigating to her complete satisfaction the misdeeds of neighborhood kids and their pets. She is an outspoken critic of Mac, who manages to impregnate her Molly on a semi-regular basis. A female in heat within five miles turns Mac's hind legs into powerful pogo sticks, and our six-foot high fence is useless to keep him in. Give him another decade and Mac will no doubt have descendants leaping fences and scratching fleas on all seven continents.

Molly, who is perpetually smitten with Mac, stirs when she sees him. She pulls against her tether and calls out to him with two passionate barks followed by a longing whine. I notice Mrs. Roberson spying out her kitchen window just in time to restrain Luke. Molly, not being in heat at the moment, warrants only the dregs of a half-hearted glance from Mac.

Only after we round the corner at the end of the block and Luke's mind moves on to other things does he finally drop the rock. "Do you think Jake's will be open?"

Luke has yet to develop a useful sense of time. *Patience.* "No—it's way too early."

Jake's Barbershop sits across the street from Luther Burbank Junior High School. Jake the barber, no relation to Jakey Blume, is a fun guy, if not a great barber. Jake is a big man with a barrel chest and huge Dizzy Gillespie jowls that shake when he laughs or growls as he loves to do whenever we show up. Plainly speaking, Jake loves people, especially kids. He is an excellent storyteller and always has a funny yarn to share.

It is impossible to walk past his shop without stopping to say hello. "Hey you!" he'll yell like thunder if you dare try to pass by without at least giving him a wave. Jake is the only barber who's ever cut our hair. He used to be a friend of Earl's. Recently, though, I suspect he's angling on Lucinda. He sure asks a lot of questions about her since word of Earl's absence has gotten around.

Luke and I have a passion of our own. We call it "sneaking," which is code for sneaking in through Jake's back door. We secrete ourselves in Jake's supply room, peek through a curtained doorway, and wait for an opportune moment. Seeing our chance, we dash through the center of the barber shop and out the front door, whooping and hollering like a couple of cowboys letting loose on a Saturday night. I think sometimes we overdo it and frazzle him a little.

Still, if we manage to scoot past Jake without him grabbing us, he rewards us with a wad of Bazooka bubble gum. It is a gamely challenge. Jake is a big man, but he is sure of foot and lightning quick. Half the time he catches us, and when he does, he slings us up into the barber chair. In forty-five seconds or less, what little fuzz we've grown since the last time he caught us is on the floor ready for the sweeper. We may be poor, but we are never in need of haircuts. Thanks to Jake's frequent army-style buzz jobs, Luke and I usually look like a couple of cue balls in search of a snooker table. Lucinda never pays for any haircuts, as far as I know.

We stop and look in the barber shop window. No Jake. Mac pads around the corner of the building, lifts his leg, and documents his visit.

"Darn dog," Luke mutters.

Down the block from Jake's is a pedestrian tunnel that burrows under Figueroa Street. It comes up on the other side of the street in front of our school, Garvanza Elementary. The tunnel has always intrigued me. I like the cool air, and the echo is fun.

Nothing exciting ever happens down there, but I always feel good in the tunnel. Something about being underground surrounded by the concrete walls makes me feel safe. I plan for Luke and I to hide out in the tunnel if the nuclear war Carl often rants about ever comes. I don't know, maybe I am part mole or groundhog.

Today, however, we determine to take our chances aboveground. Our personal crossing guard, Mac, aggressively challenges the traffic to stop, and the happy wanderers skip across the street.

The school playground slows us down. Luke is still determined to throw something, and dirt clods fly over the fence at no apparent target. Mac and I stop and watch him. I figure it's best to let him get it out of his system.

He throws one last dirt clod, ponders the sky for a moment, and then turns and looks at me. "Is Matthew in heaven?"

I never know what he is going to say or do next. Luke definitely has a way of keeping me on my toes. "I think so."

"I wonder if Lucinda knows that."

"Well, maybe. But she still wants Matthew to be here with us."

He stares at me, and I can almost hear his brain whirring. "She seems sad or angry all of the time. And she hardly ever talks to me anymore. Is she mad at us?"

"Sometimes—I guess. Mostly I think she's mad at God."

"I wish Matthew never died."

My heart hurts for him and I step closer. "I miss him a lot, too."

"I don't like it that Lucinda is sad all of the time. Yesterday I heard her crying in the bathroom. Wade?"

"Yeah."

"Do you think God knows about us?"

"If He doesn't yet, I think He will."

"How?"

"I think Matthew will tell Him about us."

His countenance takes on an almost angelic softness. "Matthew is pretty cool."

"Yeah, he is."

"You're sort of cool, too, Wade."

"I know. Are you done throwing dirt clods?"

"You know what's weird?"

"What, Luke?"

"Remember when we used to go to Sunday school?"

"Yeah."

"Well, one time, the teacher told us Jesus said, 'suffer the little children.' What does that mean?"

"I don't know."

We move on toward Kory's Market at the corner of York and Figueroa. At the intersection, I give a long look up York Boulevard to the north. The Highland Park police station is only a couple of blocks away. *Is the Sergeant keeping tabs on us today?* Kory's has a big parking lot and four checkout stands. Lucinda calls Kory's a "supermarket," which always makes us chuckle because the "supermarket" is the best place to steal a free look at the latest *Superman* comic books.

Kory's is a busy place, and sometimes we're able to take advantage of the hubbub and slip unnoticed behind the magazine racks to catch up on our favorite two-dimensional hero. On good days, we get away with freeloading for ten or fifteen minutes before the store manager spots us and gives us the boot. The free peeks are getting harder to come by.

At Luke's insistence, today we skip Kory's and beat an expeditious path the rest of the way to Three Ponds—left off York Boulevard before the bridge, down the hill on San Pasqual Avenue, and straight ahead all the way to the overpass at San Pasqual Creek. Most days offer something more to ignite a digression or lead us on another tangent. But little do we know, this day is shaping up to be like no other.

A secret known only to a few privileged local kids, Three Ponds is a hidden wilderness overlooked by time and progress. A meandering stream towered over by giant eucalyptus trees provides a peaceful, restful setting. The stream sets the pace, never in a hurry to join the larger flow of the Arroyo Seco, which feeds the larger yet Los Angeles River.

Birds and small animals thrive here protected from encroaching civilization. Early morning and late afternoon, when the animals come to drink and play, are my favorite times. If you hide downwind and crouch very still, the experience is more fun than visiting the jailed species on display at the Griffith Park Zoo. Animal tracks disperse from the ponds like wheel spokes from a hub. Always fascinated, I study the print trails and picture the little creatures sleepily snuggling in their dens.

The birds are usually in a flurry overhead. I enjoy the constant aerobatics and chatter of the jays, robins, sparrows, and finches, all of them frequently visiting the water's edge to sip, bathe, and preen.

Luke and I tend to visit during daylight hours, preferring the nonjungle terrain of Billy Goat Hill for our nighttime adventures, motorcycle gangs notwithstanding. Three Ponds is fertile ground for our hungry minds, and Luke and I are drawn here often.

The occasional appearance of an aggressive mockingbird usually disturbs the harmonious interaction of the other birds, and forever reminds me of my bad dream and Sergeant Cavendish's story of Jakey Blume's fatal fall from Eagle Rock.

A few days after the Eagle Rock incident, I decided to tell Luke about my dream of him being attacked like Jakey Blume was. He now monitors the sky like an obsessed astronomer. He's become so shadow-shy and jumpy, reacting badly to every little motion overhead, I wish I had never told him about the mockingbird dream. Truth be told, I don't like the mockingbirds any more than he does.

Today I am prepared to fulfill an oath I swore to myself to avenge the death of Jakey Blume. Armed with my slingshot, my pockets stocked with ball bearings, I am ready and able to shoot—if and when the enemy attacks. A ridiculous thought for a boy who avoids stepping on ants.

We while away the morning sitting with our pant legs rolled up, bare feet dangling in the stilling coolness of the middle pond. We examine the animal prints in the mud and trade speculations about what kinds of animals have preceded us this day. I tire of throwing sticks into the pond for Mac to retrieve, but keep it up because it's the only way to keep him from barking, which he will continue to do until he is good and ready to quit.

"Darn dog. He thinks he's some kind of bird dog."

I smile inside, sensing an opportunity to rile Luke. "You'll be wishing he's a bird dog if those mockingbirds come to visit your head again."

Luke looks at Mac. "Uh, well, you're a good dog." He reaches up and tugs on the visor of his Dodgers cap just to make sure it is there, and I am reminded of that rookie cop who nervously checked his gun the night of the hazing on Billy Goat Hill.

It was Luke who insisted I start packing my slingshot. Of late, heading deep into mockingbird territory requires special preparations. Two pocket loads of ball bearings are cached and ready, but it's a special chore to haul them, requiring considerable work to keep my pants up. What I won't do for Luke in the name of brotherly love. I fondle the bulging supply stuffing my pockets, and like that rookie cop, I double-check to see that the slingshot crammed into my back pocket is still there ready for action.

Mac finally tires of playing "Get the Stick" and ignores my last throw. This prank always rankles me. He can't just go get the stick, return it politely, and say thanks for the game. Nope. He has to make me throw the stick one more time just so he can ignore it and thereby have the last word. If only I had the power to make myself invisible. Then he would run back to where I had been and stand there with the stick in his mouth not knowing what to do—and looking stupid.

Mac sits in the mud, his rump in two inches of turbid water, his tail like a thick black water snake swishing from side to side. He arrogantly stares at me, and I hold his gaze for a moment, then look away and spit into the water. "Chase that."

He puts his head down, closes his eyes, and ignores me.

"Who do you think is better, Drysdale or Koufax?" Luke casually asks.

He is lying on his belly, creating an elaborate baseball diamond in the mud, using his finger like an artist. He's been working on it for over an hour. It actually looks pretty impressive.

"Duke Snider is the best." I know full well he is not talking about power-hitting center fielders. Already I catch a whiff of smoldering cordite.

"I'm talking pitchers, fire throwers, masters of the mound, you big dumb donkey!"

It isn't easy, but I ignore his insult, as Mac ignored mine. "Okay. Who do you think is better?"

He looks up from his muddy handiwork. "I asked you first!"

Now my fuse is burning and I fire back louder. "I asked you second!"

We are angry pint-sized versions of Abbott and Costello. *Who's on First?* Except rarely do we find humor in this non-comedic sibling ritual. Being the older brother, I try to be patient and take the high road with Luke. Admittedly though, now and then I make a wrong turn and get stuck in a quagmire on the low road.

He relishes ensnaring me with perplexing trick questions, black or white, hot or cold, up or down kinds of questions, so that no matter how I respond, he can automatically jump on the contrary side of the fence. He does it on purpose, of course he does, and the best I can do is attempt to throw off his rhythm and detour around the quagmire by echoing his question back to him. The tactic irritates him to no end, which is great fun for the big dumb donkey.

At first I decide not to antagonize him further, but then I change my mind. "Okay, Luke, Drysdale is the better of the two. But I'm glad we have Ron Perranoski in the pen."

I say this not because I necessarily think Drysdale is better, but because I know he thinks Koufax is better.

Smart-alecky as can be, Luke looks up from the mud and glares at me. "No way! Sandy Koufax is an ace!"

"Oh yeah—well Don Drysdale is the king of diamonds!" I point angrily at the mud. "Including that mucky mess of a diamond you're making with your stupid, dinky little fingers!"

Luke jumps to his feet and screams in my face. "Drysdale's the king all right! He's the king of the bean ball!"

Reacting to the rising tension, Mac starts churning the water with his tail, but he doesn't open his eyes. He's heard this a thousand times before.

"It wouldn't take a Drysdale to brush you back from the plate, you little twerp!"

Quagmire!

I step in the mud right where he's constructed his pitcher's mound, mashing my foot down as hard as possible.

Luke gasps. "Hey! You big dumb donkey!"

He clamps onto my leg like a monkey to a vine and knocks me off balance. "Whoa!" I splutter, arms flailing.

I make one futile, spastic lurch to try to right myself before I land front down in two inches of fetid water, burying my face up to my ears in the mud. Luke jumps on my back, landing hard enough to force a loud *Umph!* from my lungs. He starts shoveling gobs of slimy goop onto the back of my head.

He's knocked the wind out of me, and I can't catch my breath—putrid, muddy scum filling my mouth and nose. Mac is now barking furiously at the rough-and-tumble action. Through my moss-clogged ears, his barking sounds like someone beating on a muffled gong.

Frantic for air, I thrust my back upward in a powerful bucking arch, propelling Luke skyward like an overmatched tenderfoot bull rider. Dazed and gagging, I stand up and wipe gunk away from my stinging eyes. I feel a wiggle in my throat and reflexively cough up a big black tadpole.

Yuck!

I open my eyes but cannot focus. I bend over at the waist and blink away pond scum clinging to the inside of my lids. Straining through burning slits, I look toward the pond and spot a vague blue dot moving on the lazy current. In seconds it disappears down a smooth rock flume on the way to the shallower pool of the lower pond.

Where's Luke?

"Luke!"

I choke on a hard lump in my throat, a different kind of panic, and then dive into the water like Johnny Weissmuller rescuing Maureen O'Sullivan from flesh-craving crocodiles.

The middle pond is about twelve feet deep at its center. I have touched the sandy bottom only once before, and that was with my foot. I kick my legs as hard as I can, grab arms full of verdant liquid, and descend faster than I think possible, until I realize it isn't because of my powerful strokes.

I am sinking.

My ball bearing–laden pockets are pulling me down faster than a pair of concrete boots, and all I can think about is how I ignored Luke when he asked me to teach him how to swim.

Nearing the bottom, my ears begin to ache from the pressure. Then my feet touch down harder than I expect, startling me into action. Eyes open, I glance up through an emerald glow and strain to see the faint, rippling sheen of the water's surface.

What a way to go, lying face up at the bottom of a huge vat of lime Jell-O!

Straight out in front of me, my arms wave uselessly, fading at the elbows into handless stubs swallowed up in a murky, greenish gloom. There is so much area to cover, too much, and not enough oxygen to feed the frenetic exertion of every muscle in my body.

I snatch something in my grip that feels like it might be an arm or a leg. My heart surges, and I tug the object to my face only to see a waterlogged piece of wood, part of a tree root, not part of Luke. Angry, I kick my legs and wildly swing my arms, searching the area around me, and I know I have started to cry.

Underwater tears.

Underwater sobbing.

Underwater doom.

On the verge of drowning myself, I turn and kick off the bottom and pump hard toward the light. The sinkers in my pockets hold me down like a baited hook and it takes forever, but at last I reach the surface. As my head comes out of the water, I hear myself screaming for help. I suck my lungs full of life and immediately sink back into the watery dungeon that holds Luke captive.

Again I search, scouring the bottom with my arms and legs until I must kick hard to make it up to the surface and furiously replenish my breath. Down I go again, but Luke is not to be found. I am powerless to do more, and I must have more air before resuming my hopeless search. Keeping my face above water, I desperately try to dig the ball bearings out of my pockets, but to no avail. The moment I stop paddling with my arms, I start to sink.

More air!

God, please help me!

Gasping, choking, fighting to catch my breath, I dog paddle furiously, the stronger kick of my right leg pushing me in a wide arcing circle. Entangled in a mile-long moment of indecision, all I can do is sob.

"Luke! Luke! I'm sorry, Luke!"

Arms and legs working full throttle but rapidly diminishing in thrust, I come around to face due west and look up straight into the glaring afternoon sun. I am spent, defeated. The sun beats down, punishing my face with brutal slaps of hot accusation. I want to die.

Why, God? Some fall off cliffs? Some drown in ponds? But I'm the one to blame. I threw him in the pond. Don't take him. It's not his fault. It's my fault. Take me, God! Luke! I'm sorry. I'm sorry.

Then, just below the lower fringe of the sun's hot glare, I imagine I see something move. I blink hard. There it is again, shapes, two shapes…

"You swim worse than Drysdale pitches, you big dumb donkey!"

There on the muddy bank, with Mac proudly stationed at his side, stands a very angry Luke. I blink again, harder, and try to raise a hand to shield my eyes, but my leaden arms won't respond. Moved by the current, I come around slowly, and my face drifts under a merciful shadow, only to leave me wide open to the blunt force of Luke's petulant glare.

His freckles seem to radiate with energy absorbed from the sun, which towers over him like a giant, tangerine sparkler. And there amid my brokenness and desperation, I am, for a fleeting moment, utterly, profoundly, wonderfully relieved that my brother is safe.

Mac barks, a muffled gong; the pond pours inside me; and I go down in a swirling nebula of bubbles. Spiraling, spiraling, down I go, thankful that God has accepted the trade. I watch as the ghostly forms of Luke and Mac get smaller and smaller, corkscrewing up, up, away, and gone.

I love you, Luke.

I'm going to be with Matthew now.

Take good care of Mac.

It feels like a school of eels are wagging their tails in my face. My eyes flutter open and I swat out instinctively, missing whatever is there. I am astounded to find myself staring eyeball-to-eyeball with Mac, and the eels are actually one big sloshing tongue. I hold still for a moment and let him lick my face. It feels so good the way it affirms I am alive.

Thank You, God.

"What happened?" I feel sick to my stomach, and I groan as I feebly raise myself to a sitting position. My legs weigh ten tons. The ball bearings have turned into bowling balls.

"I think you drownded." Luke cautiously keeps a step out of arm's reach. He is not quite sure if I am mad or not. "But me and Mac saved you." He grins triumphantly but still keeps his distance.

"You mean you jumped back in the water and pulled me out?"

His grin slackens. "Well, uh, not exactly."

Given his uncanny knack for showing up at times like this, I look around half expecting to see Sergeant Cavendish. I don't see him or anyone else for that matter. My head is pounding, my ears are full of water, and the way my stomach is twitching, I think I may have swallowed a few tadpoles.

Then I belch real loud, moss flavor, and Mac gives me one of those head-cocked-sideways, eyebrows-raised looks like he always does whenever Luke or I make a mysterious noise. "Chase that." His tail instantly goes into motion, and my stomach suddenly feels much better. "What do you mean, not exactly? Either you saved me or you didn't." I shake my head from side to side, but my ears remain plugged. Mac looks at me strangely again.

"I don't know how to swim. You know that."

"Well? How did you get me out of the pond then?"

"I didn't." Luke chuckles softly. "Mac did."

"Huh?"

"Mac pulled you out, you big dumb donkey!"

"Well I'll be a bluenose gopher. How in the name of Pinky Lee did you get him to do that?"

"Easy, I just shouted, 'GET THE STICK, MAC!' and pointed at you."

"Well, I'll be dogged!"

"I think you were, Wade."

Physically, mentally, and emotionally depleted, I sprawl on the bank of the middle pond and let a large shaft of afternoon sun bake me dry. With considerable effort, I move twice to remain in the warm, rejuvenating spotlight. When finally I regain enough energy, I pull the slingshot from my back pocket and unload the near deadly ballast from my front pockets.

Still weak and shaky, I mindlessly count the ball bearings and arrange them into letters on the muddy ground in front of me. I give it my best effort, trying to polish up my downbeat mood, but soon one hundred and sixty-six silver marbles spell out the word *STUPID* in six-inch capital letters.

It's a wonder that I ever came up from that first dive. I'm not as smart as Tarzan. Jane never would have survived with Wade Parker running around bare-chested in nothing but a loincloth. With my luck, she probably would've gotten tangled up in one of my swinging vines and strangled to death.

Meanwhile, Luke seems to be enjoying a new level of kinship with Mac. For once Mac did what he asked him to do.

Thank the Lord for that!

And Mac knows he's done something important. He shows off, retrieving everything Luke can find to throw with unusual enthusiasm.

I watch them play while I rest my aching muscles. My anger at Luke has been washed away in a proselyte's conversion. I am blessed to have Luke as a brother and Mac as a friend. Turning it over and over in my mind, I keep coming back to how stupid I was to place Luke in yet another hazardous situation. I really thought he had drowned.

Will I ever learn? Maybe, but in the meantime I can't let him down by appearing weak. He needs to look up to me. I may be in chaos, but it's time to suck it up. I have to reestablish some order and remind Luke who is boss, for his sake.

"Hey, twerp, what happened to your hat?"

In all the excitement, Luke has not realized his hat is missing. In a panic, he reaches up to his head and then reflexively ducks. His eyes snap skyward like a cottontail reacting to the blip of a hawk's shadow.

"It must have come off in the water," he utters stonily, eyes to the vertical, his hand still feeling around on the top of his head.

Mac barks, impatient for Luke to throw the stick dangling from his other hand.

"Darn dog," Luke mutters, instantly reverting to his old ways.

He tosses the stick away without looking down from the sky. Mac watches the stick sail to the far side of the pond. Put off by Luke's lack of sincerity, he turns around twice and sits in the mud. Game over. I smile.

"Darn dog," Luke hisses.

"Don't worry about your hat. We'll find it in the lower pond on our way home."

"Okay," he says tentatively, looking very naked and vulnerable.

I have a thought. Like Luke, old ways are hard to change. A small smile sparks inside me and begins to multiply outward. I adopt a gravely serious tone. "You know what I would do if I were you?"

"What?" He's still looking for jet-trails or maybe a message in the clouds.

My eyelashes flutter dramatically. "I would smear mud all over my head just in case any mockingbirds are in the area." Yes, I am feeling much better. So much better, I can't resist an impulse to push beyond the line of fairness. "You know, the way your red hair lights up in this bright sunshine, you'd probably be safer walking into a bull ring with a red suit on."

He doesn't even look down. He just kneels, scoops, and smears. In a matter of seconds, he looks like a lost gopher popping up in the middle of a peat bog. Maybe I'm not so stupid after all.

The looming shadows turn the pond from an iridescent green to the color of overripe guacamole. Luke is content to sit next to me and repair his earthen headgear whenever I note a piece has dried and fallen off, while I play a restful game of word-spell with my one hundred and sixty-six ball bearings. Just as I discover I have enough ball bearings to spell *Mississippi* if I don't dot the *i*'s, Luke squeals like somebody pinched him.

"What's your problem?" *Can I make smaller letters and have enough ball bearings for Massachusetts?*

"Look," he whispers, rapidly patting more mud on his head.

I look up, hearing fear in his voice. "What?"

He keeps smearing. "Over there."

"Where?"

His lips scarcely move as he hoists a muddy finger and points across the pond. "Two mockingbirds just landed—" *whimper*— "in that bush over there. Get your slingshot."

I choke back a giggle and look where he is pointing. "Where? I don't see any birds."

"Get your slingshot!"

"Okay, okay. Take it easy."

I force myself not to laugh at the streak of goop working its way down his forehead. I pick up the slingshot and take a ball bearing from the second *s* in *Mississippi*. I prepare the ball snugly in the leather sling and pinch the load firmly between my thumb and forefinger.

I've never hit a thing I've ever aimed at with this stupid weapon, and now I'm supposed to hit a bird I can't even see from a hundred feet away? Right.

"Where are they?"

I have about as much chance of hitting a bird as I do to meet Duke Snider. Those birds, if there are any birds, are safer than raw liver crumpets at a Shirley Temple tea party.

"They're right across the middle of the pond. Look on the top branch of that smallest bush next to that L-shaped rock."

He couldn't be more precise. "Oh yeah, I see them." I squint harder. "You're absolutely right. There are two of them, and they're checking out your head, I think."

Luke's neck disappears down inside his T-shirt. Now he looks like a turtle, a scared little mud turtle.

"Kill them," he nervously urges, oblivious to the little chunks of mud now slipping off the end of his nose.

Mac dozed off earlier. He is whining in his sleep, dreaming of

Molly, no doubt. It is just as well that he doesn't see my shot miss. He can be very judgmental.

Luke is about to come out of his skin. "Hurry up! They're getting ready to attack!"

I prop my left elbow on my knee and raise the slingshot to eye level. The birds look to be a mile away as I position their faint little shapes at the center of the yoke. Slowly, I pull back on the black rubber straps, back, back, as far back as I can. My shoulder trembles and the muscles in my forearm bulge from the strain. I hesitate, held back by an itch of guilty sympathy for the birds.

They are so small and I'm so big. It doesn't seem fair. Am I Goliath aiming the slingshot at David? That's not how the story goes.

Luke is nearly apoplectic. "Shoot, Wade! Shoot!"

Aw heck, I ain't gonna hit them anyway. I close my eyes and let go.

Thwack! The ball bearing sizzles forth, singeing the air over the water, and instantly a puff of feathers floats around the bush. In stunned disbelief, I watch as the feathers settle on the leaves like fake snow in a Sears Christmas window display. The recoil of the rubber straps snaps the slingshot out of my hand and flings it into the pond, where it dips and bobs away in search of Luke's Dodgers cap.

"You got 'um!" Luke roars. "You got 'um both!"

He's right. No more birds. *I'm a murderer!*

Mac opens one eye, winks at me, and goes back to sleep.

Luke dances around in a circle, a fearsome warrior celebrating a fruitful hunt, and then takes off upstream toward a spot where he can cross over to the other side without having to swim.

"Wait up, for crying out loud!" Still fazed with a strange mixture of amazement and regret, I hurry to catch up with him.

On the other side of the stream, we hurry back downstream to the middle pond. Out of breath and full of excitement, we jostle through the undergrowth until finally we stand side by side at the feathery bush. There are lots of feathers, but no birds. Puzzled, we push farther into the thicket, scouring the branches and ground as we go.

Robbed of the prize, Luke turns sour. "Some bird dog Mac is.

Look at him lying over there snoozing in the mud. He could be helping us, you know. But he's not even interested. Darn dog."

"Why do you always have to pick on Mac? Just be quiet and keep looking. They've got to be around here somewhere. Birds can't possibly fly with that many feathers missing."

I feel guilty. I am sure they have to be dead, at least one of them anyway.

We push our way deeper into the brush, maybe thirty or forty feet, and come upon a small open space. No birds.

"Darn, Wade. I bet they're hiding and getting ready to launch a counterattack. I need more mud."

"What could have happened to them?"

"Hey, what's that?"

Luke points to a piece of cardboard big enough to use for sliding at Billy Goat Hill. It's standing on end leaning against a waist-high rock, looking quite out of place in these undisturbed surroundings. Noticing something even more peculiar, I step closer and observe a perfectly round hole in the cardboard, exactly the same diameter as my ball bearings.

"Look at that."

We step closer. I lean down to peek through the hole. Luke reaches over and grabs the cardboard. The cardboard falls over.

We both scream!

My face wavers inches away from a man's face. He's sitting upright, legs outstretched, torso leaning back against the rock. His mouth is open as if frozen in mid-speech, his glazed eyes staring in disbelief. And there for the whole world to condemn is my killer ball bearing buried down a bloody vent in his forehead. I see the shimmering sphere lodged one knuckle deep in the finger size hole. Flies already flit around the wound, excited by the early smell of death.

The realization of what I have become rampages to my very core, driving a pile at the pit of my stomach and slamming up my spine to my brain, where a silent scream builds to a mental roar raging to split my skull wide open.

I am a murderer!

A moment later, Mac stands bracing against my weakening legs. He sniffs cautiously at the dead man's shark skin pant leg and looks up at me, his big brown eyes flooding with worry, as if to say: *This is not good, Wade. Not good at all.*

Before I faint, there is an instant of revolting sickness, then a hallucination of me softly descending into the safe, protective arms of my father. But Earl does not catch me. Instead, my head crashes hard on the rock next to the dead man.

five

It is nearly dark when I come to. I am lying near the overpass at San Pasqual Creek. I do not know why I am here or how I got here from the middle pond. *Did I somehow get to my feet and stumble to the road on my own power?* Mac sits next to me, my amazing friend. *Maybe he dragged me this far and then got tired?*

I am dizzy and my head hurts. I feel a plum above my right eye—otherwise, I seem to be in one piece. After a minute, I get up, take a deep breath, and start walking home. Three blocks later a patrol car pulls up behind me and stops at the curb. My heart is vibrating. I am too scared to run but certain I am about to be arrested for murder.

The cop waves me over to the car. "We got a report of somebody lying by the road."

"Yes, sir, it was me. Uh, I mean, my dog accidentally tripped me, and I sort of fell and bumped my head."

"Nice shiner."

"Yes, sir. It hurts, but I'm okay. I'm, uh, on my way home now."

"It'll be dark soon. You better get moving."

The cop is satisfied and drives off. Stunned, I stare at the police car and wish he had been the Sergeant. I think I would have told him the truth. Instead, I throw up on the sidewalk.

Lucinda buys the story I make up about banging my head on a low branch. She is very upset about us losing our tennis shoes, though. Luke panicked, I fainted, and we both ended up at home barefoot. I lie again and tell her some big kids swiped our tennis shoes. Luke isn't talking at all.

Later, Lucinda takes the coffee can down from the crawl space in the hall ceiling. She doesn't know I am in the bathroom with the door cracked open. I hear her crying and know there isn't enough money to replace the tennis shoes and still buy the new pair of high heels she needs for work. Too ashamed to face her, I stay in the bathroom for a long time.

I finally marshal the courage a week later, with my heart quaking to rival the San Andreas, to creep back to Three Ponds to see if our shoes and the man are still there. It is awful. A stabbing pain in my stomach nearly forces me to chicken out halfway there.

At the scene, lots of footprints have been cast in the mud, not from animals, from humans, and more than I remember ever being there before. Everything else is gone: our shoes, Luke's Dodgers cap, my slingshot, all of the ball bearings, the sheet of cardboard with the hole in it—and the dead man.

A knot of nerves in my middle comes up in a sick whoosh, dropping me to the ground in a thicket of bushes amid the only remaining physical evidence of my crime, a scattering of dull, lifeless feathers.

I am so sorry for everything, God.

Weeks pass. Each seems like a century. Rampant guilt consumes me from the inside out in a lonesome, protracted torture of conscience. Methodically, bit by bit, like a carcass hauled away by ants, I am being dismantled. What little that is positive about me melts away, shrivels down to nothing, absorbed by the gluttonous sponges of fear and remorse. I long for Earl to show up and beat a confession out of me, knowing I will feel so much better after it's over. And what if he kills me? Well, so much the better.

The knot above my right eye is gone. A faint bruise remains, like a smudge that won't wash off. That my injury was only minor serves to compound my guilt. I should have at least lost an eye.

Luke is making progress. Yesterday he came out of the house and sat on the porch for a whole twenty minutes. His young conscience bothers him, too. He feels bad for running away and leaving me lying there. I tell him not to worry about it, that I am proud of him for not fainting, like I did. Still, he is suffering, and I don't know what to do for him.

The scene churns in my mind, like I'm flipping through photographs from a homicide file. Cardboard shifting, gaping mouth, horror-filled eyes, and the shiny ball bearing staring, staring, glaring out at me like an angry silver bumblebee wedged deep in a bloody hole in a cadaverous telephone pole.

And there is the nightmare that won't quit. It's always the same. I dive into the pond to save Luke, and a chrome-eyed Cyclops wearing Luke's Dodgers cap grabs my feet and pulls me down to the bottom. I try to swim but can't because somehow my tennis shoes are stuck onto my hands with the laces tied together like handcuffs. At the end, I'm drowning alongside Luke's lifeless body with Mac swimming in circles around us underwater. He's barking furiously, but what I hear sounds like he's screaming, GET THE STICK, MURDERER! I cry out for help, and billowing streams of mockingbird feathers flow from my mouth. I awake drenched and shivering.

The darkness has conquered and occupied my dreams; the invisible foe nearly has me beat, and unless there is a beautiful sky in the middle of this storm, I don't think I can take any more.

It takes me almost thirty minutes to decide not to write a note. After watching him sleep for a while, I leave Luke snoring peacefully. I order Mac to stay with him before easing myself out into the moonless night. I look back through the open window one last time and silently grant Luke full dominion over the room and our meager treasures. Mac whimpers when at length I quietly slide the window shut. He senses the dark sadness in me and is driven by an instinctive need to protect me. He is angry that I won't let him come, but I can't let him interfere.

My sandaled feet get soaked as I cross the wet grass—I left my brand-new tennis shoes, half of Lucinda's sacrifice, behind for Luke to grow into.

It is so dark, but I have made my decision. Yet as I stand on the sidewalk looking back at the house, I can't help wishing that Luke and I were sneaking out once again to bask in the nocturnal beatitude of Billy Goat Hill. We had some good times, Luke and I. One last glance toward the bedroom nearly stops me cold. Mac is framed in the window, his big brown eyes pained, desperate. Fearing he may break the glass, I sternly motion for him to get back from the window. He stares for a long moment and then dejectedly complies.

Walking down the hill of Ruby Place, I feel more alone than I ever have before, like the last boy on earth. At Mrs. Roberson's fence, Molly barks once, and it occurs to me I will never hear that sound again. The dead man's face whips through my mind, telling me he is already there where dogs don't bark.

I cross Figueroa to the east side of the street and begin my trudge north. Like a captured soldier prodded along by an abusive captor, I lean forward at a disconsolate angle and march. Wretched, forlorn—I mark a steady pace toward my self-imposed fate.

At some point along the way, I look up and catch myself longing for that sparkling miracle, the beautiful tangerine sun that delivered Luke back to me at Three Ponds. No such luck. Not even one last shooting star to light my deserted path. It doesn't matter. There is no need for beacons, benchmarks, or moonlit maps. I know the way to Suicide Bridge.

The ebony sky seals my loneliness within me.

At each cross street, I call out its name from memory—

Myosotis, Roy, Springvale, Saint Albans, Delphi, Oak Crest Way, La Prada, Hillandale, Burwood, Strickland, Poppy Peak, Annan Way, Tipton Way, Crestwood Way, Buena Vista Terrace, Glen Arbor, Rockdale, Yosemite Drive, Lanark, La Loma Road and at last, Colorado Boulevard.

Eagle Rock looms in the darkness above me as I push on up the hill toward the bridge.

I sit on the curb in front of Henry's Rite Spot and catch my breath. A faint light shimmers inside the front window and a good memory steals a moment. I think about Henry's quart-size strawberry shakes—the best. Earl used to treat us to those shakes once in a while, back in the good old days when he and Lucinda got along. My brain cruelly teases me with the taste and scent of strawberries.

Earl had his good points. I have missed him something fierce, but I never let on. I didn't want to make things worse for Luke. No sense crying over spilt milk shakes anyway. I stand up and resume my lonely march.

The lights on the bridge snap into my field of vision, warm and welcoming like faithful candles in a window. As bright and disarming as Miss Cherry's lovely smile but dangerously insincere, the lights are a clever disguise obscuring a grotesque monster. The bridge is a huge dolmen tomb for an exquisite covey of wayward souls. Now the youngest to take the solemn oath, I am seduced by its arches whose promise to quell my anguish and despair brings hope and comfort to the ultimate capricious act. I hear the bridge whispering my name, and I am not afraid.

I accept the unholy invitation and plod out to the middle of the span, sure that there is nothing left to do but wait for the sun to appear as my witness. I have arrived early. Waiting for the box office to open has always been painful, and here I am the first one in line again. I lean against the railing and try to will the dead man out of my mind. I don't want him to jump with me. This is private and personal, and I don't even know his name.

All of this flits around in the last part of my brain not yet petrified by ravenous guilt as I look down at the unforgiving concrete channel glistening in the dawn two hundred feet below. I under-stand how the bridge earned its name. Now I know how the dozens of tormented souls that have gone before me felt just before they solved their problems.

Suicide Bridge plays the part well, its hideous architecture per-fect for a classic Gothic horror movie. Constructed of two Model-T width lanes of aged, discolored concrete, the bridge looms high above a threatening gorge. It is not a cheery place, but quite suitable for those in a beaten and hopeless state of mind.

A short way up the draw is a venue famous for some of the most jubilant celebrations of modern times, the Rose Bowl. From where I'm standing, I can just make out the top of its magnificent oval protruding out of the daybreak mist. The vision reminds me of when Earl took me with him to the '55 Rose Bowl game. I was going on five at the time…

Two minutes into the third quarter I announce that I have to go to the bathroom. Earl is already drunk, and it angers him that I hadn't gone to the restroom during halftime. Not wanting to miss any of the action, he sends me off to find the facilities by myself.

I get lost in the crowd. At first I am frightened, but after a few minutes of aimless wandering, I merge into an adventure. I circle the stadium two, maybe three times, for the most part enjoying the crowded festivities. The football game is nearly over when I finally spot Earl and sit back down on the bench next to him. He barely glances at me, unaware that I've been absent for nearly an hour. *How can someone who looks so much like me not care about me?*

The bridge seems to understand.

The majestic vision of the Rose Bowl evaporates when the dead man's face flashes into my consciousness, a pasty-gray contorted ver-sion of Ricky Ricardo's face. He just sits there leaning against the rock at Three Ponds, staring at me. My mind bumps down a stair-case of questions:

Who are you?
Did you have a wife?
Did you have any children?

Did you ever take them to the Rose Bowl?

What were you doing there under that piece of cardboard?

Why were you so well dressed in a sharkskin suit and expensive shoes?

Questions, questions, questions, but for me there never seem to be any answers.

Wincing pain throbs behind my temples, like it does when you eat freezing-cold ice cream too fast. I can't get the dead man out of my mind. He's been tormenting me nonstop since Carl, right on time, fired up his Chevy and headed off to bake and wrap his daily quota of twenty thousand loaves.

Minutes tick away. Nobody gets in line behind me. The bridge lights shut off, changing shifts with the first glow of daybreak. Distant sounds of awakening commerce signal the end of the city's slumber. Soon I will not be alone. I look down again and watch while a morning mist crawls out from the rocks and drapes the channel with fresh-smelling linen custom-made for my weary bones. It won't hurt—I'll just jump into bed, pull up the covers, and go to sleep.

I think of Mac, and a tear rolls down and falls away from the tip of my nose. I watch it plummet and prepare to follow. My wounded mind closes in on itself, incapable of distinguishing anything except the final critical task, and one last selfless thought. My lips tremble over the words. "I'm sorry, Luke."

Overriding the oppressive sorrow, I begin to form the intent, the mental instructions.

It is time.

The muscles in my right leg respond...lift up over...the rail. *Please forgive me, God.*

So deep am I mired in my gloom, I do not hear the car that has come across the bridge and stopped not ten feet away from where I stand.

A man's voice booms loud over the drone of the motor, startling me out of my trance. "Hey, kid! You're out and about kind of early, aren't you?"

My leg slumps back down on the deck. I turn around and see an unfamiliar car. A big car, bright-white and full of energy, like an ivory stallion out on a morning run. Embarrassed that my face is a picture of pain and sorrow, I sit on the curb and put my head in my hands. I am ready to kill myself, but I am not ready to cry in front of a stranger.

The driver leans across the front seat to the open passenger window. "What's the matter, kid? You got problems?"

I nod without showing my face, like a silly toddler playing a game of peek-a-boo. The man turns off the motor and gets out of the car. I steal a look and quickly wipe my eyes.

It's him! He's in his uniform, which looks out of place and strange in contrast with the civilian vehicle. I note the familiar spit-shined, black knee boots as he approaches from around the back of the car.

It has been a year and a half, but when he sees my face, he recognizes me right away. "Wade Parker? Kind of far from home, aren't you?"

I nod again. It is so good to hear his voice again. It warms me a little. "What are you doing way over here, sir?"

"I'm on my way home. I used to live in Highland Park, but I live in South Pasadena now—not very far from here. I've got a little place off Fair Oaks."

"Oh. I thought you had to live in Los Angeles."

"That used to be the rule, but not anymore. Say, you're not related to Chief Parker are you?"

"No, I'm not an Indian." I do not intend to make a joke. It just comes out that way. I chuckle sarcastically to myself, my emotions splitting wider than the Grand Canyon. Perplexed at first, he gets it and smiles.

A car starts across the bridge in the same lane that the Sergeant stopped his car. The big white stallion will have to gallop on or let the car go around.

He opens the passenger door. "Come on, get in."

I hesitate for a moment and then do as he orders. He slams the car door, hurries around the hood, and jumps in behind the wheel. Gunning the engine, he puts the stallion in gear and the rear hoofs yelp. "She's got great traction."

As if I know what that means.

We cross into Pasadena, and I look out the rear window at the bridge. My solution has been stolen away from me. *I'm not worth spit.*

He makes a few turns, and a blurry five minutes later swings the big white car around to the back of a restaurant called the Den.

He cuts the engine and sets the brake. "I just brought her home yesterday."

"What? Oh, you mean the car."

He grins proudly. "She's a 1956 Buick Special—far from new, but just barely broken in. I got her for a pretty good price from a White Rock beverage salesman over in Highland Park." He's still grinning. "Like her?"

"I've never been in a car this big before."

He strokes the steering wheel. "I haven't picked out a name for her yet." He looks at me, inviting a suggestion. I shrug.

"I know. I can't think of anything either." He rolls up his window and motions for me to do the same. "Come on, let's go get some breakfast."

I move slowly. My stomach isn't interested in food. My mind is still back on Suicide Bridge.

We enter the building through a rear service door and tramp down a dim hallway that smells of animal fat and stale produce. I slog along behind him like a mindless drone. A couple of turns later, we emerge through swinging doors into a cramped but clean, well-ordered, brightly lit kitchen. My eyes narrow to adjust to the light.

An elderly baldheaded man no more than an inch taller than me, and thin as can be except for a bowling ball shaped gut, stands at a stainless steel sink full of bobbing potatoes. His back is to us and he turns abruptly, startled by unexpected visitors. I immediately notice an array of tattoos on the man's wet forearms. It's impossible, even in my spiritless mood, to look at this little man and not smile.

"Well, praise God! How are you doing, Lyle?" The little man cackles. He flashes a smile that is way too big for his elfish face and quickly wipes his hands on an apron tied snugly below his round belly.

I watch with fascination as the tattoos on his forearm appear to move when he reaches to shake hands with the Sergeant. I look closer and recognize the tattoos are all of Jesus, the same on his other arm. I see Jesus by the seashore, Jesus standing near a well with a woman, Jesus standing before a crowd of people, and Jesus on the cross.

"I couldn't be better, Rodney. How are you?"

"It doesn't do any good to complain. Praise the Lord anyway— that's my motto." He cackles again.

I am still very distraught, but I can't keep from smiling. This little man isn't a dwarf, but his high-pitched laugh and spunky disposition remind me of the Munchkins in *The Wizard of Oz*, my favorite movie.

The little man turns his grin on me. "And who might this young colt be?"

He hobbles over and thrusts Jesus at me. His eccentric gait suggests the presence of an invisible barrel between his legs, his knees splayed three times farther apart than his ankles. To say he is bowlegged would be an understatement.

I shake his hand. "My name is Wade Parker, sir. It's nice to meet you."

"Rodney Bernanos. It's a pleasure to meet you, too. Just call me Rodney, if you please. You're nearly as tall as me so you can save the *sir* for teachers, preachers, and jail keepers."

"Huh?"

He clips short another cackle when a gray cat leaps from some unknown springboard and lands gracefully on his right shoulder, where it proceeds to sit perfect as a parrot on a perch.

Intrigued by the man and the cat, I watch them both as a trace of an impression tickles my consciousness. *Bernanos? Why does that name sound familiar?*

Rodney reaches up as natural as can be and commences scratching the cat behind its ears, as if the cat had been there all along. This motion stands the tattoo of Jesus on the cross in an upright position and makes the cross appear to move as though swaying with the wind. My stare is flagrant.

"Like my tattoos, do you?" A warm acknowledgement twinkles in the little man's eyes.

I stammer, unsure if my curiosity is impolite or rude. "Sorry, sir."

"Don't be sorry, son. It's a good thing to want to look at Jesus. Jesus changes lives, you know. I used to have naked lady tattoos on my arms. When Jesus came to live in my heart, everything changed. So it was off with the naked ladies and on with my Lord and Savior."

"Really?" Is he pulling my leg? I glance at the Sergeant and then look a little closer at the tattoos.

In Rodney's eyes I see truth and sincerity. Something about this strange little man makes me feel good, makes me feel like I belong, even if I do outweigh him. I think of Miss Cherry that night on Billy Goat Hill. Her special warmth and caring made me feel the same way. Drawing upon a new ripple of confidence, I continue my inspection of Rodney's unusual artwork. "Why did you have naked ladies on your arms?"

Rodney cackles with delight and holds up both arms, inviting an even closer look. "It was one lady, actually—my devoted wife, Doris. God rest her soul. It was during World War One, and I was a young freedom fighter in France who desperately missed his equally young wife. A Parisian tattoo artist worked from photographs and the vivid visions in my head. The tattoos of my beloved Doris helped keep me alive during the worst of it. You might say Doris stood at the door of death with old Rodney several times."

"Wow!"

He cackles again. "We were quite a couple, inseparable, and crazy about each other. Oh, how we loved to dance." He frees a mirthful snicker, and his eyebrows wiggle in remembrance of young romance.

As though spying baby birds in a nest, the cat perched on Rodney's shoulder furtively watches his eyebrows for additional movement. Its mouth twitching, the cat is clearly ready to pounce. I glance again at Sergeant Cavendish. He notices the cat's intentions, too, and his face blooms in a mixed bouquet of smile and grin.

"You wouldn't believe my one and only Doris. What a wonderful woman she was. But, Lord of all that is sacred..." He shakes his head sharply. "Sometimes that woman would push me harder than a starving jockey on a three-legged nag."

Jockey? Rodney Bernanos? Earl always used to talk about betting the ponies. He mentioned the name Bernanos before. Well I'll be, this funny little man used to be a jockey.

"But, I have to be honest with you. I do miss Doris something fierce." He holds his arms out in front of him and gives them a wistful look. His animated face slackens. "You understand about covering her up, don't you? You see, she's with Jesus now."

"I think so."

Then he jumps on a fresh horse faster than a Pony Express rider running behind schedule. "But by golly, you could seal that mighty mouth of hers in a burl wood box, bury it with the pharaohs, and I'd still be able to hear her screech when she called me."

I step back, a little shocked. "Screech?"

"Oh, could she screech. She never appreciated her likeness on my arms, no sir, not one bit. She died not long after the war. To be honest with you, Wade—and Lyle knows all about this—I didn't want to go on living without my Doris. For a lot of years after she passed, I was lost and eaten up inside with sadness and loneliness. Then one day God worked a miracle in my life. He took away my hopelessness. And not long after that, I decided to cover up Doris with Jesus."

I am mesmerized by this man. "Those are real fine tattoos, sir."

Rodney flexes his forearms and cackles again. The cat hunches low on his shoulder watching the bird nests for the slightest sign of movement.

"I can hear her right now. 'Rod-*neee*!'" he screeches. "That's just how she'd say it. 'Rod-*neee*!'"

Rodney is something to behold—the bald head, the bowling ball belly, and the cat on his shoulder—all the while cackling like a chicken that just laid a three yolker. The cat, annoyed by Rodney's screeching, gives me a salty look, as if to warn me that the eyebrow nests are all his, and then refocuses on his potential prey. I need to sit down before I fall down and scoot onto a stool next to the sink full of bobbing potatoes.

"'Rod-*neee*! You don't know which way you're going unless you're on a crazy horse running in a circle! Rod-*neee*! Those darn horses are smarter than you!' She was right about that." He grins and takes a deep breath. "'Rod-*neee*! You love those horses more than you love me!' Lordy that woman could hurt a man's feelings when she wanted to. Well, you know what?"

"What?" I am holding my breath to suppress my laughter.

He calms himself and returns his fingers to the backs of the cat's ears. "Old Rodney always knows where he's going now. And once in a while, when I feel just a little bit lost or lonely, I hold up an arm, right or left, left or right, and my sweet Lord Jesus points me in the right direction."

The eyebrows wiggle again, and this time the cat is ready. It flicks out a hard left jab, followed by a right cross, then another hard left jab, and then leaps from Rodney's shoulder to my lap, where it promptly curls into a tight ball of purring fur.

The pummeling leaves Rodney's bushy gray-brown eyebrows in a muss. I can't contain myself and slide to the floor in a heap of laughter, the stool toppling over to the floor beside me. The cat rides down with me, unflappable in his prowess and victory. The Sergeant is practically gagging he is laughing so hard.

Rodney, with no loss of dignity, casually spits on his fingers and smoothes his eyebrows back into place. He gives the cat a respectful look. "You can see why I named the feisty little palooka Rocky. Only the boldest of rodents come around with a cat named Rocky Mouseano in the ring, uh—" *cackle*—"kitchen I mean."

I roll on the floor as months of repressed emotion burst from me in a geyser of joyful release.

Composure comes slowly to the raucous gathering. The Sergeant and I sit on the floor as Rodney keeps us all acting goofy and silly. I look at the Sergeant sitting next to me, and he's laughing and smiling as much or more than I am. It's been a year and a half, yet the strange bond I previously felt with him seems as strong and mysterious as ever. When that motorcycle gang thundered to the crest of Billy Goat Hill I was scared half to death, only to be mesmerized when he ripped the latex prop from his face as we stood in the dark at the top of the Crippler. I was stunned when he appeared at Eagle Rock like a ghost from the past, then captivated by his cryptic message of caution and responsibility. Now he shows up like only a guardian angel could and whisks me off of the bridge of no return, only to five minutes later introduce me to the kindest most fascinating person I have ever met. *How can this be?*

It's a magical moment here in this kitchen with these men. I am alive. I want to be alive. I am grateful to be alive. And I feel sure, looking at the Sergeant and not seeing the police uniform but only the man, that our special bond has now been forged of iron. He looks at me and smiles. Is he reading my mind? He gives me the thumbs-up. I return the signal. To me, the deal has been sealed.

As Rodney lays out the fixings for an incredible breakfast feast, I privately wish for the courage to tell the Sergeant about the dead man.

Rodney Bernanos, by his own account, cooks better than he ever raced horses. Already well past seventy, his riding career occurred long before I was born. But he certainly proves his mastery of the culinary arts this morning.

The Sergeant hangs back and lets me and Rodney get better acquainted. I learn how to make *horsecakes*—buttermilk batter with a palm of oats, diced apples, and four sugar cubes mixed in thoroughly, tail up when you plop them on the preheated griddle, and a whinny when you flip them over. The entire procedure is carried out while dancing in place to an adolescent rhythm closely resembling the great American classic, "The Hokey-Pokey." Rodney's demonstration is priceless.

He explains that his secret horsecake recipe helped him woo Doris. "She fell in love with my horsecakes first, and then she fell in love with me."

While he supervises me at the stove, he shares stories from the racing world, critiquing some of the more famous jockeys like Eddie Arcaro, Bill Hartack, Willie Shoemaker, and Johnny Longden. He claims to have taught Longden everything he knows about jockeying, plus some. When he moves on to the horses, his heart swells with pure passion and his little eyes glow like flares. He lauds mounts with odd names such as Kelso, Round Table, Nashua, and Citation, none of which, he makes very clear, he ever had been blessed to ride. He particularly raves about a newcomer named Carry Back, making news for his sensational late rushes in the stretch.

But his all-time favorite is a magnificent horse named Silky Sullivan, which he claims is the greatest come-from-behind thoroughbred of all time. "Silky Sullivan has heart, Wade. More heart than most men I have known." His glowing eyes shine with moisture. "Sometimes in my dreams I hear Doris telling me that I have a heart like Silky Sullivan. Imagine that, me with a heart like Silky Sullivan.

"Well, actually my old heart isn't so strong anymore. I tell you, as hard on me as Doris sometimes was, that woman also knew how to make a man feel proud. She had good points and bad points, like all of us, I guess. Yes, my one and only Doris was a very special woman. When you grow up, Wade, I pray God will bless you with a wife just like her."

"Does her name have to be Doris?"

Cackle. "What would you like it to be?"

"How about…Cherry?"

"Oh, so you've met Cherry, have you?"

"Yes, sir, just once."

Rodney gives the Sergeant a strange look that I don't understand.

The three of us sit in an upholstered leather booth in the main dining room of the Den. I catch on that we are special guests when

I realize there are no other customers or employees present. The Den is strictly a dinner house open for business at 4:30 p.m. seven days a week. It's an upscale place catering to the type of clientele who appreciate candlelight and fancy napkins. Stylish but well broken in, a decor of thematic elegance sits like bait in an alluring trap, ready to capture the fancy of artful equestrians and rueful horsemen alike. Horse racing memorabilia sets the ambience, each booth a shrine to a specific famous horse or jockey as evidenced by spotlighted photographs and oil paintings.

We sit in the Sir Gordon Richards booth and enjoy our horse-cakes smothered with apple butter and hot maple syrup. With Rodney's permission, I taste coffee for the first time in my life. I pretend I like it.

Halfway into the meal, my thoughts drift during a lull in the conversation. Maybe an hour has passed since I leaned over the bridge railing and watched that tear drip from my nose and fall like a tracer bullet leading the way. I envision myself lying in a bloody mangled mess, cold meat and crunched bones waiting for some hapless mortal to come along and be marred for life by the grisly discovery. I shiver and try to shake the image.

I should have been bothered with thoughts of Lucinda. I should have thought about how she would have second-guessed every child-rearing decision she ever made, how she would have tortured herself with self-blame—the very affliction I know so much about. And poor Luke, how he would have floundered through years of resentment, his broken heart festering, raw, the wounds of desertion and betrayal refusing to heal.

And then there is Mac, my trusted confidant, my noble protector. Loyal beyond death, he would have faithfully waited for the boy who said "stay" and then never came home. A day, a week, a year—however long it took—he would have followed my scent through a thousand nuclear battlefields to get to that point on the bridge, from where, with his tail wagging and his heart filled with love, he would have jumped. I close my eyes. *Thank You, God, for not letting any of this happen.*

Not only am I still alive, I am being fed and entertained by a jokecracking ex-jockey restaurateur who almost needs a booster chair to see over the stack of horsecakes piled on the plate in front of him. I sit here in amazement, radiating energy like a crystal in the sun. Instead of recrimination, I feel perfect, in harmony with the universe, my symmetry complete, as if molded from the purest of elements by the hands of a loving and forgiving Creator. A short ride in a slightly used Buick captained by a Sergeant named Lyle has delivered me from the balustrade of despair to the open gates of the future. I feel special. I feel chosen.

Rodney covers his mouth to belch, then shovels in a last big forkful. "Want some more horsecakes, Wade?"

"Just one more—please."

Cackling with delight, he gets up and heads for the kitchen. Rocky trails after him, his tail straight up in the air like an antenna alert for important signals.

"Pretty neat guy, isn't he?" the Sergeant says once Rodney is out of earshot.

"He's really wild, sir. How did you meet him?"

"Rodney kind of saved my life a long time ago."

"Really, how did he do that?" *If the Sergeant says, "He saved me from jumping off a bridge," I'm leaving.*

"It's a long story. Maybe I'll tell you about it sometime."

"So, you've known each other for a long time?"

"I've known Rodney all my life. He knew my mother and father. They died in 1934 in a fire. After that, Rodney raised me. I lived with him except for a couple of years during World War Two."

Something in his voice makes me think he doesn't want to talk about his parents. "Did Rodney save your life by pulling you out of the fire?"

"No. Rodney had nothing to do with the fire."

What an odd answer. I didn't think Rodney set the fire. No way would I think that.

Rodney reappears with a final horsecake big enough to choke a horse. He sets the large platter down in the middle of the table. "That's the last one, gents. Eat what you can."

The three of us pick at the pizza-size horsecake and talk some more.

Rodney feeds small pieces to Rocky, who sits on the floor performing for his master. "He's not as smart as a horse, but he's a good animal. Do you have any pets, Wade?"

"Yes, sir, I have a dog named Mac. He's very intelligent."

"What kind of dog is he?"

"Shepherd and Doberman mix."

Rodney thinks for a moment. "Does he still have his ears and tail?"

"Yes, but he doesn't like us to tease him about it. We couldn't afford to get him clipped and cropped."

Cackle. "No, I guess he wouldn't appreciate being teased. Boy, did I ever learn the hard way not to bad-mouth horses." He grins. "Well, not to their faces anyway." *Cackle!* "I caught a ride once on a hot-blooded three-year-old named Abdulla. She was fighting the gate real hard, and we were about to get disqualified. Out of frustration, I told her she wasn't fit to make dog food." *Cackle!* "She threw me in the mud two lengths out of the gate and won the race without me. It's best not to antagonize animals. Isn't that right, Rocky?"

He gives the cat another morsel and thinks a little bit longer. "This dog of yours, Mac, you say?"

"Yes, sir, Mac is his name."

"Well, your Mac wouldn't happen to have a noticeable scar on his right hindquarter would he?"

"Why, yes he does. How did you know that?"

"I heard a racket in my neighbor's backyard one night some months back. I knew my neighbor wasn't home so I grabbed my flashlight and went out in my pajamas to investigate. I saw your dog, Mac, playing connect the dots with a lovely young Dalmatian by the name of Antoinette. Unbeknownst to me, my neighbor paid a stud fee the next day hoping for a lucrative litter of mascot pups for the Glendale Fire Department."

We are laughing again, this time on a full stomach.

"You should see the little buggers." *Cackle!* "They look like Picasso's worst nightmare. I told my neighbor he ought to try to sell them to the police department instead. Maybe they could use them as undercover dogs." He gives the Sergeant an accusing look. "They should make fine cop dogs. They'll probably change their spots."

I do not get Rodney's meaning, but I read well enough between the lines to know it can't be good. His odd reaction to my having met Miss Cherry combined with this comment about the puppies has me feeling a little tilted and confused. I glance at the Sergeant. He looks uncomfortable, maybe even a little pale. He doesn't respond to Rodney's jab. Rodney turns back to face me and replaces a cold look with a warm smile.

"I might keep one pup for myself though, now that I know they were sired by your dog Mac."

"So, you live in Glendale, sir?"

"I sure do, right below Adventist Hospital." *Cackle!* "Your Mac covers a lot of ground doesn't he?"

"Sometimes Mac is a very busy boy."

Rodney crows like a rooster. "I couldn't have put it more delicately myself!"

The Sergeant just shakes his head and remains quiet.

For the next few minutes Rodney's crack about the puppies making good cop dogs rolls back and forth inside my head.

The time comes for Rodney to get on with his workday. I wish we could stay longer, but I settle for his promise that we will get together again soon. We say our so-longs and load our full bellies back into the Buick. I have started to worry about Luke being home alone, even with Mac on guard, and gladly accept the Sergeant's offer of a ride home. I wave to Rodney as we pull out of the parking lot and hope that I really will see him again. Earl always said he would see me again, too.

The sun is out in full glory. The mist in the Arroyo has retreated back to wherever it comes from. And as we cross back over Suicide Bridge, I feel queasy about beating the odds.

Why am I still alive? I don't understand it, but naively I believe some understanding will come to me later. I watch uneasily as we pass by the spot that nearly claimed my life barely two hours earlier. A lifetime ago. I turn and look over the seat through the rear window.

"Never look back, Wade."

I let go of my thoughts and look at his face. "What do you mean?"

The corner of his eye crinkles as he gives me an all-knowing smile. I've seen the expression before. He understands more than he is saying. He must have realized why I was there on the bridge and what I was about to do.

In placid silence, we drive on, the soft vibration of the big Buick engine gradually settling my emotions back to neutral. I sense his eyes on me several times, but I can only look straight ahead and watch the street signs go by in reverse order of the litany I had earlier chanted to the dismal death-march sky.

I had not expected to see any of this again, and now in the healthy light of this glorious new day, every tree, every house, every beautiful blade of grass sparkles with the invigorating shine of renewal.

Meeting Rodney Bernanos has borne a tonic effect, but the Sergeant literally saved my life. I would have jumped if he had not come along. His showing up on the bridge at that critical moment couldn't have been a simple coincidence. It had to be part of a plan. It just had to be.

Ruby Place. Before, the name of our street always conjured up visions of a loud and obnoxious woman who chewed gum and wore bright lipstick. Now the word whistles from my lips with reverence for the precious gem that it is. I am filled with a strange new appreciation for everything. Wow! Imagine that. I am privileged to live on Ruby Place.

My imagination soars as the big stately Buick ascends the hill. I am a prince returning to my castle. Regal curb feelers fore and aft trumpet the arrival of my royal coach.

"Queenie," I say.

The Sergeant gives me a puzzled look. "Queenie?"

"She is a girl, isn't she?"

"Who?"

"I thought you were a trained investigator."

"I am." His forehead scrunches.

"You asked me to think of a name for something." I pat the seat to give him a hint.

"Oh yeah." He grins. "Queenie—I like it. Queenie she is."

Hah! I named his car! Cool!

The screen door slams open, and Luke bounds off the porch like he is greeting rare company. His spirit seems miraculously lifted as well. "Hey, you big dumb donkey! Where in the heck have you been?"

You'd think I was the ice cream man giving out free Popsicles the way he's grinning at me. "I went for a long walk this morning. The Sergeant gave me a ride home."

"How come you didn't take me?"

"I don't know. I guess I needed to be by myself." I am hoping he'll let it go at that. I don't want to have to lie to him.

"Hi, Mister Scar. Cool car."

"Thanks, Luke. You can call me Lyle or even Mister Cavendish, if you like."

"Okay, Mister Crabfish." He is in a rare mood.

"Say. What do you guys think about letting me take your picture in front of Queenie?"

"Queenie is the car's name," I inform Luke, proudly adding, "She's got great traction."

The Sergeant gets out of the car and opens the trunk. He removes a camera case and ushers Luke and me to the front of Queenie, where he positions us standing in front of her massive grill. He makes us feel special, like two little Buick Specials posing with the Queen Mother herself.

Lucinda could never get us to stand still and have our picture taken, but Luke and I pose for the Sergeant like professional models.

We patiently wait while the photographer gets ready for the shot.

Luke watches him fiddle with the camera, and I can tell he is thinking about something. Then, without warning, out it comes. "Do you ever take pictures of dead bodies with that camera?"

The shutter clicks, the flashbulb explodes inside my brain, and reality drives home not in a royal coach, but more like a sledgehammered wedge of tempered steel driving into petrified oak. I split in half. Dry me, stack me, burn me, and scatter my ashes to the wind. I'm still a murderer!

The picture the Sergeant takes shows a boy who by all appearances looks well-balanced and happy. A picture is worth a thousand words? I doubt anyone will ever look at that picture and say anything other than "cute kids" and "nice car."

"Yes, as a matter of fact I have, Luke."

It sounds like an accusation to me. Luke is on another planet. He seems to make no connection between Lyle, Mr. Policeman taking pictures of dead bodies, and our real-life horror show at Three Ponds. I must look whiter than Queenie as I stare off into space, my short-lived hold on happiness suddenly frozen, repressed by living, breathing fear.

The Sergeant looks me in the eye. "What's the matter, Wade? You look like you just saw a ghost."

In my mind his words are marinated with innuendo. *Do they handcuff ten-year-old boys?* "I guess I ate too many horsecakes."

Luke looks at me funny. "Horsecakes?"

"I'll tell you about it later, Luke."

The phone rings inside the house. "I'll get it!" Luke bounds toward the house. "It's probably Lucinda calling to see if you showed up. She was in a snit about going to work and leaving me at home alone."

The Sergeant puts the camera back in the trunk. "Well, Wade, it's been quite an experience. But I better say so long for now."

I am flooded with adrenaline. I don't want him to go. I want him to come into the house, sit on the sofa, and hear my confession. But I can't speak. I am scared to death, afraid that he won't like me anymore, fearful that the government will ship me off to Sing Sing or Alcatraz. Or worse yet, to the bottom of a pond filled with the syrupy green blood of a million Martians where I'll live forever, breathing in goop through gaping gills like a giant carp.

He starts up Queenie.

Inside my mind I am screaming, *PLEASE WAIT!*

Luke yells from the front door. "Wade, it's Lucinda! She wants to talk to you!"

I glance at Luke and nod.

The Sergeant rolls down his window and motions me over to the car. I rock closer on numb stilts. He holds out his hand to give me something. I present my open palm and look for a sign of forgiveness in those all-knowing eyes.

Holding his closed hand over mine, he speaks in a foreboding tone. "Have you boys ever been to Mississippi?" He lets something drop into my hand.

I shake my head.

He stares at me for a moment and then eases Queenie out slowly and pulls away from the curb. I see his eyes in the rearview mirror. I glance down at my outstretched hand, and there to my horror is a shiny silver ball bearing, the one from the second *s* in *Mississippi*, the gouged-out eye of the Cyclops.

I want to throw it all the way to Barstow, but it won't let me. In a stupor, I put it in my pocket and watch Queenie make her stately descent down the hill of Ruby Place. The Sergeant raises an arm out the open window. Powerless to do otherwise, I raise an arm in return. And then he is gone.

"Wade! You better get the phone. She's madder than a hornet."

I go into the house and pick up the receiver. "Hello…Yes…I'm sorry…Okay…I promise…Bye." I hang up the telephone and walk like a zombie toward the bedroom.

Mac, sitting exactly where I had ordered him to stay so many hours before, wags his tail. "Come," I whisper.

I lie down on my bed, and he jumps up next to me and plops his head on the pillow. "You are Toto and I am Dorothy."

He licks my cheek.

"There's no place like home with you, Mac."

No longer in control of my dreams, deathly afraid that the dead man Cyclops is waiting for me, I close my eyes and repeat the words over and over inside my head.

Never look back, Wade.

Never look back, Wade.

Never look back, Wade.

I am still a murderer, but it seems my meeting with Rodney has some lasting benefit. Because for the next twelve hours, Doris and Jesus help me and Rodney peel, cook, and mash four bushels of potatoes. I wish I would never wake up.

Six

The Grim Reaper's scythe had come close enough to shave me, if I had any whiskers, that is. The bridge was a tool of my guilt, luring me to the brink of eternal damnation. Inexplicable forces intervened, and all I know for sure is that I want no more of that business. I had gone way beyond harmless contemplation. Indeed, I had readied myself, the dagger of mortality poised, all nets of rationality removed, nothing in the way save the final impulse—only to be pulled back from the edge of darkness because of some larger plan to which I am not privy, nor remotely equipped to understand. I have to face my demons squarely. Unfortunately, knowing and doing are not the same thing. I find progress wherever and whenever I can. Most important, I pledge I will never ever think about killing myself again.

Yesterday John Fitzgerald Kennedy was elected the 35th president of the United States. If I had been old enough to vote, I would have voted for Richard Milhous Nixon because Election Day was marked with a brief appearance by our dad.

Me and Luke came home from Billy Goat Hill, and there was Earl's sandblasted, sun-bleached car parked out front. We could hear the shouting from the front yard, so we stayed out on the porch and overheard the whole thing. Lucinda was crying, and Earl swore out loud that he'd sooner vote for Nixon than pay another dime in child support. Earl stormed out of the house, the screen door slamming behind him. He took one look at us and never even said hello. As much as his indifference stung, I mostly felt sorry for him. He looked terrible —tired, unshaven, sweaty, and reeking of alcohol—and it is to be the last image I have of my father.

Everything is turned upside down and backwards. I've lost my perspective; I can't find my compass. I feel so abandoned that had I been a ten-year-old boy living in early Nazi Germany, my bitter and vulnerable state of mind might have made me an easy recruit for the Hitler Youth. Thankfully, I was born in another decade near the Arroyo Seco, not the Danube, Elbe, or the Rhine.

I manage to shore up my collapsing world in large part by frequent visits with Rodney Bernanos. Lucinda lets me take the bus alone to see him, though she has not yet allowed Luke to join me. She thinks together we are more likely to get lost or into trouble. She won't let Luke stay home by himself either, which limits me to visiting Rodney only when she is available to stay with Luke, which is not as often as I'd like.

There is no school today, and Lucinda is home cleaning. Remarkably, she offers to drive me to see Rodney if I'll take the bus home. I am excited as she drops me off at Rodney's restaurant but feel sorry for Luke, who is sulking in the backseat and doesn't even want my front seat position when I get out of the car. Lucinda is still too overprotective when it comes to Luke, him being her youngest now.

Passing a stack of vegetable crates near the rear door, I enter the Den through the same dark hallway as before. I find Rodney in the kitchen as usual. Rocky greets me with a purring rub against my pant leg.

"When do I get to meet your brother?" is the first thing Rodney says.

"I don't know. My mom still won't let him come."

"Well, one of these days, maybe."

"Maybe."

"Want to earn some pocket change today?"

"Sure."

"My produce man just left a delivery out back. I missed him by five minutes, or he would have brought everything in the kitchen like he usually does. Will you bring the crates in for me?"

"Yes, sir."

Hefting three flats of tomatoes, six crates of lettuce, two bags of onions, six sacks of potatoes, and an assortment of cartons containing carrots, cabbage, radishes, and a few unidentifiable leafy items will earn me fifty cents and a cold soda.

When I finish, I sit in the kitchen and note that Rodney is listening to a preacher on the radio while he works. "Who is that?"

"That's Billy Graham. He's an evangelist."

"What's an evangelist?"

"A preacher who preaches the gospel. Billy Graham travels all over the world preaching the gospel."

"Oh—what does *the gospel* mean?"

Rodney looks at me and smiles. He's been stirring something in a big ceramic bowl. He stops stirring, puts the bowl on the counter, and sits himself down next to me. "The gospel means…the Good News, as told in the Bible in the New Testament books of Matthew, Mark, Luke, and John."

"Matthew—how about that. That was my baby brother's name. And Luke gets his name from the Bible, too."

"Yes, he does."

"Who was Matthew?"

"Matthew lived in the time of Jesus. Of all things, he was a tax collector. He became a follower of Jesus."

"My baby brother was named after a tax collector?"

Cackle! "You could say that. And Luke was a physician, a doctor."

"Sheesh! Luke Parker is named after a doctor in the Bible. That's a good one."

"The thing is, Matthew and Luke, as well as Mark and John, wrote down some stuff that's very important to know, Wade. Together, they tell us the story of Jesus Christ, and that's what evangelists like Billy Graham talk about."

"And he even gets to be on the radio in Los Angeles? Do you think Billy Graham will ever come here?"

"He's been here. I went to hear him once. And I'm sure he'll come to California again sometime."

"Really? Maybe someday I'll get to see him."

"I hope you do."

For the better part of an hour, I listen to Billy Graham talk about how God so loved the world He gave His only Son, so that everyone who believes in Him will not perish but have eternal life. Rodney smiles and watches me listen with rapt attention to the radio, while he continues with his routine preparations for the afternoon restaurant opening. The telephone rings a few times, though he ignores it, making me feel like my visit, and Billy Graham's message, is what is most important to him.

The radio program ends. "Well, thanks for the soda and the fifty cents, Rodney. I guess I better be heading home now."

"You're welcome. Leaving so soon?"

"Yeah." I chuckle. "Doctor Luke is waiting for me, and my mom probably wants to go to work."

"Work is what I have plenty of, too. Almost time to open up for the early dinner crowd. It was good to see you. Thanks for stopping by."

"Good to see you, too."

Rodney gives me a hug at the door. "Take care, Wade."

"I will." I turn to go, but a feeling deep in my heart stops me. I look back at Rodney, and he smiles. "I love you, Rodney."

"I love you, too." He hugs me again.

As I walk to the bus stop, I feel warm and good about my visit. There sure is something different and special about Rodney, something I am drawn to. Exactly what it is I cannot say. I just know I am comfortable in his presence and better for having spent time with him.

The peaceful mood stays with me while I wait for the bus. But oh, how quickly things can change. On the ride home, I see someone I had hoped to never see again. We are moving down Figueroa Street at a fairly fast clip, but there's no mistaking the vision that steals my peace.

I shiver as Lieutenant Shunkman roughs up a man already restrained by handcuffs. The man in handcuffs fearfully glances toward the passing bus and seems to make eye contact with me. In that fleeting moment, I see the man cry out when Lieutenant Shunkman slams his knee into the man's back. The man drops to the pavement, and Shunkman looks up, grinning like a madman.

"Oh my gosh! Did you see that?" the woman sitting in front of me blurts.

My stomach hurts, and I turn in my seat and stare straight ahead.

When I get home, I try to shake the image of Shunkman. *Should I tell the Sergeant what I saw?* He is around some, also making me feel special—though he remains a mystery in many respects. The mystery overreaches him, at times spilling over into his relationship with Rodney. I sense something isn't quite right between them, and I worry that it might have something to do with me. *Maybe telling them what I saw will make things worse.*

They're both looking out for me, protecting me, I repeatedly reassure myself. I need to believe in them. I have to.

Today is one of those rare days of smog-free splendor that almost justifies living in Los Angeles the rest of the year. Rodney has invited Luke and me over to play with Kirk, the spotted son of Mac and Antoinette. Kirk is named after Rodney's favorite actor. Believe it or not, Luke finally has Lucinda's permission to make the trip. It is Saturday, but she is working as usual and cannot give us a ride.

The lumbering but lovable trolley cars of Los Angeles have gone the way of the dinosaur, driven to extinction by a conspiratorial tire-and-rubber company. I retain a vague but fond image of the old Red Cars. But the free-wheeling, fume-belching, rubber-tired buses that now scurry over the landscape like fleas on a mongrel suit me just fine. The buses give me range and mobility at an age when the system works against you, and I take full advantage.

I know the routes of northeast Los Angeles better than some of the bus drivers, and getting to Rodney's house in Glendale is almost as easy as walking to Suicide Bridge.

We arrive just before noon, laughing and hamming it up as we approach Rodney's newly repainted house. Coming up the front walk, I glance through a large undraped window and see all the way through the interior of the house to an open back door and a sun-drenched yard beyond.

I spot Rodney in the backyard. Something is wrong. I stop halfway up the walk, confused and unsure of what we might be interrupting. Luke collides with me, and I momentarily lose the bright, sunshiny image of Rodney. I could swear I just saw his arm lash out as one would do to slap someone in the face. Worse yet, I think I saw a figure retreating from Rodney, only a blur of motion, but enough to associate with the unmistakable outline of the Sergeant.

What is happening?

This is Luke's first introduction to Rodney, and he's very excited. On the bus ride over, I repeated all of my favorite Rodney stories for Luke, psyching myself up as well in the process. All of that is gone now—replaced by uncertainty. If I saw what I think I saw, how can it be so? I look again and see Rodney standing alone, staring at some unknown corner of his yard, his back to me now.

What did I see?

"Come on," Luke says. "What's the matter?"

"Wait just a second."

I spread my arms wide to hold him back while I try to gather my wits.

What in the heck did I see?

I allow Luke to move ahead to the porch. He looks at me with a question, I nod, and he rings the doorbell.

A puppy barks, followed immediately by Rodney's trademark cackle—and I am tremendously relieved. Disavowing any need to know, I willingly let go of my fears and wait with a heart full of joy as the nicest, funniest friend I have ever known hobbles to let us in. What a great day this is going to be after all!

A moment later the door opens. "Hi, guys!" *Cackle!*

"Hi, Rodney—this is my little brother, Luke."

Rodney looks at Luke. He grimaces and squeezes his eyes shut strangely. He clutches his chest and bends his knees with a jerky motion as though he's been clipped from behind by an unsportsmanlike tackler.

Luke stares at him, not sure what to make of this odd behavior. I am taken aback as well. Rodney hasn't yet unlatched the screen door, and it stands between us like a barrier separating inmate from visitor. In stunned disbelief, I watch as he drops to the floor. His body goes rigid against the screen door as he paws at his chest and neck, fighting to breathe.

A moment of futility passes during which I hope and pray that he is just kidding with us. Rodney loves to mess with me, but never anything like this. Perhaps he's playing an outrageous prank—goofing around and pretending that the first sight of Luke causes him to have a heart attack or something? But this isn't a joke. He is in serious trouble, awful pain, and there is nothing I can do except linger at a standstill, ambushed.

"Get my neighbor next door!" Rodney gasps.

I scream at Luke to run next door, and he takes off like a shot.

"Rodney, what's the matter? What's wrong?"

"Wade!" he calls out to me from some distant dimension, his eyes rolling around as though disconnected from their sockets.

My throat constricts in sympathy with his tortured breathing. I wheeze, "Yes, Rodney?"

I kneel down as close to him as I can get, my face and hands pressed hard against the metal screen as I try in vain to reach to him, to touch him. Tears flood down and off my face, pelting the newly painted threshold I want desperately to cross.

His whole body trembles as he struggles to speak, and for one brief moment he focuses on me, his pained eyes conveying how sorry he is. "Remember, Wade, Jesus is the best friend you can ever have. He loves you very much. Only Jesus can set you free." Then his eyes roll up, leaving white blanks between fluttering lids.

From inches away, I watch him let go, the terrible pain softening, the tenseness in his body slackening, his face drifting to an expressionless, nonexistent state. Last, his arms fall away from his chest, and one final breath hisses slowly over his lips as he peacefully settles on his side.

It happens that fast.

Seized by panic, unable to move, my mouth opening and closing with convulsions of silent screams, I look on in horror as Kirk whimpers and nudges Rodney's limp hand. At some point before Luke comes back with the neighbor, my mind halts, shutting off like a burned-out lamp.

I feel myself rocking back and forth to an inner, pulsing, pounding rhythm as Rodney's words repeat in my mind like an insistent echo. *"Remember, Wade, Jesus is the best friend you can ever have. He loves you very much. Only Jesus can set you free."*

Please don't go, Rodney. I want you as my best friend. Please don't die! I don't want you to leave me. I need you.

I imagine he replies. *The Father has called me home, son. It's my time. Don't be sad. I'm here with Doris, but I'll never be far from you. Remember, Wade, Jesus is the best friend you can ever have. He loves you very much. Only Jesus can set you free. I love you, Wade.*

But, Rodney, there is something I need to tell you!

I am with Him now, son. Believe on Him with all your heart, and we will be together again.

But there's something I need to tell you, and now it's too late. It's not fair!

Then I remember something Billy Graham said. *"Seek Him, trust Him…and you will know the Truth."*

And again I imagine I hear Rodney's counsel. *Remember, Wade, Jesus is the best friend you can ever have. He loves you very much. Only Jesus can set you free.*

It's not fair!

The ambulance drives away slowly—no siren, no lights. Luke would have preferred emergency flashers and squealing tires. I sit on Rodney's porch, weeping, not understanding, wanting to lash out at something, anything, everything. The neighbor is inside Rodney's house talking on the telephone. He is a nice man. He says he's known Rodney for over twenty years. He says Rodney told him all about me and that Rodney loved me very much. With a longing as deep as the ocean, I sit with my head in my hands, my chest aching with the worst of all things—a broken heart.

Kirk scratches at the screen door, whining and wanting to come outside and play. He is young and doesn't yet know how to behave at a time like this. Mac would know. I wish Mac would come and comfort me.

The neighbor hangs up the telephone and lets Kirk out on the porch. The puppy goes straight to Luke, and the two of them head for the lawn. Luke is eight now, old enough to realize what has happened, but he didn't know Rodney. Somehow, perhaps because he's in his own kind of shock, or perhaps thanks to a small miracle, he doesn't cry. It's better for me that he doesn't cry.

The man comes out on the porch and sits next to me. He's holding a Bible. "I know your heart is breaking, Wade. Mine is, too. Would it be okay with you if we just sit here and pray together for a bit?"

I nod. "Rodney told me a lot about Jesus. Do you think he's with Jesus now?"

His eyes are red and puffy like mine. "Yes, I do. We can say a prayer for Rodney right now, if you like."

"Okay."

I look over at Luke and then close my eyes.

"Dear Father in heaven, we praise and worship You. Thank You for blessing us with the privilege of knowing our precious friend and brother, Rodney Bernanos. We trust in You, Father, and we know that all things work for Your purposes and according to Your will. Comfort us in our loss and sorrow, and help us to live our lives with the same love and joy for others that Rodney so freely gave to us. We pray in the holy name of Jesus. Amen."

"Amen." I appreciate this man. He seems a lot like Rodney.

"I think old Rodney's heart just finally gave out," the man says, sniffling. "He had two heart attacks last year. I'm going to keep Kirk for him." He put his arm around me. "We both lost a very good friend."

I nod, shaking uncontrollably from the staggered gasps and bitter chills that come from the unanswerable *why* of life and death. The prayer did comfort me, but I feel crushed by the weight of the unanswered *why*. The only rationale my mind can convey is beyond unbearable.

Maybe God has taken Rodney Bernanos away from me as punishment for killing that man at Three Ponds.

I whisper, "I n-need to go h-home now."

"Okay. Someone is coming to pick you guys up."

"Who?"

"Sergeant Cavendish. They were able to reach him by radio. I gather he happened to be close by. He should be here soon."

It must have been him in the backyard. But how can I possibly ask him about it?

"This was Rodney's Bible, son. I think he would have liked you to have it."

"Okay."

For the next few days, Luke takes good care of me. He is proud that he didn't run away this time. As for me, I just don't see how I can go on.

Four long days have passed since Rodney's fatal heart attack. Having his Bible, knowing where it is and that it now belongs to me, has helped to buffer and soften the worst of the loss. I haven't opened it or attempted to read any Scripture. I just let the knowledge that I have it comfort me.

The Sergeant and Lucinda have just met for the first time in person. I suspect they have spoken on the telephone before, though neither has said so. Yesterday, Lucinda finally agreed to let me attend the funeral with the Sergeant, but only after insisting she had to be here to meet him when he picked me up.

I sit in Queenie with Rodney's Bible on my lap while they chat on the front porch for a couple of minutes. Seeing the two of them talking face-to-face makes me nervous. The Sergeant knows things. One wrong word from him, the slightest innocent slip of the tongue, and Lucinda will turn into the last thing I need right now.

We are well on our way to Rodney's funeral when the Sergeant speaks to me for the first time. We have shared a respectful quiet up until now. The important thing is that Lucinda smiled and waved to me before we drove off, which gives me a high level of confidence that the Sergeant said nothing to betray me.

"Your mom is pretty." His cheerful tone is as much for his benefit as for mine.

"She works and cleans too much."

"Oh."

I am too depressed to see or hear the bright side of anything. Caught up in my own grief, I don't realize how much the Sergeant is hurting. I have lost a very important new friend, but he has lost his closest loved one. I am not capable of thinking about it that way.

"How come Miss Cherry didn't come?"

"She didn't really know Rodney. They only met once several years ago."

She didn't know him? That seems strange. I am surprised Miss Cherry, as close as she is to the Sergeant, didn't know Rodney. But that certainly isn't a reason for not coming along. She should be here, at least to lend moral support. But I sense it's a sore subject with the Sergeant, so I don't push it. My curiosity slowly disperses in a somber cloud of fresh memories of Rodney as Queenie glides on.

The funeral looks like a reunion of Gulliver's Lilliputians. Twenty-five jockeys enter the church dressed in full riding gear. It is a colorful tribute to their departed friend, though quite a bizarre sight. It pleases me immensely to witness such admiration, to know Rodney was liked and respected by longtime friends from his horse racing days.

Beautiful Queenie, polished to an ivory sheen, looks out of place in the funeral motorcade—a white sheep in a family of black sheep. We ride along solemnly, the minister's powerful invocation still governing the mood. The Sergeant tries to cover his tears so as not to upset me further, but it is a long, sad ride to Forest Lawn, too long for me to keep quiet.

I want to tell him I saw him in Rodney's backyard right before Rodney collapsed and see what he has to say about it, but the nerve won't come. My desire to speak up gives way to gutless reticence, and the trip becomes excruciatingly long. When finally we turn in the main gate at Forest Lawn Cemetery, there is no relief from the layers of melancholy besetting me.

The long procession of cars winds up a grassy, headstone-crowded hill. We stop, Queenie the eighth car back from the long black hearse carrying Rodney. I look back at the crawling line of vehicles trailing far down the slope. The people at the end have a long walk up to the gravesite. We wait while Rodney's friends and extended family mournfully trudge up the rise, all of them except the jockeys wearing the black apparel of death.

Standing at the gravesite with all of these people, I feel like a stranger. But I'm glad I am here. I go numb when they lower the casket into the hole. It is so final.

I give a small wave good-bye to the descending coffin and wonder if Rodney has seen Matthew, maybe said "I love you" for me.

Rodney's grave marker reads:

RODNEY LUIS BERNANOS
"A child of God…In the home stretch."
1884–1960

Back in Queenie, neither of us has much to say, both of us thinking to ourselves how much we already miss Rodney. I almost ask the big question, then chicken out and turn the car radio on instead. The dial is full of Christmas music and commercials touting the appearance of Santa Claus at a dozen different places at the same time. It only serves to further set the pessimism solidifying within me. I turn off the radio in the middle of Bing Crosby's "White Christmas."

"I'm not in a Christmas mood either," the Sergeant says.

Finally, I decide to speak up. I will try to work my way up to the hard question. "Do you remember that first morning at Rodney's restaurant, the morning you picked me up on the bridge? You said sometime you would tell me about when Rodney saved your life. How about telling me now?"

The Sergeant looks at me, and his face lights up. "You're quite a kid, Wade Parker. Were you reading my mind?"

"No, sir, I'm not a mind reader." I smile at him. "I guess maybe we both were thinking about the same thing, about Rodney I mean."

"So, you want to hear the story, huh?"

"Yes, sir—if you don't mind."

"Okay…ahem," he says, clearing remnants of funeral emotion from his voice. "When I was about your age, I guess it was a year or two after Jakey Blume died, I got myself into a real jam one day." He laughs heartily, and the atmosphere of the funeral vanishes. "I mean a *real* jam!" He laughs harder yet, his eyes growing big.

"What kind of a jam?" I start to giggle.

"Well, let me see. As I remember it, a friend and I were walking down York Boulevard one day. It was April, and it had been drizzling off and on for days, just enough to keep things damp. So we paid no mind that the sky had turned angry with black clouds aching to burst. I had a silver dollar my dad had given me. I always carried it with me like a good luck charm. You know what I mean?"

I nod and reach into my pocket to touch the ball bearing.

"I had been flipping the silver dollar in the air, and my friend was calling heads or tails. You know, just goofing off, something to do. I kept trying to toss the silver dollar higher and higher, and eventually I dropped it. Off the sidewalk it rolled, over the curb, into the gutter, and down into a storm drain."

"Oh man! I lost a couple of baseballs that way."

"That's just the thing. I was determined not to lose my good luck charm."

"Yeah, right—tough luck."

"Nope. I went down the drain after it."

I'm not sure if I should believe him or not. He seems serious though, without that little give-away twinkle in his eye that I have come to know so well. "Are you talking about those little skinny openings in the gutter where the water from the street goes?"

"Yes, water and everything else that people don't want, but most important, my silver dollar."

"I don't think I can fit my body through those openings. How could you?"

He smiles crisply, his lips pinched tight in the middle. "You don't believe me?"

I fear I may have made him mad, and it knocks down the nerve I have been building up to ask him my question. I try to rephrase. "Well, I'm just saying—"

But he cuts me off. "I was a skinny little runt, much smaller than you, more the size of Luke."

I bristle inside. *Luke's not a runt!* It is obvious he doesn't appreciate being doubted. "Isn't it dangerous to go down there with all the garbage and spiders and who knows what else?"

"Isn't the Crippler dangerous?"

"Yes. But it's fun."

"That's my point exactly."

"I don't get it. What's wrong with having fun?"

"There's nothing wrong with having the right kind of fun. Like I said before, you're quite a kid, and I think you're smart enough to figure these things out for yourself."

"Figure what out?"

"Confused?"

"Yes—a little, I think."

"What I mean is—sometimes when we're kids we know when something is dangerous, and we do it anyway. It's when we don't know that something is dangerous that we can really get into serious trouble."

He has me going in circles, and I give him a blank look.

"Okay, forget about that for now."

Forget what? I feel stupid.

"Anyway, inside the gutter opening, it dropped down into a concrete box that was about four feet long, three feet wide, and just deep enough to stand in. It was very wet in there, but I easily saw my silver dollar lying on the bottom. I squeezed through the opening and dropped down into the box, and that, my smart friend, is when my problems started."

He grins at himself in the rearview mirror, glances over at me, and then turns his attention back to the road.

"Well, what happened?"

"I dropped to the bottom and accidentally kicked the silver dollar. It slid into the drain pipe that empties the water from the box down to the big storm drain pipes that lie thirty feet or so below the street."

"That's where my baseballs went, I suppose. So long silver dollar, too, huh?"

"Nope. I went down the pipe after it."

"Geez! Were you crazy or what?"

"No—not crazy. I just failed to think clearly and realize the danger."

A light turns on in my head. "Okay, I get it."

"Good." He nods with satisfaction.

"So what happened next?"

"The pipe was just big enough for me to squeeze my shoulders in. It was dark and spooky, and I was very nervous, but I figured my silver dollar hadn't gone far. So I pushed with the toes of my shoes, inching my way into the dark pipe with my arms outstretched in front of me. All the while, my fingers were feeling around trying to locate my good luck charm. I got in there about six or seven feet and finally found my silver dollar."

"Boy, you sure were lucky."

"I wish."

"What do you mean?"

"What do you think, smart guy? I was stuck, which might not have been so bad—if the clouds had held their load. The rain started coming down in buckets!"

"Geez Louise! How did you get out?"

He looks at me for a long moment, and then he answers my question in a tone deeply respectful of the incredible hero we both loved. "We just finished burying the guy who saved me from that storm drain."

How amazing. Then, almost against my will, the words jump from my mouth. "Sir, can I ask you something important?" My stomach flip-flops and I stop breathing.

"Sure."

"Were you in Rodney's backyard right before he had the heart attack?"

Clearly startled, he glares at me with a look of anger I have never seen directed at me before. "No. Why?"

He was there! "Well, the thing is…I thought I saw you—saw Rodney slap your face in the backyard."

"What? That's pretty ridiculous, don't you think?"

"I guess." *Why is he lying?*

"I don't know what you think you saw, but I even had some detectives look into…well, let's just say everything looked normal at Rodney's house. After he passed away—I mean. You know?"

"I guess." There's no use pushing it further.

He clears his throat again, quite differently from the way he cleared it a few minutes before. "Would it be all right with you if I finish the story now?"

"I guess."

Shifting moods like a chameleon changes color, he gives me

one of those careful, cryptic grins, like that night on Billy Goat Hill, and instantly I am reminded of Miss Cherry. Thoughts of her seem to visit me whenever I am feeling low, or when the Sergeant displays a mannerism or expression I associate with the first night we met.

Not at all intending to change the subject but relieved to have my mind on something else, I ask, "Do you think I could see Miss Cherry again sometime?"

"I thought you wanted to hear the rest of the story."

"I do. It's just that sometimes you make me think of Miss Cherry."

"You know, the other day she asked me about you and Luke."

"She did?" My spirits zoom skyward. The look on my face gives me away.

"You like her, huh?"

A tingling blush crawls all over my cheeks. "Yes, sir, I think she's real fine."

It no longer matters that he was in Rodney's backyard. I trust that he has his reasons for not telling me the truth.

"I like her a lot, too." He pauses for a moment, thinking, and then blurts out, "I plan to ask her to marry me!"

I turn sideways in the seat to face him. He looks so happy. "Really?"

"Yep. You're the first one to know—well, not counting Rodney. I told him last week."

I am pleased on all three counts—that he wants to marry Miss Cherry, that Rodney knew about it before he died, and that the Sergeant likes me enough to tell me.

"Do you think she'll say yes, Wade?"

An elaborate idea pops into my head, and suddenly I'm the one clearing his throat for dramatic purposes. "No, sir, I think maybe she's going to marry someone else."

He chokes once and fights off a coughing spasm. Red faced and watery-eyed, bona fide worry etched deep into his brow, he says, "What!" *Cough!* "Who?"

Gotcha! That'll teach you not to lie to me. I turn away from him and gaze out the side window, trying my hardest to look like a person struggling to find the least painful words to express some terrible news.

Queenie hums along, sharing a silent giggle with me. I feel him glaring at the back of my head. Finally, when he can't stand it any longer, he slaps me on the shoulder, harder, I'm sure, than he means to. I flinch.

"Spit it out, Wade."

I turn around and face him squarely. "Well, sir, as you know by now, I get around this part of town pretty darn well—for a kid, anyway."

"Yes, you most certainly do. Too much for your own good, I think."

A faint threat in his eyes, combined with the implication veiled in his choice of words, seems to make the ball bearing in my pocket vibrate like a weather vane signaling the approach of a storm. I am thrown off balance for a moment.

"Well, *ahem,* the thing is, Luke and I, well, sir—sometimes we like to hang out near the Highland Park police station."

"So?"

A lighthearted, aw-shucks, what-the-heck, I-think-I'll-change-the-subject kind of aloofness comes over me. I give him a great big false smile and head for the gold. "Maybe one of us will turn out to be a police officer when we grow up, like you, sir."

"Yeah? Well that's just peachy. So what does that have to do with Cherry marrying somebody other than me?"

"Miss Cherry works with you at the O.C., uh, whatever you call it, doesn't she?"

"O.C.I.U., Organized Crime Investigation Unit. What about it?"

I have definitely found his weak spot, his athlete's heel, or whatever you call it. He is starting to fume, and I delight in the fact that he's being played by a ten-year-old kid.

"Well, sir, I guess a lot of the officers at the Highland Park station know you O.C.I.U. people, including Miss Cherry."

Queenie turns the corner at Ruby Place.

The Sergeant is blistering now, his imagination flinging his temper wildly from its normal realm of cool and calm. I allow a lengthy pause just to needle him.

"Get to the point, Wade."

Queenie glides to a graceful stop at the curb.

Mac is napping on the front porch. He raises his head, verifies that the car and its passengers are authorized objects, and then returns to his slumber. Luke's head pops up in the bedroom window. He waves and I smile at him while I discreetly unlock the car door and casually reach for the door handle.

"Well, sir, I overheard some of the officers talking a couple of weeks ago."

I am beginning to impress myself with my acting. The seriousness in my voice might even fool Lucinda.

"Talking about what?"

"Not what, sir. About *whom* would be more to the point."

He looks ready to choke me. But then, with great effort, he relaxes himself and forces his mouth into the shape of a tolerant smile. "Okay, Wade, about *whom* did you and Luke overhear my fellow officers at the Highland Park station talk about?"

I want very much to say, "Pardon me, but would you kindly rephrase that to avoid any possible misinterpretation on my part?" but I am sure he will smack me if I do. Instead, I say with the solemnity of a reluctant bearer of bad news, "Miss Cherry said..."

He tenses noticeably. "What about Miss Cherry?"

He forces his face into another artificial smile, and I glance toward the house. Luke, still standing at the window, is now motioning for me to come in the house. I nod to him and return my attention to the Sergeant. I give him my most sympathetic look. "I'm really sorry to be the one to tell you this, but I think you should know so you don't end up making a terrible fool of yourself."

He looks about ready to burst into tears. "Go ahead...tell me."

"We heard the officers talking about Miss Cherry being in love with someone other than you."

I reach over with my left hand and give his arm a comforting squeeze.

I feel wonderful, giddy, soused on an exhilarating rush of sweet revenge. I am paying him back for all of the roller coaster rides he has taken me on. For the unnerving scene that night on Billy Goat Hill when Scar and his gang challenged the cops and scared me and Luke half to death; for that moment of horror when he peeled away his face like a half-human lizard shedding its skin; and for the time up on Eagle Rock when he told us the heart-tugging tale of Jakey Blume, mockingbirds, crimson red hair, and all, as if he were a gypsy fortune teller revealing the hypnotic visions of my dreams from the dark center of his mystical crystal ball.

But most of all, I feel like I am handing back to him the atrocious ball bearing that he so cruelly dropped into my hand. Yes, I'm giving him back all of the evil in me and keeping only the good. But instead of all that, I am only playing a joke. No, not just a joke—a *great* joke. The kind of joke that close friends use as building blocks in the mutual construction of trust and respect.

"Did they say who the other guy was?"

"Yes, sir—I'm afraid they did, sir."

I touch his arm again and he flinches. "Who is he?" He closes his eyes to lessen the sting.

"Are you really sure you want to know?"

He opens his eyes. "Yes, I'm positive." He closes them again.

The moment of truth has arrived. "We heard them say Miss Cherry is in love with—ME-*e-e-e-e-e*!"

I bound out of Queenie, slam her door, and sprint to the house. I want to stop on the porch and look at him so I can squeeze out all the pleasure I can, but I don't have the nerve. I don't dare even glance over my shoulder as the back of my neck prickles from the deadly glare of a rancorous male Gorgon, painfully hankering to turn me into a pre-acne towheaded pillar of stone. I hide in the bedroom until I hear the soft thrum of Queenie fade down the hill.

Oh well, I guess I'll hear how Rodney pulled him out of the storm drain another time.

Then, like a Drysdale fastball high and inside—it hits me. If it's the last thing he ever does…he will get even with me.

Regret closes in faster than Mac on a scent leading to Molly's house.

seven

Christmas 1960 comes and goes like a train passing through an abandoned station. Despite Lucinda's best effort, Luke and I are less than grateful for our meager bounty. Luke complains the loudest and the longest. Eventually, I decide to step in and get a little tough with him after he makes Lucinda cry. Later, I realize my aggressiveness has more to do with the stress I'm under than anything Luke might deserve. What's done is done. He'll get over it.

I am also disappointed the Sergeant doesn't come by to say hello during the holiday. A Christmas card shows up in the mail a week late. It's a religious one, which surprised me. Some spiritual residue from Rodney might explain it, I don't know. I do know there was no return address on the envelope. He must be mad at me for the Miss-Cherry-being-in-love-with-me stunt. Some of us can dish it out and some of us can take it, I guess. I wonder if he'd told Miss Cherry what I said.

There are times when I sense that the Sergeant is near. I get a spooky tingle on the back of my neck and find myself looking around to see if he's watching me from the shadows. I can be most anywhere when the feeling comes over me—standing in the school-yard, walking on the sidewalk, or hanging out on Billy Goat Hill—but I never spot him. I wish it would stop. Having your hopes dashed so regularly is not a good way to live.

Here it is the middle of February already, and I haven't seen or heard from him since the day I slammed the car door and ran into the house scared to death to turn around and look at him. I plan to say I am sorry for the stunt if and when I ever get the chance. I miss him a lot, him and Rodney.

The ball bearing still bangs around in my pocket. As the weeks limp along, it gradually takes on a different significance, transform-ing itself into an object of remembrance, a cherished keepsake that symbolizes my withering relationship with the Sergeant. I can't go anywhere without it, and I constantly check my pocket for fear that I might lose it and have my only connection to the Sergeant fizzle away completely.

The haunting little silver ball has become *my* silver dollar, and I vow that I will never let it fall into a storm drain. I think I would slide down a hole to Hades if necessary to keep it. Ever so slowly, I am learning there may indeed be a hole to Hades, and its sides may be greased with deceit.

Time drags on in a sun-up to sun-down drudgery of existence punctuated by frequent bouts of anxiety about the mysterious dead man of Three Ponds. The worst days end in a losing battle to stay awake for fear the dead man awaits me just beyond the edge of slumber. As soon as I drift into his realm, he starts railing at me, always accusing, accusing, accusing.

But a countervailing voice also inhabits my dreams, and it speaks to me when I listen very carefully. Rodney's voice, always steady, never shouting, gently reminds me how much Jesus loves me. When I concentrate on my memory of Rodney's voice, I can also hear Matthew chattering nearby. I picture him wiggling with excitement as he looks up bright-eyed and smiling at the colorful mobile that dips and dangles above his crib. The way that Rodney and Matthew give me comforting thoughts, they must be together in heaven.

My waking hours are also full of extraordinary influences. Last week Luke and I were sitting on the porch with Mac when our next door neighbor, Carl the baker, had one too many beers and walked out into the middle of Ruby Place with his tarnished but venerable antique rifle.

"Yuri Gagarin, you lousy red commie!" he yelled between long pulls on his long-neck bottle. "Come down from there!"

Staggering badly, he pointed the rifle up at the smog and lined up the sights like he was actually aiming at something. Then he let the old bolt action single shot rip…*Boom!* Mac howled every time Carl fired off a round. Man oh man, I didn't know what to do, but given the odds against one of the slugs falling back to earth and hitting us, which were worse than the odds of old Carl actually hitting the first man in space, we were never in any danger.

He put on quite a show until the police came and hauled him away. A reporter from the *Los Angeles Herald* showed up in time to snap a picture of four very nervous cops engaging and disarming Carl. Of all the people standing around watching the once-in-a-life-time show, the reporter picked me out of the crowd to ask questions about the incident.

I am sure I was misquoted: "Wade Parker, age ten, said his neighbor, Carl the baker, was (envious, ed.) of the Russian's high quality Rye bread."

Luke claims the paper got it exactly right.

Another development is taking shape. Luke and I have formulated a plan to install a network of candles along the walls of our newest Shangri-la, the storm drains under northeast Highland Park. Cavendish Caverns becomes the code name, a phrase Luke coined after seeing pictures of Carlsbad Caverns in a back issue of *National Geographic*. I liked it the moment he said it, and right then and there we decided it was most fitting that we dedicate our newest playground in honor of the man who gave us the idea. After I told Luke Sergeant Cavendish's silver dollar story, we found a different moral in the storm drain rescue tale. Adults should be mindful of the stories they tell to children.

Our first hurdle is to find another way into the storm drain system. Going in through a curb drain proves a physical impossibility for me, and I am not about to send Luke down there to reconnoiter. I suspect the curb drain route poses some unknown hazard, the exact nature of which isn't clear because the Sergeant hasn't been around to tell me the rest of the story. I don't yet fully understand how the storm drain system actually works; all I know is water drains from the streets into the openings in the curb and disappears. I guess it all ends up in the rice paddies in China.

The challenge of trying to figure another way into the storm drains helps keep my mind occupied. The loss of Rodney and my apparent disaffection from the Sergeant and Miss Cherry together with the dead guy add up to a burden too much for my young heart to bear. I need a remedy, and instinct tells me I have to step outside of myself and find something with restorative power in order to survive.

In my imagination, I romantically reason that magic medications can be found in the dark, fortress-like dispensary of Cavendish Caverns. Necessity has led to the invention of a new frontier, one that exists entirely underground and well below the radar of reality, which meets rather well with my notion about being part mole or groundhog.

We discover a storm drain discharge tunnel opening in the concrete side slope of the Arroyo Seco quite by accident—literally. The revelation comes about when two cars collide on the York Boulevard Bridge, which traverses the Arroyo Seco and the Pasadena Freeway. Luke and I have just gotten the boot from Kory's comic book section for the umpteenth time. We are standing outside the store, both of us highly incensed that we have been invited to leave so quickly. We are not yet finished making rude faces at the manager through the storefront window when the red flashing lights of two police cruisers stopped in the middle of the bridge catch Luke's attention.

"Look at that," he coos.

I can take them or leave them, but Luke is always mesmerized by flashing emergency lights. The cyclical flicker of the strobes has a Pied Piper effect on his brain. Like a moth to a flame, there is no stopping him. The fireworks of Independence Day are a veritable feast for his eyes, but for some arcane reason, flickering flames do not have the same effect. Thank God for that, or I'd be spending the rest of my childhood as a permanent member of a bucket brigade.

I am still peeved at the store manager and don't give Luke my immediate attention. He tugs my shirtsleeve, and the next thing I know we are standing on the bridge staring with morbid fascination at two mangled cars. The drivers, dead or alive we don't know, have already been whisked away in ambulances, and traffic has been detoured away from both ends of the bridge.

As we stand gaping at the carnage, two rattletrap tow trucks appear like half-starved mongrels scenting the waftures of road kill. The drivers crawl out of the rusted wreckers and amble over to inspect the auto carcasses, which appear to be fused together by the head-on impact. The tow truck drivers are a rueful sight. Like inbred cousins from some distant hollow, they both stand there scratching their heads, as if the friction might warm their wits enough to figure out how to separate the cars.

The flashing lights go off, and with the euphoria not yet cleared from his eyes, Luke walks straight over to Festus and Jethro. I follow, staying three steps behind. I don't want to get too close—they look downright diseased. Luke moves right in and performs one of his priceless Lukeisms, as I have come to call them, an outlandish absurdity of the type I previously strove to discourage but recently have developed an appreciation for. Kind of like an acquired taste, a term I learned from drinking Rodney's coffee.

"You gentlemen give me a quarter each, and I'll tell you exactly how to solve this problem," Luke announces.

The little mercenary sounds like he has a Ph.D. in mechanical engineering. I start to reach for his arm to pull him back, afraid they might smack him one for being a smart aleck. But then I see them digging down deep in their greasy coveralls and smiling kind of goofy like, both of them oozing makeshift cleverness like they are getting a VIP discount. They each deposit two bits in Luke's little pink hand.

The taller one of the two, a Tennessee Valley baritone, speaks first. "Okay, young feller…" He snorkels a cubic foot of air in through hair clogged nostrils, which sounds like the snore of a congested whale, and then expels something from his throat so vile I can't possibly describe it. "Tell us how ta untangle these mules."

The man breaks into a slovenly grin, revealing a greenish tangle of broken teeth. I take a couple of steps to the west to get out of the stream of his breath. Luke stands his ground.

The other tow truck driver chimes in. "Yeah. I hopes we don't haffs ta put the a-cet-a-lean turch to 'em."

Luke peers up at them with his angelic baby blues and speaks with the sincerity of Billy Graham. "Put a hose on them. It works with Mac every time."

He deposits the quarters in his pocket, turns smartly, and walks away. I bust a gut while Festus and Jethro resume scratching their heads and pondering at a snail's pace whether or not they've received fair value for payment tendered.

Luke hasn't an inkling how funny he is. He's the perfect straight man. He isn't serious and moody like I often am. His mind travels a zone I can never enter, and I wish I could gain access to his easygoing state of inner peace.

As time rolls on like the steady flow of the Arroyo Seco, I begin to look up to Luke, at times envying him for his steely nerve and philosophical armor. That he could fearlessly approach two scary looking men and advise them on the art of auto uncoupling, two men who look like they eat little kids as in-between meal snacks, that he can get away with something like that just dazzles me.

And I envy his apparent immunity from nightmares. Certainly he has cause to entertain ghosts same as me, what with his plight with the mockingbirds, not to mention our shared encounter with the dead man. Yet, such appears not to be the case. I admire and love him for his crazy daring. I shake my head as we walk over to the bridge railing. Behind us, Festus and Jethro begin to tinker with the mangled autos.

Luke stands at the railing casually looking down at the Arroyo Seco. Seeing him there, I am reminded of that morning on the "other bridge" when I stared down into the inviting mist. Man, I wish I could find a way to be less affected by things. I have remained the oldest chronologically while somehow Luke has grown beyond me.

"Look." Luke points downstream toward a county flood control truck parked on the concrete bed of the Arroyo Seco.

"Well, well, well. I think we may have found the entrance to King Tut's tomb."

"Nope—it's Cavendish Caverns." He grins, stretching his freckles to the limit. "Just like those pictures I saw in *National Geographic*."

If the pictures included a warning about the dangers of caverns and other dark places, Luke sure didn't mention it.

Luke walks upright with plenty of freeboard while I have to stoop slightly, crook my neck, and tuck my chin to my chest or I'll end up with a bald spot. A continuous trickle of contaminated water moistens the bottom of the tube. Some kind of slimy life-form marks the concave walls, its varying stages of hydroponic metabolism staining the concrete with striations that remind me of the horizontally scarred shoreline of a fickle lake. We observe the strange phenomena with passive curiosity, ignorant of its foreboding message—just indecipherable hieroglyphics decorating the walls of an ancient cave. Such obvious signs of a changing water level fail to trigger a warning.

We previously observed the flood control workers use a special tool to open the massive metal discharge cover. The cover is designed, I suppose, to make it next to impossible for tunnel rats like us to get in. It's like the door to the nest of a giant trap-door spider, free swinging, suspended from a single monstrous hinge, and actuated by force applied from inside. A moderate amount of water opens it an inch or two, while a lot of water will push it open several feet. The first time I get a close-up look at the door, I conclude it is a hopeless idea. As it turns out, we are not to be defeated—the tire jack from Lucinda's trunk works perfectly.

Animals may not possess the logic-based reasoning ability that we humans supposedly have, but they often display remarkable instinctive judgment that some of us, namely me, could do well to observe. Mac quickly demonstrates that he's no relation to Cerberus, the hound of the underworld, as he absolutely refuses to enter the storm drain. He takes one look at the precarious way we have propped open the huge discharge door and slams his rump down on the ground like a pack mule on strike. No amount of cajoling or ridicule will change his mind, and he insists on taking up a post just outside the tunnel opening. There he sits—humorless, stoic, and as rigid as a carved stone statue. Without question, he is the best looking mixed-breed sentinel in all of the Arroyo Seco.

Admittedly, Lucinda's car jack is strained to its limit and looks like the equivalent of a toothpick propping open the mouth of a great white shark. If the toothpick should snap during ingress or egress, there won't be a second chance. No more hazardous than a late night showdown with the Crippler, I reason.

We test our nerve to the limit on our first voyage into the tunnel. Apprehension marks each step as we edge our way into the darkened crypt. An ominous semblance hangs in the dank air, like a sign saying—*Danger Go Back!* But we proceed into the crypt anyway, plodding ever so slowly as we imagine we are knowingly going against the wishes of the dead.

Behind us a circle of light gradually dims, giving inverse rise to our growing unease. My Flash Gordon flashlight, an unreliable gadget at best, isn't powerful enough to make us feel secure.

Luke hooks a finger through my rear belt loop and shuffles along behind me, his sneakers making sucking noises each time he lifts his feet. After we have penetrated the hole about the length of a football field, I stop and glance back toward the dwindling spot of light. I try to absorb a few additional rays of courage. Seeping blackness has nearly closed the void behind us, and we continue along the gradual incline at a slower pace than before.

Soon my flashlight starts to flicker, and Luke begins to feel uneasy, judging by the increasing resistance pulling my pants back against my middle. Already leaning forward to keep my head from scraping the top of the tunnel, I shift my center of gravity a little farther forward, offering more tug and encouragement to help him along.

Luke could stand face-to-face with those tow-truck drivers and bamboozle them without batting an eye, but delving into this kind of unknown is a different trick altogether. Suddenly he panics and puts the brakes on. My belt loop snaps, and Luke falls backward, landing on his backside with a sloppy splash. With all of my momentum, I sail headlong in the opposite direction. I try to catch my balance but end up executing a full-stretch landing that is almost graceful. My flashlight takes it much harder when it hits the deck like the lights-out-loser in a Sonny Liston fight. I slide on my belly for thirty yards, something akin to a wet seal sledding on oily ice—and thus we make another fantastic discovery.

The magic of this place encompasses me with a strange new sense of security—back in the womb, blindman's bluff without the blindfold. Exhilarated by the unexpected foray into the slithery wet blackness, I shout, "Wow! That was fun!"

Wow! That was fun! A hollow but happy echo immediately agrees, launching me into a much needed giggle.

I sit up soaking slimy-wet and squint back in Luke's direction. Far away, a wanton circle glows, flirting with the darkness like an impassioned but very demure moon. At some inestimable distance in the foreground, a starkly contrasted silhouette of Luke shifts like a geometric shape imprisoned in the cylinder of an infinite kaleidoscope. Attempting to curb a new wave of anxiety, I laugh out loud and think to myself—*there is light at the end of the tunnel!*

"I'm okay, Luke!"

"I'm not!" Luke's silhouette rapidly retreats toward the safety of the loving moon.

During expedition number two, we perfect the concept of placing candles in the tunnel. Luke comes up with the best method, and his freckles seem to glow in the dark when I compliment him for thinking of something good.

Every fifty feet or so, we locate little imperfections in the otherwise smooth wall of the tube and use them as sconces to hold the candles. We find a notch above the midpoint of the tunnel wall, melt some wax on it for stickum, and post a candle. Pinpoints of flame lick at the concrete leaving odd tear-shaped soot marks, while swaying flares embrace shadowy partners that silently dance on the curvilinear walls. The captivating ambiance fits my imagination like a glove, and soon we become masters of our endless medieval dungeon.

We are fully adapted by the end of our third trek into the cavern. We move about with surefooted confidence, firmly in command of our strange new environment. I have found the perfect escape from the surface world, a world that has revoked my right to happiness and become darker than the light I have found in the darkness below ground. Down here I feel privileged and free from the haunting images that reside in the scenery above—the gruesome images of the dead man that show themselves only to me. There is no scenery in Cavendish Caverns.

Luke seems happy enough just to be wherever I am. However, Mac, stubborn beyond all belief, has not altered his position on tunnel frolicking one iota. We have taken to calling him Mr. Party Pooper, but he is immune to childish insults. Wise beyond his years, he continues to guard the storm drain opening with suppressed trepidation, while Luke and I have become mercurial in our actions, buzzing in and out of our honeycombed hive like bees jazzed with the feverish pace of spring.

As the surface dwellers suffer through the blast furnace of summer, we enjoy the cool, damp darkness of our secret hideaway. We have become moles shunning the light of day and the attendant clatter of the normal world to enjoy the serene isolation of our exclusive subterranean kingdom. For me, the tons of compacted earth overhead serve as perfect shielding from everything that is bad. And Luke, well, he is just glad there aren't any mockingbirds in the storm drains.

By the time the dreary, overcast mid-June skies over Los Angeles have once again tarnished the myth of sunny California, Alan B. Shepard, Jr. has restored Carl the baker's pride, Sam Yorty is preparing to move into City Hall, Chavez Ravine has become synonymous with Dodger Stadium, and Luke and I are spending more time in our cave than hibernating bears in the dead of winter. Overriding Mac's obvious displeasure, a great period of emotional prosperity ensues. I hope it lasts.

Lucinda left for work very early this morning, which affords Luke and me a quick start on the day; a lucky break because of the rain showers forecast to hit in the late afternoon or early evening. Thanks to stories told about rescues from storm drains, I have enough sense to know we do not want to be down in the storm drain during a flash flood. I advise Luke that we'll have to call it quits at the first sign of rising water. He assures me that that's fine with him.

We wolf down some Wheaties, the breakfast of champion cardboard sliders and tunnel riders, and hastily pack some munchies in a knapsack. Grabbing a fresh can of motor oil and Lucinda's tire jack from the garage, we head off for another thrilling day in the wet and wild blackness below.

We keep the rest of our tunnel riding gear squirreled just inside the tunnel opening. In our full riding attire we look like a couple of drillers after a good day in the oil field. We wear old sweatshirts and dungarees soaked with motor oil, a kind of slick friction-free husk worn between skin and concrete. Luke calls our slimy getups greased pigskin. It does occur to me that oil-soaked clothes, candles, and matches might be a dangerous combination. But we never seem to have any flammability issues. Human Molotov cocktails we are not.

"I'm tired," Luke announces after a couple of hours of vigorous sliding.

"Me, too."

"Can we stop for a few minutes and eat some of our goodies?"

"Okay." I am out of breath and also a little hungry. "But let's walk back up to the starting gate first so we'll be ready to make another run after we rest."

The "starting gate" is the name we have applied to a particular inclined section of pipe. I did a little homework on storm drains and found out the system is designed to utilize the force of gravity rather than electric pumps to move the water. The entire network is laid out with a gradual downhill gradient that routs the water toward outlets that discharge it directly into the Arroyo Seco.

After much exploration, the starting gate proves to be the optimal point from which to start a run. It works like a Pinewood Derby ramp or a ski jump ramp, and we use it as such with a good running start to boot. We probably achieve speeds on the order of twenty-five miles per hour at the bottom of the ramp and then slide down the pipe for nearly a quarter of a mile. It is pure fun and an exhilarating sense of freedom blasting like a projectile down the longest cannon barrel in the world. Depending on how fast our start is, we finally come to a stop anywhere from three to four hundred feet from the tunnel outlet, feeling charged up and raring to hustle back to the starting gate and do it all again.

We try different styles—feet first, head first, belly down, belly up, sitting up frontward, and, weirdest of all, sitting up backward. Sometimes we even hook together in tandem like a two-man toboggan, although this style is much slower than making the run individually. There are occasional collisions, too. They happen when the one walking back up the tunnel fails to spread his legs in time for the one coming down.

Boy do we have fun—marvelous, carefree, timeless fun.

'Twas a life not for the fainthearted.
But such innocent foolishness, when
compounded, leaves young rascals
well confounded, or…maybe even
with the dear departed!

We sit at the top of the starting gate leaning against the wall of the tunnel with our legs arching over the silent trickle that flows continuously—the perpetual lifeblood of our eventide sanctuary. Resting, munching, talking, and at times just sitting quietly, we listen for the cavern's voices and manfully nod or smile when we hear something we haven't heard before.

The caverns speak frequently in mysterious, invisible rumbles and soft, aimless echoes that float on gentle tunnel breezes. Different sounds come and go that after a while all sound the same. I am intrigued how the tunnel voices travel like messages sent across time from unknown universes, communications never answered but heard and appreciated nonetheless. Sometimes the voices seem to speak directly to me—distant manhole covers groaning under the weight of the world, or the resonant vibrations of misplaced baseballs yearning for the game, or the chime-like knells of silver dollars calling heads-or-tails like lonely loons lost in the dark.

I, the boy manslayer banished from above, have found residence deep in the soul of the City of Angels. And it is wonderful to share this refuge with my brother. Me and Luke, the greased-up little moles that we are, nestle together in our burrow of safety, comforted by the soothing beat of our underground mother's gentle heart. Yes, life is good down below.

I sit here looking at Luke as he casually reposes opposite me. My younger brother, my only remaining brother, looks so innocent. He realizes I am looking at him and he grins at me, his freckles shimmering in the quivering candlelight.

Does Luke ever have such convoluted thoughts as I? He has problems—sure he does, some of the same ones that I have, in fact. Yet, he seems so able to take things in stride. *Talk about convoluted... Maybe if I had an older brother, if I weren't the oldest and therefore not the responsible one, I would be able to take things in stride, too?*

Luke is human—of course he is. He reacts at the time that something happens; but on the whole he is far more lenient with the world, with life's imperfections than I am. I sit here resting, looking at him and admiring him and wishing I could figure out how he does it.

He stares back at me with no specific focus, apparently deep into his own confidential accounting. After a while, he says, "I think I should get a new cap."

We never retrieved his Dodgers cap from Three Ponds, and he has been hatless since. Still, his pronouncement, coming on the heels of my own long rumination, seems ridiculously profound. While my searching mind is lost in a kind of metaphor-seasoned philosophical soup, Luke deftly whips up a tasty baseball cap broth. *How convoluted can I get?*

"A new cap? Why?"

"Because, you big dumb donkey, I can't stay down in these tunnels forever."

I think about that for a moment. "True enough." I assume he must be leading up to something. "Are you still worried about the mockingbirds?"

"I figure I need to be more practical about the mockingbird problem."

"What do you mean?"

He smiles judiciously, making me feel as though I have asked him to reveal the secret of life. "Well, I've been doing some research." The careful smile remains. "Did you know that mockingbirds are also sometimes called catbirds?"

"No, I didn't know that." *Maybe he is as strange as me.*

He nods. "Haven't you ever noticed how their call kind of sounds like the meow of a cat? Meow, meow," he croons, attempting to sound like a mockingbird mimicking a full-grown cat, but sounding more like a half-dead mockingbird mimicking the *mew,*

mew of a malnourished kitten. Nevertheless, it does vaguely resemble the annoying squawk of a mockingbird.

I bury a laugh. He is being far too serious to appreciate the humor I see in this. "Yes, I see what you mean, Luke. Would you like to stop off at Kory's on the way home? They might have some Dodgers caps."

"Well, the thing is—I don't want another Dodgers cap."

"Hey, wait just a darn minute! If you think you're going to wear a Giants cap, you can forget about being my brother!"

He laughs hard at that one. "No way, you big dumb donkey. I want a cap from that university down in Georgia, the kind that has a bulldog on it."

"What?"

"You heard me."

"Why?"

"The way I figure it, no catbird is going to mess with me with a big, mean, ugly looking bulldog on my head."

He is deadly serious.

I laugh so hard I nearly wet my pants. Geez, what a comedian. He has absolutely no idea how funny he is, naturally funny, without even trying to be funny, funny. At first he is offended by my irreverent reaction, but the virus of laughter is very contagious and soon he's laughing along with me. It takes a while for us to calm down.

"Are you ready to do another slide, Luke?"

"Yep. Can I go first?"

"Sure."

As we start to get up we are startled by a tremendous BANG!

The rumble comes as a shock wave from the direction of the tunnel opening, a wicked metal-against-metal scream that reverberates up the tube at the speed of sound. The candles near us flicker and sway as a shift of air brushes by my face. I am badly shaken by a surge of adrenaline.

Luke gives my arm a desperate shake. "What was that?"

"I don't know."

Denial throttles my mind, and I can almost feel my brain hardening like some yet-to-be discovered organism whose only defense against the perils of the wild is to turn to stone to keep from being eaten. *Here I go again. Why can't I just react? Why does my mind launch itself into some kind of out-of-control hyper-thought that pulls a total vacuum on my very being and sucks the marrow right out of my bones? Get a grip, Parker!*

I can smell my own dread oozing from me like blood from a bullet-ridden body. An aching urge to repent enshrouds me in a chrysalis-like crust, closing me in, locking my petrified mind in a prison that might not open for a thousand years. *Get a grip, Parker!*

We have trespassed in the medieval mines of Mephistopheles, the worst of the seven devil chiefs, and now he hath come to exact a toll! Death to all transgressors! *Get a grip, Parker!*

I become conscious of my own labored breathing. I focus on it, slow it down, and forcefully steady myself against the tremors of fear tempering my hapless thinking.

"You big dumb donkey, don't you think we should go see what made that noise?"

I swallow a gulp of air as deep as I can. "Yes."

Loosening my arm from Luke's grip, not wanting him to feel my trembling, I consciously conjure up my real imaginary friend, Duke Snider. *I need your help, Duke. I can't bear to lose this game!*

Power of the mind gives me a quick burst of resolve upon which I brace myself and bravely stand up. A big mistake. I am so rattled I've forgotten the first rule of Cavendish Caverns. I bump my noggin hard on the ceiling overhead and sit back down faster than an obsessed competitor in a game of musical chairs. I see twinkling silver ball bearings, not stars.

Luke cringes. "Geez, are you all right?"

"Ugh!"

"Your head sounded like Lucinda testing muskmelons at Kory's, except at least ten times louder."

Watery eyes squinting with pain, bile bubbling in my throat, my mouth wide open as if to scream, I reach up and delicately feel for an egg—an ostrich egg. "Oh man, I darn near busted my head wide open. Ouch! Ooo-ah! Hold on a second, I need to sit still for a bit."

"Sure, geez man, take your time." He sits next to me.

After a few deep breaths I decide my head is okay, but a fierce soreness rising from my shoulders tells me I've jammed my neck. *Way to get a grip, Parker!*

Luke saddles up behind me at the starting gate and we cautiously push off, but not a fast running start like we normally do. Sliding along, like a steam locomotive out of steam, coasting in neutral trying to stretch it out to the next water tower, I scan the narrow pinpoint horizon ahead, while Luke strains his neck to see over my shoulder. Our perception of distance is thrown off by our reduced rate of speed, or so I try to convince myself. But, when at last we come to a complete stop, I know we are in serious trouble.

We are close enough to the tunnel outlet that the absence of that glorious spectral beacon that has always been there waiting with Mac can only mean one thing—the worst has happened.

Denial goes down in one big gulp of stomach-punching reality, and my head begins to throb with each titan pulse of my quaking heart. Luke clings to my back, his breath hissing in my ears in short gasps of fear and long wheezes of terror. His desperate SOS stabs deep into the heart of my failed sense of responsibility.

Motionless silence closes around us until at length Luke releases me from his backward bear hug. He stands, and I pivot a quarter turn and lean against the wall. Dejected and hopeless, I am unable to stop the charge of guilt percolating in through all of my pores.

"The jack must have collapsed, Wade."

I guess he had to say it. The audible truth rips me wide open, and I resist looking up at him, ashamed to meet his gaze. When I do look up, I see he is nearly smiling, his face aglow in the soft, lusterless hue of the candlelight. He reminds me of the picture of Jesus in Reverend Bonner's office, the Son of God posed in serene muted tones, as though the painter had created the masterpiece by candlelight. And that leads me to think of Rodney.

"Remember, Wade, Jesus is the best friend you can ever have."

I wish Rodney could tell me how he rescued the Sergeant from the storm drain.

We walk to the end of the tube and confirm it is now sealed shut by a cast-iron monster. Only a weak sliver of light rims the outside edge of the circular barrier. Mac is out there, very angry and barking incessantly. The jack must have taken off like a rocket, but Mac sounds okay.

Thank You, God, for not letting the jack hit him.

He is whining, sniffing, and most assuredly listening. He knows we are here now, just on the other side of the door from him. I put my mouth close to the door. "Mac! Quiet down! We're okay, boy!"

Even under the duress of the circumstances, he obeys like a well-trained dog of the silver screen. But this isn't a movie, Mac isn't Rin Tin Tin or Lassie, and he's not going to valiantly run home and bring back help. There is no intermission, no commercial break, and probably no happy ending.

"Tell me the story again," Luke says.

"What story?" My throbbing head and sore neck are competing with each other.

"Tell me the story about how Rodney saved the Sergeant from the storm drain."

"Geez, Luke, I told you before...*he never finished the story!*" The screaming makes my head throb worse.

"Okay already—you big dumb donkey."

"I didn't mean to yell at you. I'm sorry."

He sits next to me. "Don't worry, Wade. We're going to get out of here." He speaks so confidently he almost sounds cocky.

Suddenly he is above the line of reason and I am below it. *Terrific. And just what does that say about me?* On the other hand, maybe he has a plan. *Yeah, right, like the catbird boy and his magic bulldog are going to work a little sleight of hand, maybe just snap a finger or two and voila! We'll find ourselves standing outside next to Mac. Maybe he'll want us to wear groundhog hats so we can find our way out of here by the first day of spring.*

Meanwhile, I'm the one responsible, the older brother, the one who should have known better. This is just great. Maybe I should go ahead and strangle him. *Yeah, why not, because when they eventu-*

ally find our bodies, I'll be blamed for the whole thing anyway. Let the big dumb donkey's record show it: Wade Parker—Convicted, 1961, Fratricide (Posthumously). Get a grip!

All I can do is sit here and think myself into bigger and tighter knots.

With Mac quieted down, a new sound emerges from the background. I put my ear to the cast-iron monster and listen. "Luke…do you hear something?"

"Yes, I do."

"What does it sound like to you?"

"Rain."

Uh oh, I mouth.

"It's raining hard, Wade. Mac doesn't like to be out in the rain, you know."

Great! Now the dog's getting wet, and I'm to blame for that, too. How am I going to explain this to him? "Listen to me. We've got a serious problem here. It's raining outside. I don't want to scare you, but do you know what that means?"

"Yes, I do."

"What do you think is going to happen?"

"Well, pretty soon this tunnel will fill up with water."

He floors me completely. "And you're not scared?"

"No, not really. Are you scared?" He grins, and the candlelight makes him look like a subterranean gremlin full of mischief, enjoying watching the boy from upper earth sweat.

"Yes, I'm scared! Geez, you're something else!"

"Look, you big dumb donkey, I don't see a problem here. All we have to do is sit tight and wait for the water to push the door open, right?"

It doesn't matter whether he's right or not, because the cavern instantly fills with the *siss-s-s-s* sound of an approaching wave. It is only about eighteen inches high, but it hits us with sufficient power to knock us both off of our feet. The wave crashes into the iron door and curls back over the top of us, embroiling the entire space in a churning cauldron of foam.

The door doesn't budge one inch.

I am more startled by how fast the wave has come than the getting knocked down part. Under any other circumstance, getting knocked down by a little old wave would be fun. But this is terrifying.

Luke gets back on his feet and helps me up. He actually laughs, and I can't believe it. I have a mouth full of nasty water—even swallowed some—a foulness coating my tongue, and Luke is laughing like a hysterical hyena. This ought to keep his catbirds away!

"Shut up!" I splutter and gag, spitting out as much of the vile taste as I can.

"Okay, okay. Are you all right?"

"No! Darn it, Luke! We're going to drown in here!" I choke and cough and nearly throw up while Luke calmly suggests that maybe next time I might want to close my mouth. *Next time?*

The water is already up to Luke's waist and he still shows no sign of fear. *Is there something wrong with me? Or is my little brother insane?*

"The door is going to push up anytime now, Wade."

Then I notice how quiet it has gotten, and I hear the sound of thousands of bubbles rising and bursting at the surface. It's like being inside a big aquarium with a powerful aeration pump humming below. The water keeps coming, and to make matters worse, the combination of the stress and the gag reflex from choking on the tunnel water triggers a world class case of hiccups.

"I ho-*u*-pe the door pushes up soon, Lu-*u*-ke!" I sound like a sick Chihuahua.

My mental knot pulls tighter when it occurs to me that the door might have been damaged when the jack gave way. Maybe that's why it isn't opening. I want to tell Luke what I'm worried about so he can argue against it and make me feel better. But I think better of it, realizing the situation will only worsen if I make him panic. Just then, the cast-iron jailer groans, and a burst of light flares from the bottom of the aquarium—the crescent moon of Atlantis offering rays of hope.

Luke squeals, "I told you! I told you!" But the water keeps rising. It is now up to the middle of his chest.

I look back up the tunnel and see many of the candles are still burning. Strange new multi-colored reflections play across the shrinking distance between the rippling water and the concave ceiling. It looks so weird, surrealistic—the tunnel, the water, the candles, the strange reflections. I imagine we are caught in the swamping passageway of an antediluvian monastery.

The door groans again! *A waxing moon! Yes! Let the tides recede!*

"Luke! Come closer to the door."

"Okay—Wader." He splashes closer like a playful puppy.

"Wader? Real funny. If the door opens just a little more, I think you can fit through."

"Ten-four—Wader." He smothers me with a concurring grin.

"When I yell *go*, you take a deep breath, hold your nose, and push yourself down as hard as you can toward the light."

He nods like he is acknowledging basic instructions he has heard many times before. "Roger—Wader."

"As soon as it opens a little bit more, I'll come along right behind you."

"Wilco—Wader."

He is excited and laughing and not scared in the least. You'd think we were next in line for the roller coaster at an amusement park. "This is better than the Crippler, ain't it, Wader!"

I am scared to death. "Much better."

Another groan! More light!

"GO! GO! GO!"

Down Luke goes in a furious whirlpool of bubbles, disappearing faster than a scrap of soap sucked down a bathtub drain. I scream out victoriously and picture him shooting out in a gusher on the other side. Luke has been born again unto the everlasting light of day! *Thank You, Jesus!*

Now I am alone with my fear.

I am bigger than Luke and can only hope that the door will open wide enough to set me free, too. The candles begin extinguishing one by one, no match against the rising tide. I want to let go, dive toward the light and push on the door, but I'm afraid I will get hung up in the opening and drown. That will be my last option. Until then, I'll wait and pray that the door opens further—and in time.

Pray?

I don't know how to pray. No one ever taught me how to pray. Besides, what exactly is praying anyway? Do you have to start a prayer a certain way? Say certain words or follow certain rules? Why can't I just talk to God? I mean, if I just say, "Hi, God," won't He listen?

Maybe I should try to cover all the bases, just in case. Maybe I should cry out to God and Jesus, and throw in a respectful shout to Poseidon and Neptune, maybe even Johnny Weissmuller and Popeye the Sailor Man. They all seem to know their way around water. Heck, maybe a direct appeal to my hero Duke Snider will help get me out of this jam.

Get a grip, Parker!

With the entombing liquid swelling up to my aching neck, I finally surrender and follow my heart. I think of Rodney.

"Remember, Wade, Jesus is the best friend you can ever have."

"He loves you very much."

"Only Jesus can set you free."

"Yes, Father, in the name of my best friend, Jesus, who loves me very much, please set me free from this place. Amen."

Saying the prayer helps to calm my mind and shut off the fear. I start to feel light-headed and—buoyant. A few seconds later, the water lets go of me and gives way to a strange mystical vision…

The Stygian onslaught subsides in a Moses-like miracle, and sud-denly the water is gone without so much as a puddle left behind. Down the passageway coming slowly toward me I see a single file line of hooded monks, each tapping lightly on a tabor hanging from straps looped over their necks. The monks are chanting a motet that is further complicated by an echo bouncing off the tunnel walls.

The monk at the front of the line is a high priest. He carries a swaying censer, the fumes from which confuse me—first smelling of incense, then horsecakes and apple butter, then the wonderful clean scent of Miss Cherry. The monks stop at a distance and fall silent. The high priest comes forward, pulls back the cowl from his mummified face, and stares at me with rheumy centuries-old eyes.

In his eyes, I see a prophetic vision of his own death, and the purchase of my freedom. But I do not understand. Slowly, his arm rises up from his side and levels at my face. He wags a bony accusatory finger as his tightly pursed lips part, and he speaks to me in a raspy, penetrating monotone utterance—"Equus Asinus Gigantus."…

"Huh? I don't understand."

Bubbles gurgle from my lips as I strain upward. I mash my nose against the concrete and attempt to thieve one last deep breath. Pounding heartbeats string together like links in a chain holding me down, while my last breath tightens its grip in my chest and fights to stay with me.

I sense a gentle pulling at my feet, a comforting feeling that I do not resist. Slipping down, I hear the last candle extinguish with a kisslike hiss, and the watery unknown beyond calls out my name.

I embrace it with bleary passion…

Luke and I are seated together on a hard wooden bench. It's very uncomfortable, but we wait patiently in the anteroom adjoining the office of E. Townsend Parker, Esquire. We remain quiet, not talking, not fidgeting, and behaving in strict accordance with the stern instructions given to us by an unfriendly secretary.

We arrived ten minutes early for our appointment; still, we were told Mr. Parker would see us only if time permitted. Luke discreetly tugs at his stiffly starched collar while I nervously glance about the lavishly decorated room.

Two hours later, I look up and see ruby-red lips slowly pull taut in a duplicitous smile. "I'm sorry, Master Wade, Master Luke, but the Earl of Barstow will not be able to see you. He suggests you make another appointment for some time in your next life. Good day, boys."

We trudge out to a million dollar lobby and look down into a marble pool full of rare, exotic fish.

"I hope somebody hangs him," Luke says.

Embarrassed, tearful, I say nothing.

"Are you all right, Wade?"

After-rain air engorges my lungs, oxygenating my blood and restarting my brain—the sensation of light-headedness, faint and pleasurable.

"Are you all right, Wade?"

My eyes crack open to billowing white clouds bobbing in a sea of blue. *Am I dreaming?* Something shakes me, perhaps pulling my arm, I am not sure.

"Wade! Are you all right?"

Woof!

Not quite back over the line of consciousness, I think the fish in the marble pool are barking at me.

"Wade!" Luke slaps my face repeatedly.

I'm alive! I bolt up to a sitting position, look quickly for the wizened finger-pointing monk, and start coughing uncontrollably.

Woof! Woof! Mac zealously informs Luke that I am all right. *Woof!* He climbs on top of me and sloshes his tongue all over my face.

"Okay, boy," I sputter, trying to push him off.

As I attempt to hold Mac away from my face, my eye catches something in the distance. I think I see a man hanging by the neck from the catwalk under the old A.T. & S.F. trestle. "*I hope somebody hangs him*"? Am I still dreaming?

"Mac, quit! Get off!" Luke yells.

Mac reluctantly climbs off of me.

I close my eyes tight and rub the lids. When I open my eyes again, the man is not there. *Geez.*

I look at Luke and can tell he's been crying. "I'm okay." I give him as much of a smile as I can.

He breaks down completely, blubbering and shaking, deep breaths catching in his throat as he tries to speak. "I-I-I thought you-you-you were dead!"

I pull him down to me and put my arms around him. I feel him shudder hard and surrender the tension in his body as he melts into me. "I'm okay, Luke." I pat his back.

He whimpers, "I love you, Wade."

"I love you, too." I begin to cry as I hold him.

Mac sighs and looks straight at me, as if to say, *I told you so.* Then he lays himself out across my legs, the stoic sentry still doing his duty.

Over Luke's shoulder, I see our knapsack and the rest of our debris. Hundreds of candle remnants are scattered about like wreckage on a beach. We huddle together drenched and crying, sprawled out on the wet concrete like worthless mullock dumped outside the mouth of a dangerous mine.

Cookie cutter shadows drift across us, then bright sun and instant steam rising off the concrete, followed by more shadows. The vacillating sky epitomizes my entire state of affairs.

What do I do now? I'm not worth spit. I guess God is still punishing me for killing that man. What else could explain this?

Whatever happened after I blacked out in the tunnel, the trauma has left my body aching and sapped of energy. The knot on the top of my head throbs unmercifully, but at least I can remember how that happened. I know my physical body will recover, and the emotional deadening I experienced from the first near drowning at Three Ponds was measurably worse than this. This flogging by dunking was less severe because I assumed Luke's safety had been obtained.

But am I building up a tolerance or becoming immune? Or have I merely beaten the odds and benefited from blind luck? My will, my purpose of mind, isn't even part of the equation. My will is locked in paralysis and my very life, although apparently buoyant in the presence of water, is at a standstill. The roots of failure have riddled the soil of my existence, and I have become nothing more than a stubborn, noxious weed barely clinging to life.

Our reunion becomes unbearable as I listen to poor Luke, tears streaming down his face, relate how he waited outside that stubborn metal hatchway. "I prayed for you, Wade. I prayed real hard."

"I'm glad you did."

"And God answered me. The door burst open! And water gushed out like a giant garden hose!"

He witnessed me shooting out of the tube and onto the deck as lifeless as a defeated salmon tossed to the rocks by a raging rapid. He relates the details with such two-dimensional emotion and affection that it sounds more like a wild cartoon than a violent near death experience. But I know better. My bumps and bruises, physical and mental, are real.

The worst part is seeing with my own eyes how Luke nearly died of sadness. He lays his head on my chest. "I don't want to live without you, Wade."

Some older brother I am.

We slog up from the arroyo on a slick, narrow switchback, the path topping out on a brushy ridge straddled by a hole-ridden chain-link fence. We breach the fence and appear on the street out of wind and looking like a couple of sewer rats seeking the safety of higher ground.

My legs are wobbly, my stomach is even less steady, and my mind is in a tangle over what to make of the entire episode. I wish Festus and Jethro would come and tow me home and put me to bed. Luke, on the other hand, is fit as a fiddle, fully recovered and ready to tackle the next adventure on the agenda.

"Let's stop and sit for a minute, Luke. I need to rest."

"Sure. Do you want me to go up to Kory's and get you a Royal Crown?"

"Do you have any money?"

He grins. "Nope. But I can swipe some empties from around back and cash them in."

"That might work at Sal's, probably because Sal lets us get away with it, but don't try it at Kory's. We already have a bad name there. Thanks anyway. I just need to sit for a bit."

"Okay." He sits on the curb next to me.

Mac had lagged behind us coming up the path. Now he sits on the other side of me, rump on the curb, front legs in the gutter.

"Hi, boy."

"Darn dog," Luke mutters. "He thinks he's a person sitting like us."

I give Mac a long scratch behind both ears. "I think Mac might be smarter than both of us put together."

Mac's tail starts up, acknowledging the compliment. He gives my cheek a lick, which I take as forgiveness for ignoring his warnings about the storm drain. No matter what I do, no matter how stupid my behavior is, Mac always loves me and forgives me.

Resting quietly at the curb, I think about the Sergeant. *"I failed to think clearly and realize the danger."* I am amazed I'm alive to have those words haunt me now.

I dig my fingers into the furry folds of Mac's shoulders and massage my way up his neck. "Good boy, good dog."

Mac may have forgiven me, but I have not forgiven myself. Contrition weighs heavy on my shoulders, and no one is volunteering to massage mine.

The walk home has never been longer. Each step treads hard on what little is left of my gossamer ego. I am convinced I have evoked the wrath of God. Being driven out of Three Ponds and flushed out of Cavendish Caverns proves it. Superstitious worry has turned into wary veneration. And now fear is compounding at an alarming rate, filling me with foreboding that the worst is yet to come.

We arrive home to an empty house—no note from Lucinda, no singing Carl to sooth my battered spirit. The three of us sit on the front porch in silence until the sun goes down. Luke falls asleep on the steps, and I get him on his feet and walk him to his bed. We both reek of tunnel sliding, but baths will have to wait until tomorrow. It matters not that the fridge is nearly empty—we are too tired to eat anyway. I'll make horsecakes for Luke in the morning. If there's no milk, I'll use water for the batter.

As I tuck myself in bed, I try to banish a sinking feeling. I need to create a positive mental countermeasure before facing the dead man. I imagine that I possess an ampule of concentrated bravery. I apply a tourniquet, find a vein, and give myself a massive dose. It puts me to sleep, but I do not rest.

The good news is the dead man of Three Ponds has the night off. The bad news is he has a substitute tormentor. The hanging man appears swinging like a pendulum from the catwalk under the train trestle. All through the fitful night, the rope groans—calling my name.

eight

Nineteen sixty-two takes forever to come, or maybe it is 1961 that takes forever to leave. It seems Carl the gun-toting baker is suffering the same lethargic passing of time that I am. He is on probation for disturbing the peace and unlawfully discharging a firearm within the city limits. He mopes around looking long in the face, attending three AA meetings per week by order of the court. Recently his spirits have revived some thanks to Friendship 7 and John H. Glenn, Jr.

Carl claims he's quit drinking, but Luke and I know better. We watched him stash several cases of Brew 102 behind the old fig tree in his backyard today. He saw us peeking through the fence and then pretended not to see us.

"Bottled bread yeast," he sang out plenty loud enough for us to hear.

Luke and I giggled and hunkered down behind the fence.

"*FIG*-ure that," Luke whispered.

His pun cracked me up so that I had to get up and run around to the other side of the house.

Carl is not a healthy role model, but he has always been relatively harmless. I have been extra considerate of him since the day he tried to shoot down the Russian cosmonaut. Strange as it might seem, even given how much his drinking problem serves as a painful reminder of Earl, on some murky level I identify with Carl. Truthfully, I don't believe he is any less stable than I am. In fact, I think Carl is a hardworking, intelligent man. And he sure can sing. The difference is I haven't yet been tempted by the curse of alcohol, and I hope I never am.

But there is another difference between Carl and me, a big one. Carl enjoys the unconditional love and support of a wife, who by everything I can tell must be eligible for sainthood. Carl is more than a handful—the whole neighborhood knows that—but despite his legendary cantankerousness, his wife never seems to lose patience with him. She doesn't give up, and I admire that about her. Lo the burden that Carl can be, she truly seems happy and content.

Sometimes I watch her work when she tends her flower garden in their backyard. Half the time she seems to carry on a conversation with a nonexistent workmate. Once I dared to ask her who she was talking to.

"Who am I talking to? Why, my best friend." She smiled.

"Really? Your best friend…who?"

"Jesus. He's a very good listener."

"Really? I should tell Him that I hope someday I have a wife who loves and cares for me as much as you love and care for Carl."

"My goodness, that's just about the nicest thing anyone has ever said to me. Bless you, Wade."

"My friend, Rodney, told me a little about Jesus."

"I'd say you have a good friend."

"He died."

"Oh, I'm sorry."

"That's okay. I have his Bible."

"That's good. Do you read it?"

"No. But I like having it."

"I'm glad you told me about your friend."

"I like talking about Rodney."

"He sounds like he was very nice."

"Yes, ma'am, he was. Can I ask you something?"

"Of course…anything you want."

"I was wondering—why does Carl hate the Russians so much?"

She appears slightly surprised. "My goodness, Carl doesn't hate the Russians. As a matter of fact, he *is* a Russian. He was born and raised near Moscow and fled during the revolution. He made his way to the west and eventually became an American citizen. But he misses his homeland very much. It's the Soviet government and communism that he has a problem with."

"I didn't know that."

"Well, I'm glad you asked. Answers come from questions. That's how we learn things."

"Yes, ma'am. Well, real nice talking to you."

"Nice talking to you, too. Give that Bible of yours a little reading when you can. It's full of good answers."

"Yes, ma'am."

No wonder Carl gets so worked up. What do you know—he's a Russian. One thing is certain, the story of Carl attempting to shoot down a Soviet spacecraft will be told at least a thousand times.

April Fools' Day 1962 finds me prepared to detect and thwart any and all attempts by Luke to trick me. I feel certain he is trying to set me up for a fall of some kind, and I've been careful to note his every move. Like Carl, I have been moping along, struggling with my demons one day at a time, so I'm used to keeping my guard up.

Before the day is over, I may indeed be proven a fool. But today there's an enlivening newness about and I am enjoying some especially rare good cheer. I have good reason to be upbeat and happy—it is springtime and the smell of baseball is in the air.

I'm sitting on the bedroom floor annoying Mac, who is in the middle of one of his random naps. Tickling the tufts of fur between the pads of his paws is one of my favorite pastimes.

I start to tell Mac one of my best Duke Snider tales when Luke bounds into the bedroom all out of breath. "Guess what! I know you won't believe me—but the Sergeant just pulled up out front in Queenie!"

I look at him cross-eyed. "Oh, come on now. You do better than that." He's been trying all kinds of unimaginative nonsense since we got up this morning, but this takes the cake.

"No, really, I'm not fooling. It's the Sergeant for sure. The tree is blocking the car, but I'm pretty sure I saw another person with him."

Yeah, right. He does seem quite serious, but I am absolutely not falling for it. Mac hasn't raised an eyebrow, which is a highly reliable indication that no interlopers have entered Parker territory. "Okay, let's see... I know—you go tell *the Sergeant* that Miss Cherry and I have gone to Hawaii on our honeymoon."

"I'm not going to say that."

"Go on—just tell him."

"Are you sure?"

"I'm sure."

"Okay, if you're sure that's what you really want me to say."

"That's what I really want you to say." He spins on his heels and leaves the room as quickly as he came in. *Easily defeated twerp.*

Mac grows weary from my prolonged pestering and makes a halfhearted attempt to nip my hand. He adds a weak growl before laying his head back on the floor. With one eye open, he watches me apply a piece of floor lint to the tip of his moist black nose. His tolerance for this kind of abuse does have a limit. If I keep it up long enough, he'll concede the space to me and retreat to another part of the house. End of game. Following him is not a good idea.

Something startles Mac, and he snorts out a burst of air that sends the lint sailing in a perfect loop-the-loop. In the same fraction of a second, he's up on his feet displaying an erect ridge of fur down the length of his spine.

"Geez, take it easy boy. I won't tease you anymore."

His glaring deep-brown eyes pierce the space I occupy like parallel X rays.

"Aloha, tough guy. I thought you were in Hawaii."

Scar!

Mac relaxes and puts a little wag in his tail. I turn around slowly and mouth the words, "April fools?"

He gives me that handsome grin. "How have you been, Wade?"

"Uh—fine, sir. How are you?"

Luke leans his head in the door. "I told him what you said."

I give Luke a stern look, and he sticks his tongue out at me.

"I'm good, Wade. I've got someone out in the car who would sure like to see you guys."

Mac jumps up on the bed and peers out the window. His tail goes into high gear, and he starts whining. "Molly, uh, the dog from down the street must be out there."

"No—it's Cherry." The Sergeant nudges me with his elbow. "You did say you wanted to see her again, didn't you?"

My jaw drops. The mere mention of her name sends me reeling. My hope of seeing her again has been dormant all this time. Now it comes surging back in a trove of giddiness that spills forth and fills me with an urge to bolt. "Miss Cherry is out there?"

"Come on, tough guy. It's not wise to keep a beautiful woman waiting. Remember that." He tugs me along by the arm.

A debilitating bashfulness comes over me as we walk out onto the porch. There she is standing by Queenie, both of them radiating beauty in a dramatic shaft of afternoon sun. Miss Cherry smiles and Queenie shimmers, their complementing stylish contours blending to perfection. The picture could have come out of a four-color Buick brochure—a gorgeous blonde leaning against the comely-lined four-wheeled work of art. *Buy this car and you're sure to meet a beautiful lady like this!* But this is much more than a subliminal advertising message; this beautiful lady is real!

I feel her smile from all the way across the yard and fall helpless to the magic of the moment. My wits stripped bare, something dashingly mature to say dangling just beyond my mind's reach—I try to think faster.

Mac reaches her first. His pretense is to assess her as a possible threat, but I don't buy it for one minute. His behavior is farcical, although measurably better than my own. I watch as he gallantly tenders himself at her feet and gazes up with unabashed adoration. The scorpion of jealousy stings my heart as I watch him receive a caress behind the ears for his adroit opportunism.

Worse yet, as if he has preeminent rights, Luke slips under her other arm and confiscates a generous hug. I make it to within six feet of her and stop in my tracks. I yearn for both of her arms to close tightly around me, but alas, all I can manage is a shy stare.

"Hello, Wade."

The beauty has spoken directly to me. A reply is now mandatory. "Hello, ma'am. Um, you look real sharp, ma'am." *Oh for crying out loud, what a doofus!*

She giggles. "You look pretty neato-keeno yourself."

I do? Blue jeans with patched knees, faded striped T-shirt, old sneakers caked with storm drain scum. I do? "Gosh, um, thank you, ma'am." My cheeks begin to tingle, and one of my shoes sort of digs its toe into the sidewalk.

"Well, come here. Don't you want a hug?"

I step closer, biting my lip to stop myself from saying, *Gee, that would be real sharp, ma'am.*

She lets go of Luke and grabs me, immersing me in an exhilarating teddy bear hug. Dandled and steeped in a stupendous embrace, I am rendered light-headed and flushed. Blissfully adrift on a sea of blithe confusion, I am in that cocoon time between boyhood and manhood when female tenderness can turn gears that don't quite yet mesh.

She holds me tight, lingering longer than I expect, pressing me like a precious flower in her book of special memories. Rocking me in her arms from side to side, she lulls me, frees me from all of my unearned burdens.

I want desperately to tell her how much I've missed her, but I'm afraid if I do I'll start to cry. Instead, I turn my head to the side and look at the Sergeant. I fish for a signal—a wink, a nod, even a raised eyebrow—anything that will tell me to bunt, take, or swing away. He only grins, but I see what I want most to see. He isn't mad at me for my outlandish practical joke about Miss Cherry wanting to marry me. At least that is my interpretation. The hug is over, and suddenly it's only half as long as I would like it to be.

She stands me back from the car door. "Lyle and I brought you each a surprise to show you how much we, well—how much we *like* you." Her voice is candied with a tantalizing lilt. She softly clicks her perfect teeth to tease us further.

Luke squeals and dashes closer. "What surprise?"

"Hmm, let me see now." She feigns perplexity to build the suspense. "I wonder who should get the first surprise. What do you think, Luke?"

"Me first, me, me, me!" Luke yips and skips about in a wild caper, and then prances in front of Miss Cherry like he used to do outside the bathroom when waiting for Earl to finish one of his marathon sessions.

The Sergeant starts mimicking Luke's dance. Miss Cherry swats his shoulder and tells him to quit it. He clowns with her by covering his face with his arms like a boxer inducing an opponent to waste punches.

Finally, the Sergeant settles himself down and turns to me. "I thought I'd let you know I spoke to your mom about this first—and she said it was okay with her."

Bringing us presents is certainly unexpected, but I am more surprised that he would feel the need to seek Lucinda's permission. I feel certain the gifts are not overgenerous—maybe some baseball cards or a kite perhaps.

Luke is a different story. He is really revved up, high steppin' at six thousand rpm. Put him in gear, pop his clutch, and he'd burn rubber for a quarter of a mile. "You better give Luke his present first before he explodes."

"Thank you, Wade! Yes! Me, me, me!"

Luke has always been impossible to take on Christmas mornings. I just wish I could be as free with my emotions as he is. Not me. Mister keep-it-all-inside Wade.

Miss Cherry opens the car door, and I see two brightly decorated packages complete with curlicue ribbons sitting on the front seat. One is shoe box size, the other slightly smaller. She leans inside the car, pulls out the shoe box shaped gift, and hands it to Luke.

To my surprise, Luke suddenly turns circumspect and stares strangely at the package. It takes me a moment to realize he's looking specifically at the designs on the wrapping paper. He is clearly uncomfortable, possibly even on the verge of tears.

I touch his shoulder. "What's the matter, Luke?"

"It's c-c-covered with birds-s-s," he splutters, the word *birds* hissing through his teeth with heavily salted disgust.

The Sergeant chortles but quickly puts a hand over his mouth, while Miss Cherry clips short a peep-like chuckle and offers Luke an overly sweetened smile.

Incredulous, Luke just stands there rigid as a redwood. The effrontery has stolen his glee, and he holds the offensive box away from his scowling face as though it were a smelly diaper.

Miss Cherry becomes the picture of regret, and I surmise they must have picked out the bird-patterned paper as a joke. *Hey, wait a second. How do they know about Luke's mockingbird problem?* The Sergeant attempting to play a joke is one thing, but Luke is far too cute for Miss Cherry to tease like this.

Birds in the all-inclusive sense have become a serious subject with Luke, and Miss Cherry and the Sergeant obviously didn't realize that joking about such a thing would be cruel. The moment turns awkward, and I can see they don't quite know what to say.

I look closer to inspect the feathered specimens and quickly note the gift wrap design is a *Birds of the World* pattern. "No catbirds, Luke."

"Are you sure?"

I point at the different shapes and spout the names of whatever winged creatures I can think of. "I only see quail, pheasant, grouse, turtledoves, a couple of bobolinks and maybe one cassowary." The truth is, I don't know a pelican from a parakeet.

"Oh…okay." He needs only to hear the right assurances from his big brother.

Secretly, I bank a certain April Fools' Day sort of satisfaction from their prank. I glance at Miss Cherry, and she gives me an appreciative wink. *Yes, I'm a hero!*

Luke rips off the offending paper, throws it to the ground, and we move beyond the immediate crisis. It *is* a shoe box. He removes the lid, lifts back some tissue paper, and with his face beaming bright as a searchlight, he proudly displays a brand new baseball cap. "Wow! Look, Wade, a Georgia Bulldogs cap!"

I get it…the bird-patterned paper makes sense after all.

Luke quickly pulls the cap down over his vulnerable red hair. Above the visor is a caricature of a muscular bulldog smiling shamelessly as though he has just eaten, you guessed it, a catbird.

I finally figure out that Lucinda must have blabbed about Luke's mockingbird problem and probably offered some specific gift suggestions. While to the best of my knowledge Lucinda knows nothing about our lives as storm drain troopers, she does know about Luke's desire to own a Bulldogs cap and the hilarious reason why. What she possibly might have told them to get for me, I can't begin to imagine.

Miss Cherry sees the opportunity for an apology and adopts her most sympathetic tone. "Sorry about the wrapping paper, Luke. I hope you're not *too* upset with us."

She comes across a bit contrite for the Sergeant, and he rolls his eyes.

I think she is just being nice, maybe even a little motherly. Either way, Luke is glowing, sanguine-faced, and fanciful. He's up beyond the clouds in a respite from worry, his new cap auguring a future free from attacks from on high. And he doesn't hear a word Miss Cherry is saying.

I elbow him a little harder than I mean to. "Come on…what do you say, Luke?"

"Hey, you big dumb donkey. Watch it!"

"Well, Miss Cherry is talking to you and you didn't even say thank you for the cap."

He frowns at me and then quietly says, "Thank you."

Immediately his hands go up to touch and stroke his new hat, his new pet, his new defender. And seconds later he is gone again, eyes glazed, off in a mental utopia where I envisage he is sitting around a campfire like a pompous nobleman roasting mockingbirds on a wooden spit and listening to his jowly bulldog bodyguard recite Shakespearean sonnets in perfect King's English.

Miss Cherry watches him as he slips back into his reverie. She smiles, pleased that he is so taken with his hat.

"Hey, what about Wade's present?" asks the Sergeant.

"Well, let me see here. What have we brought for big brother?" She reaches back into the car for the other gift and hands it to me along with the blessing of one of her captivating smiles.

"Thank you very much."

"Lyle picked it out. He said we had to get the best for Wade Parker."

"Thank you again, ma'am…and sir." I am so happy with all of this unexpected attention it could be a box of snakes, and I'd still be full of appreciation.

"You're welcome, honey. Lyle and I hope you like it."

I look over at the Sergeant, now sitting on the grass scratching Mac's belly. I glance at Luke, and his eyes tell me he is still frivoling in a fantasy dimension, his mind hooked to a helium-filled balloon that has not yet returned to earth.

The gift is heavier than I expect. For a moment, I relish imagining what it could possibly be—something in parity with a Bulldogs cap. I shake the package and listen for telltale clues to its contents. Silence.

But then I yield to a pinprick of caution. Given their choice of wrapping paper for Luke's gift, I can't stop myself from scanning the box for renderings of the dead man of Three Ponds. I only see freeze-framed images of Emmett Kelly and friends engaging in various antics with confetti and seltzer water dispensers—no dead man. *Whew!*

Luke suddenly slips back from his coma-like sojourn. "Just open it, Wade. Maybe they got you a cap, too."

"I don't think so. They know you're the hat wearer in the family, not me."

I glance at the Sergeant. He offers me a supplicating smile that does little to ease the disquieting concern gnawing at the back of my mind. I can't suppress the memory of the last time he gave me something. It turned out to be spurious, not a gift at all, more like a dire warning. The little chromium marble he dropped in my hand has clung to me like a pilot fish since, and it's probably the force that holds me in the tangle of troubling dreams that plague me to this very day. I look askance at the clowns, hesitating like a dieter trying to abstain from eating sweets but not wishing to offend a gracious host.

The Sergeant tries to goad me. "Maybe we should give his present to the dog, Cherry. Wade seems to think there's something in there that might bite him." The comment makes me even more suspicious.

Mac has been lounging on the grass preening his fur and relishing his belly rub. At the mere mention of his species he sits up at full attention, ready, willing, and able to rip open a hand-me-down gift. He stretches his legs, does one of those *get-the-kinks-out* whole body tremblers that start at the head and flow like falling dominoes to the tip of the tail; then prances over to me, or rather to the gift I'm holding; and gives it a thorough sniffing. Finding no hint of edible treasure within, he shambles back to the Sergeant and settles for a continuation of his belly rub.

Lost in the moment, I watch Mac with envy. His is such a simple existence. I stand here frozen in my own ridiculous reverie, doing the same thing I had just chastened Luke for doing. Miss Cherry no doubt notices a disturbing trend, a genetic trait implanted in both Luke and me. *Parker's Syndrome: Stupidity in the presence of gifts.*

I have gone completely silly over all of this. My eyes, too, must have glazed over, because Miss Cherry takes hold of my arm and gently pulls me out of my dingy stupor. "Wade."

"Huh?" I grin—stupidly. "Oh, sorry, ma'am."

"It's okay, honey. Just go ahead and open it."

At length, the clowns are properly drawn and quartered. Another wink from Miss Cherry confirms her influence over me as I become the proud owner of a brand-new transistor radio. "Wow! Neat!"

Mac turns his head away in disgust, but Luke is sufficiently impressed. "Hey, cool, can you get Vin Scully on that?"

The Sergeant chimes in. "You sure can, Wolfman Jack, too—clear as a bell all the way from Mexico. I checked it over real good, Wade. It picks up all of them, static free—KRLA, KHJ, KFI, KNBC and KMPC."

I look over the pudding box size receiver with the scrutiny of a jeweler inspecting a new shipment of diamonds. It has the smell of brand-new—solder, wiring, and plastic—and it seems to be very well made. But then I notice the label on the back, MADE IN JAPAN, and I can't keep from frowning. To me MADE IN JAPAN means throw this junk away.

I turn the radio around and look at the manufacturer's brand on the front. An American company—now I am confused. "It says the Japs made this on the back."

Carl has come out of his house and sits on the steps of his front porch. He leans his head behind the solid banister that encircles his porch, and I deduce he is probably nursing a beer. He looks over at our little gathering and waves to us like a well-behaved probationer and polite neighbor should.

I wave back.

The Sergeant says, "The Japanese are going to own the electronics market someday, Wade. We all better get used to it. The fact is, Japanese quality is improving all the time. Reputable American companies wouldn't put their names on it if it wasn't any good."

"Is that so? Well, somebody should tell Earl."

Earl claimed to have been captured by the "Japs" during the war. I gather they did not treat him well. Mistrust of Japanese people, "those sneaky, slanty-eyed creeps," as Earl was given to call them, has left a bigot's imprint.

And speaking of bad influences, Carl definitely has some contraband hidden behind the banister. I watch him lean twice more. Come to think of it, speaking of the war with Japan, Carl once told me he lost a nephew at Pearl Harbor.

"In fact, Wade," the Sergeant goes on, "some folks believe the Japanese will own this country someday."

A mischievous impulse clicks inside my head. I'll have to pick the right time, but I can't wait to inform Carl that someday he'll be making his mortgage payments to the Bank of Hirohito. Just to get his mind off of the Soviets, of course.

We all sit around on the front lawn talking, Luke still on cloud nine with his new cap, me running up and down the dial finding more radio stations than I ever knew existed. Miss Cherry and Luke meander over to the fence to chat with Carl, who has abandoned his comical effort to hide the beer. In another thirty minutes he'll be singing patriotic songs to the entire block. Mac has drifted off to sleep stretched out between the Sergeant and me, nap number five or six probably.

I have thoroughly enjoyed the surprise visit, and I'm pleased that they decided to stay the entire afternoon. The Sergeant seems relaxed. I notice he carries an unusually nice tan for so early in the year. Where has he been spending his days to get so brown? If he's been going to the beach, I wish he would invite Luke and me to go with him.

For the first time since they arrived, I find myself sitting alone with the Sergeant. It's great to share the same space with him, pass some time together, and enjoy each other's company. Something like a father and son feeling stirs in me, and I am acutely aware of how much I've missed him. I can't help wondering if he has missed me too, or whether he's even thought much about me at all. I guess the gifts answer that question, but it sure would be nice to hear him say it.

No one is more content than Mac. He is dreaming, whimpering softly, his feet twitching just like they do when I tickle them to annoy him.

I settle on one radio station, and after a while the Sergeant gets up and sets Queenie's radio to the same place on the dial. "Hi-fidelity sound," he says as he settles back down next to me.

"Enjoy it while you can. It won't be long before Carl's singing drowns out everything."

"Maybe we'll just sing along with him then. You know, when they give you lemons you make lemonade."

"Carl's voice isn't sour. He has a sweet, wonderful voice. It's just deep and loud—real loud. Carl is strange, but in his own way, I think he's brilliant."

"Maybe he's a kind of savant."

"A savant? What's that?"

"A savant is a person with profound and rare knowledge or ability. An unusually gifted or wise person, I guess you could say."

"I don't know how wise he is, but he sure can sing."

The Sergeant laughs and rubs the top of my head. Then out of the blue, he looks right at me. "You know, I kind of missed you, Wade. I'm sorry it's been so long, but I guess I've been keeping to myself a little too much since Rodney died."

My heart soars and dips. "I missed you too, sir. I think about Rodney just about every day."

"You don't have to call me *sir* all the time, you know. You can call me Lyle if you like."

"Yes, sir, I know. Maybe to some people it's kind of corny, but I just like to call you *sir* because I respect your being a policeman and all."

His face turns solemn, almost ashamed, confusing me completely. He looks away, as if to keep from revealing more. Something sure seems wrong, and my confidence falters like a sail slackening in shifting wind. He coughs, and I take it as the kind of cough you make when you want to change the subject.

I switch gears, trying to keep the hurt out of my voice. "Where have you been all this time?"

Now he really looks uncomfortable, skittish. "Well, some of the time I had to be away on business."

That sounds a little strange. A Los Angeles cop going away on business? But I don't have the nerve to question it. I am disgusted with my lack of courage. "Oh. I was afraid—well, I was thinking maybe you were mad at me and that was why you didn't come around."

"Why would I be mad at *you*?"

A ball of desperation clenches in my gut. I want so much to tell him the truth—that I know he knows all about me killing that man, that I'm glad he didn't arrest me or turn me in, and that I thought he was mad at me and didn't want to see me because of what I had done—but I don't say a single word about it. *Coward!*

"Well, um, sir, do remember the last time we saw each other?"

"Yes—the day of Rodney's funeral." His mood turns melancholy, and I realize I have dredged up unpleasant feelings for both of us.

"That's right. Well, do you remember when you dropped me off at home that day?"

"Yes, sort of, I think—what about it?"

Jeepers, do I have to go through the whole thing? Suddenly I remember what I told Luke to say to him when I thought Luke was just April fooling me…about Miss Cherry and me being in Hawaii on our honeymoon. *He must be playing dumb and pulling my leg.* "Well, if you remember, I kind of, well, actually—I played kind of a dirty trick on you."

Now I am painfully conscious of the possibility that he might have told Miss Cherry about my prank, and specifically that I had claimed she wanted to marry me. *Geez!* Nervously, I glance in her direction.

"A dirty trick? I don't remember that." His face is full of interest, as though this is the first time he's heard anything about this.

I move around to the other side of him and position my back to Miss Cherry to make sure she doesn't overhear us. "Don't you remember? We were sitting in Queenie." I point at the car. "She was parked right where she is now."

I am whispering and I don't like that I am. The secretive vibration in my voice tantalizes Mac out of his slumber. He doesn't open his eyes, but rising brows and quivering ears are sure indications of eavesdropping.

The Sergeant gives Queenie kind of a stumped look. "Yeah. So what? I always park there, don't I?"

I hold his gaze for a bit, watching for the crack of a smile and stalling for time. A Coca-Cola commercial playing on the radio ends and the disk jockey segues into "Poor Little Fool," by Ricky Nelson: "...*and here's Ozzie and Harriet's little baby boy with an April Fools' Day lament...*" I glance over my shoulder and note Miss Cherry's hips beginning to sway with the music.

Carl has apparently swallowed enough artificial courage, because he's in the middle of telling Miss Cherry about his day of infamy and his unfortunate incarceration. He gets louder, his arms darting about punctuating his speech with animated flair. The way she laughs, Miss Cherry seems to be enjoying his lowbrow humor. Carl has been generous with his supplies, as I can see Miss Cherry now cradles a beer of her own. He has also produced a cream soda for Luke.

Out of the corner of my eye I see Carl's patient wife peeking through a slit in the curtains. Such a sweet lady she is. She's probably bracing herself for the concert that is sure to begin soon.

Before resuming my whispering, I tap the radio volume knob for a little more background noise and move a little closer to the Sergeant. "Come on, sir—you know you remember. I told you I had heard some talk at the Highland Park police station."

He gives me a blank look. "Really?"

I am annoyed with the whole charade. I can tell Mac is becoming annoyed, too. Ricky Nelson is doing a good job obscuring my voice, but I lean in even closer. "You said you wanted to marry Miss

Cherry, and I told you that she wanted to marry someone else."

He just stares and shrugs—no memory whatsoever.

Ricky's final refrain fades to silence, and I get to my feet. Exasperated, dizzy with frustration, and completely unaware of the quiet lull, I shout at the Sergeant before I can catch myself. "I told you Miss Cherry wanted to marry me!"

The Sergeant's face jells with pure pleasure as the heat of utter humiliation sets mine ablaze. I glance at Miss Cherry as my cue comes over the pudding box radio—the intro to Del Shannon's "Runaway." My brain says flee from this place of shame and confusion. *Run! Run! Run!* But my legs won't respond. I am frozen solid, entrapped in a crystalline glacier that isn't moving anywhere. I am on public display like a statue in the park. *Bring on the pigeons!*

A second or two of eternal length expire before my synapses rejoin my legs with the will to move. But it is too late.

"April fools!" the Sergeant bellows.

"What!"

With lightning quickness he lunges, grabbing my legs and pulling me down on top of him. My humiliation flashes away in a frothing frenzy of uproarious laughter, hilarious squealing, and frantic attempts to escape. Not a chance. I am hopelessly ensnared in the powerful clutches of a human grizzly determined to tickle me beyond the bounds of oblivion.

He howls and roars, all the while laughing equally as much as me. "I remember every word you said—you little trickster! But I've got you now!"

Miss Cherry and Luke run over and jump on the pile, and Mac prances and barks as he jumps in and out of the roiling ball of arms and legs. Carl laughs and claps and whoops and hollers as he dances a Russian jig. The fence separates him from us, but he is not about to be left out of the merry scrum.

His wife, still peeking through the drapes, is delighted to see him so energized and happy. So much so, she comes out of her house and hurries over to the fence. Carl locks an arm around her waist and waltzes her around his front yard until she finally squirms free and scurries back inside the house, but not before collecting up an armful of empties.

Batteries drained, limp as a tuckered out trout ready to be reeled in, I slump into a wheezing, giggling mass of arms and legs.

The Sergeant is as exhausted as I am. He grins and makes a breathless declaration. "We're even, you trickster. But you did put up a heck of a fight."

Relieved that my fears about him being mad at me are unfounded, I squeak out a tired thank you and privately count my blessings.

Miss Cherry ends up next to me in the pile. Now we lie side by side on our backs, looking up at the first twinkling hints of dusk. Luke untangles himself and resets his cap, while the Sergeant sits up and brushes a few blades of dried grass from his hair. Mac wallows on his back, snorting and snuffling in the grass. He nuzzles the Sergeant's leg with his snout, and the Sergeant obliges him with a firm caress behind his ears.

As though responding to an announcer's cue, Carl begins a remarkably soft and dulcet rendition of "God Bless America." It is strange how the ambiance has shifted from an almost violent cater-waul to sublime calm. Lying here so close to Miss Cherry, I feel like a circus tiger soothed by the trusting presence of my trainer. As the sky blushes toward nightfall, Carl's melodic praise of God and country is lifted up on a gentle breeze and sent as a sweet gift throughout the neighborhood. I'm thinking maybe Carl is a kind of wise savant, the way the Sergeant said. It takes a wise man to know just when to sing.

As I gaze above and behold the most beautiful orchid sea, I am immersed in a wonderful sense of security. I feel so loved—a feeling I want to last forever, want to be real. Maybe I just need to know when to sing.

Miss Cherry takes my hand in hers. She turns her head to me, her lips very close to my ear, and speaks with a soft, mother-like tenderness. "You know, if I weren't already betrothed to Lyle, and you were twenty years older, I'd marry you in a minute."

He did tell her.

I want to ask her what *betrothed* means, figuring it must be a term from the secret language of undercover cops. Instead, I decide to ferret it out later. "That's real sharp, ma'am," I say, for the moment beguiled into feeling nothing at all like a doofus.

"Lyle and I won't be having any children. But I love being around kids, especially you and Luke."

"Lucinda wouldn't mind sharing us with you."

With the crickets of spring providing a cacophonous background score for Carl's loyalist medley, we lie here enjoying the performance like concert patrons at an evening on the green. We gaze to the heavens with the same awe and wonder that human beings have been experiencing for thousands of years. To me the brightest stars are symbols of my innermost thoughts, and I scan from horizon to horizon reviewing the events of the day. Like the earliest astronomers, I scour the constellations in search of the paradigm that will make it all add up.

I wish I could find my guiding star, or at least a way to uncross my star-crossed life. My biggest problem is I am only eleven years old, and try as I do, I lack the intellectual maturity to solve the complex riddle of emotions that overflow from every cell within me. The adults lying in the grass beside me have made an important impression, but I need more, so much more. I need grown-ups permanently engraved in my life. I wish I could find the strength to tell them how I feel. I wish it all could be so as I ruminate over the vast galaxy above.

I sit up for a moment and allow myself to float with the sunset.

Miss Cherry sits up next to me. "This is my favorite part of the day. This is the moment of mellow transition when the day's events merge into the stillness of the vespertine."

"Vespertine…I like the sound of it. What does it mean?"

"It's a fancy word for the evening. I think of the vespertine as that magical instant between dusk and twilight. If you blink, you'll miss it."

This is a magical moment for me, my vespertine. Someone up

there must be watching out for me; I just know it in my heart. I close my eyes and try to picture a twinkling stellar solution for all my woes, and thoughts of Rodney float across my mind. *"Jesus loves you very much."*

Memories of Rodney's voice ripple across the sky of my soul. In the form of a prayer, I silently proffer myself as a votive child in hopes of bringing Miss Cherry and the Sergeant closer to me. For deep down in my loneliest of places I know that the truth I desire cannot be found, or understood, without the abetting love of a wise mentor. I just wish it were possible to stay here with them forever.

The moist chill of night has already fogged her windows when finally the Sergeant puts the key in Queenie and fires her up. Luke and I stand at Miss Cherry's window. I feel awful not knowing when I will see them again. On top of that, there is no escaping my cowardice in missing the opportunity to confess my sins to the Sergeant.

It has been a very good day, the best in a long time. But the reality of April fools comes like a slap in the face when Miss Cherry smiles, reaches through the open window, and hugs me one last time. "Good-bye, Wade. I'm very happy I got to spend some time with you."

"Me too, ma'am—bye."

I try my best to be a man, but I can't stop the uncooperative tear that trickles down onto the pudding box radio tucked snugly to my chest. I take a quick step back from the car and turn the radio up louder, desperate for a happy song to bring me back under control.

I am in trouble from the opening drumroll. The greatest rock and roll crooner of all time opens my floodgates wide, his bittersweet empathy burning into me like lashes from a whip. He sings of the painful side of love, of desperate longing for things that can never be, of pitiful crying when pitiful crying is the soul's only defense against crushing abject sorrow.

A modicum of leftover pride compels me to turn away and walk toward the house, my head hanging low, Roy Orbison my singing guide. I close the front door and slump to the floor. Tears flow to beat the Arroyo Seco, and only Roy understands the depth of my misery.

Luke stays by Queenie and handles the last farewell. I turn off the radio, get up from the living room floor, and go into the bathroom to blow my nose. When Luke finally meanders into the house, I am sitting on my bed with my eyes closed. He hums something upbeat and cheerful as he comes over and sits on his bed directly across from me. Two inches separate the toes of our sneakers.

Mac strolls into the bedroom and jumps up beside me. He licks my cheek, not to be sympathetic or affectionate—he just likes the salty tear trails.

Carl has stepped it up a notch and is now blasting out a thunderous interpretation of "Wild Blue Yonder." He usually finishes up on a religious note, probably a strategic move to mollify his wife. Tonight I am sensing he's in the mood for "Onward Christian Soldiers."

Behind my closed eyes I am thinking, *What a way to live.* My life has become a topsy-turvy ride down a churning rapid of wild emotion. In fact, I'm not really living at all. I am more like a slave with no hope for a better future or a better life. Except *my* master does not pop a bullwhip or wield a club to beat me into submission. My master is a wicked trio of guilt, loneliness, and heartache.

I know Lucinda loves me with all her heart, and my condition is not the result of her failings. I do not begrudge my mother. If I were capable of blaming anyone other than myself, it would be Earl—but I don't even blame him. I am my own worst enemy, and deep down I know that I'll have to find a way to negotiate an armistice with myself. I have enslaved myself, so I'm the one who must find the way to freedom. *Only the dead are not slaves*, a poet once said. I hope that isn't true.

I can handle the days; it's the nights, the dreams of Three

Ponds that keep me in a choke hold. I need my good dreams back, the ones that used to star me and Duke Snider. I need to dream of Miss Cherry and the Sergeant. I need to keep them with me at night, inside these closed eyes. I must try harder to overcome my guilt.

And still, as I sit here on my bed wrestling with my thoughts, I feel Luke's presence and know that there is some purpose and good in my life. If not for Luke, I surely would have turned to dust long ago.

Meanwhile, the silver ball bearing rages like a tempest in my pocket. It does not approve of my taking solace in brotherly love or playing dream ball with the Duke. It does not like me partaking of anything positive. Like a hexed amulet, it tenaciously throbs with disapproval and blocks the forgiveness I so desperately want. The battle rages on.

Luke sits quietly on his bed and patiently respects my feelings. When finally I sigh and shift my legs, he speaks. "They gave me this, Wade."

I open my eyes, and he hands me a sealed, plain white, business-size envelope. "What is it?"

"I don't know. They said to give it to you. That you should open it because you're the oldest."

I look at the envelope and wonder what it could possibly be.

A final good-bye note?

A subpoena?

An arrest warrant?

It is torturing Luke that he's not the one designated to open the envelope. "They said we—um, you I mean—could open it anytime you want."

"Well—what do you think this is, Mac?" I hold the envelope to Mac's nose and let him sniff.

"Geez! Don't let the darn dog slobber on it."

"What do you think, Mac?" He sneezes, and I, too, notice the smell of Miss Cherry's perfume on the envelope.

"Come on you big dumb donkey, open it!"

"Let's not be hasty now—it might be a trick or something."

"Oh, for crying out loud!" His face puffs and mantles under his new bulldog coronet.

Teasing and baiting Luke is good medicine. The bigger the rise I get out of him, the more it recharges my batteries. He is glowing red as a beet, his britches full of ants, and thanks to him I feel a thousand percent better than I did five minutes ago.

I look at the envelope again. It is addressed: *To Luke and Wade*, in cursive handwriting with bright blue ink—definitely a feminine hand. I note that Luke's name is before mine. Being the oldest carries with it an obligation to be magnanimous once in a while. "Here," I say, surprising the heck out of him. "You open it."

Now it's his turn to surprise me. He pulls out his peewee pocketknife and carefully slits open the envelope, rather than the usual barbaric shredding I expect. He removes a single folded sheet of bond paper and lets the envelope fall to the floor. He unfolds the paper, holds it out in front of himself, and carefully scrutinizes its contents, as though he were censoring a note from his teacher to Lucinda.

The top half of his occasionally cherubic face appears above the sheet of paper. His eyes change from an expression of curiosity to either ecstasy or horror, I am not sure which, as the paper slips from his fingers and joins the envelope at our feet. There before my very eyes is what can only be described as a true miracle.

In Luke's impish little hands are four, third-base-side box-seat tickets for the opening game at the brand-new house that O'Malley built—Dodger Stadium. A million volts of *ec-c-c-static* electricity zap through my body. "Wow!"

Luke screams loud enough to drown out Carl, and Mac howls to his ancestors with the power of a hundred full moons. Luke leaps off of the bed and hops around the room. He whoops and squeals with the vehemence of a rainmaker challenging a ten-year drought. Mac and I join the rumpus in a wild romping effort that is not to be outdone by Luke. I grab my new radio and crank the volume knob all the way up just as Bobby Darin's "Splish Splash" comes over the air.

Luke hands two of the tickets to me, and we parade from room to room holding the precious little documents high above our heads like the honored regimental standards of a proud cavalry. Two uproarious bantlings we are, strutting little peacocks, lucky leprechauns flaunting the proverbial pot of gold.

The radio blares out instructions like a coach on the sidelines inspiring his team to victory. We go crazy with excitement, dancing with each other, imitating what we've seen on *American Bandstand*. The songs pour out from the radio, and we respond accordingly, doing "The Twist" side by side, wiggling our behinds and snapping our fingers and pounding on our knees like make-believe bongos. Finally, in one huge encore, Johnny and the Hurricanes launch us into a frenzy that completely wears us out. Beyond the point of exhaustion, we crash back on our beds where the lofty celebration began. Our private party has lasted for over an hour.

The sweat of my unbridled joy evaporates slowly, cooling me down, leaving more salt crystals for Mac. I watch Luke's chest rise and fall. He is fast asleep, probably deep into a catbird hunt with his new bully bird dog leading the way. He smiles in his sleep as I work at a stubborn knot in my shoelace.

I gently remove the tickets still clutched in his hand and match them with the ones that I've been revering. I study the four tickets, put them in numerical order, and read and reread all of the important information printed on the front and back sides. I stare at them for a long time. *They really are real tickets. Amazing.*

I put them with my Duke Snider baseball card collection that I keep in an old oxbow chest of drawers in the corner of the room. I tuck them under a pair of oversize corduroy pants that I won years before in an audience raffle at the *Pinky Lee Show*.

I debate whether to slip under the covers or wait up for Lucinda to tell her about the miracle when I see the sheet of paper and the envelope still lying on the floor. Mac jumps up on the bed as I pick up the paper. There's some writing on the paper that I didn't notice before:

Dear Wade,

Lucinda said it was okay. "C" and I will pick you and Luke up plenty early so you can watch the players take batting practice and warm up. We'll have a real blast!

Your friend,

Lyle

PS. I have to go back to Miami for a few more days.

PPS. Never look back, Wade.

Miami…so that's where he got the tan.

"Never look back," I say out loud.

Then deep inside my spirit I hear Rodney's voice. *"Remember, Wade, Jesus is the best friend you can ever have."* I smell horsecakes and smile while I put the piece of paper in the envelope and place it in the drawer with Duke and the tickets.

"Never look back," I mutter again. *What in the heck does that really mean?*

Mac looks at me with droopy eyes. "Move over, boy. I'm tired, too."

I shuck off my jeans, turn out the light, and slip under the covers. Lucinda won't mind if I don't wait up for her tonight.

"What a day, Mac. What a day."

He thumps my leg with his tail and licks my cheek.

Outside my window, Carl croons on.

I lie here in the dark and listen to Carl pour out his heart. It is kind of sad, really. I understand now that he misses his native Russia, and this is how he expresses his longing. I am his audience, and I realize more than ever how much I identify with him. I reckon we are both misunderstood souls, savants of the vespertine maybe, who are forever seeking but never quite finding our place in the mysterious order of things—life.

Then I decide I don't like the idea of being anything like Carl. Carl is a drunk, just like Earl, and I certainly don't ever want to become a drunk like them.

I turn the radio on low and hold it by my ear. As Santo and Johnny play "Sleep Walk," I drift off in a dream of being there when Duke Snider hits three home runs in one game for the third time in his career. And briefly, my discontent and self-pity are driven back into the darkness where they belong.

Lucinda comes home about an hour after Carl's vocal chords give out. She isn't alone. She and a "guest" tiptoe into the house, but vigilant Mac detects them easily. He jerks up in bed on full alert, knocking the radio into my head and awakening me from a light slumber. "No barking," I whisper.

Mac settles down, but he is far from happy about a stranger being in the house. Lights go on in the living room, and I hear muffled voices and giggling. *Three, two, one,* the bedroom door opens, and I know she is looking in on us. I hold Mac still and pretend to be asleep. She leaves the door open a crack as usual.

Mac could easily barge his way into the living room and confront the stranger, but he chooses to obey my command. A few minutes transpire while I attempt to listen to more muffled conversation.

This is the first time Lucinda has brought someone home with her, as far as I know. I don't like it. Earl has been gone for over two years now, and in all this time Lucinda has never shown any interest in men. I thought she was only interested in her work, nothing more.

Curiosity forces me out of bed. I silently order Mac to stay put and then listen at the door. I gain little information—the sound of ice cubes tinkling against glass, more giggling, and Lucinda's voice saying what possibly sounds like the name Fred or Ned several times. Then the living room lights go off, and moments later I hear her bedroom door click shut.

My curiosity grows. In T-shirt and underpants, I creep out into the hall and make my way down to Lucinda's bedroom door. A moment later the light at the floor beneath her door disappears, leaving me standing in total darkness. I hear the man talking now, not so muffled. The voice sounds vaguely familiar, but I can't place it.

The man says, "You're not going to say, 'April fools'…are you?"

Then I hear lots more giggling.

Wait a second! That voice sounds like that mean cop, Shunkman, from that night on Billy Goat Hill. No way, it can't possibly be that guy. Now I'm playing April fools' tricks on myself.

I slink back to the bedroom feeling rattled and powerless. In the dark, I carefully slide the dresser drawer open and reach under the corduroy—just to make myself feel a little better. I slip back in bed feeling as uneasy about being awake as I feel about what usually visits me in my dreams. Some choice. I close my eyes and soon surrender to fatigue.

Just before the dead man of Three Ponds jumps out from behind the cardboard and shouts, "Hello there, murderer, have you missed me?" Miss Cherry's voice echoes down from the direction of Billy Goat Hill… "Lieutenant Theodore Shunkman, how nice it is to see you out and about on this lovely evening."

At precisely midnight, Carl and his Chevy save me from my nightmare. I awake with a start. I hide under the covers the rest of the night until I hear the guest leave just before dawn. When sunrise has sufficiently brightened the room, I lower the covers. Mac sits on the floor, watching and staring out the window. Something tells me he's been sitting there on point all night long.

I pity the poor burglar who ever makes the mistake of picking this house to plunder.

nine

I have risen up some from the nadir of my dilemma. When Luke flashed those Dodgers tickets, it gave me some hope, something to look forward to. I check under the corduroy pants no less than a dozen times per day. The drawer handle can't take much more.

I struggle over whether to quiz Lucinda about her late night guest—just to see what she might have to say. I suppose no good can come from raising the subject; I expect her to tell me some sort of elaborate fib, and I'm not sure I want to set myself up to be punctured that way. I probably don't have the nerve anyway.

I have asked her several times about the unexpected daytime guests—the Bulldogs cap, the transistor radio, and the amazing Dodgers tickets. She remains very hush-hush, except to say that she approved the visit and the gifts, including the baseball tickets. I find her measured silence strange and unsettling. It's as if she is taking her lead from the Sergeant, the great mystery man, the one who rarely gives me a straight answer about anything. When I get this kind of shuffle treatment, it makes me feel bad, like I'm unworthy of the truth.

The Sergeant is always impossible to figure out, but this time Lucinda does reveal something about what might be inside her. When circling around my question, she gives up a pained smile that seems to hint of regret or hopeless resignation, or possibly even camouflaged hurt feelings. Maybe deep down Lucinda is saddened by my general enthusiasm for the Sergeant and Miss Cherry? Our mother is so disengaged from our daily lives, never having returned to us after Matthew died, that it doesn't seem possible she might feel jealous about her remaining sons becoming attached to another adult. Who knows, maybe she wants to go to the Dodgers game with us? I can't figure her out.

I do not believe Luke and I ever consciously exclude her from anything. We simply coexist on a parallel dimension and the independent nature of it obscures any thoughts of inclusion. Like so much missing or unmarked on the charts of my small inward existence, this is beyond my ability to navigate. So I turn further inward, retrim my sails, and try my best not to let it run me onto the rocks.

We arrive at Chavez Ravine two hours before game time. My stomach is plagued with butterflies over the possibility of seeing Duke Snider up close. When Queenie saunters up over the rise on Stadium Way, my heart swells with pride. Despite all the anticipation and my powerful imagination, the first glimpse of the new stadium catches me completely unprepared.

My eyes behold a beautiful sight, a gleaming Brooklyn-blue castle grandly shooting skyward, launching the dreams of Abner Doubleday far into the future. The stadium is so far beyond what I had pictured, I cannot grasp the full splendor of what I'm seeing. I am in awe—or perhaps in Oz. *So this is how Dorothy felt when she first set eyes on the Emerald City!*

As I peer out the car window at the newest wonder of the earth, utter bliss tickles my insides with a sugary rush of excitement. "Man! This is as good as life gets!"

Luke is equally dumbfounded. "Yippee! Look at that, Wade!"

"It is absolutely amazing!"

My mind reels as I imagine the Duke already sequestered some-where inside the castle, royalty that he is.

The splendor of Dodger Stadium is rivaled only by the stun-ning beauty of Miss Cherry. Riding in the front seat ahead of me, she occasionally looks back and smiles. Every time her eyes meet mine, my heart speeds up. This is becoming the best day ever!

Queenie hums across a sea of newly laid blacktop and delivers us through a phalanx of wooden sawhorses and concrete barri-cades. She noses her way up to a security gate upon which a sign hangs that reads: AUTHORIZED OFFICIALS AND PERSON-NEL ONLY. The Sergeant shows his police badge to a guard, who seems to recognize him, and the guard immediately waves us through.

As we move past the smiling sentry, the Sergeant glances over his shoulder at me. "This is where the players park." He nods up ahead and cranks the wheel to the right. "That's Duke Snider's Corvette over there."

A tingle rattles down my spine, and I giggle from an overflow of nervous energy. I never thought I'd get this close to Duke's Corvette. Two seasons past, Luke and I ventured to the Coliseum for Duke Snider Night, when Duke received the car and other gifts in honor of his outstanding career.

"I'll remember this night for the rest of my life," he had said in an emotional address to the crowd.

I stood in the stands and cried as my heart overflowed with respect and honor for my great hero. "I'll remember this night for the rest of my life too, Duke," I called out to him from deep within the throng of over fifty-one thousand admirers.

It was a doubleheader. Duke didn't play in the first game, but in the second game we got to see him hit a smash homer over the centerfield fence before an usher caught us and roughly expelled us from the Coliseum. We didn't have tickets for the game and had managed to slip through the turnstile by crowding in with a family with a bunch of kids. We used every penny we had for bus fare, but it was well worth it.

As we roll past the Duke's sporty carriage, I am almost close enough to reach out and touch the fender. I feel compelled to bow and renew my pledge of fealty as Queenie finds a vacant stall and eases herself in.

I open the car door and hesitate for a moment before placing my shoes on the pavement. I am about to step on hallowed ground and want to savor the moment before taking what feels like the final step of a lifelong pilgrimage. I say a private entreaty of esteem and thanks, take a deep breath, and slowly get out of the car. *Wow! I'm at Dodger Stadium!*

"You're awfully quiet." The Sergeant sidles up next to me on the ramp climbing up from the parking lot.

I smile as one might smile while beholding a renowned work of art. "This is the greatest day of my life. Thank you for making this possible, sir."

He puts his arm over my shoulders and squeezes me in kind of a fatherly hug. "It's my pleasure, son. I know this means a lot to you and Luke."

The word *son* rings loud and sounds more than wonderful. I try it on for size, knowing full well he only meant it as a figure of speech and did not intend to imbue the special meaning I would dearly welcome.

"I really appreciate it."

He squeezes my shoulder again. "I think you and Luke are in for a special day indeed."

I catch that all-knowing look and can't help but wonder what he really means by *special.*

We walk to a turnstile with an overhead sign that reads: VIP CHECK IN. A portly man dressed in bleach-white pants, an equally bright starched white shirt, blue blazer, and a dashing red tie gladly checks our tickets.

Friendly as a car salesman, he says, "Field level box, row one, third base side." He laughs heartily, almost like Santa Claus, and gregariously chimes, "You'll be able to hear Mr. Alston *think* from these seats."

"Oh…my gosh!" Luke blurts.

I glance up at the Sergeant, shock smeared all over my face, and mouth, "Row one dugout seats?"

He nods and grins just the way he did at that cop, Lieutenant Shunkman, the night of the hazing on Billy Goat Hill. "We want only the best for the Parker brothers."

I do a Luke and squeal at the top of my lungs and dance in place till my feet hurt.

Programs, popcorn, and peanuts in hand, we gleefully head into the infield tunnel. This special tunnel is no storm drain under Highland Park, nor is it a subterranean dungeon or illusory playground offering false hope to wayward souls. In this tunnel there will be no flash flood or visions of hooded monks. The light at the end of this tunnel is brilliant with the beaming animus of baseball, luminous enough to brighten my spirit and fill my needy heart with monumental satisfaction.

Luke is beside himself, too.

Man oh man, this is so great!

As we emerge from the interior portal, a whole new level of awe pours over me. I am seized in the grip of a baseball epiphany. My eyes roam like voracious conductors taking in everything, flooding my already overloaded brain with images of a great sports icon. My concept of *Oz* now appears glamorously before my dazzled senses.

A meadow of emerald green abounds far and wide, a living carpet so rich and luxurious only a wizard could have made it so. The sight of the infield makes me giddy. Hybrid clay, groomed to perfection and warmed in the life-giving sun, glows with radiating tinges of conquistador copper. The base pads stand out like mother-of-pearl tuxedo buttons, formal, resolute, classy adornments in the honored wreath of competition. Ivory talc baselines converge at home plate, like a twin-tailed comet resting its head on the seat of business. And out in front, fain to commence the cannonade, the pitcher's mound sits as a solitary bulwark centered in the field of battle.

Oh, baseball—what a magnificent game you are!

Slowly I turn and nourish myself with the majestic panorama of Dodger Stadium. "My gosh," I whisper as my eyes fill with the massive decks, staggered four high, looming like a stair-stepped mountain behind home plate.

The stands fan out in a gargantuan horseshoe from foul line to foul line. And hovering high above are towering stanchions of artificial sun that shine all around the glorious field. Bleacher sections, standing proudly left and right of centerfield, wear matching scoreboards surmounted with giant orange Union 76 globes. Bunting elegantly draped from nearly every horizontal place declares through its colors that we are in the land of the free and the home of the brave. Old glory, the California Bear and brightly colored baseball pennants everywhere, lazily wave in the breeze. The colorful decorations are nice all right, but unnecessary carnival trappings, mere window dressing. The true beauty is the game itself.

I do note one thing that is less than perfect—the outfield wall. It is clearly a pitcher's helper. Not the distance, the color. Baby blue just won't do; it is far too light. Of course, I favor the hitters, and hitters need contrast in their field of vision. It's difficult enough to hit a small white ball with a round stick when it's coming at you at ninety-five or one hundred miles per hour. If it were up to me, I'd paint the outfield wall a darker blue. *Not to worry, Duke will tell them.*

Dodger Stadium. It is all so perfect, antiseptically clean, comfortable, and secure. I am safe here inside this temple of baseball, my new citadel. Nothing else matters at the moment.

"We're this way," the Sergeant announces after consulting with a smartly dressed usher.

"Oh gosh—it's a ways down there, isn't it?" says Miss Cherry.

The Sergeant leads the entourage, and I traipse along following Miss Cherry. Luke has been straggling four or five paces behind me since we left the parking lot. I glance back at him often, remembering my own folly with Earl at the Rose Bowl seven years earlier. I don't want to waste one minute hunting for Luke today.

As we make our way down the steeply paced stairs, members of the Cincinnati Reds trickle out of the first base dugout and gather around the cage set up at home plate.

The Sergeant pipes up. "Batting practice, boys."

I take a gander toward the field, and my eyes momentarily leave my footing. I stumble forward down the steps and regain my balance only by inadvertently grabbing Miss Cherry's waist. It is an involuntary reflex, completely unintentional, and wholly embarrassing.

Miss Cherry's startled squeal echoes off the underside of the mezzanine deck like feedback from the public address system. Her popcorn shoots up in a volcanic plume showering down around us like flash-cooled buttered pumice. Luke flinches hard, fearing for an instant that a squadron of deadly catbirds has amassed for an all-out blitzkrieg. The Sergeant, caught at mid-sip, dumps half of his icy beverage down the front of his shirt. And me, well, I do the only thing that makes any sense under the circumstances—I sit on the steps and laugh…nervously.

Miss Cherry turns around, unflappably calm. She leans over, bending at the waist, preparing I fear to vehemently chastise me for my ungentlemanly behavior. I sense a coming monsoon, but it is too late to skedaddle now. To my surprise she only smiles and playfully wags her finger in my face.

"Sorry, ma'am."

I giggle at the popcorn decorating her new coiffure. She recently cut off her beautiful long hair in favor of a stylish new look. I don't really care for it—short, straight, tucked behind the ears and swept across the forehead. The popcorn doesn't help, and I can't contain myself—I laugh some more.

The Sergeant turns around toward the commotion. He is dripping wet, soaked from chin to knees. If this had happened to Earl, he would be furious, and I would be looking for someplace to hide. But one look at the Sergeant and I laugh even harder. He grins and starts laughing, too.

"I tripped, sir."

He booms back in the unmistakable voice of Scar. "He says he tripped, so how come I'm the one who got drenched!"

Then he wiggles his eyebrows just like Rodney Bernanos, and Luke busts a gut. Luke surely would have loved Rodney.

I spot him immediately. He is very close, standing just outside the dugout smiling and talking with Jim Gilliam. He removes his cap, and for a moment the sun lights up his head in a flash of silver. I am startled to see just how gray he really is.

I am sitting next to the Sergeant, and he nudges me to make sure I notice him. "There's the Dukester."

"Yes, I see him." It is all I can do to keep the sudden build up of excitement inside me from breaking out in a scream.

"He's looking awfully gray around the muzzle, isn't he?"

"He's always been gray," I respond testily.

"Okay, already." He gives me a wary look. "You're a little wound up, aren't you?"

"Sorry."

"Hey, no sweat—as long as you're happy."

"I'm more than happy, sir."

"Good. Duke is the pendragon this season. Did you know that?"

"What's a pendragon?"

"It means he's been appointed team captain, which is one of the highest honors in team sports."

"Oh, cool."

My hero is only yards away. At one point Duke looks in our direction. He seems to spot someone and waves. My heart pounds and the Sergeant can tell I am squirming in my seat.

"Don't get too excited. His wife and kids are sitting right behind us about four rows."

I want to turn and look but can't work up the nerve. I have started to sweat. Restrained delirium best describes my state of mind.

The Reds finish their batting practice, and now it's the Dodgers' turn. Tommy Davis, Frank Howard, Johnny Roseboro, and Maury Wills all take their turns in the cage. Then Willie Davis, Ron Fairly, Wally Moon, and Larry Burright take some swings. All the while, Duke Snider stands off to the side, watching like an omniscient fox nestled in the grass.

Each player makes a point of talking to Duke after he finishes his turn in the cage, no doubt checking with the master for any words of wisdom.

Don Drysdale walks over and says something that makes Duke double over with laughter. I find myself laughing along with them, as if somehow I am privy to the joke.

Soon it is time for Duke to step into the cage, and my heart races a little faster. Yes, he looks a little long in the tooth, but dare tell that to the first ball that sizzles toward the plate. *Smack!* There is no sweeter sound on this earth.

"Incoming!" shouts one alert person standing among a group of blue-coveralled men huddling in the right field bull pen. I can hear the guy all the way across the field. Members of the grounds crew scatter like shadow spooked chicks in a barnyard as the leather-bound projectile slams into the ground right where they had been standing.

Frank Howard, both Davis's, and Wally Moon have gathered around the cage ostensibly to heckle their esteemed captain. Now they howl with delight. Frank Howard, the giant power hitter, especially loves it. He grabs the chain-link screen and shakes it much like a caged gorilla might do to display his fearsome power. The Duke cracks up and apes back at his teammate.

I am surrounded by laughter and look around. Then I realize I have jumped to my feet and put on quite a display of my own mimicking Frank "the gorilla" Howard. Instantly embarrassed, I sit down to the applause of a dozen fans who have filtered in behind us. Chagrin contains me for the next few minutes.

"Hey! There's my buddy, Leo!" The Sergeant scrambles to his feet. "Leo!" he shouts over the railing. "Leo, over here!"

Leo "The Lip" Durocher turns around and scans in our direction. Recognizing the Sergeant, he waves and comes directly over to where the Sergeant is leaning over the railing. They shake hands, laugh, and chat like old chums, while I watch with great surprise. The Sergeant looks over at me as though pointing me out to Mr. Durocher, then turns back and chats some more, laughs some more, shakes hands with Leo again, and then comes back to his seat, and sits down.

Miss Cherry is surprised, too. "What was that all about?"

"Leo's a friend of mine." The Sergeant leans close to Miss Cherry and whispers something in her ear.

I never did like whispered secrets, and this time is no exception. Whatever he tells her, it makes Miss Cherry squeal almost as loud as she did when I tripped coming down the aisle, except this time she clamps her hand over her mouth. Then, with genuine surprise in her voice, she says, "Really?" The Sergeant nods and Miss Cherry promptly plants a big kiss on his lips.

Very weird. I sit and stew, knowing it's no use asking them what is up.

Duke Snider keeps swinging and making solid contact with nearly every pitch. Several more baseballs sail over the right field wall. One threads the bleachers in centerfield, bounces hard in the staging area some 450 feet from home plate, and rebounds over the outer fence into the parking lot. All in all it is an amazing display of the awesome power still contained in the body of my number one baseball hero. In my heart and mind, I am swinging with him on every pitch.

When he finishes his workout, Duke cradles the Louisville Slugger on his shoulder, tips his cap to his youthful understudies, and strolls with the elegance of a peacock back to the dugout.

Leo Durocher intercepts him, and the two legends stop near the on-deck circle and talk. Number four has his back to me, but I can clearly see Mr. Durocher's face and can tell he is doing most of the talking. My eyes are riveted on them and I wish I could read Leo's lips, but nobody has ever been able to do that.

Leo probably knows Duke's swing better than anyone. Since Duke is expected to play today, Leo is no doubt mentioning some subtle nuance about Duke's stance or swing.

Fascinated, I gamesomely fancy I am a child prodigy, a phenom, the youngest rookie in major league history. I suit myself up in full Dodgers battle dress and step up to the on-deck circle right beside them. For the next few minutes I absorb much wisdom from two of the greatest sages in the game.

The opening day sun pushes through a diaphanous morning haze and spreads its thermal blessing over the inaugural scene. I close my eyes and turn my face up toward the warmth, feeling as though life aboveground is good again—if only for a day. My face begins to glisten as I give myself to the sun's goodness, and a heady sensation merges into a feverishly sweet delirium. Overwhelmed by the totality of the moment, I feel as though I am no longer in my seat but floating. I become less and less aware of my surroundings—the murmur of the growing crowd, the cries of prowling vendors, the popping of glove leather on the field below—all of it slowly fades away.

Like a christening spirit establishing occupancy, my physical body turns to vapor and disperses into the ambient surroundings, where I lay claim to my rightful place in the new milieu...

Leo Durocher points, Duke Snider turns around and stares, Leo makes a beckoning wave with his arm, the Sergeant stands up, Miss Cherry squeals again...and before you can say *Hocus-Pocus,* I am being hoisted over the wall and down into the solid arms of Edwin Donald "Duke" Snider, the pride of Compton, the Silver Fox, the Duke of Flatbush, future Hall of Famer, and MY HERO! A snapshot impression slices through time eternal.

Duke sits me down on the field and gives my hand a firm shaking. "Well, young man—I hear you're my number one fan."

My feet and legs are functioning, but I feel as though my body is levitating, probably because of the gallons of adrenaline displacing my blood supply. A grin wider than Los Angeles distorts my face, and my bladder quivers in response to an emergency pee-or-flee signal from my conflicted brain. When Duke lets go of my hand, my fingers instinctively toy with the sticky, honey-like residue of pine tar.

I can feel my head nodding up and down in the affirmative and I hear someone who sounds unmistakably like me say, "You're the greatest, sir." I am hopelessly starstruck.

Duke laughs shyly, and I notice an endearing modesty about him that I hadn't expected. He is human, just like me. "Let's hope Mr. O'Malley thinks so after the season is over."

He winks at Mr. Durocher, who is standing within earshot. "What's your name, son?"

It must be the excitement, but now I really do have to go to the bathroom. I lick my dry lips. "Wade Parker, sir."

"Wade Parker—boy, that sure sounds like a ball player's name. Matter of fact, we've got a young man named Wes Parker in our farm system. We think he's going be a heck of a ball player in a couple of years."

I can't believe this is really happening. I will be dancing like Luke again if I don't do something soon to relieve the pressure in my bladder. "Duke, sir—um, Mr. Snider, I mean." I sound like I have a mouth full of marbles. "I'm really sorry, but I have to go to the bathroom."

"No problem. Have you ever been in a big league clubhouse?"

"No, sir."

"Well, how 'bout we pretend you're a young sportswriter or something. That'll be fun. Come on, follow me."

My heart rate triples, and my smile wraps around to the back of my head as Duke Snider leads me into the Dodgers' dugout. *Unbelievable!*

The Dodgers' manager, Walter Alston, is standing in the dugout near the clubhouse entrance. He's talking on a telephone and looks up startled to see a shrimp like me in his dugout.

"It's okay, Walt. He's a cub sportswriter from the *Los Angeles Times*. He's with me."

Mr. Alston nods and keeps talking into the phone.

We enter the clubhouse just as someone yells: "Infield practice!" The booming voice startles me. Big men wearing baseball uniforms head my direction, and I feel like an indecisive squirrel in the middle of a road, unsure which way to dart to avoid being run over.

My senses are just beginning to stabilize when I bump smack into Johnny Podres. "Oops! Sorry. Excuse me, sir."

"Hey there, kid, how are you doing?"

"Fantastic, sir. Good luck today."

Podres is pitching the historic first game in Dodger Stadium. It is quite an honor. He smiles and gives me the thumbs-up.

It's about an hour before the pregame festivities are scheduled to begin. Activity in the clubhouse is frenetic. Ball players, trainers, real sportswriters, and team executives scurry about the clubhouse with no evident organized purpose. I find the hubbub very exciting.

"The urinals are that way." Duke points beyond where I am standing wide-eyed and marveling. "Go ahead. I'll wait right here for you." He smiles reassuringly.

I head down a corridor past a dozen players, recognizing some, not recognizing others, and turn a corner into a bathroom and shower area. I step up to the trough and unzip. Alone for the moment in the belly of Dodger Stadium, I try to convince myself to be calm and accept that this is really happening. I am almost positive I am not dreaming. After about ten seconds my euphoria bursts out in a nervous giggle. *Who would believe it!*

Major league chatter, metal cleats gnashing on concrete, raucous laughter—the symphony of the locker room resonates off sparkling tile walls. Standing there at the urinal, I am wound up so tight with amazement I really have to concentrate to go. I need to reach up a little by standing on the balls of my feet. *This can't be a dream. If I were dreaming, I would dream myself to be tall enough for a major league urinal!*

Then, an amiable voice startles me so I almost fall over. "Rookies are getting younger every year."

I turn my head toward the voice and look up, way up. Don Drysdale stands towering over the trough less than ten feet away.

"No, sir, Mr. Drysdale. I'm not a rookie. I'm a reporter with the *Los Angeles Times*."

I am so unnerved I almost lose my balance. I dip my knees to keep from rolling over backward, which causes me to splatter on the front edge of the porcelain trough. I must look something like a newborn colt trying to stand up for the first time. There is nothing I can do to recover my dignity.

Mr. Drysdale chuckles. "You can't be a reporter, kid, you're much too polite." He winks, tucks in his jersey, cinches his belt, and adjusts his cap. "Don't forget to wash your hands, kid. See ya."

Back out in the locker room, I find Duke talking with Sandy Koufax. A twinge of sadness scurries through me as I think about how thrilled Luke would be if he were here with me now. Luke has been unhappy with the Dodgers since they traded Charlie Neal to the Mets, but he still thinks the world of Sandy Koufax. Maybe, out of kindness, I won't tell him I saw Sandy Koufax. Not a chance.

Duke spots me. "Hey, Wade, come here and meet Sandy Koufax."

I stick out my hand and realize too late that I haven't rinsed all of the soap off. I'm not accustomed to washing my hands every time but wasn't about to go against Don Drysdale's orders.

Mr. Koufax smiles warmly and shakes my hand. If he notices the soap, he doesn't say anything. "I hear you're a sportswriter."

"Not really, sir—I'm too polite to be a sportswriter."

Duke and Sandy are momentarily speechless. Then they look at each other and crack up. Mr. Koufax pats me on the back. "You know something, Duke? This kid is all right. Maybe he'll bring us some good luck today."

"Yeah, maybe we should have Podres rub his head a little."

Still laughing, Sandy Koufax rubs the top of my closely cropped noggin and walks away shaking his head. "Hey, Perranoski! Wait till you hear this one!"

Duke continues to chuckle as he leads me back out to the dugout. Mr. Alston is still on the phone and doesn't pay any attention to us. We walk back out into the warm sunshine, and I feel completely charged up, rife with enthusiasm—so alive. And I'm not at all nervous anymore.

Mr. Durocher is over by the wall talking to the Sergeant. I look up in the seats and see Luke and Miss Cherry waving to me. I grin but am feeling way too cool to wave back.

Duke notices them, too. "Is that your mom and your brother?"

I am uncomfortable with his question and not quite sure how to respond. I like it that he thinks Miss Cherry is my mother, but at the same time it makes me feel guilty and disloyal to Lucinda. "That's my brother. His name is Luke." I try to ignore the other part of his question.

"Your mom is very pretty. I'm not wild about her hairdo though."

I giggle in agreement, noticing a couple of popcorn kernels still nested on top of Miss Cherry's head. "She isn't my mother. She's a real good friend of ours."

"Oh. Is that your dad talking to Leo?"

I am caught off guard again. This time his question gives me a little stabbing feeling, and I know it's already too late to mask the pain. "No, sir. He's also a good friend. Earl, um, our father, abandoned us a few years ago."

Duke doesn't say anything, but a sympathetic sadness fills his eyes. It seems he's gotten the whole picture from that one word, and he glances up to the seats where his own family sits. The life of a professional baseball player requires a lot of travel. Maybe he has some regrets about being away from his wife and kids so much. I stand there feeling like a textbook example of abandonment.

Duke puts his hands on my shoulders and turns me around so I face toward the field. The Dodgers' infielders have taken their positions and are in the process of stretching and limbering up. One of the coaches has arrived at home plate and is preparing to hit some ground balls.

Duke kneels on one knee and puts an arm around my waist. "Do you think you might want to play in the big leagues someday?"

"Not really. I'm just an average athlete. I might want to be a policeman, though."

"Police work can be kind of dangerous, don't you think?"

"Yes, sir. But not nearly as dangerous as facing pitchers like Bob Gibson or Don Drysdale."

His eyes turn serious. "You've got a point there, my friend."

"My brother is a big fan of Charlie Neal." I release a sarcastic chuckle. "He's not very happy with the Dodgers for trading him."

"Charlie's a friend of mine. Baseball is a tough business. Sometimes players get traded. But going to the Mets isn't necessarily a bad thing for Charlie. He's from Brooklyn, and it's always a big deal to play for your hometown team. Like me growing up in Southern California and getting to play ball for the Los Angeles Dodgers. Charlie will help them win some games, but it'll be some years before the Mets are a competitive ball club."

"I hope the Dodgers never trade you, Duke."

He smiles and gazes wistfully toward center field. "I'm a Dodger, Wade. I might not know how to play baseball in any other uniform."

"I think you're the greatest center fielder of all time, sir."

The silver fox grins. "You think so?"

"Yes, sir, I sure do."

"Boy, I don't know about that, Wade." The modesty shows again. "There are some exceptional center fielders in the game right now. There's Willie Mays and Mickey Mantle, for example."

"They are terrific players. But I happen to think you're a little better."

"Boy, you are my biggest fan, aren't you?"

"Yep."

"Well, I sure do appreciate that. But just between you and me, and strictly off the record, Mr. Baseball Writer, I believe Joe DiMaggio is the best center fielder of all time."

Duke stands up, signaling the end of our chat. He looks over to Leo and the Sergeant and gives them the high sign with his eyebrows. "You know something, Wade? Well, I hope you don't mind

me offering a little advice about your father and all. Sometimes I
can be pretty hard on myself, and, well, there's a little saying I
learned along the way that has helped me through some rough
spots. We must find a way to forgive, or we only end up blaming
ourselves."

A feeling of great trust wells up in me, and squinting there in
the wonderful Dodger sun, I look at him. "But what if it's me who
needs forgiving?"

"Hmm? Boy, now that is a very important question. I guess if
we really think about it, the whole world needs forgiving. But you're
a young man, Wade. If you're already carrying something heavy on
your shoulders, chances are whatever it is probably doesn't belong
on your shoulders anyway.

"I was thinking more along the lines of your father taking off
and abandoning you. That's an awful thing for a father to do, but
who knows what troubles he might have on his shoulders. I'm not
making any excuses for him, but if you can find it in your heart to
forgive him, it will be a good thing for you."

Duke smiles as I consider his meaning. *But Earl doesn't deserve
forgiveness.* I struggle with the core of his advice. Realizing I will
have to chew on it, I just look at him, and he smiles and squeezes
my shoulder.

I flip-flop over a wild notion to tell him about the dead man of
Three Ponds, and the image of Duke Snider suddenly dissolves…

"Wade!"

"Huh?" Startled, I snap my head around.

"Are you all right, honey? You look a little pale." Miss Cherry
places the back of her hand on my forehead.

I was dreaming! "Yeah—I'm okay. Sorry, I guess I was thinking
too hard or something."

"I guess so, sweetie. Lyle's been calling you. He wants you to
come over there by him." She points and nudges me out of my seat.

I see the Sergeant motioning to me to hurry up. Miss Cherry
looks electric with pent-up enthusiasm, like she is in on a big secret.
I pick a popcorn kernel out of her hair as I slip by her toward the

open aisle. I look back at her and Luke once more, and then cautiously make my way over to the Sergeant.

I am still numb from my midday fantasy as I approach the Sergeant, but I perk up some as I come under the influence of his captivating grin. I walk up next to him and put my hand on the railing. "Yes, sir?"

"Ah, here he is. Wade, I'd like you to meet—Duke Snider."

I start to slump to my knees and have to grip the railing with both hands to steady myself. My heart bangs and clatters, I blink hard, swallow harder, and peer over the railing straight down into the face of my real live hero.

He raises his arm and offers his hand to me. "Hello, Wade. I'm Duke Snider. I'm very glad to meet you."

I have enough sense about me to reach over the rail and take his hand. I squeeze firmly and grind as much pine tar into my pores as I can, planning never to wash my hand again. "It's a great honor to meet you, Mr. Snider." I got that out in a surprisingly clear and forceful voice. I immediately notice the bat he used for batting practice is still resting on his shoulder.

"Wade here is going to be twelve years old next month, Duke. My fiancée and I brought him and his brother to the opener as a treat, and kind of an early birthday present for Wade."

"No kidding. What day is your birthday, Wade?"

"May 30, sir."

Duke warms with an obvious twinkle in his eye. "You know something, Wade? May 30, 1950 was a very good day for both of us."

"Yes, sir, it surely was. You hit three home runs in the second game of a doubleheader against the Phillies at Ebbets Field that day. And the Dodgers won. It was a Tuesday."

Duke's mouth hangs open.

The Sergeant appears proud of me. "Pretty special kid, huh, Duke?"

"I'll say. Wade, it seems me and you are kind of connected."

His words make me light-headed. "Wow—thank you, sir."

"I've been blessed with a lot of good fans, especially back in Brooklyn. And you're right there with the best of them."

My heart soars and hovers around the third deck. "I think you're the greatest center fielder of all time, Duke." My words of praise ring forth like a familiar echo. It seems to me I rehearsed that line just a minute or two ago.

Duke's winning smile grows bigger and better than the Sergeant's best grin. "Tell you what, Wade. How would you like to have this bat as an early birthday present?"

"Really?" My face beams brighter than Queenie in the noonday sun, and my hand grasps the handle of the bat so quickly I startle myself.

"It's yours."

"Thank you!"

"You're welcome, son. Have a great birthday."

Suddenly my eyes pool up. Embarrassed and confused, my male conditioning quickly checks the outburst. *Is this really happening? Or am I still in the middle of a daydream?*

But the Duke's regal scepter, tightly gripped in my sweaty little hands, is as real as real can be. It peals true and solid like the Duke's advice about forgiveness as I tap it firmly on the concrete deck. A therapeutic vibration travels up my arm and ripples across my chest, magically giving me power. The sound and the feel of that simple shaft of lathed wood instantly fills a good portion of the bleak void in my soul.

Since long before Earl ran off to Barstow, a dearth of love has battered my psyche and left my heart raw as an open wound. My mind and spirit have been festering ever since. Now a gift from the noblest of all baseball royalty commences a painless debridement of my wound. At last the tide is turning. At last I am moving in the right direction. At last my wound has begun to heal.

The Sergeant brushes his hand over the top of my head. His reassuring touch triggers the tears again, and overpowered by joy, I break down completely. Through eyes blurred like rain-streaked windows, I gaze down at Duke Snider. Glorious Dodger sunshine pours across his mirth-filled face, making his silver-stubbled cheeks sparkle with glitter. His compassionate smile tells me everything is going to be okay.

In his eyes the message is implicit: *I must find a way to forgive, or I'll only end up blaming myself.* But to me this is a conundrum of untold scale.

The Dodgers lost the opener six to three. But I was so enamored with the bat, I didn't really care who won or lost. My favorite Dodger got the historical first hit in Chavez Ravine. He also hit the last two home runs in historic Ebbets Field.

Hero worship had some therapeutic benefit, but bad dreams cannot be offset by fantasies forever, not even by fantasies come true. Even after that glorious day in the sun, the little silver sphere came back around with the certitude of an orbiting planet ruled by the unyielding laws of physics. I just can't help thinking about the dead man. Because of me, he will never get to see Dodger Stadium.

It is all too much for the bruised mind of a boy not yet twelve. Something has to give; and when it does, I fear I will be looking at the beginning of the end of the world.

The missiles in Cuba can't begin to compare.

ten

Me and the bat are hanging out in the garage. Man, I love this bat. It's been three months; still, every time I look at it, I relive the entire day at Dodger Stadium—the best day of my life. I keep it next to my bed at night. The smell of the pine tar comforts me and helps me get to sleep. The bad dreams have been fewer and farther between with the bat sleeping by my side. I think some kind of magic is working for me. Good magic. Duke Snider magic.

I hear Lucinda yelling for me. *What now?*

I walk outside and close the garage door behind me. Lately, Mac has found a cool place in the garage, and he keeps trying to get in there to relax away from the afternoon heat. He really likes it, and I've been meaning to make a spot for him with an old blanket so he doesn't have to lie on the oil stained floor. I haven't gotten around to it, though.

"Coming!"

She beckons me up to the front porch. She is dressed for work and ready to leave, and I can see she is agitated about something. "I want you to go get your brother. Something very important has come up, and I need to talk to both of you right away. Hurry up, go find him right now."

Three sentences, that ties the record for the amount of conversation my mother has directed toward me in weeks. "I don't know where he is."

"I don't care—I said go find him right now!"

"Yes, ma'am. You don't have to yell." *This can't be good.*

I guess correctly and find Luke two blocks away. He's been around the back side of Jake's Barbershop, where he discovered a half-empty bottle of Clubman aftershave lotion in Jake's trash bin. He has managed to soak himself with the stuff. I actually smell him before I see him. The scent is so strong my eyes are watering. I send him on ahead of me and fret about what might be on Lucinda's mind. *She is overdue for a good rampage. Way overdue. Maybe she's heard something about the dead man?*

Lucinda is pacing like a wild animal in the living room when Luke and I finally settle side by side on the sofa. She's been crying, and my first thought is that Earl must have come around again and upset her. The sinking feeling starts to come over me, the feeling that I seem to live with most of the time, the awaiting execution feeling.

I brought the bat in the house with me intending to put it away in the bedroom closet, but she didn't let me get past the living room. I'm holding the bat between my legs, my sweaty hands gripping the handle for courage. Luke sits next to me, reeking like a florist shop full of dead flowers.

Being sat down together on the couch and addressed like this feels uncomfortable, threatening. For so long, Lucinda has been here physically, but her spirit has gone elsewhere, searching harder than ever for Matthew. All this time she hasn't communicated with us much more than to say hello and good-bye; now all of the sudden she has something important to tell us. *This sure can't be good.*

She doesn't sit with us on the sofa but stops her nervous pacing and stands off to one end of the room, about as far away from us as one could be and still be in the same room. She looks drained and tired, like a person overworked, short on sleep, and long past the need for a vacation. For the first time, I wonder if her nights might be possessed by bad dreams, like mine. She really looks terrible.

Convulsively, she blurts, "We have to move away from here right away."

Stunned, disbelieving my own ears, I stare at her.

"No way!" Luke cries. "I like my school!"

"I'm sorry—but that's just the way it is, Luke. We are moving, and I need you guys to start packing for me."

I stand up, my hands clenched tight around the bat handle. "What do you mean? Today? Right now?"

"Yes. We have to go immediately."

Huffing and puffing, Luke pulls his hat down over his eyes, slumps deep into the sofa cushions, and refuses to hear anything more.

I move a couple of paces toward her, the bat swinging from my right hand. "Well, why, Mom? What's going on?"

"There's nothing to discuss, Wade. It's just a fact—we are moving tomorrow. I'll be back with some boxes, but then I have to go to work. So I need you guys to really pitch in and get all of your stuff ready to load. It would be great if you could pack up some of the kitchen things as well. When I get home tonight, I'll work on the rest of it. A truck will be here in the morning, and some men will load the heavy furniture for us, but we need to have everything else ready before they arrive."

"What men?"

"Just some men!"

"This is crazy. Won't you at least say where we're moving?"

"Glendora—but that's all I can say right now."

"Glendora? Where the heck is Glendora?"

She exhales a partial surrender and gives in to tears. "Wade, I can't go into anything else right now. I'm sorry, but that's the way it is. I'll be back soon with the boxes."

And just like that she heads out the door.

From under his hat Luke mutters, "This sucks."

Lucinda comes back a little while later with lots of cardboard boxes: new ones tied ten to a bundle. She tries to drop them off without subjecting herself to further questioning, but I scoot out the back door and around the side of the house and manage to pin her out by the car. "Do the Sergeant and Miss Cherry know about this?"

"As a matter of fact they do."

I am taken aback. "Well, what did they have to say about it?"

"I told you I don't want to go into this right now. I just can't deal with any more questions."

"But this isn't fair. It's not right. What did the Sergeant say? Did he...tell you anything...something bad about me? This is my fault, isn't it?"

She looks at me with tired, angry eyes. "For that matter, you can't see the Sergeant anymore either."

"What!"

"I know you think the world of him and Miss Cherry, but we have to cut off those ties now. I have made an agreement with them, and they know they are not to have any further contact with my sons."

I hold on to her arm. "Agreement? What agreement? What in the heck is going on? This can't be right!"

She removes my hand and gets in the car. "I'll be back tonight. Please pack."

I stand with the bat in my hand and watch her drive away. I look around and wish I had someone to complain to, to argue my case to. I want to smash something with the bat, but there is nothing to smash. I sit on the curb and try to stifle the rage that has nowhere to go. *They made an agreement?*

Uninspired and with great reluctance, we dutifully pack all of our things. We also make a good dent in the kitchen items as directed. Luke and I don't have much to say throughout the afternoon and evening, both of us wrapped in the depressed colorlessness of mourning. Drained from the packing and the stress of the dastardly news, we decide to hit the hay a little early—but not without a plan.

At about 10:30 p.m., we hear Lucinda pull in the driveway. She looks in on us, and by the sound of her movements about the house, spends about an hour packing. Shortly after midnight the lights go off.

Luke whispers, "Are you ready?"

"Yes. Let's do it."

Out of pure defiance, we head out for one last hurrah at Billy Goat Hill. Not knowing how far away Glendora is, we figure it could be a long time before we see Billy Goat Hill again.

There is no moonlight sliding, no laughter, no playful arguing over the finer points of baseball. We sit next to each other at the top of the Crippler, depressed, confused, and more than angry. Even the crickets show reverence for our funeral-like mood and keep their whirring low and dirgelike.

Luke throws a pebble down the incline. "I think she's found us out."

I stare straight ahead, believing I know exactly to what he is referring, but we have never had this conversation, and I don't want to have it now. I want my murderer status left unspoken. I want the burden of all that it entails kept within me, and me alone. I want to continue to protect him from "it" as I have all this time, and for as long as possible—forever.

But, I also know Luke. That he would speak of it now means that he has completed his unfathomable process of logic and has arrived at a point of understanding, and having arrived at that understanding must now speak about it. He will explode if he doesn't. I can't just stare ahead and say nothing and allow an explosion.

"She had to find out sooner or later, I guess."

"What are we going to do? I don't want to move."

"We don't have a choice, Luke."

"This really sucks!"

I look around for Mac. I need him here by my side. "Mac! Where are you!"

"He went back to the house."

"I thought he was following us."

"He went back."

"For sure?"

"Yes, I saw him go back."

"Darn!"

"I've been thinking, Wade—what if we promise her we'll give up Cavendish Caverns?"

My heart stops and I look at him with relief and amazement. *He thinks she found out about our storm drain escapades, not the dead man!* "I'm pretty sure she isn't open to negotiation. I'm afraid we're just going to have to do what she says."

I see the reflection of the moon in his teary eyes. "I'm scared, Wade."

"We'll be okay."

I wish I had said it with more conviction, but I have always hated lying to him. He scoots over closer to me and halfheartedly throws another pebble into the darkness.

We come home at four-thirty in the morning to a very scary scene out in front of the house—four police cars with lights ablaze and neighbors milling around in their robes and slippers. Carl's wife is out on her front stoop in her nightgown and appears to be praying toward our place. Luke goes into a stupor over the flashing lights.

I run to the house and a policeman tries to stop me, but I dodge him and rush inside to find Lucinda lying on the sofa. She is crying hysterically. Another policeman is trying to calm her.

She sees me and cries out, "Wade! I'm so sorry!"

My heart pounding hard in my chest, I turn around in a panic. *Where is he?* And then…I see him.

The tiny little light left shining in my soul is savagely snuffed out by a massive sigh of pitiful desperation. Mac, my great protector, my true loyal friend, is lying dead in the corner behind the front door, his tongue lolling from his mouth in a circle of blood on the floor. I see a big hole in his chest.

"Noooo!" I fall down beside him. Sobbing, I sit there petting his head and rubbing his ears. "I love you, Mac. I love you, Mac. I love you, Mac." My hand touches the blood on the floor. It is still warm.

Evil has broken into our house in the middle of the night. Mac is dead. Lucinda has gone insane because she couldn't find us. And I want to run away from everything, but I can't.

The cops leave me on the floor with Mac. After a while I get up and go into the bedroom. I pull my bedspread off of my bed and drag it into the living room. No one gives me a hard time, and I ask two of the cops to help me pick Mac up. We carry him out to the garage. I want to make a nice spot for him with my bedspread. I want it folded just so and spread out smooth for him so he doesn't have to lie on the oil spots. The two cops seem to understand why this is important to me, and they help me fold and position the bedspread. We lay Mac down, and I ask them to leave me alone with him.

They nod to each other, and one of them says, "I'll wait for you outside the garage door. We'll need to take him away in a little while, son."

"Why, sir?"

"I'm sorry, but we need the bullet."

"Oh."

"You can be with your dog for a few minutes."

"Is Sergeant Cavendish coming here?"

"No he's not, son. Your mom made it very clear she doesn't want him here, and he's tied up with some other problems anyway."

Other problems? "Is he okay?"

The two cops seem to exchange a worried look while my question floats away in the dark. They step outside the garage, leaving me staring at the empty doorway.

I sit next to Mac and pick up his front paw. I feel the soft tufts of fur between his toes. I remember how when he was just a pup he would chase big mean neighborhood dogs away from our yard, and how he always wanted to play Get the Stick with the biggest stick he could find, and how when I was sick he would stay by me on the bed until the fever broke—what a tough guy he was, even as a pup.

"I love you, Mac. You're a good boy—the best friend I ever had. You did your job. Thanks for protecting Lucinda." I lie down next to him and wrap my arms around him. Has he gone to where dogs don't bark?

After a while, I leave Mac's body in the garage and walk outside to the front yard. The sun is rising, and all of the neighbors have gone back to bed, all except Carl's wife. She sees me and comes over to the fence.

I walk over to her, and she reaches over the fence and hugs me. "Somebody killed my dog."

"I'm so sorry, honey."

Her kind words and her gentle smile do give me some comfort. "We are moving away from here."

She takes my bloody hand in hers. "Yes, I heard. I'll miss seeing you boys."

"I have to go check on my brother."

"Okay, you take care of yourself."

I start to turn away, but then I stop and look at her. Tears welling up again, my eyes meet hers, and something inside keeps me there at the fence. "Everything is all messed up, ma'am."

"I know, honey." She touches my cheek. "I believe somehow all things work for God's purposes, and I just want you to know I will always keep you and your family in my prayers."

"I never knew your name."

"Esther. My name is Esther. Do you still have your friend's Bible, honey?"

"Yes, ma'am."

"Good. Try to keep it with you."

"Okay. Good-bye…Esther."

"Good-bye, Wade. God bless you."

I leave Esther standing by the fence with tears running from her kind eyes.

A few minutes later, Luke and I watch as two police officers carry a black bag from the garage to a van parked out front. I sit there on the porch with my arm around Luke, wondering what sort of darkness awaits us in this place called Glendora.

An impenetrable distance into which coolness has settled defines the relationship between Lucinda and me. I'd never even heard of Glendora, and with hardly a day's notice I find myself living here. I have questions, lots of questions, all prefixed with the word *why.*

Why did we have to move?

Why the hurry?

Why Glendora?

Why did Mac have to die?

Why can't I see the Sergeant anymore?

Why can't I see Miss Cherry anymore?

Why won't you answer me?

There are many ugly battles, and Lucinda always ends up in tears. But she never once gives me a plausible answer to any of the core questions. Luke tries his best to stay out of it. Worst of all, I have not heard from the Sergeant or Miss Cherry. I obey Lucinda and do not try to contact them.

For a while, I harbor hope they will find me and do something about this terrible injustice. I believe they will come and help me, but months pass, during which every ring of the telephone and every knock at the door sends my heart skipping with the hope that it is them. They never call. They never come. Not even a note in the mail. Eventually, my pride kicks in, and I begin to lie to myself and pretend that I don't need them.

The initial shock of the violence at Ruby Place slowly wears off, but I am left mired in a thick sludge of resentment that lays heavy over the prior layers of my troubled existence. I no longer trust

Lucinda, or anybody else, for that matter. For a while, I try to accept things as they are. I truly try to make it work. But after everything else that has happened, my litany of misfortune, I can't help seeing Lucinda as the bad guy, the person who ripped me up by my precious few roots and jammed me into another universe without so much as one word of explanation. Like layers of fallen leaves beneath an old dying tree, season by season my bitterness deepens.

A price is paid by all. Lucinda seems to age ten years overnight, though I feel no compassion for her. Frustrated and hamstrung by her derisive silence, I knowingly, ever so gradually, separate myself from her, until it becomes clear we are living in opposing camps. To me, Lucinda is the enemy.

My only power in the whole mess comes when I absolutely refuse to go along with her ridiculous proclamation that, coinciding with the move, we have to start going by a different last name.

"What do you mean we have to change our name?"

No answer.

"What do you mean from now on our last name is Gelson?"

No answer.

"No way, Lucinda! Earl was a complete jerk, but I'm not changing my name from Parker to Gelson! No way! What in the heck is going on?"

No answer.

For a while after the move from Ruby Place, Lucinda tries to spend more time with us. She claims things at work have changed and she can afford not to work so many hours. How can that be? She has the same job, as far as I know. I don't bother to ask…she won't tell me anyway. She seems always on edge, and we all feel the tremors building toward a cataclysm. Our new home in Glendora is a darkening sky. A showdown is coming.

The fuse of rebellion sizzles and sputters for four long years, until I can't take it any longer. The time comes to make a decision, and I believe I am doing myself, and probably Lucinda too, a big favor. I have to target my anger somewhere, and Lucinda is the bull's eye.

Tomorrow, June 3, 1966, three days after my sixteenth birthday, I shall emancipate myself. And unlike most runaways, I know I will never go back. Having made my decision, the thing I now dread most is telling Luke what I must do.

"But, I want to go with you!"

"I can't take care of you by myself, Luke."

"You don't have to take care of me. I can take care of myself."

"No. You have to stay with Lucinda. It'll be bad enough for her with me leaving. I won't go far. I'll still see you often."

"But I don't want you to go."

"I know—but I just can't stay here anymore. I have to get out on my own. In a couple more years you can fly away too, if you want to."

This goes on for hours. He cries. I cry. In the morning as I prepare to leave, he refuses to look at me. He lays on his bed, his back to me, and stares at the wall.

I have a gift for him, a little book about small airplanes and flying, which I lay on the bed. He ignores it. Finally, I say good-bye.

"I hate you," he hisses as I close the door.

The worst of this new life is the sting of missing Luke and the shame I put on myself for running out on him. Luke suffers from the separation as much as I do. We are linked sprites pulled apart by a cruel mystery, and it is no longer the same between us. With me gone, Luke catches the brunt of Lucinda's reaction. He tells me she has become paranoid and fearful that he will leave, too. I talk to him often, that is, whenever the enemy doesn't answer the phone.

It's not easy living on my own, but I quickly gain experience. It's amazing what a person can do in order to survive. Mac's heroic death had nearly killed me, and leaving Ruby Place was hard, but the worst thing I struggle with is my anger and resentment toward Lucinda.

"You can't see the Sergeant and Miss Cherry anymore." It was the way she had said it, almost like an afterthought, and so cold and

heartless. It poisoned my heart toward her. She became jealous of them, after all. Lucinda, my own flesh and blood mother, viciously turned against me. No consultation. No questions allowed. Period! She is a traitor!

I have no clear memory of the actual physical move from Ruby Place. I just remember swallowing my rage.

The Huntington Car Wash in Monrovia provides everything I need to survive: a job. I figure it will take me six weeks at the car wash to scrape up enough money to put a roof over my head, which I am going to need soon. It has been threatening rain for several days, and the guys at the car wash have been grumbling. In the car washing business, rain means no work. While my coworkers complain, I fight off images of flash floods and storm drain doors. I am living on the streets with little in the way of possessions, but my mind is rich with memories both good and bad. I get lonely but never bored.

After a full day of work, I gather up as much cardboard as I can find. Under an overhanging bush against a cinder block wall which backs up to the railroad tracks, I stash my precious few belongings and make my nest. The rain comes and so do the trains every couple of hours.

Eventually the cardboard soaks through and sags down all around me. Wet, cold, miserable, and very lonely, I think about quitting and going home. I miss Luke terribly. I imagine I hear the Sergeant whispering, "*Never look back, Wade.*" I remove the plastic I use to protect Rodney's Bible from the elements and open the book to a random page. It's too dark to read, but I place my palm on the open pages and close my eyes.

I am dozing fitfully about an hour before daybreak when something grabs the front of my jacket and jerks me to my feet. A hulking ghostly form towers over me, its foul breath of cheap wine and rotting teeth stinging my nostrils. Gnarled paws close around my neck and I can't breathe. I am terrified that the dead man of Three Ponds has returned to carry out his revenge. I am sure a third eye of wicked silver is staring with sinister clarity deep into my psyche.

A voice, barely human, hisses like a serpent in my ear. "Got any money-y-y, boy-y-y?"

In a reflex of its own, the Louisville Slugger comes up from my side, over, and down with such savage power that it must have stored the awesome energy of the Duke's last swing. The serpent goes down hard and slumps with a horrible hiss against the wall, a murky dark ooze tracing down its neck.

My compressed larynx spasms and then relaxes enough to allow me to gasp in some air. "No!"

I kick the slumping torso as hard as I can, slipping in the process and falling down next to it. I scream again and then realize another train is screaming by at sixty miles per hour a few short yards away.

I run, bat in hand, as fast as my trembling legs will take me. I make it maybe ten blocks, and my throat swells up, nearly cutting off my breathing completely. Wheezing terribly, I stop and try to gather my wits. I survived, though I had to leave my few possessions behind, including some food—and Rodney's Bible. I am thankful for the miracle of Duke's gift, without which the serpent would have surely eaten me.

Three hours later I am in the car wash owner's office begging for as many hours as possible. I desperately need to earn enough money so I can afford to sleep behind the safety of a locked door. Six weeks is a long, long time.

I have been on my own eight months now. Suffering from loneliness and obsessed with memories of a better time, I make a long-contemplated decision. I will try to find the Sergeant and Miss Cherry.

On a rainy day when car wash labor isn't needed, I thumb my way west on Colorado Boulevard from Monrovia through Pasadena over Suicide Bridge and down past Eagle Rock to Highland Park. The journey takes most of the day, but the last ride drops me off right in front of the Highland Park police station. I am a nervous wreck, very tired, and too scared to immediately enter. I hang around outside for over an hour, hoping one of them might come out. Finally, I go in and plant myself at the front counter.

A burly desk officer approaches. "What can I do for you, kid?"

"I was wondering if it would be possible to see Sergeant Cavendish, or, Officer, uh, I'm not sure about her last name, but her first name is Cherry, uh, please, sir." I am sweating under my shirt and feeling sick to my stomach.

He gives me a long, careful look. "Webster."

"Pardon?"

"Webster. Cherry's last name was Webster. Cavendish and Webster." He scratches his forehead. "What do you want with those two?"

"Nothing. They're old friends of mine. I would like to see them please."

"I'm afraid you're a few years too late, kid."

"What do you mean?"

"They don't work for the department anymore."

My heart sinks. "Why not?"

"Well, now. That's really none of your business, kid. Anything else I can help you with?"

"Do you know where they live?"

"Couldn't tell you if I did. Department policy."

I must look pitiful as I start to turn away, because he leans forward across the counter, glances around, and then whispers to me. "You best forget about those two. They both got into some trouble a while back. Big secret investigation. Caused a whole lotta grief for the big brass. You seem like a good kid. It's best you don't have anything to do with those two."

I am in tears before I get outside. I don't want to believe him. They're O.C.I.U. undercover cops. He's just making up a story because he can't tell me the truth about them.

Up the block from the police station is a phone booth. I dial Luke. I need to hear his voice.

"Hey, you big dumb donkey!"

I feel so much better. "How are you?"

"Okay."

"How is she?"

"The same. What's going on with you, Wade? Still looking for ghosts?"

"Not funny, Luke."

"Where are you?"

"Actually, I'm over in Highland Park."

"No kidding? You really are looking for ghosts."

"I went by the police station and tried to see them."

"And?"

"I was told they haven't worked there in years."

"Sorry. Are you going to let go of it now?"

"No."

"Thought so."

"Do you think she'll let you go with me to a Dodgers game when the season starts?"

"I don't ask for permission anymore. I just go. Let me know when you have tickets."

"Okay. You still mad at me for leaving?"

"Yes."

"Thought so. I love you, Luke."

"I love you, too, you big dumb donkey."

Near dark, I find myself walking up the hill at Ruby Place. Molly, her muzzle now a wintry gray, is barely able to walk. She no longer cares about barking at passersby. She looks at me with sad disinterest. It seems, other than Molly, not a soul who ever knew me still lives in the neighborhood.

I sit on the curb in front of our old house. The place needs paint, needs Carl to sing a song, needs Mac to snooze on the porch. No lights on yet. Looks like nobody is home. My misplaced childhood appears to be a thing of the distant past.

The sun is fading fast, and the idea of hitchhiking back to Monrovia in the dark seems less sane about now than sliding down the

Crippler in the dark. *Maybe I ought to leg it up to Billy Goat Hill and sleep out under the stars tonight, that is, if it doesn't start raining again.*

"Wade Parker?"

I turn around and see Carl's wife, Esther, standing on her front porch. Unlike Molly, she looks exactly the way I remember her. "Hello, ma'am."

She smiles and cranes her neck to get a better look at me. "My goodness, praise the Lord, it is you."

"Yes, ma'am."

Using a cane for balance now, she takes one careful step at a time down off the porch. "You're practically all grown up. Come over here and let me get a good look at you."

I walk over to the fence. "It's nice to see you, ma'am."

"My heavens, you're so tall and thin. Are you eating enough? You're a bit too skinny, you think?"

"Yes, ma'am. I live on my own now, but I get enough to eat."

"On your own? Well, honey, you can't be more than sixteen. You're not living with your mom anymore?"

"No ma'am…not for a while now. I'll be seventeen pretty soon. I do okay for myself."

"Well, I'm sure you do. I always thought you were a resourceful little boy. You were always making things work somehow, weren't you?"

"I guess."

"It sure is nice to see you. It's a blessing from the Lord to know you are doing well. It was such an awful thing that happened that night. I still pray for you and your family."

"Thank you, ma'am."

"Of course, honey. How is your brother doing?"

"He's fine. I talk to him fairly often, just today, actually. He's become interested in flying airplanes, and he thinks he might want to get his private pilot's license some day."

"Imagine that. Flying of all things. Didn't he used to be afraid of birds?"

How did she know that? "Yes, he had some hang-ups about

mockingbirds for a while. That was my fault, really. Kind of funny though, isn't it?"

I manage a small smile and she laughs. "Our heavenly Father does have a sense of irony and humor. In my eighty-odd years of loving the Lord I've been fascinated to observe how God's wisdom works in the lives of people."

"I guess so. How is Carl, ma'am?"

Her smile softens. "My Carl passed away in January of '64. He was never the same after President Kennedy was killed. He loved the president very much, and all the speculation about the Russians being behind the assassination took quite a toll on him. Goodness, if he were here now he'd be quick to correct me. I mean the Soviets, not the Russians."

"I'm sorry he passed away, ma'am." *I can't believe how I used to wise off to Carl about the Russian stuff.*

"No need to be sorry. The good news is my Carl had quit drinking for over a year before he died. He had been going to church with me every Sunday, and he accepted Jesus as his personal Savior. Carl was born again in the Lord. I believe we'll be together again in heaven, which gives me tremendous comfort."

Born again? "Well, it was good to see you again, ma'am. I better get going though. I've got a long walk ahead of me."

"Are you sure? Tell you what, how would you like to have supper with me? I don't get much company, and it would be a real treat for me to serve you a nice meal."

"Well, uh…"

"Unless you have a date lined up with a pretty young girl, this old girl would love to have supper with you. I already have a nice little pot roast in the oven, and there is plenty for two."

My mouth is instantly watering. "Well, um…"

"No *uhs* or *ums* about it. Come on around the fence here."

How can I say no to this sweet old lady? "I guess supper would be fine, if you're sure you don't mind."

"Good then—it's settled. I might even have a big slice of blueberry pie for you, too."

Blueberry…my favorite. "Maybe you have a little work I could do, or something that needs fixing. I'm pretty good at fixing things."

"Don't be silly; you're my guest, not a hired hand. So what brings you back to the old neighborhood? It's so nice to see you, honey. I think about you and Luke all the time."

Esther is making me feel better than I have in a long time. "I was looking for some old friends, but I didn't have any luck finding them."

"Oh, well, maybe you should pray about that. You just never know, the Lord might help you find them. I know He would sure like to hear from you."

He'd like to hear from me? Right. "Couldn't hurt, I guess."

"Have you heard what they're doing to Billy Goat Hill?" She opens the gate and pulls me through.

"No, ma'am—what?"

"Well, you wouldn't believe it. They've started building houses up there. Not much cardboard sliding going on anymore. Most kids have these skateboard contraptions now. They zoom by the front fence all the time. It looks like a lot of fun riding on those skateboards, and a lot of skinned knees too, I think.

"Well, come on in now. You know, not too long ago I sold Carl's old '55 Chevy Bel Air. Do you remember that noisy thing? What an old clunker that thing was. Carl was never much for vehicle maintenance, but the young man who purchased it was quite excited about it. Three hundred dollars' worth of excitement, to be exact.

"Goodness me, Carl used to start that awful sounding motor up every night when he headed for the bakery, and it used to worry me that the racket would wake up the neighbors. Were you kids ever bothered by that noise?"

"Not really…"

"That's good."

She loops her arm through mine and moves us toward the house. This is the first time I've ever been in her yard, much less in her house. I am curious to see the inside.

"Let me get the door for you, ma'am."

"Thank you. I had a little stroke last year, but praise God, I bounced back just fine. My new friend Mister Cane here keeps me steady, but he does get in the way sometimes. Say, guess who I saw at Kory's Market a few weeks ago, and he asked about you boys?"

"Who?"

"Jake—you know, from the barbershop."

"Really? Jake asked about us?"

"He most surely did. Say, I bet you'd like to see Carl's old antique rifle. And by the way, do you still have the bat that meant so much to you?" She giggles. "I guess you can tell I knew a thing or two about you boys."

"Yes, ma'am, I can tell."

Esther's pot roast was meant to be in my stomach. I've never felt so completely satisfied in my entire life. A home baked piece of heaven describes the blueberry pie. Sitting at her kitchen table watching her clean up the dishes, I am overcome by a feeling of appreciation and thanks. It has been forever since I experienced this kind of caring and attention. It would be great to feel like this all the time, to belong, to matter to someone.

Esther's kindness rekindles some hope in me. I came here to find the Sergeant and Miss Cherry, and instead, I find a friend who I am beginning to think maybe I always had but didn't know it.

Esther dries her hands and drapes the dish towel over the faucet. She pauses for a moment, scratching her wrinkled chin, and then looks at me with eyes so sparkling and warm I can feel the love in her heart.

"Do you mind if I ask you something, Esther?"

"I always enjoy a good conversation."

"We got to talking about other things, but earlier you said Carl was…born again?"

"Yes?"

"What exactly does that mean?"

"That is a wonderful question." She removes her apron and sits

at the table with me. "Well, first I should tell you I have been reading the Bible since I was twelve years old, and I'm still learning
about how much God loves the world."

"I've only read bits and pieces of the Bible. A friend of mine
died a long time ago. I had his Bible. But I lost it one night when I
got…uh, I accidentally left it behind."

"I remember you told me you had your friend's Bible. I think
you said his name was Rodney."

Amazing. "Yes, ma'am, Rodney. I forgot I told you about him."

"That's a shame about the lost Bible. But all is not lost that's
misplaced, you know. Let's hope it came into the hands of someone
who needed to know the Lord. Well, my goodness, things do happen, don't they?"

"Yes, ma'am, they sure do."

"I have not had an easy life, and I don't mean the challenge of
being married to Carl, but I have had a wonderful and wonder-
filled life. For all the troubles I've ever faced, I've always found
answers and instruction in the Bible. I pray you will be inspired to
read more of it."

"So, what about being born again? What does it mean?"

"The term *born again* comes from the Bible. Jesus said, 'No
one can enter the Kingdom of God without being born of water
and the Spirit.' You see, Wade, by His boundless mercy, God offers
everyone the privilege of being born again…by accepting that we
are His offspring, His children, and He is our true Father in
heaven."

"Oh. Where could I find that in the Bible?"

"I recommend you read the book of John, first."

"Okay."

"You'll learn that God loved the world so much that He sent
His only Son, Jesus, to die and be raised again to bring salvation to
the world—and that means Jesus died for each and every one of
us."

"Even me?"

"Yep. Simply put, the Bible says when a person makes the decision to accept Jesus as his personal Lord and Savior, then the Spirit of Jesus begins to live in him. At that very moment, the person is born again into the Kingdom of God."

"Wow, and then what?"

"That's another very good question. Accepting Jesus is the beginning of experiencing true peace and happiness right here in this life on earth. I see life as a sort of quest, and quests are a form of a test and often involve surprise and mystery." She grins. "It has been my experience that God seems to enjoy testing me, and He has definitely thrown a lot of surprise and mystery my way.

"Having you here in my kitchen is certainly a surprise and not without some mystery, wouldn't you say?" She grins again.

"So you think God brought me here today?"

"I know He did."

"Huh, that's kind of cool."

"That is very cool…if old ladies are allowed to say *cool*. One more thing about your born again question."

"Yes?"

"Let me get something for you, just a second." She gets up and shuffles into the adjoining pantry. She returns with a piece of paper. "Here, you keep this. It's 'The Sinner's Prayer.'"

"Lord Jesus Christ, I come to You now, because I am a sinner.…" Hmm…maybe I'll read the rest later. "Thank you, ma'am."

"You're welcome. You keep that paper, and I'll pray for the day when you truly feel it in your heart to pray the prayer out loud for God's ears to hear. When you do, I promise He will hear you."

I feel a warm tingling inside my chest. "Okay."

She smiles with great satisfaction. "Would you like to stay here tonight, Wade? I always keep the spare room ready for company, just in case. I don't have any family of my own, but once in a while I get to host a church visitor. How do a hot bath, a good night's rest, and a wholesome breakfast in the morning sound to you?"

How could I possibly say no? It would break her heart. "Yes, ma'am, I would appreciate that."

"Praise God. You know, I think you could fit into some of

Carl's old things. I've been slowly giving away his clothing, but I still have a trunk full of clean socks, undershirts, and such. You're welcome to anything you want."

"Thank you."

She yawns and looks at the clock above the sink. "My goodness, is it ten o'clock already? I'll have to call it an evening. Your room is to the left there, and the bathroom is at the end of the hall, complete with towels and such. You just make yourself at home, and I'll see you in the morning. Sleep in if you'd like. I'll be here whenever you get up, and we'll have a nice breakfast together. Okay?"

"Sounds good. Thank you."

Esther hugs me and says good night.

I sit at the kitchen table and try to absorb the contents of the day. Rain. No work at the car wash. Hitchhiking all day. Eight different rides. No Sergeant. No Miss Cherry. An eighty-year-old angel named Esther. Blueberry pie. Carl's socks and underwear.

Who would believe? Is the unknown unfolding with certain randomness…or…is all of this part of God's plan for me?

A light washes in through Esther's kitchen window, and I look out to see a car has pulled into our old driveway next door. A man and a woman get out of the car and open the rear doors on either side of the vehicle. They both lean in to the backseat, each coming up with a sleeping child. I watch with fascination as they carry the kids into the house. *Do they have a dog?*

From the comfort of Esther's kitchen, I am able to view the scene with a degree of detachment and objectivity. I see a good house. But a house is not a home. I hope my former house is a better home for them. *Perhaps a little prayer couldn't hurt.*

I enjoy the luxury of nightmare-free sleep until the bacon smell surrounds the bed. For a fleeting moment I think the dead man has managed to set me on fire. *Geez.* I get up and slip on Carl's old robe.

In the hallway the bacon smells wonderful.

"Good morning, Wade."

"Morning, ma'am."

"How did you sleep?"

"Very well, thank you."

"Have a seat. How do you like your eggs?"

"Over easy, please."

"Coming right up."

Out Esther's kitchen window I see a border collie. *They do have a dog. Good.* "How do you like your neighbors, ma'am?"

"A very nice young couple, Bert and Marilyn, with two kids, Jared and Melody. Bert works for the gas company, and Marilyn is a full-time mommy. They go to my church."

"Really?"

"The dog never barks. They call him Barney. I don't suppose you drink coffee, do you?"

"Yes, I do. Black, please."

I notice a Bible and an envelope with my name written on it sitting on the table. "What's this?"

"Open it."

She sets down a steaming cup of coffee, and I think of Rodney Bernanos. The envelope contains what appears to be a lot of money. I look at her. "What's this for?"

"It's the money I got from selling Carl's Chevy. I know that old car must have bothered you pretty near every night all those years. You take that money and keep it for an emergency, a little nest egg."

"Three hundred dollars? I couldn't…"

"You can't say no to me, young man. But I am willing to make a little deal with you, if you like."

"What kind of deal?"

"Well, the way I figure it, it's a shame that we didn't get to know each other better while we were neighbors all those years. I would like you to take my phone number so you can stay in touch. Check up on this old lady now and then, maybe come by and see me when you have a chance. I bet we can make up for lost time."

Make up for lost time? Is it possible to make up for that much lost time? "You don't have to give me money to do that. It would be great to stay in touch with you."

"Well then, you'll just have to accept the money as a gift from God. But far more important than the money is the Bible there I'd like you to have. That's the copy Carl studied for the year or so before he died. You'll find some of his notations written in the margins. I hope you'll do some reading and find the same joy and comfort in it that Carl found."

"Thank you very much, ma'am."

"After breakfast, there is one small favor you could do for me before you go, if you don't mind."

"Sure—anything."

"Carl used to think he was getting away with something hiding cases of beer behind the old fig tree in the backyard."

I laugh. "Luke and I were aware of that."

"I'm not surprised. Alcoholism carries with it a lot of shame, you know. Drinkers often try to fool themselves into believing they can hide the problem. Anyway, these old wobbly legs, even with my cane, can't get me around in the backyard anymore. I used to love to tend to my flowers and such, but I've had to let it all go to seed. The weeds always win in the end, don't they?

"Anyway, there are two cases of beer still stowed under the fig tree, and I worry that some rambunctious neighborhood kid will eventually find it." She hands me a bottle opener. "Would you go out there and pour all the beer onto the ground and bring the empty bottles up to the back porch?"

"Sure."

"Thanks, honey."

The tree is badly overgrown and the weeds so high and thick, I don't think anyone would ever have found Carl's hidden beer. I have to push my way in under low-hanging branches and brush away years' worth of dead leaves to find the beer. The wood crates are rotted, and the labels have long ago peeled loose from the bottles, but sure enough each bottle is full of amber liquid.

As I pop the bottle caps and start pouring, the chamber created by the surrounding branches fills with the aroma of stale beer. At first the smell is mildly offensive, but soon I find myself enjoying the unique scent. Too much so, as halfway through the dumping project I become tempted to taste the beer.

Then I hear the muffled laughter of children coming from the other side of the fence, from my old backyard, and the temptation is replaced by a strange feeling of shame.

I pop the last bottle cap and pour, and as I do, a sudden flutter and flapping of wings is in the branches above my head. I reach back for a slingshot that is not there as feathers float down at my feet, like fake snow in a Sears Christmas window display.

Walking down the hill of Ruby Place with the Bible under my arm bookmarked at John 3:16 by Esther, her phone number and three hundred dollars in my wallet, I decide to loop back around the block and have a nostalgic look at Billy Goat Hill. The path up the hill, worn smooth by generations of youthful bare feet, is still there, but looking up toward the top of the hill, I see clear indications of construction activity. I stand there at the trailhead halted by doubt. Do I want to satisfy my curiosity and snoop around the construction site? Or do I want to keep the memories of my childhood playground unspoiled? I decide a climb up the hill will only yield sad feelings and regret. *Never look back, Wade.*

Instead, I turn around and head for Monrovia. It looks like a good day for washing cars. I stick my thumb out and start north up Figueroa Street toward Eagle Rock. In no time, I catch a ride that takes me all the way to the Huntington Car Wash. The driver says he is the pastor of a church in Arcadia and doesn't mind going the extra two miles to drop me off at my destination. I think he is impressed by the Bible under my arm.

During the ride I keep thinking about how good the stale beer smelled. *One ride, forty minutes…yesterday it took all day. I've got to get myself a car…and maybe a cold beer.*

Three nights later, the angry young man in me, the one who was angry enough to leave his only brother behind, decides to accept the first beer he is offered. It tastes nothing like the stale aroma I inhaled under Esther's fig tree. It is good and smooth and friendly. Three bottles is all it takes for me to sing patriotic songs and warn about the evils of communism. I feel like a jerk when I think of Esther, but my new friend pushes her away with promises of everything I've ever wanted. In fact, one more bottle of this delicious stuff, and I believe I'll be ready to shoot down a cosmonaut.

eleven

*J*ohn Fogerty's lament floats around the moonlit room evoking my soul, beseeching me like a sportive wraith beckoning from the shadows. Creedence Clearwater Revival mixed with a quart or so of Red Mountain wine, stirred lightly—my recipe for passage into the zone of subconsciousness wherein I've been tarrying more and more of late. Rock music and alcohol—in them, their worldly combination, I find a sad but effective form of sympathy. Artificial sympathy, yes, but better than no sympathy at all for a needy twenty-two-year-old man.

In the dimness, my transistor radio still looks new. So many years have fallen by the wayside, yet every time I look at the radio I think of the Sergeant and Miss Cherry. His claim that the Japanese had achieved an acceptable level of quality was correct after all. But thinking about it only makes me feel sorry for myself. Often, I wonder where they are and hope time is treating them well.

The wine buzzing just right puts a silly sardonic smile on my face, and I reckon the radio signal is so clear because I rarely used the FM function. Now FM radio is the rage. They call it Underground Radio, a term which seems to speak directly to me. The MADE IN JAPAN sticker is long gone, but I haven't progressed at all.

That's not exactly true. I have been blessed to meet a wonderful woman, fall in love, and get married. Her name is Melissa, and she is half Japanese, half Caucasian, which sheds forever one of Earl's lousy legacies. Love washed away the imprint of bigotry. What would Earl say about that? Esther always talked about God's sense of humor.

My wonderful wife notwithstanding, I have been on a long downhill slide. It began when Esther died. Losing her was a terrible blow that brought back the pain and loss I experienced when Rodney passed away.

Esther never gave up on me, always glad to hear from me, always giving me encouragement, always gently attempting to talk with me about the Bible and God's grace. Once after a spirited discussion about forgiveness, I came very close to telling her all about the dead man of Three Ponds. In the end, I just couldn't bring myself to do it. Instead, I finished off the night getting drunk in a Pasadena bar and sleeping it off in my car behind a Shell gas station.

The last time I saw Esther, I had stopped by her house to show her my new used wheels, an ivory 1966 Mustang. She was very impressed, and she surprised me when she asked me to take her for a ride. "Let's go to the beach!"

We drove down to Malibu and strolled barefoot in the surf. She was a spindly tidal crab hobbling along with her cane scraping the sand. I don't think she had ever walked on the beach before, and it was such a joy seeing this sweet old lady with a childlike sparkle in her eyes. We even saw a couple of movie stars, an aging one whom she recognized, and a young one whom I had recently seen on the big screen.

We talked a lot about suffering that day, how some of us experience so much of it in this life, and the unfairness of it all. Matthew and Mac came up at one point, and I tried to steer the conversation in a happier direction. But she worked hard to get me to grasp the notion that people who suffer more than their fair share of pain and heartache can receive a great blessing, the realization that more important than our need for answers is our need for God Himself. She told me the story of Job from the Bible.

At one point, she picked up a surf-worn shell and held it up to the sun. She looked at the shell with a kind of wonderment mixed with knowing recognition, as if it contained some powerful message that God had planned to wash up on the shore at the precise moment of our passing. "You know," she said. "Most of the time we are blinded by our own wants and desires, and we can't see beyond our immediate suffering or troubles. But God has a plan for each and every one of us. And if we believe in Him and trust Him, and if we can manage to be patient and wait for His perfect timing, He allows us to appreciate and understand the fullness of His plan for us."

That's the thing about Esther that will stay with me as long as I live. She suffered, she trusted, she believed, like Job. We had a good time at Malibu, cherished moments that I keep folded and tucked close to my heart. I wish I had visited Esther more, listened to her more, trusted her more. Maybe, just maybe, I wouldn't be on the slippery slope that I am on now.

My wife loves to use my arm as a pillow. Not wanting to wake her, I resist moving as long as I can; slowly my hand goes numb, like my mind on the wine, and it is time to turn over.

"Ouch!" My shoulder-length blond locks are always getting caught in the wickerwork headboard.

"Huh?"

"Nothing. Go back to sleep, babe."

Melissa turns over, mumbles femininely, and snuggles closer. Ten thousand pins slowly leave my arm in search of another cushion.

Moonlight sifts in through the window bathing our bed in a soft lambent glow, tantalizing and energizing the natural violet highlights in Melissa's herbal-scented raven hair. The strands shimmer iridescently against the whiteness of her pillow, beguiling me, deluding me in the most pleasing sense. It was her long beautiful hair that sparked my initial attraction to her, though her physical beauty cannot be broken down into individual attributes. When combined with her transcendent personality, she is the sum total of any man's notion of a beautiful woman.

The sheer curtains in the bedroom had not been my choice. Melissa insisted that she be in full charge of decorating the bedroom, and I soon found out why. Melissa's passions escalate in the moonlight. She says the moon is a romantic and mysterious orb. She has a way with words—colorful, precise, and direct. Full moons at our house are welcomed, indeed. Now I love the curtains.

Enchanted by her warmth, her scent, the soothing rhythm of her breathing, often I lie awake at night and watch her sleep. With tender fascination, I observe the beat of her gentle, loving heart, pulsing quivers that ebb in the delicate dip between her collarbones.

I have been crazy about Melissa since the day we first met. She thought I was crazy, but I sensed in her an interest that she wished to explore. Before Melissa came along, I had become a shameful purloiner of female affection. I was love starved and love shy at the same time, which I'm sure had everything to do with Lucinda's treason, the trauma of suddenly losing contact with Miss Cherry, and the loss of my dear friend Esther—the only three women I had ever been close to. Consequently, my romantic relationships had been episodic and compulsive, and in hindsight—unhealthy.

Melissa suspected much about my prior escapades, which made it tough for me in the beginning. But as time went by, she began to see through the case-hardened exterior that I lugged around like a full suit of armor.

One night early in our courtship, she discovered a small chink in my breastplate. We were sitting in a pizza parlor, both feeling uneasy, self-conscious, not chewing our pizza the way pizza was meant to be chewed. Conversation had been strained, a little too forced, superficial at best. We tentatively probed for themes of common ground. She flirted with her eyes and I with my voice as we plowed over some of the same ground covered during our previous date.

I was beginning to slip into self-defeating doubt that she would ever decide she liked me, and then she asked what would turn out to be the perfect question—the needed nudge to start the wheel of conversation turning. "What's your favorite movie?"

New ground. "You mean my favorite of all time?"

"No, only those made between 1960 and 1965. Of course, I mean of all time."

Her smile is a carbon copy of how I remembered Miss Cherry's smile. I have been noticing how much she reminds me of Miss Cherry. Except for her hair color and skin tone, they could easily pass for mother and daughter.

"No question about it, my favorite movie of all time is *The Wizard of Oz.*"

Her eyes shimmered with approval. "You're kidding?"

"Your favorite, too?"

She nodded and smiled a little more invitingly than before. "I adore *The Wizard of Oz.*" My radar blipped in reaction to an alluring shift of her posture as she leaned across the table toward me.

It turned out we were an incredible match on *Oz* trivia. Neither could stump the other as we dazzled back and forth, trading our knowledge of obscure details. We even agreed on the most controversial aspect of the movie. The shift from black and white to color was a stroke of genius.

Inhibitions dissolved, we bartered over who should eat the last slice of pizza. "You win," she said, after I negotiated successfully for a pepperoni-flavored kiss.

Matched halves of a wondrous geode we have become, and lying here sharing Melissa's moonlight, I am filled to repletion, aching memories distanced, supplanted by the calming intensity of her.

Melissa sleeps, as I learned she always will, after we make love. Now, watching her slumber, her skin rippling in hues of gray with the breezy shifts of the curtain, I think only of the good things from my past. I smile at the ceiling. This is my paradise, her sleeping, me watching her sleep and feeling wonderful.

Melissa guessed correctly—I identify with the Tin Man. I am the Tin Man. Jack Haley does a perfect rendition of me. With a heart like Dorothy's, bigger than Kansas, Melissa takes me into hers and shows me that she has more than enough heart for both of us. I marvel over how she so skillfully presses me to reveal my feelings. While she busied herself with that last slice of pizza, I gobbled up the attention as any fool would—though I feared that I had made a real fool of myself.

She loves the Tin Man, of course she does. She is the embodiment of Dorothy, and her Dorothy-like sweetness and empathy utterly overwhelm me. No woman has ever opened me up in this way…and soon she has me in tears. The Tin Man character is a metaphor of my life. Like the Tin Man, I am so emotionally rusted I cannot move. Then Melissa comes along with the oilcan.

She shifts in her sleep and gradually awakens. "Can't sleep?"

I nod.

"Want to tell me the story again?"

I gaze appreciatively into her eyes, and I begin at the beginning, knowing she will listen with such faith that when I am done, I'll once again see a beautiful sky in the middle of the storm.

Again, I tell her everything.

Again, she understands…everything.

Matthew…

Earl…

Lucinda…

The murder…

The Sergeant…

Miss Cherry…

All of my misgivings, failings, guilt…all of it vents like molten lava, spewing from deep within my tormented core, flowing into my sea of ruin, churning and boiling an ocean of pain into steam.

She holds me tight and takes it all off of my shoulders with eyes so comforting—windows of wisdom, pools of compassion, two-way mirrors that both absorb and reflect my deepest feelings. Her loving spirit envelops me, and I truly feel as though she were with me through all the bad years, sharing my losses, my pain, and my need.

The only time she ever cries—and even so she does it with great strength—is when I completely break down and tell her, again, how Mac died.

She drifts back to sleep under a blanket of moonlight, and her breathing plays upon my ears like a lullaby. She is beautiful, smart, incredibly honest, sensitive, and kind. But in my long-entrenched mode of self-punishment, I struggle not to think of her loving me as an undeserved gift. I lie here next to her, counting my blessings, thankful for having her, but I cannot pretend that everything is okay.

I know full well that Melissa's loving me does not mean I am healed. Even with Melissa and everything she represents as good in my life, I still find myself coveting the childhood I lost. As cancer is to tissue, so unshriven sin is to the soul, and not even the love of a great woman can absolve me of my sin.

The radio sits next to me on the nightstand. I remember how I kept it on my pillow that April Fools' night after Luke and I celebrated our good fortune—the Dodgers tickets. I treasure the radio most of the time as a symbol of the precious memories, the minority memories that are forever seeking to be heard over the clamor of guilt, resentment, and regret. But the radio is also capable of conjuring up painful images from the past, and I have come close to smashing it to bits more than once. An inanimate object made in Japan, well made in Japan the Sergeant had argued, whose mere existence is at times an act of complicity in the perpetual haunting of Wade Parker.

A far more dependable friend is leaning in the corner of the room, a friend as faithful as Mac and always within arm's reach— the bat Duke Snider gave to me. I can just make it out in the shadows. I smile as the images of that magnificent day at Dodger Stadium rewind and replay in my mind. The bat is a symbol, too. It stands for truth and virtue. It is my private treasure, my personal proof that some dreams can come true. What would Duke Snider say if he knew the bat had been used for more than just hitting baseballs? I smile at the ceiling again.

I wonder about Miss Cherry and the Sergeant. I have never let go of them, and they rise up now as I toy with the little silver ball bearing. Not long ago, I drilled a hole through the ball bearing and turned it into a piece of jewelry. I wear it around my neck on a leather thong. Melissa likes the way it dances on her skin when I hover over her in the dark.

She knows all about the ball bearing and isn't afraid of it at all. "Superstition is born of ignorance," she likes to say. "Someday, when you're ready, you will get rid of that thing."

I take another swig of Red Mountain and glance over at the bat. I get a sudden rush of sorrow—Duke Snider hasn't made it to the Hall of Fame. I wanted him to be elected in his first year of eligibility. *You'll get in Duke, one of these years…when those idiot sportswriters are ready to acknowledge your greatness. If they only knew what you did for me.*

Another big gulp of wine pushes me beyond the special zone. My pattern of self-punishment has become pathetically formulaic, and my drinking is steadily getting worse. *Why am I so powerless to do anything about it?*

Luke is worried about me. "Don't let the booze get you like it got Earl, Wade." If I've heard him say it once, I've heard him say it a thousand times.

"Don't worry, I'm nothing like Earl, or Lucinda," I tell him, but he sees right through me.

"You drink like Earl, and you refuse to talk about it like Lucinda. How much more like them can you get?"

He has no idea how deeply that truth hurts. "I love you too, Luke."

Watching Melissa sleep, I know it's not for the lack of a good woman that I cannot heal my pillaged spirit—that much had been established way back when Miss Cherry was involved in my life. Yet if there is no cure for me, at least watching Melissa sleep is a temporary remedy. It treats my symptoms.

She turns again, fussing like a snoozing feline trying to get comfortable lying on her stomach. The way she shifts around in her sleep makes me chuckle.

Slowly she opens her eyes. "Still can't sleep?"

I smile and nod. "I love you."

"I love you, too."

For the first time since the tragedy of Three Ponds, I have someone I trust, someone who loves me despite knowing about my unspeakable secret. While men are walking on the moon, I thank God for my one special blessing. I think I can go on…as long as I don't lose Melissa.

Sometimes certain things you hear stick in your mind and won't go away, ever—even when you're drunk. There was a guy I knew, a drinking acquaintance, who while sitting at the bar one night turned to me and said, "Alcohol is a strange poison. Short of causing you to run your car into an abutment or a tree, it kills you slowly, while being your very best friend."

Later that night, he flipped his car into a ditch and broke his neck. He left behind a loving wife and five wonderful kids. It sticks in my mind, what he said—I, too, have become a husband, and now a father. Melissa and I have a beautiful baby daughter, Kate. But—I keep drinking.

The truth is, alcohol has become a ubiquitous force in my life. In a vicious partnership with the nightmares that never went away, it has seized control of me, and my existence is gradually filtering down to the dregs of saloon culture, one step above but only a short stagger away from the gutter.

Carl, you were a better man than I. Earl, you're still in third, but I'm slipping fast.

Melissa continues to prove her love for me on a daily basis. She is a persistent soul, harmonizing with Luke to drive me up the wall with their constant urging that I get counseling.

"We don't want to lose you," they say.

"You both worry too much."

"I worry for Kate, honey. What if she lost her daddy? I know you don't want that to happen."

"What about me, Wade? You're the only brother I have."

A couple of guiltmongers. "I don't want counseling."

My argument is steadfast and logical. I don't believe in psychology. It's nothing but unscientific mumbo jumbo, a so-called profession teeming with charlatans more twisted than I. Any treatment of what ails me—whether by a shrink, a priest, a gypsy, or an extraterrestrial being—will require my confessing that I have committed the heinous crime of murder.

No. The atrocity at Three Ponds, as I have come to think of it, must remain my private sin. To me, it sounds like the title of a true crime novel—*The Atrocity at Three Ponds!* It sickens me to think that I could be the villain in one of those pitiful blood-and-gore tomes.

So here I am, pestered by my wife and brother, while destined to run with the boys in the bottle—Beam, Walker, Grand-Dad, Turkey, and Parker, the den of fools—until something, somebody, somehow, someday rips my wings off and puts me inside the bottle like the guilty insect I have become. No question about it…I am the offspring of Earl and Lucinda Parker. Earl—the drunk, and Lucinda—the stubborn mute. And now, ladies and gentlemen, I give you Wade—the drunk who refuses to talk about it.

As accurate as Melissa and Luke are, I try not to think about turning out just like Earl. In the comparison I find a brutal shiv of truth, a razor sharp burr that cuts away at my heart and unravels my poorly knitted pride.

On the outside I am, of course, the life of the party. Only Melissa—my sweet, beautiful, kind, loving Melissa—knows the depth of the guilt that holds the mortgage on my sanity and cruelly shuffles the index of my dreams. At times I feel even Duke Snider, along with the Sergeant and Miss Cherry, have abandoned me. I think of all of them often, especially at night as I prepare to battle against my dreams.

Sometimes I imagine them as my guardians, my protectors. I make them into powerful scarecrows and station them around my field of slumber. They are supposed to ward off the incessant, airborne carnivores that feed on my mind and rob me of much needed rest, much like Luke's mockingbirds of lore swarmed about his crimson crown. My rapacious oppressors are crowlike thieves, attracted to all things shiny—silverware, jewelry, buttons, and the omnipresent ball bearing, which now hangs around my neck on a sterling silver chain.

One of the worst nightmares involves a hideous, foul-smelling vulture whose head is that of the dead man of Three Ponds. The vulture circles me for hours, days, tormenting me from the sky, its shadow looping around me, around and around, hypnotizing me until finally I can no longer stay awake. Then, in a dream inside the dream, the huge vulture lands on my chest, its talons pinning me to the ground, and rips the tendons out of my neck as it attempts to steal the shiny ball bearing. I wake up from the dream inside a dream screaming through a ragged gash in my throat, while the dead man-vulture laughs at me. If only I could remove that symbol of my crime and cast it into the sea. *Would then I be free?*

Melissa has faith. "One day you'll be able to let go of the past. I know you will. I'll always love you, no matter what." She tells me that more often than Luke repeats his warnings.

The only thing "in the past" is the medicinal value of the alcohol. Now the booze acts as a turbocharger in my brain, a distilled catalyst inciting my nightmares to heightened levels of torture. Even during my waking hours I slip deeper and deeper into a semi-lucid, leper-like state of isolation. My internal psychologist, whom I despise, tells me I am teetering dangerously on the psychotic.

Luke continues to warn, Melissa continues to urge counseling, and eventually they do get to me with the Kate-losing-her-daddy argument. Why I have to lie in order to deal with it I don't know, but I end up concocting a story about having a close call with a telephone pole one blurry night. With my fingers crossed behind my back, I promise Melissa I won't drink and drive anymore. A self-serving ulterior motive lurks within the false promise. It means she will have to come to the bar with me, something I have long been hoping for. Except for a sip or two of wine at home, Melissa doesn't drink, which makes her an ideal chaperone for a fun-craving alcoholic.

She takes the bait. "They can call me an enabler if they want to, but I'm going to do everything I can to keep a telephone pole from taking my daughter's father away from her."

In actuality, our daughter, Kate, probably spends more time with Luke and his new bride, Trish, than she spends with us. They found out Luke was sterile after a year of trying, and Luke almost seemed relieved when he delivered the news. Always the philosopher, he laughed it off, proclaiming himself to be the last in the Parker line to suffer the curse of the mockingbirds. Uncle Luke adores Kate, and the free supply of baby-sitting gives Melissa complete freedom to baby-sit me. In the mirror I see something worse than a self-serving drunk; I see a shameless drunk. I see Earl.

It would break Esther's heart to know how much like Carl I've turned out to be, a happy drunk and usually harmless, except perhaps to myself. Putting aside the one infamous shooting-at-the-cosmonaut incident, Carl was a functional, punctual, reasonably responsible drinker. I, however, am known to occasionally end up in the sheriff substation drunk tank, especially when Melissa is not available to accompany me to the tavern. The only thing that saves me from being shipped out to the Los Angeles county jail downtown is a deputy sheriff by the name of Bob Serrano.

Bob is a recovering alcoholic, who, for reasons only he and God know, goes out of his way to watch out for me. Bob always manages to intercede and make sure I'm kept in a substation cell to sleep it off. County jail is no place for a nice guy from Highland Park like me, according to Bob. Some might argue Bob does more to enable me than Melissa does.

Booze is a strange poison, and its insidious, cumulative wear is taking a toll.

They say a drunk has to hit bottom before he can start to climb back up. I slammed on the bottom one night at a place called Buster's Bonanza Room, a classic neighborhood watering hole in San Dimas, California. It had not been a good day, beginning with a minor fender bender in the morning caused by another one of my "odd sightings."

Over the last several years and on as many as a dozen occasions, I believe I may have seen Miss Cherry. If it is her, and I no longer believe it is, she is usually just a blur of motion, a fleeting ghost skirting along the limits of my peripheral vision. Other times she is a vague but annoyingly familiar human form that I am convinced is purposefully watching me from a distance. I used to get excited and chase after the mirage, never to catch it. Everyone knows mirages always escape, and I no longer have the courage to tell Melissa when it happens.

Another odd sighting this morning distracted me enough to cause me to lose the rhythm of stop-and-go traffic. The guy I rear-ended was nice enough, and the mutual bumper scratches were not worth any lost time or paperwork hassles. He did ask if I had been drinking, and when I said, "Not in years," it was plain he didn't believe me.

It was the pity I saw in his eyes that triggered the ruin of my day. The man saw me the way I used to see Carl. I white-knuckled it till mid-afternoon, then needed two quick belts to quell the shaking before I called Melissa from the pay phone at Buster's. She showed up at five-thirty based on my telephonically sworn oath that we would play three games of pool, have dinner, and then go home.

I am finishing drink number six when Melissa shows up at Buster's. I'm just starting to feel normal. Three hours later, Buster himself is behind the bar swearing he will cut me off if Melissa goes home without me, which she has been threatening to do for the past hour. Buster's disapproving frown only amuses me.

With another refill in hand, I turn around and shout across the crowded bar to Melissa. "R-r-rack'm up, baby!"

I have to steady myself to keep from falling down. My inebriated gyroscope is bumping strangely, and for a moment there is a Babel of confusion when something pops inside my head followed by the sound of bad static. After a brief blackout moment, I manage to get my coordinates and tack my way back to the pool table.

"Come on, honey, maybe it's about time we head for home," Melissa urges for the umpteenth time.

"Soon, baby, soon."

"It's a full moon." Her eyes twinkle solicitously.

"Just one more game, beautiful."

She tries everything she can think of to gain my cooperation. But her best efforts are all in vain. I am too far over the edge, and on this night I cannot be charmed or reasoned with.

In the larger context, deep down I feel I am too far gone to be saved. Worse, I don't believe I deserve to be saved. Once in a while, I hear Rodney's voice or Esther's trying to break through. But I have fought all my life against the voices of dead people, and it's too hard to pick and choose the good voices over the bad.

The curse of man, the liquid destroyer, the poisonous genie of blended grain mash is out of the bottle and washing away all of the voices. I am into the voice repellent big time tonight, and nobody, not even sweet, loving, wonderful Melissa has the power to put the genie back in the bottle.

I brush Melissa off and draw back my cue, my eyes blinking to find some focus. I let the cue rip, nearly falling down in the process. The cue ball slams into the wedge just as Melissa removes the rack. I see Carl shooting at cosmonauts as a horde of billiard balls collide in a nuclear carom, the sound of the impact clanging off the walls and reverberating with the pounding beat of the jukebox. Melissa flinches and curses at me, her patience dwindling and then gone. She glares across the table, angry as a carnie working the midway caught in the line of fire by an impatient kid hungry for the big prize.

Nearly as jangling as the scattering of the billiard balls, my senses collide, throwing my already anesthetized perception into total disarray. Palpable tremors signal through my bones sending crabs of alarm scurrying around in my gut.

The room begins to move, like a merry-go-round starting up, and the jukebox wails an ominous warning as "Mama Told Me Not to Come" by Three Dog Night blares from the far end of the room. The eerie message thumps throughout the smoke-filled bar, a musical harbinger announcing the accession of an alcoholic's madness.

The room tilts sharply with a spine-jarring jolt that causes my legs to buckle and the billiard balls to topple off the table. Like oversize marbles, the balls clunk hard on the floor and disperse randomly around the barroom. Squinting through the smoke-laden air, I watch in disbelief as the balls, now far more than sixteen in number, begin to scrabble around and arrange themselves at my feet.

To me, the floor appears as a muddy flat. I recoil and gasp as the balls slowly shift into forms, shapes, characters—letters of the alphabet! First an *M*, then an *I*, then an *S*, until the word *Mississippi* holds statically, coagulated in a paste-like muddy gruel. Then, in a dizzying, anagrammatic, kaleidoscopic swirl, the balls reconfigure to form the word—*MURDERER*! Horrified, I stare at the floor as the accusation throbs in my face like a blinking neon sign.

I fall back and try to shake off the vision, but it won't go away. As suddenly as before, the balls rise up from the floor and hover miraculously in a precision V formation two feet above the pool table. Weaving back and forth, my wobbling legs barely holding me up, I rub my red-rimmed eyes and try desperately to blink away the apparition. But my eyes grow wide as the numbers and colors drip off of the billiard balls and splatter on the pool table like melting wax, leaving behind blinding-silver metallic eyes that taunt me with sporadic charges forward and back. My hallucination is as real as the panic sweating out of my cramping body. I hear Three Dog Night howling for my blood, and I begin to cry.

Then, in a sudden fit of terror-induced rage, I lunge forward and wildly swing my stick at the ghostly balls. They scatter about like plump rats evading an attacking broom. The cue stick shatters violently on the edge of the pool table, a large splinter rebounding up to the ceiling where it sticks like an arrow meeting its mark.

My darkening fate looms all around me as the silver balls take up a radial formation and begin circling like blood-sniffing sharks. They poise to strike, filling me with dread, pushing me down, down, deep inside my fear. I blubber out a cowardly whine and then scream out, cursing incoherently at the demons only I can see.

In the mirror behind the bar, I see a face white with panic and wet with the desperation of brain infesting fright. I wrench myself around and lunge toward the door, sure that the army of silver fiendish eyes will chase me to my death. I stumble through the crowded bar knocking aside people, chairs, and drink-laden tables in my path. I am frantic to make it to my car, to the trunk, to the only weapon that offers a defense against my helpless paranoia.

The music keeps at me, pounding from behind as I charge out the door. But the silver balls do not follow me into the night. Instead, I fear they have tricked me into my retreat only to take my precious Melissa prisoner. The warped manifestations of my hounding guilt have come to strip me of my only link with reality—my Melissa!

From out of the trunk comes the Excalibur, the magic sword of the Duke of Flatbush. In my muddled mind, I recall how it had been handed down, bequeathed from a Royal Duke to a simple peasant boy, a fatherless ghetto rube whose lonely destiny had been forged in the heartless shires of the City of Angels. Like the sacred sword, I have been heated white-hot and hammered true on the anvil-like hill of the sacrificial goat, and quenched in the second of three baptismal ponds, and blessed by the high priest of the Caverns of Cavendish.

I stand here shivering and cowering in the dark parking lot, my alcoholized blood oxidizing with each rapid gulp of night chilled air. Alone and scared, I begin to mutter fragments of the Paternoster as one of faith might do in preparation for death. Slowly I focus my intent. With all of my might, I grip the bat firmly in both hands and plead for an end to the madness.

A faint electric hum emanates from the bat. A tingling vibration enters my hands and climbs up my arms. Growing in intensity, the energy marches across my chest, swelling my muscles, then jolting me with a strange surge of rejuvenating power. Instantly, I am cleansed of all fear and now see clearly what my destiny requires of me. I was born to be Melissa's knight in shining armor.

An alcoholic's pathetic nirvana floods into my heart, and my psychosis takes me on a quantum leap propelling me past the present to the future and beyond. I clutch the wooden avenger firmly and feel my strength swell tenfold. Empowered with newfound courage, I prepare to answer the call. Excalibur hoisted high in the night sky, poised to sever the head of the dragon called guilt, I charge back into the smoke-filled abyss.

Booze gives breath to my slobbered battle cry. "I'll save you, fair Mi-s-s-sala!"

I, Sir Wade of Ruby Place, stumble forth in search of another drink, determined to rescue the beautiful maid in distress—my darling, sweet, beautiful, loving Melissa.

I am a lonely wayfarer, a lost fool who has strayed so far from home I no longer know who I am. My soul is thrown away and I am without hope. If only I could find a safe place, a protected haven away from and untouched by the madness of this world, I would convert to it. For in this darkness I am alone. Won't someone help me—please? I didn't mean to do it. It was an accident. I didn't know the man was there. I didn't mean to kill him. I'm sorry! Please forgive me!

I fall back through the barroom door, the bat flailing wildly in front of me. I hear Melissa scream and strain my eyes to see her, but the darkness has me by the legs and is pulling me down. Just before everything turns black, I imagine I see angels who know me from days gone by...

"Do you think God knows about us?"

"Luke, is that you?"

"Never look back, Wade."

"Sergeant Cavendish, is that you?"

"Remember, Wade, Jesus is the best friend you can ever have."

"Rodney, is that you?"

"By His boundless mercy, God offers everyone the privilege of being born again..."

"Esther, is that you?"

No, Wade, it is I.

"What? Who's there? Who are you?"

Who do you think I am?

"I don't know. Who are you?"

Seek Me and you shall know Me.

"How?"

Knock and I shall answer the door.

"I don't understand."

You must open your heart and let Me come in.

"But why would you want me?"

Because I love you, Wade.

"But I am no good. I've done something terrible."

All men fall short of the glory of God.

"But, I'm a...murderer!"

I know you as I know the truth of all things. I have a plan for you, but you are the one who must choose to change.

"How? How can I change what has already been done?"

Trust Me.

"Hey, Parker!"

The clamp around my skull instantly twists a full turn tighter. "What!" An astringent belch makes its way to freedom.

"Rise and shine, Wade—this isn't a Holiday Inn."

With considerable effort, I raise my face off of a cold fiberglass plank. A gelatinous string of drool stretches between the plank and my swollen lower lip as my eyes focus just enough to make out a human form. I am pretty sure it belongs with the voice. "Bob—is that you? Am I in the tank again?"

Deputy Bob Serrano intentionally clangs his collection of keys on the steel cell door. I can see enough to tell his bushy, black mustache is turned down in a severe frown. "I'm afraid so."

I met Bob Serrano one night at Buster's Bonanza Room not long after Buster's had become my newest home away from home. He and his partner were doing a routine walk-through. It was a quiet night on the beat, and we ended up talking for a while. He came back later without his uniform and patiently listened to my long, carefully edited cop story about the mysterious Sergeant Lyle Cavendish.

Bob started hanging out at Buster's, I soon found out, after his daughter died of leukemia. Though now a Christian and a recovering alcoholic, he continues his regular walk-throughs and goes out of his way to stay in touch. There must be something about me that cops can't resist. They always seem to want to keep tabs on me. Anyway, Bob sees a lot more in me than I've ever seen in myself. All of the regulars at Buster's are friends of mine, but none quite like deputy Bob Serrano.

"Easy with the keys—please, sir."

"Oops. Gee, am I bothering you?" He bangs the keys again, except harder.

I wipe a bare forearm across my mouth. The spittle leaves a gooey snail-trail from elbow to wrist that instantly begins to dry. From the way my head is throbbing, much less the damage to my face, I conclude it must have been a bad one. "Did I hurt anybody?"

Bob swings the jail door open and steps inside the tank. "Yes, well—not seriously, anyway. Melissa's feelings are a different story, though."

I look up at Bob. "Aw, she's okay. She probably won't talk to me for a day is all, maybe two."

My bloodshot eyes clear enough to see the disgust plastered all over Bob's face. He can't resist stating the obvious. "You don't deserve a woman like Melissa."

He is right, but it isn't the first time he's said that. "Shoot, Bob. I don't deserve a friend like you either, do I?" My lip is badly swollen and the grin I show him isn't worth the pain, but it does force his stern-set gaze to give way to a half smile.

"Nope, you sure don't."

I want to lay my head back down, but I am afraid to give Bob another reason to yell or bang his keys. Grunting, I haul myself up to a sitting position. "Did I do any damage?"

Bob hooks both thumbs in his gunless gun belt, the holster empty in accordance with jail rules. "According to Buster, you owe him three hundred bucks."

The hard stare he's putting on me causes the skull clamp to tighten another turn. "Geez...what'd I break this time?"

"You don't remember any of it, do you?"

There is a suggestion of pity in Bob's voice that I don't care for. I guess a part of my ego isn't fully pickled yet. I shake my head and feel stiffness in my neck. "No, Bob. I guess I don't remember a thing."

He sighs and clenches his jaw. "Wade, you really outdid yourself this time. According to forty-plus witnesses, you went out to your car, got that Duke Snider bat of yours, and proceeded to belt a billiard ball through every one of Buster's windows."

"Cleared the place out, did I?"

"Don't sound so proud of yourself. When you finally ran out of balls, you went outside and tried to get everybody to sing 'Take Me Out to the Ball Game' with you."

"Good grief." I wearily try to rub the kink out of my neck.

"You caused some grief, all right. The watch commander says I have to charge you this time."

"Geez." I close my eyes and will against a sudden pang of nausea.

"You know how many times you've lain on that bench sleeping it off?"

I shake my head and start to tune him out. His message already sounds too much like a lecture. "I haven't kept a count."

"You've had nine public drunkenness detainments in the last two years."

His poorly veiled disdain cuts me. I know it will sound stupid, but I say it anyway. "I'm sorry, Bob."

"Oh, I'm sure you are, but that isn't all of it."

Give me a break. "What?"

"Buster says you darn near took Melissa's head off with that bat of yours."

"What!" I feel the blood drain from my face.

"That's right—you should be scared. Apparently she tried to stop you. You were out of control. Everybody knows you didn't mean it, they all know how much you love her. But for the grace of God, Wade, you could have killed her." He clenches his jaw again and looks away, signaling something worse is coming.

"What? Tell me."

"Buster says the bat clipped one of Melissa's pierced earrings and ripped her earlobe in half."

"Oh no!" Panic floods my veins. I struggle to get up on my feet.

"Sit down!"

"Huh?"

"You haven't heard the worst of it yet."

"What?"

Now I see pain in Bob's face. He can't look at me as he says the words he knows will rip my heart right out of my chest. "Melissa took off. She's left you, Wade."

I start to my feet again, but a sledgehammer of dread hits me in the solar plexus. I can't breathe. Bob says something about bail being a thousand dollars and then disappears, leaving the jail door standing wide.

He returns with a Dixie cup of water and hands it to me. In shock, I take the cup and drop it, water splattering back up in my face. Bob backs out of the cell again, but I don't notice.

I slip off the bench to the floor, water dripping from my face, and in my mind I am suddenly lying on the bottom of the middle pond. I frantically rip at my pockets, sure they are full of deadly ball bearings, holding me down, drowning me. Then my hands are stuck and I can't get them out of my pockets and this time I know Mac can't save me—he's been dead for thirteen years!

"Here," Bob says, handing me another cup.

"Huh…what?"

"Come on, pull yourself together. Don't spill it. You're shaking like a frightened animal."

I manage to raise the cup to my mouth, but I can't drink. To me the water looks as green as the water in Three Ponds. I set the cup down on the floor. Bob grabs me under the arms and raises me back up on the bench. "I'm pathetic," I mumble.

What Bob hears is a muffled whimper, a cry for help. He sits down next to me and hands the cup to me again. This time the water looks potable. I down it.

I need a drink, I think to myself, not daring to say it out loud.

"What you need is God, Wade," Bob says with the consoling tone of a friend. "I know you've heard this from me before, but it's the truest thing I can ever say to you." He looks straight into my ashamed eyes. "You have got to get straightened out, and you are not able to do it on your own. I couldn't do it myself, either. I was a discarded, rusty, bent, twisted-up old nail lying in the dirt. To tell you the truth, I wanted to die.

"But one day, after someone who is now one of my dearest friends sat down with me for the hundredth time and said the same thing I am saying to you now, I decided to take a chance on God. I got on down on my knees and told Him I needed Him and that I couldn't make it without Him. I surrendered my will to His and asked Him to help me." Bob squeezes my shoulder. "I finally agreed to go with my friend to an AA meeting. It was very hard in the beginning, but the Lord helped me through.

"But I lost my wife because I didn't get help soon enough. I don't think it's too late for you to get Melissa back."

"Do you really think so?"

"Yes, I do. God taught me to believe in miracles."

I sit here letting what Bob said soak in, remembering that the last time I talked to Luke he made a speech of his own. "I hate to say it, Wade, but you are a drunk just like Earl."

"You were too young to remember anything about Earl," I argued, knowing full well if I remember Earl's drunken tirades, Luke remembers them, too.

"What time is it, Bob?"

"Trying to change the subject?"

"Give me a break, will you."

The desperation in my eyes wears him down some. "Two in the afternoon. It's Saturday, in case you're wondering."

I endure another turn of the clamp. "Why didn't you rouse me earlier?"

"You got bail money on you?"

"No."

"There's your answer."

Bob sits next to me, patiently waiting, allowing me to think. He is right, of course. I have to do something about the drinking, but not AA, for crying out loud. *Hello, my name is Wade. I'm an alcoholic. HI, WADE!* "Geez."

"It's not geez, Wade, it's Jesus." He grins.

"You're not going to let up, are you?"

"It's your life we're talking about here, and I'm willing to fight for it."

"Did you see Melissa?"

"Yep."

"Did she say she was going to her mom's house?"

"Nope. She mentioned San Diego, though."

"Yeah, her mom lives in San Diego."

"Good."

At least I know where to find her. Her mom didn't like me much before and I figure this debacle will drop me about fifty more rungs on the ladder. The lady has a very long ladder. "How much is my bail again?"

"A grand."

Assuming Melissa hasn't cleaned out the bank account, I figure I can probably get my hands on about two hundred dollars. "Which bondsman will cover me if you tell them I'm your friend?"

"Well now, here's where the good news comes in." He grins. "Your bail has already been made."

"Well golly gee whiz, praise the Lord, Bob."

"Exactly, though let me tell you from personal experience, the Big Guy would rather you avoid the sarcasm."

"So? Who put up the bail money?"

"A woman—she's waiting outside for you."

"What woman?"

"She's a friend of mine. I know her from AA. She's a recovering alcoholic. I'm thinking maybe she can do you some good."

"Geez."

Bob grins again. "Try saying Jesus."

"Jeee-susss. Happy now?"

"It's a start."

I stand up, and my stomach reminds me just how much poison is still in me. Wino shakes turn into nervous shakes as I try to focus my mind on Melissa. Out in the hallway, I spot myself in a polished metal mirror. I look like a badly trampled throwaway from some skid row alley.

"Can I borrow your comb, Bob? I guess if some woman I don't even know is bailing me out of jail, the least I can do is show a little respect and comb my hair."

Bob reaches into his back pocket and gives me his comb. "In case you were wondering, nobody hit you in the mouth. You banged your lip on the bench last night, after we put you in the tank."

"What? No police brutality?"

I show him a real grin, and he shakes his head, implying I am hopeless. I hand the comb back to him and he nudges me toward the cell door. "Remember, AA, a meeting. I'll take you anytime. You just say when."

"Thanks. I'll give it some thought. I promise I'll really give it some serious thought."

"I'm praying for you every day."

I hear echoes of Esther's voice.

I take a deep breath and walk out into the holding area. Another deputy hands me a manila envelope with my name printed on it, has me sign a receipt book, then gives me the pink copy of what I signed. Bob walks me to the rear door of the jail.

I stop suddenly at the door, my heart kicking hard from a new jolt of panic. I turn back to Bob, my red eyes pleading, hoping. "Do you know what happened to my bat?"

He shakes his head and gives me a look that strongly suggests I am beyond his ability to help. "I was hoping you'd forget about the bat."

"Never."

"It should be locked up in evidence, but I put it in the trunk of your car last night. It's still parked in front of Buster's. Your car keys are in the envelope."

"Thank you."

"You can thank me by going to a meeting with me."

"I'll tell you this much, I'll do whatever it takes to get Melissa back."

Bob swats the back of my head and backs away, giving me my leave. I stand at the back door of the jail shaking enough to rattle the keys in the envelope.

"She's right outside the door, Wade. She's been waiting for almost an hour. Go on, I think you'll be quite surprised by how much she cares."

I push on the door. "Thanks again."

"God bless you, Wade," Bob calls from the echoing innards of the jail.

Why would a stranger shell out a thousand dollars to bail me out of jail?

twelve

My breath catches in my throat. *Not again.*

This time the mirage is no more than twenty feet from me. It turns toward me and smiles. I close my bloodshot eyes and open them again. The mirage is still there. "Miss Cherry?"

"Hello, Wade."

This isn't real...I have to quit drinking...Bob doesn't know the half of it. I stare in disbelief. I reach out and run my hand through the image, expecting it to ripple away like vapor. She waves back and steps toward me. *She is real!*

She looks much older, but still exquisite. I picture her as I saw her that first night on Billy Goat Hill, climbing off that big motorcycle and standing in the circle of headlights. She was a beautiful angel descending from paradise. I relive the rhapsody of her first words to me. "*How old are you, honey?*"

So many years ago it was, and still the smell of her perfume stored away in a vial somewhere deep in my brain releases and flows over my memory. I breathe deep and recall the pleasure and the terror of that first encounter. The mix of emotion is the same at this very moment.

I have longed to see her, as a lost toddler must long to be reunited with its mother, but I am so shocked by this unexpected revelation she may as well have thundered down on me in the darkness of my dreams on a motorcycle embroiled in a billowing cloud of dust. This is a miracle.

"How?…What?…Uh, I never expected to see you again."

"It's been a long, long time. How do I look?"

Her voice is exactly as I remember it, so familiar to my ears that the years of separation seem hardly more than a week. I am speechless. My mushy brain can't process what is happening fast enough. I walked out of the jail wanting to immediately find Melissa and beg for her forgiveness. But this development is such a shock my priorities are suddenly tangled and conflicted.

I darn near say, "Real sharp, ma'am," but somehow manage a coherent sentence. "As beautiful as in all of my dreams."

The compliment suits her, possibly makes her blush, though it could be the bloodshot filters I'm looking through. "I can't say the same about you, young man. You've grown into a handsome prince. Except right now you look like you've been to hell and back."

"Maybe I have."

She hugs me and it is strange, not the way I remember her hugs. I am much taller than her now, the reverse of the last time she hugged me.

"Thanks for bailing me out—I guess."

"I want to hear all about it."

"How much time do you have? It's a very long story."

"For you, I have the rest of my life."

With less than a modicum of shame, I ask, "Would you like to go have a drink somewhere?"

"I can see we have our work cut out for us, don't we?"

"I need to find my wife. I need a drink. I need to get my car. And I need to apologize to Buster, the owner of the bar I terrorized last night. Maybe not exactly in that order, though." My mind is spinning.

"Come on." She takes my hand. "My car's over there. You can show me the way to this Buster place. I guess we can accomplish three of those things in one stop."

"I really screwed up."

"I've been there."

"Do you remember the bat that Duke Snider gave to me?"

"Ha! How could I forget it?"

"They say I beaned my wife with the bat, but she's supposedly okay. I must have completely lost it. I don't remember a thing."

"I know all about what happened. Your wife already told me."

"You've talked to Melissa?"

"Yes, at length, and she sounds like a wonderful lady."

"She is wonderful. But how did you know about this? I mean, you showing up here is amazing. It's too good to be true."

"I'm an investigator, or was, anyway. Remember?"

That angers me. "No way, ma'am—that's not good enough. The Sergeant always used to put me off that way. I'm not a dumb, naive kid anymore. Well, I'm not a naive kid, anyway."

"I'll tell you this much, Wade. You need help. And I think I can give you some, if you're willing to accept it. Your wife asked me to bail you out, but she's not coming back to you. Not just yet, anyway. She and your daughter are staying with your mother-in-law. She doesn't want to talk to you right now, not until she's convinced you are serious about cleaning up your act. So it looks like you're stuck with me for the moment. Okay?"

Feeling angry and powerless, I look away from her. "Yeah? Well, why should I trust you? Why should I believe anything you have to say? Where have you been all these years?"

"Not far away."

"Doing what?"

"Trying to keep my head on straight—staying sober."

"So it's true then, you're not a cop anymore?"

"That's right."

"Why?"

"I'm sorry, Wade, but I can't really talk about that."

I look back toward the jail door. At least I knew where I stood in jail. I feel like walking away from her, leaving her right here in the parking lot. She sounds way too much like Lucinda. No answers. But what am I going to do, run away from home? Get a job at a car wash? I turn and look at her again. "Can't talk about it or won't talk about it?"

"Wouldn't you rather focus your mind on how to bring your wife and daughter back home where they belong?"

"What about the Sergeant, then? Do you happen to know anything about him—that you care to share with me, that is?"

Now she looks away. "No. We split up long ago."

"I tried for years to find both of you. The way things happened, the way my mom made us move from Ruby Place and wouldn't let us see you guys anymore, really hurt me. Now, after all these years, you find me a drunken jailbird and say you want to help me?"

"We have all the time in the world to get to know each other again." She takes my hand and tugs me toward her car. "Tell me how to get to this bar of yours."

Her hand is warm and soft, just as I remember it. It is not possible to stay angry with her.

In the car the initial shock dissipates, and my emotions level back to somewhere this side of numb, normal enough to remind me I have a fat lip and a major hangover. "Your last name is Webster?"

"Yes."

"I tried to find you once."

"I'm sorry for all that you've been through."

"I went to the Highland Park police station. They wouldn't help me, but they did tell me it would be best to stay away from you, that you and the Sergeant got into some trouble. What was that all about?"

"Maybe someday I'll be able to talk about it, but I've been working hard to put that part of my life behind me. I have lots of regrets, lots of guilt, and some good memories, too."

"Did you and the Sergeant ever get married?"

She shifts in her seat and looks at me. I see pain. "No, we never did."

"So, you never had any kids either?"

"No."

"You would have been a good mother."

"Maybe." She looks at me, her face red, eyes tearing. It might as well be Lucinda sitting there.

"So, everything went wrong. I don't understand any of it. I guess you knew about the break-in at our house and about Mac?"

"Yes, I did. But Lyle and I, for administrative reasons, were not allowed to work the case."

"Administrative reasons?"

"Because we knew you, your family. It's standard procedure not to assign investigators who have a personal relationship with the victims."

"We were victimized alright. None of it has ever made any sense to me. The first half of my life was shrouded in mystery and the second half isn't a heck of a lot better—so far."

She tries to smile. "There is the future."

"Yes. Depressing, isn't it?" *I need that drink.*

"It certainly is if you continue to drink yourself to death."

"I'll be all right. I'm a survivor."

I look out the window and tears begin to flow. She pulls to the curb and parks the car. No more words. We both just sit there and cry for a few minutes.

A guy from a glass company is up on a ladder, removing broken glass from the front window of Buster's Bonanza Room when we drive into the parking lot. My car is parked at the far end of the lot. We enter through the back door. I don't deserve to use the front door.

Buster is none to happy to see me. "Are you here to pay for the damages?"

"I'm here to apologize and to have a drink. This is Cherry Webster."

Buster looks at Cherry. "No offense to you ma'am, but...Wade, you're no longer welcome here. The next time I see you, I expect it to be the last time, and you better have three hundred dollars in your hand when you come through the door."

"It's your place."

"Yes it is, and your failure to respect that is the reason you are banned from *my* place for life."

"I've been banned my whole life, Buster. But for what it's worth, I am sorry for what I did last night."

"Apology accepted. I hope your wife heals up fine."

Cherry opens her purse and lays three hundred dollars cash on the bar. "I would prefer he not come back here ever," she says.

She gives me a determined look, and her eyes say any protest by me will be a total waste of breath.

Buster smiles and picks up the cash. "We're good then."

We exit the bar and walk to my car. I pop the trunk to make sure the bat is there. It is. *Thank you, Bob.* I stand there feeling empty and lost, beyond the comfort of thoughts about my childhood hero, Duke Snider.

And all at once the totality of my circumstance comes in a flash of sad clarity. I have been banned from my favorite watering hole, but more important I have hit a new bottom, a bottom lower than I ever thought possible. If I fall any lower I will be dead. I think of the two people who tried to help me in the past, Rodney and Esther, and the spiritual thread that links them as one in my mind. I see them both, hear their voices and their hearts crying out to me, and there, standing at the back of my car in the parking lot of a saloon I am no longer welcome in, with a woman who once meant more to me than my own mother, I realize just how powerless I am to save myself. I still may not be able to say it out loud, but inside myself I admit I am defeated.

Miss Cherry is very quiet, her eyes are closed, and I'd say she is praying, if I weren't so sure I thought I knew better. She leans against the car fender, and despite my woe I am again struck by how beautiful she still is. A question spills over my lips and startles me as much if not more than it does her. "What do you know about—God?"

She opens her eyes, and I think possibly she was praying. "Well, through AA I've come to believe God is real, but I'm still working on understanding who He is. I believe God helped me admit I was powerless over alcohol and gave me back my sanity, yet I'm still defiant and haven't completely turned my will over to His care."

"Do you pray?"

She looks at me and warms my heart with a shy little smile. "Yes, but not often enough. Mostly I pray for wisdom to surrender and allow Him completely into my life."

"Do you really think you can help me?"

"With God's help, I promise I'll do everything in my power to help you, but only you can decide when you are ready to be helped."

"I don't know where to begin."

"I began by talking to God."

Geez. "I don't know if I'm ready to do that."

She grins. "What are your options?"

Part of me wants to grin back, but what's left of my pride won't let me. A ridiculous shrug and an equally intelligent, "I don't know," is all I can come up with.

"Well, we both know life is an adventure, and my mother always used to say all great adventures must begin with a feast. How does the idea of putting something solid in your stomach sound?"

"That would be a good thing, I guess."

A few minutes later we get situated in a back booth at a Denny's. No cocktail lounge on the premises. "How is your mom these days?" Miss Cherry asks.

"Okay, I guess. We didn't speak for many years. I was very angry with her, still am. The way she refused to explain or give reasons for anything—well, I still blame her for a lot. I ran away when I was sixteen and never looked back."

"Is her health up to code? Is she happy?"

"She's never been happy since our little brother died. As far as I know, she's physically healthy."

"Do you see her?"

"You still act like a cop."

"I'm just interested in you."

"Lucinda was invited to our wedding, and she and Melissa hit it off pretty well. Melissa worked on me for several years and ended up mediating something of a truce. At first I did it only to appease Melissa and make her happy. Now I talk with my mom on the phone on occasion, and we've gotten together by ourselves a few times. I try to keep things superficial, or I end up getting frustrated and angry. She still refuses to talk about the past."

"I see. That's better than nothing."

"Not much."

Our food arrives at the table. Miss Cherry seems as grateful for the break as I am. She says a short prayer of thanks over the food and continues the interrogation. "So—tell me about your daughter."

"Her name is Kate. She's five and cute as can be. She looks so much like her mother it's spooky. Kate has become a connecting point for my mom and me. My mom adores her only grandchild."

"That is way better than nothing, it's wonderful!"

"Yeah, my mom and I do spend some time talking about Kate. She says Kate's personality reminds her of me when I was that age. A little schemer, she calls her. I will say this, Kate is very resourceful."

"That's a good word to describe the way I used to think of you—*resourceful.*"

"How so?"

"For one thing, you had to be resourceful to slide down the Crippler in the dark."

I just about choke. "You know, I never did do that—in the dark, I mean."

"I won't tell." She laughs. "You were the champion cardboard slider though, and I'd say that is the accomplishment of an incredibly resourceful person."

"I'll accept that."

I feel relaxed and I'm enjoying our lunch. She has managed to divert me around my most immediate crisis and get me to open up some.

"Seriously though, you were an amazingly resourceful kid. You were the older brother who held up under the stress and strain of a collapsing family. What you did to keep it together for yourself and your brother is amazing."

"I'm not so sure I did as well as you suggest."

"You were fantastic, but you also paid a heavy price. I think perhaps we're seeing the effects of your sacrifice now."

"I didn't make any sacrifices—I didn't have any choice."

"You could look at it that way. But I saw how you took care of your brother. You stood up, you took the fire of the circumstances, and you made it work. But I think you're paying for it now. The self-destructive behavior, the booze—it's pretty classic stuff."

"How about hereditary?"

"Maybe, but it's not an excuse. How about your father? Do you ever hear from him?"

"I don't know if he's dead or alive."

"You said you made an effort to find me. What about him? Did you ever try to find him?"

I exhale a deep breath. "No."

"How come?"

"You can't be serious."

"I am serious." She gives me an assessing look. "How do you feel about the idea of forgiveness?"

"Maybe I've done things that can't be forgiven. Why? Do you need to be forgiven for something?"

The question really seems to throw her, so much so I can't help wondering what nerve I've touched. "I wasn't thinking about *you* needing forgiving, Wade. I was wondering about your ability to forgive. I am very interested in the subject of forgiveness."

I think of Duke Snider. I speak his words out loud. "We must find a way to forgive, or we only end up blaming ourselves."

She stares at me like I just shouted over a loudspeaker the combination to the lock on the vault of her most private secrets. "Yes, that says it quite profoundly."

"Someone told me that once."

"Someone?"

An awkward moment follows, leaving me perplexed and uneasy. I feel like I just walked in on a forbidden conversation. Not that the last twenty-four hours have been normal, but something about this reunion has already gone askew, and I can't for the life of me grasp a single thread of what it might be. I want less mystery, not more.

"Look, I really appreciate your showing up. For years I've dreamed of seeing you again. To be sitting here with you is a miracle in itself. I appreciate your bailing me out of jail and paying my debt with Buster. I'll pay you back as soon as I possibly can, but…"

"But what? There doesn't have to be any *buts*. I'm here—and you need help. What you just said—I agree this has all the earmarks of a miracle. Let's go with it. Let's see what God has in mind. I'm only a couple of steps ahead of you in this God thing, but from what I've experienced already, the changes for the better in my life, I don't think there is anything God can't do. With God all things are possible, and it's never too late. I'm an example of that."

"But…"

"Look—I think we should pray."

"Maybe tonight I'll give it a try. 'Now I lay me down to sleep'…I think I remember how to do it."

"How about right now?"

"Here—in a Denny's restaurant?" I look around, trying not to show how self-conscious I feel. I can lose my mind and break the windows out of a bar, I can nearly skull my own wife with a baseball bat, I can wake up on a fiberglass jail bunk and brush aside the pity of a concerned friend, but to suggest that I openly pray in a public restaurant—now that is something I can't do.

She spreads her hands out on the table. "Right here and right now."

"I don't think so."

"Sit there with your eyes open if you want."

"Wait a sec…"

"Dear Lord, it's me, Cherry again…"

Geez. I close my eyes.

"…and I'm here with Wade Parker. Father, You are the Creator of all things. You are holy, and we worship You. Lord, we need Your help. We cannot do this by ourselves. Only You have the power to right what is wrong. Father, please help Wade turn away from the darkness of alcohol. Draw him in toward Your loving light. Help him to adopt a heart of forgiveness so that he may relinquish the past and look forward to the future. Father, please forgive our sins and help us to sin no more. We ask these things in the precious name of Jesus—amen."

"Uh, amen." I open my eyes, and to my surprise, a tear spills down my cheek. I feel warm and kind of safe-like. Esther tried to get me to pray with her many times, but I never gave it a sincere effort. I wish I could tell Esther I am sorry.

"How do you feel, Wade?"

"I don't know, warm, I guess, a little emotional. I'll tell you one thing for sure, I haven't thought about a drink since you started talking this spiritual stuff."

"Another miracle, maybe?"

"Maybe. What will really be a miracle is if Luke still speaks to me after he finds out what I did to Melissa at Buster's last night."

"Why don't we go call him?"

"He won't believe it when I tell him about you."

"Let's pray about it. Just kidding," she says with a grin. "I'll pray for you. Here's a quarter; the pay phone is that way."

"Just kidding"? But I did feel something. God, if You are real, if You can hear me, I am sorry. Please forgive me. Please help me. Please bring Melissa back to me.

The way Luke says hello, practically shouting into the phone, makes it pretty clear he is furious with me. I figure he's already heard about the show at Buster's and is ready to read me the riot act. Miss Cherry stands next to me at the open phone booth door, lending moral support.

"Where in the heck have you been, Wade?"

"I know, I know. I really screwed up this time. You've been right all along. I'm just as bad as Earl was. I've got to do something drastic, AA maybe."

"What are you talking about?"

"Yeah, right—like you didn't hear what I did to Melissa? I'm really going to need your help this time, little brother."

"I've been trying to find you. You haven't answered your phone. I went by your house and left a note on your front door."

Good. He's already talked to Melissa. "I know she's probably so mad right now she won't talk to me. But she'll listen to you. I need you to tell her how sorry I am. And you're never going to believe who bailed me out of jail."

I look at Miss Cherry, both of us anxious to tell Luke about her.

"Wade!"

"What?"

"I don't have a clue what you're talking about."

"Come on, Luke. Don't mess with me. I've had a rough weekend. You said you left a note for me. What? Have you heard from Melissa?"

"No. I haven't been able to reach her, either."

"I guess she's really mad. It's going to take some real doing to get back on her good side."

"What did you do?"

"You mean you really haven't heard what happened at Buster's?"

"No. I don't know anything about Buster's."

Miss Cherry offers encouragement with her eyes. She nods her head, gently nudging. "I figured word would be all over town by now. Me and my bat put on quite a show, so I've been told anyway."

"No, nobody said anything about you and your bat. I've been all over town trying to find you."

"Oh." It finally sinks in that something other than my idiotic behavior is on his mind.

"Wade?"

"Yeah—what is it, tell me."

"I'm afraid I've got some real bad news."

The cracking edge to his voice scares me. Miss Cherry takes my hand, sensing the wrongness of the conversation. "What is it? What's happened?"

"Lucinda—is dead."

thirteen

Melissa comes home right away. A death in the family, unpleasant as it is, brings people together who might otherwise refuse to acknowledge the need to speak to each other. In this sense, my mother has delivered a final kindness to me. Her untimely death brings the return of my wife and a new beginning to my life—a strange exchange for a spiritual fledgling to grasp. I asked God to bring my wife back, not take my mother away. The grand mystery continues.

Melissa places one condition on her return. I must join AA. I agree to this requirement with the understanding that it will likely take a long time to fully win her back. If I have gained one thing from my unorthodox beginnings, all those years of watching out for Luke and nearly two decades of waiting for the dead man's reprisal—it's patience.

Miss Cherry is concerned that my impetus for starting AA be unencumbered by false motives. How can winning my wife back be a false motive for sobriety? I think any reason is a good reason, if it guides me into the program. We shall see.

Melissa was instrumental in smoothing the jagged edges of my estrangement from Lucinda. Her efforts, coupled with the ameliorating influence of time, had brought me around to a let-bygones-be-bygones frame of mind. I invited Lucinda out to dinner one rainy night not long before her death. The dinner went well. We had been a long, long storm, my mother and I, and to be settled and calm was an amazing achievement. We enjoyed several subsequent visits before her accident froze the status of our relationship midway to full reconciliation.

Mistaking an off-ramp for an on-ramp, a drunk driver hit Lucinda head-on on the San Bernardino Freeway near the top of Kellogg Pass. There must have been a preceding moment of horror; save that, her demise was instantaneous and painless. I felt the added sting of irony when I learned my mother had been killed by a drunk driver, a member of my own dangerous legion.

As a part of my program in AA, I met with and forgave the young woman who took Lucinda's life. By then, Miss Cherry's fascination with forgiveness had already taken root in me, or I never would have been able to do it.

Miss Cherry encourages me to reconcile my thoughts about Lucinda, to let go of the bad and keep only the good.

Although I am no longer angry with her, the door to the Lucinda part of my past still does not quite lock. Occasionally, winds of resentment rise up and rattle the door open. There remains a nagging feeling that Lucinda was trying to work up the courage to tell me something—something vital. That I will never know what was bothering her only compounds the already burdensome feeling that my life is based on some arcane punishment; that I am the product of events, circumstances, human influences, and things of mystery far more complex than slingshots and mockingbird feathers.

Like an unscratchable itch, the unknowns of the past remain as irritants to my otherwise improving existence. It is also the mulch from which my newly germinated seed of forgiveness sprouts. This is the way it is. "With God's help," Miss Cherry says, "you shall endure the past, relish the present, and look forward to the future."

Patience and endurance—one more respectable character quality and I'll have the beginnings of a list of virtues. One day at a time, as we recovering alcoholics say.

Deputy Bob Serrano and Miss Cherry are my sponsors in Alcoholics Anonymous. With their unflagging help, I finally openly admit I am powerless over alcohol. Empowered by their friendship and Melissa's love, I am coming to realize just how unmanageable my life had become.

As the haze of alcohol slowly evaporates and hindsight becomes clearer and clearer, I begin to see just how hard I have slammed on the bottom. Inversely, I begin to see how blessed I am to be in recovery. As I accept the truth about my strange, poisonous, deceitful friend, that it has defeated me, I take my first step toward liberation. Miss Cherry assures me the God who I still do not know is right here by my side.

In the beginning, it was humiliating. "Hi. My name is Wade...*I'm an alcoholic!*" But I am finding there is noble virtue in humility, not in humiliation. The older brother is becoming more like the younger brother, a philosopher. Growing stronger, I'm moving closer to the idea that true peace comes not from the feckless friendship of alcohol, or from material things, or even from the love of other human beings. The big dumb donkey is slowly letting go of the fear that does not want him to believe that true peace resides in believing in and relying on God.

The prayers of Rodney and Esther and the steady conviction and dedication of Luke, Melissa, and Miss Cherry are contributing mightily to the restoration of my soul.

Miss Cherry plays a pivotal and ongoing role in my program. Our one-on-one testimonials help create open-mindedness. She tells me of her struggle with the pressures of police life. And though always in an oblique manner, she shares bits and pieces of her relationship and eventual breakup with the Sergeant. I am fascinated with every new speck of information, each precious little fit in the million-piece jigsaw puzzle.

She confides that there have been other boyfriends, but that no other man has been able to take the Sergeant's place in her heart. She often speaks of her life with the Sergeant in terms of its consequences. She left him—that much she makes clear. But she also describes her life after him in terms that I find most curious. It is almost as if the downturn of her life had been expected, part of a deal, the agreed-upon price that had to be paid.

Sometimes she describes herself and her "consequences" in ways that make me think of her as a soldier ordered to do something that exceeded her conscience, and rather than carry out her duty, or perhaps to stop carrying out her duty, she deserted or resigned in shame. Whatever it was, it took a toll.

As we spend more and more time together, I begin to sense that, like mine, her conscience still bothers her. About what, I do not know. Something though, perhaps an unspeakable dark secret like my own, has eaten away part of her spirit, leaving her empty and aching inside. Her passion for the study of forgiveness is driven by this, I think.

She remains beautiful on the surface, like a pearly nautilus. But loneliness, her unscratchable itch, has crept inside and taken up residence in the lovely shell.

She tells me how her drinking gradually got out of control and landed her in Alcoholics Anonymous. I find all of this easy to relate to as I embrace the same outcome, which doubly roots our camaraderie in a common history.

We talk about many things, though on the subject of the Sergeant she remains careful, guarded. When I probe too deep, she changes the subject, but just enough to keep from turning me off or discouraging me in my own quest for sobriety.

She isn't the only one to hold back secrets. I am equally incomplete with my candidness, as I, too, resist crossing the big line when exploring the great plains of my past. It is crazy how adept we both are at walking that line, even dancing on it once or twice, but never crossing over.

As time passes, she and I whittle away at the layers of our his-

tory. I remain mired in the perspective of the adoring boy infatu-
ated with the beautiful mother figure. She walks the beat of the lady
cop concerned about the welfare of two young hooligans naive of
the hazards on the wrong side of the tracks. A hundred times we
talk into the wee hours of the morning, long after Melissa and Kate
have gone to bed. We whittle and whittle and whittle, and always I
am left floating within the margins of my unease, nagged by the
sense that something unspoken still holds the key to the dark mystery of my childhood.

It is much the same as my impression of Lucinda in those short
months before she died. She wanted to tell me something—I know
she did—and I can't seem to shake it. Unspoken truths are like spirits stuck in limbo.

Like long-term passengers in a private elevator, together we ride,
up and down, down and up, sharing the journey with great mutual
affection. Almost always we have fun. Almost like a loving mother
and an adoring son dancing every dance at a fairy tale ball. But never
does our elevator stop on that certain forbidden floor, where the
Devil plays a waltz for erstwhile dancers with sub rosa pasts.

Notwithstanding my progress in most other areas, my secret
life as a child murderer stays buried deep in my psyche, an indelible
tattoo that my timeless timidity has conspired to emboss under
layer upon layer of scar tissue. In prayer, I whittle away at the scar,
but I just can't bear to let Miss Cherry see the tattoo. It is quite a
dance.

About all of this I pray—day after day, week after week, month
after month. I ask God to give me continued endurance and the
patience, and He seems to be bringing me along. So far so good, I
guess. He must know what He is doing. *I wish you would tell me
what I'm doing wrong, God. What is missing? What have I left out?*

Today, I'll clean the garage in the memory of my mother. I remember how Lucinda used to clean when she was upset or frustrated.
Clean and work, that was her. Man, did she clean a lot after

Matthew died. After Earl left she literally scrubbed the kitchen linoleum down to bare wood in a couple of places. Luke and I had to watch out for splinters.

An hour into the garage clean-up, Melissa comes out to check on my progress. "Want some lunch?"

"Thanks, but I'm not hungry."

"You've made a good start. Is that the throw-away pile?"

"Yep. You might want to look through it first."

"What's that box over there?"

"That's my Esther keepsake box."

"Can I see?"

"Sure. I haven't looked at the stuff yet. I was going to go through it later."

"Want to take a break and look together?"

"Okay."

We avoid an oil stain and sit together on the concrete floor. Instantly, I remember that night when the cops helped me lay Mac down on the garage floor, and how after a while I went outside and talked to Esther by the fence. "*I believe somehow all things work for God's purposes, and I just want you to know I will always keep you and your family in my prayers.*" My eyes turn wet and glassy as I begin to remove other memories of Esther from the box.

Melissa puts her arm around me and kisses my neck. "You loved her very much, didn't you?"

"Yeah. I've always felt like I let her down."

Melissa hugs me. "You're doing so well now, honey. I'm so proud of you, and I think Esther would be very proud of you, too."

"Did I ever tell you how you remind me of Esther?"

"No. You say I look like Miss Cherry, except for the hair color and skin tone."

I grin. "You are gorgeous like Miss Cherry, but you remind me of Esther in a different way. She was so full of grace and kindness. I think she put the whole world before herself. I've talked about her husband, Carl, a million times, what a handful he was. Esther used to love to tend her backyard flower garden, and sometimes she would carry on conversations with an invisible person while she worked. I could hear her through the fence. One time I asked her who she was talking to, and she said, 'Why, I'm talking with my best friend, Jesus.'

"I told her I hoped someday I'd have a wife who cared as much about me as she cared about Carl."

Melissa smiles. "I guess I am like her…I talk to Jesus, too."

"What does Jesus tell you?"

"He tells me to never give up on you." She kisses my neck again.

Melissa removes Carl's Bible from the box and hands it to me. It's been a long time since I've held Carl's Bible in my hands. I open it, and the pages separate where they are marked by a faded sheet of paper.

"What's that?"

"It's a copy of the sinner's prayer. Esther gave it to me when she gave me the Bible."

An envelope slips from the Bible and drops in my lap. Melissa picks it up. "There's money in here."

"Three hundred dollars. Esther gave it to me when I was sixteen and living on my own. She made me take it. Her kindness meant so much to me at the time, I could never let go of the money. Many times I went hungry, but I just couldn't dip into Esther's gift."

Melissa hugs me again. "You sure have come a long way."

"Do you really talk to Jesus?"

"Yep, all the time."

"I didn't know. Since when?"

"Since Kate was born. The first time I laid eyes on her, I knew God was real."

I love this woman so much. "I'm sorry you couldn't share that with me then. I'm sorry for everything I've put you through."

"I know, honey."

She reminds me so much of Esther it's as if I were sitting at her kitchen table on Ruby Place.

Melissa opens the faded piece of paper. "Have you ever spoken these words to God?"

I close my eyes and I am there in Esther's kitchen. "*You keep that paper and I'll pray for the day when you truly feel it in your heart to pray the prayer out loud for God's ears to hear. When you do, I promise He will hear you.*" Tears spill forth and drip on the pages of Carl's Bible that Esther had bookmarked for me all those years ago.

Esther's love pours over me, and I know deep in that place in my heart that she touched all those years ago, that the gift that I am now being given is an answer to all of her prayers.

I look down at Carl's Bible, and my eyes are drawn to the answer that has been there all along…"For God so loved the world, He gave His only begotten Son, so that everyone who believes in Him will not perish but have eternal life."

"Wade? Are you okay?"

I look at Melissa, tears streaking down my face. I rise up on my knees. "Yes, just be here with me. I believe God has answered my question. I know what's been missing. I want to pray this prayer with you holding my hand."

Melissa smiles. "Okay, honey." She gets on her knees next to me and takes my hand. "Can I say it with you?"

Together we go forward united for the rest of our lives. "Lord Jesus Christ, I come to You now because I am a sinner. Today, Lord Jesus, I repent of my sin, I turn away from my sin, and I turn to You. I believe that You died for me. I believe Your shed blood covers all my sins. I believe no one else can save me but You, Lord Jesus. I ask You to come into my heart. Wash me, cleanse me, and make me Your child. I receive You in my heart by faith. Please help me to live for You until You come again. Thank You, Lord Jesus. Amen."

We sit there crying and hugging until Kate wanders into the garage. She finds us laughing and happy in a way she has never seen us before. "Oh good," she says grinning. "I was beginning to think you guys had forgotten."

"Forgotten what?" Melissa says.

"Today is my…birthday."

I reach for her and pull her into my lap. All three of us squish together in a wonderful hug. "Today is Mom's and my birthday, too."

Kate giggles. "Presents for everyone!"

It has been a year since that blessed day in the garage, and a lot has changed. I turned thirty not long ago; praise God, I am finally living in a kind of peace I never thought possible. We joined the church where Miss Cherry and Bob Serrano belong, and recently Luke and Trish have started coming. Melissa teaches Sunday school, and I am on the worship team, singing and playing guitar.

Regular Bible study continues to give me answers to questions I have contemplated since I was a child. My faith is deepening, and my trust in God has helped me gain some perspective about the bad memories and unhealthy tendencies of the past. I understand God has forgiven me, but I haven't fully released the contents of the deepest chamber of my heart. I still feel a final confession is owed, and I pray that God will give me the courage to speak of it and set it free. While the one remaining item on my spiritual to-do list is a huge one, based on the remarkable progress of the past year, it is hard to imagine that anything could go wrong.

This year we decided to celebrate Kate's birthday on Saturday, though she actually turned seven last Wednesday. Kate wanted to wait for the weekend so Miss Cherry could attend the party. Miss Cherry's car is scheduled to be in the shop over the weekend, so I agree to pick her up early to allow time to go present shopping.

Miss Cherry complains of a headache when we're browsing in the toy store and takes something for it. I am a little concerned for her but know she is a trooper. Soon we are making our way home with birthday presents safely hidden in the trunk.

"How's Luke these days?"

"Luke is Luke, fine all the time."

She nods but doesn't smile. "It will be good to see him."

"Is your head feeling any better?"

"Worse."

"Maybe I should take you home. Kate will get over it. One look at all the presents, and she'll be oblivious anyway."

"No. I'll be fine. It just takes a while for the aspirin to work."

As is always the case when I spend time alone with Miss Cherry, the past and my desire to speak with her about it flutter like moths feeding on memories stored in the closet of my mind. They drive me crazy, flitting about, stirring up dusty images. If I could just do it, pry open my head and let those moths out, I'd be done with it. Somehow, I have always felt Miss Cherry should be the one to hear my final confession. One of these days.

Deputy Bob keeps telling me about a Christian workshop he thinks would be good for me. It deals with spiritual bondage, and how to overcome negative thinking about the past. If I could just let those moths out, I could probably teach the class.

All I know is I am always watching, always sizing up the moment, always flirting with the possibility of revealing my last secret. I want to shed the burden of Three Ponds so badly, yet I always fall short of finding the nerve to do it. Always, always, always.

The impulse to do so strikes me again for the ten thousandth time, and with little confidence that I will actually say anything, I turn my head and look at Miss Cherry. There is always a glimmer of hope that my mouth will take charge and spill the beans for me. "We have a little extra time. Would you like to stop somewhere and have a cup of coffee?"

She gasps and puts her hands to her head. I touch her shoulder and feel tremors moving her against her will. I turn the car around, furious that the nearest hospital is at least ten minutes away. I try to keep her talking, the pain in her head making that impossible as she screams out twice, tears streaming, hands pressed tight to her temples. Then, still more than a mile from the hospital, she slumps unconscious against the car door.

Everything seemed so right this morning. Kate put us in a celebration mood at the crack of dawn by jumping on our bed and
making us all sing "Happy Birthday." But slowly, the day unfurled
its fronds of trickery, intimating nothing coming of extraordinary
magnitude. Sneaking killer earthquakes give little or no warning.

I see the hospital's emergency entrance up ahead. *Please God,
don't let her die!*

Even with the untimely death of my mother and the warning it
portended, it never once crossed my mind that a time like this
could come, a time when it might be too late to tell Miss Cherry
everything. Now faced with that daunting possibility, I feel as if I
have been banished from our private elevator and stranded in a
stairwell that climbs and descends but never ends in either direction.

I pound on the car horn as we screech to the curb and come to
an abrupt stop behind an unattended ambulance. Hospital person-
nel respond immediately, and within a minute Miss Cherry is
placed on a gurney and rushed inside. I call home to Melissa, and
soon the entire family huddles in a vigil in the waiting room.

I am fine when I shake Miss Cherry's doctor's hand and introduce
myself. I sit across from his desk staring blankly past him at rain-
streaked windows. Then something—his professional
comportment, the massive desk, the expansive collection of books
lining the shelves, the plaques, the certificates—gives me permission
to drop my guard. The drizzle set me up. I can't help myself. I let it
out in a downpour.

The doctor sits quietly unaffected while I rein in my sorrow.

When I speak, my throat is tight, constricted by heavy-hearted-
ness. "She's only forty-eight years old. I thought strokes were
something only old people had."

I look around the doctor's office absorbed in my frustration,
despondent. A single unforeseen event has brought back old adver-
saries—powerlessness and despair. The urge to take a drink wages a

dishonorable war against my weakened resolve. I fight the war with the only weapon I have, the one Miss Cherry helped me obtain, three AA meetings per day for the past fourteen days, and prayer—the most powerful medicine for a most powerful disease. Miss Cherry would be proud of me.

The doctor taps a pencil on the file folder lying open on the desk before him. "Yes, Mr. Parker, strokes are generally associated with the aged, but there are many different causes of stroke. In your aunt's case…"

I had told him I was Miss Cherry's nephew and only living relative—a lie, but not too far from the truth.

"…we believe the weakness in the blood vessel in her brain was due to a congenital defect. Her hypertension no doubt also contributed to the stroke."

The doctor's bearing is forthright and businesslike, which I appreciate. At the same time I am a little put off by the clinical detachment in his tone. After all, we are discussing the condition of Miss Cherry, someone I love, not a damaged car that has been towed in for repair.

"I didn't know she had high blood pressure."

"Nor did she, apparently. That's the terrible thing about high blood pressure. Often there are no symptoms."

My mind drifts momentarily. I am angry that something like this should happen to her, especially after she worked so hard to kick the booze habit.

"It's been two weeks. What's your assessment of her long-term prognosis?"

Since the day of the stroke, I have spent every evening at her bedside. The entire right side of her body is paralyzed—leg, arm, even her facial muscles. Her once beautiful face now lists to one side in a dour snarl that seems to be getting worse. She cannot speak, though it is clear she can still hear and to some extent understand.

We have worked out a rudimentary way to communicate. With considerable effort, she is able to answer simple questions with yes or no responses by extending one or two fingers on her left hand. I have to keep my chatter very simple, almost childlike phrasing, or she doesn't seem to comprehend. It upsets me that she isn't improving. I am very discouraged.

"It's difficult to know with any certainty how any stroke patient will recover. Statistically speaking, we know that some patients will recover some, if not all, lost motor skills. Speech can also return to normal. I believe your aunt's condition is stable and that she will survive this terrible ordeal. As for her medical treatment and outlook for recovery, we'll just have to wait and see. Time will tell."

I listen carefully, doing my best to understand and accept what has happened to Miss Cherry. But I can't help conceding that the bottom line is clear: Miss Cherry might not recover from the stroke. She might be stuck in a semi-vegetative quagmire for as long as she lives.

I evidently appear as stoic as a stroke patient myself, because after some indeterminate period of time the doctor escorts me out of his office and back to Miss Cherry's room.

"It's good that you're spending so much time with her. I'm a strong believer in fostering the will to recover. Sometimes I think we practitioners of modern medicine have barely scratched the surface of the science of healing."

"That's not very encouraging."

"Ah, but the brain is an amazing organ. We should never underestimate it. Keep talking to her, Mr. Parker. I know it does her a lot of good."

The doctor pats me on the shoulder and leaves the room.

I return to the familiar chair next to Miss Cherry's bed and sit down. She is asleep. I carefully lift her delicate hand into mine. She looks pale and her hand feels cool, lifeless—frail as a baby bird fallen from its nest. Clear plastic tubing disappears into both nostrils giving her enriched oxygen to breathe. Saliva tends to pool at the unnatural, down-turned corner of her mouth, which I dab occasionally with a tissue. I dote over her for hours at a time.

Her once lovely face, contorted to one side as though some silent hurricane force wind tugs at the flesh covering her skull, still is beautiful to my adoring eyes. To me she remains as enchanting as she was the day she appeared at Ruby Place and surprised Luke and me with unexpected treasures. I still envision her as that beautiful angel standing beside Queenie, bathed in a shaft of afternoon sun. And though I know I can never go back, my mind allows time to fold back on itself.

For brief merciful moments I am that little boy again, securely embosomed by a kind and beautiful angel. I stroke the back of her hand as I recall the silly anxious heart of that naive bashful kid. I remember exactly the butterfly feelings as I hesitated, gazing from the front porch that day long ago. The fool of April spun like virgin wool yarn around a spool of adolescent fantasy. An ocean of water has passed under the bridge since then.

The bridge!

My breath catches. I haven't thought about the bridge, in what, maybe five years? I stop rubbing Miss Cherry's hand and just hold it for a little while. I shake my head when I think about how close I had come to jumping to my death. I shudder as a picture of me on the bridge looking down into the lonely mist flashes through my mind.

I remember how Mac whimpered when I slid the bedroom window shut and began my morbid march in the dark. I think about all of the stuff I would have missed—mostly bad stuff, but a lot of good stuff, too. Luke and I enjoyed our share of fun, and certainly there is wonderful Melissa and my adorable daughter, Kate. Yes, there is a lot of good. I hold some of it in my hand right now. I look at Miss Cherry lying here helpless and vulnerable, as much so as I had been way back then. *Please help her, God.*

Tears well up again as I think about how she came along as a salving force, nursing me along with her personality, her attention, her caring. I was wreckage in need of salvage, and she was a vital part of the team that collected my scattered pieces from along the shoreline of my disastrous life. She and the Sergeant, working in tandem, had quickened the rebonding of my broken pieces.

Man, what a day we had at Dodger Stadium. That was far and

away the best day of my entire childhood. Mental snapshots of that awesome experience fill multiple catalogues in my head. I smile, remembering when she reentered my world to help me break with my pathetic reliance on the poison in the bottle.

Miss Cherry was my reformation. Deeply committed to her own quest for redemption, she worked diligently to share her passion with me. Like Rodney and Esther, Miss Cherry was sent by God to reveal Himself to me. Without her taking an interest as she did, I would have always thought of myself as the murderer kid who never got caught, never was punished, and never did his time in the reformatory where he belonged. In the disturbing quiet of the hospital room, I run it through my mind again. *I killed a human being. There was no arrest, no confession, no punishment, and no forgiveness.*

How can that be?

Perhaps that's why I worked so hard to punish myself. How unmerciful I was in my masochistic campaign of self-torture, a relentless psychological blooding intended to purge the guilt that could never quite be eliminated. It seemed that no matter what I did to myself, I could not repay my debt. The man I killed remained dead forever, a fact from which I could not escape.

It was a miracle when Miss Cherry reentered my life. The way she bolstered my fading spirit came with such miraculous timing it must have been marked by God's own mysterious schedule. She understood my pain, without, I believe, understanding its real cause. Seeing her here before me as helpless as I had been not long ago, it saddens me to think I may never be able to tell her the whole truth. I owe Miss Cherry my very life, and now I may never get the chance to repay her.

I wish I could perform a miracle for her. I wish I could lay my hands on her and make her well.

The doctor's advice echoes through my mind. *"Keep talking to her, Mr. Parker. I know it does her a lot of good."*

But can she understand me? Can she really understand me? A new sense of regret begins to seep in. Unconsciously, I fondle the keys in my pocket, my fingers toying with the silver ball bearing which now hangs from my key ring on a loop of its own.

Subliminal impulses travel up my arm and blow in my ear— the voice of a demon perched on my shoulder. *Maybe Miss Cherry's stroke is part of your punishment?* It is an old familiar voice.

"Please, God, please stay with me."

I shake off the demon. These ridiculous thoughts are nothing more than the leftover ruminations of a once desperate man. As always, the ball bearing offers no helpful advice. Its signals, if there really are any signals, are only in my mind. And they are always questions, or painful reminders, never any answers—the demon's tactics for a slow, punishing defeat.

But my frustrated demon dies hard. At the far edge of my spiritual clearing, from a thicket of thorny brambles where snakes slither and hiss, he calls out to me one last time. *Where is the Sergeant now? Would he come to Miss Cherry if he knew of her plight? Would she want him to come? Are you afraid to try to find him?*

"It won't work anymore, demon. I have God on my side."

I dab Miss Cherry's mouth with the tissue. I watch her lying here, so frail, so defenseless, so much in need. I will no longer cower before demons—Miss Cherry needs me. I must be patient. I must endure.

Then, with the innocence of that little boy of so long ago, now a man, but perhaps still just as innocent, I wonder what Duke Snider would do. For one thing, he would have gotten rid of that cursed silver ball bearing a long, long time ago. I think about that one for a while.

Sitting next to Miss Cherry and holding her hand, I think about calling Luke just to hear his voice and maybe try to make him laugh. He is prematurely balding now and wide open for mockingbird jokes. The thought makes me smile.

I do not yet fully understand about the strength-giving power of prayer. But I do have faith. *Stay with me, God. Speak to me about patience. Please give me a sign. I need You.*

From far away in the back of my memory I hear Luke's voice.

"Be patient. Duke Snider waits for his pitch, you know."

I realize the TV is on in Miss Cherry's room. I look up. On the news is my old hero Duke Snider. After patiently waiting fifteen years for his pitch, he's being inducted into the Baseball Hall of Fame at Cooperstown, New York. I close my eyes. *Thank You, God.*

fourteen

The years have brought a deeper mellowing. Without a conscious awareness of it happening, I began to accept the things that I cannot change. At first, I abstractly gleaned the concept from the Serenity Prayer, an important part of the AA tradition, but with the passing of time I have reached a greater understanding. Ever so gradually, I am accepting the unsolved riddle of my Chinese puzzle youth. If part of my past is to be shrouded in mystery, so be it.

After an arduous battle with my own ego, I chose to exercise my free will and surrender it all to God. The bad dreams are still with me, though much less frequent and much less disturbing. Brooking the nightmares of darkness no longer entails sleep deprivation. Hallelujah!

At the age of thirty-eight, I find the road is becoming smoother, though seemingly faster, and I have much for which to be thankful. My marriage to Melissa, who is sweet and beautiful as ever, is more than any man deserves. Luke and I are about to celebrate five years in partnership as proud owners of a thriving travel agency, and with thanks for God's grace, I am in my twelfth year of sobriety.

My daughter, Kate, a beauty to rival her mother, has just turned sixteen. Kate is excited about starting her junior year in high school. She carries a 4.0 grade point average, and confident thoughts of college scholarships glimmer in her beautiful blue eyes. She has my eyes and her mother's hair. She looks like a sixteen-year-old version of the actress Connie Sellecca. And although the brain damage left Miss Cherry permanently disabled and relegated to live out her remaining years in a rest home, she survived her stroke and is doing well. Indeed, I have much for which to be thankful.

I am lounging on the back patio of our new Upper Bradbury home enjoying the blessings of the summer morning sun as it rides the ridgeline of the steadfast San Gabriel Mountains. Early shadows lean toward the Pacific marking a steady crawl east toward day's end. My first cup of steaming black coffee warms my insides as I scan a printout of the prior week's bookings. Luke and I are promoting an Australian vacation package, and sales are brisk thanks to Paul Hogan and *Crocodile Dundee*.

As often happens, the coffee stimulates welcome flashes of Rodney Bernanos. *Cackle!* I hear him laugh, and I quickly skirt around the memory of his heart attack and give some thought to that little puppy—Kirk. What ever became of him? Did he grow up to be the noble protector of a kind and loving owner? I hope so.

Kate opens the kitchen slider and strolls across the patio to refill my cup. My nostalgic interlude evaporates when she purposefully clears her throat to get my attention. "Daddy, can I use the Chevy this afternoon? Christina and I want to rent a video, probably that Sally Field movie *Places in the Heart*, and watch it over at her house."

I look up from my printouts into my daughter's beautiful eyes, and I am struck once again by how much I have to be thankful for. "Thanks for the refill, honey."

She leans against the recliner I cozily occupy, bumping it softly with her hip to tease me as I raise the hot, laden cup to my lips. "I'm being extra nice so you'll let me use the car, Daddy."

The ink on Kate's new driver's license is still wet, and walking has suddenly gone out of style. My free hand sneaks up and tickles her behind her bare knee. "Creepy mouse." I recite a piece of the tickle song she loved so much when she was a little girl.

"Careful, Daddy." She giggles and backs away, the coffee in the pot sloshing but steady in her hand. She smiles as she always does whenever I give her some attention.

Kate's smile is just like her mom's, and therefore just like Miss Cherry's before her stroke took it away. Those three heavenly smiles, gifts from the Almighty, are the sustaining blessings in my life.

The sun backlights Kate's raven hair, the natural violet highlights shimmering iridescently—the wonder of genetics on display. "Did I ever tell you how pretty you are?"

Her smile takes on an added glow. "About ten times a day, but I'll creepy mouse you unless, of course, you say I can use the car."

Kate's mother also contributed a monster gene for relentless persistence. I smile.

"Uncle Luke and I are going to visit Miss Cherry this afternoon. I'm sure he won't mind picking me up. I'll call him in a few minutes just to make sure."

Kate takes that as a yes, her eyes glimmering accordingly. With step one successfully completed, she now hits me with step two. "I might want to spend the night at Christina's." She tries her best to make it sound like an incidental thought. "Her mother already said it was okay. And Mom says it's fine with her, as long as you approve." She giggles surreptitiously and softens her voice. "I think Mom wants to spend a cozy night at home alone with you."

Kate is very clever. I already feel for the poor young man who wins her heart. I give her a smile that tells her I am onto her, but that I admire the ruse. Inside me there is a smile bigger than the one I am showing Kate. Having memorized the lunar chart out to the year 2020, I know a big, fat, full one is due in tonight's sky.

"If you bring me one more refill in a little while, you can stay over at Christina's…" My voice drops down to the octave of doting sternness. "With one very important condition."

Her dangerously innocent eyes brighten. "A proviso, you mean?"

"Yes, a proviso, Miss College Bound. You have to stay put at Christina's. No running around in the car—Okay?"

"Okay, Daddy. I promise."

In the house the phone rings. With an abundance of enthusiasm, Kate scampers to answer it. At her age, a ringing telephone is a thing to behold. She reappears at the door a minute later. "Daddy, it's for you. It's Uncle Luke. I already asked him if he could pick you up, and he said 'fine.'"

She is an opportunist, just like her mom.

"Okay, sweetie, please tell him I'll be right there."

A hawk hovering high above the patio appears not to be moving, in total command of the thermal riding up the pocked barren slope that ascends sharply from our rear property line. He is looking for a meal, a mouse maybe, or perhaps a little red-headed boy. As I get up and head into the safe cover of the house, I am glad not to be a creepy mouse with red hair.

Kate eagerly hands me the phone. I give her a lightning fast tickle, making her squeal and squirm away.

"Hello."

"Yes, hello. Is this Mr. Wade Parker?"

"Speaking."

"Mr. Parker, this is Duke Snider calling."

Wouldn't that be something? "Gee, Mr. Snider, you sound more like Charlie Neal."

"Ha, ha. How would you know what Charlie Neal sounds like?"

"Actually, I don't know, Luke. Could be Charlie's pushing up daisies by now."

"Well, that's a pleasant thought."

"Sorry about that. I'm sure old Charlie is doing fine. I know

Duke Snider is doing well. I heard he's working on his autobiography. It's supposed to be published sometime next year."

"Oh geez," Luke moans. "The way you've lugged around that bat he gave you for the past twenty-five years, you better buy a bunch of copies. Books aren't as durable as bats, you know."

"I've already put in an advance order for a dozen copies." I listen to Luke groan again. "Hey, come on, Red. If it wasn't for Duke Snider, I probably wouldn't be here talking to you now."

Luke laughs. "Yeah, and if it wasn't for Duke Snider, Buster wouldn't have had to replace all of those windows, either."

"Aw, heck, those windows were old anyway."

"Yeah, right. Old glass, broken or not, needs to be replaced. So tell me, who do you think is better...?"

"Drysdale."

Luke jives, "What are you gonna do, ya big donkey, throw me in the pond again?"

Luke often jokes about the negative highlights of our past, but even the slightest reference to Three Ponds can still give me a chill, possibly even ruin my day.

"So, little brother, I understand your niece conned you into picking me up this afternoon."

"Sure. No problem. Trish won't need the van; she's going to the mall with the new gal from across the street, the one who came to church with us last Sunday. Remember, she's the one I was telling you about the other day, the gal who put all the bird feeders in her yard.

"Geez, I felt like going over there and laying my fear of mockingbirds complex on her, but Trish wouldn't let me. Oh, and get this. Her seven-year-old son is named Jake. Their last name is not Blume though, it's Kimball. Of course she calls him Jakey."

"What color is his hair?"

He laughs. "I knew you'd ask. Blonder than yours, but the name Jakey and the obsession with birds is kind of a blast from the past, ain't it?"

"Yeah—kind of." I am annoyed that I still can't touch on such things with the lighthearted zeal that Luke can.

"Man, how I love a good blast from the past."

"A good blast, yes. Luke, let's get serious for a minute. I'm glad you're going with me today. Miss Cherry called me twice to remind me to be sure I brought you with me. I don't know why today is so important, but it evidently means a lot to her that we're both coming. She's been asking why you haven't been to see her in a while. I know you don't feel as close to her as I do, but it really means more to her to see you than you think. It's kind of like the Smothers Brothers. I think she always liked you best."

"Well, of course."

"No, really, Luke. You were only six years old that first night on Billy Goat Hill. She's never forgotten that. If she only knew you were actually much tougher than me, even then, maybe she would have liked me best."

"You're full of it, Wade."

"Always have been."

"I'll pick you up at three-thirty, big brother."

"Thanks. I'll be ready. See ya."

"Wait a second, Wade!"

He catches me just before I hang up the phone. I put the receiver back to my ear. "Yes, Mr. Snider?"

"Ha, ha. Listen, I've got a crazy question for you."

"All of your questions are crazy, Luke."

"Well then, here's another one. How long do you think Mac would have lived, I mean, you know, if he hadn't got killed?"

He is famous for his off-the-wall questions, but this one catches me completely off guard. "I guess fifteen, maybe twenty years at the most. Why?" I flash on a picture of Mac climbing all over me as I wake up outside the mouth of Cavendish Caverns.

Softly, Luke says, "I miss that darn dog sometimes."

My heart quavers in-between beats. Hearing him say it just that way pulls at something deep in my buried core, choking me up. My eyes turn glassy, and I have to take a moment and clear my throat. "Yeah, I think about him sometimes, too. I know he probably saved Lucinda's life, but, well, as terrible as it sounds, for a long time I wished that he'd come with us to Billy Goat Hill that last night."

"Yeah, I know what you mean. Well, the reason I mention Mac is because Trish and I have been thinking about getting a dog. We went to the Glendale Animal Shelter yesterday to look around. There's a dog there that could pass for Mac, if she was a male and didn't have any spots, that is."

I wonder if…no, it can't be. I smile to myself and don't say it. "Luke, I have the strangest feeling that you should go back to the pound and get that dog."

"Really? That's what Trish says."

"Yeah. Definitely."

"I think you're right. There was something special about her."

"Can I suggest a name?"

"Sure."

"How about—Antoinette? You could call her Andi or Toni, for short."

"Yeah, Antoinette. That's what I was thinking."

He does remember. I am pleased.

"Wade?"

"Yeah, Red?"

"I'm glad you're my big brother. I love you. See you around three-thirty."

He hangs up before I can respond. *I love you, too, Luke.*

Kate comes in from the patio carrying the coffeepot. "I warmed your coffee for you, Daddy." She notices the moisture in my eyes. "What's the matter? Did Uncle Luke tell you another one of his funny stories?"

"Yes he did, but I think I just got something in my eyes, honey."

"Yeah," she says beginning to tear up. "I have that problem, too. I must get it from you." Kate puts her face to my chest and gives me a hug worth millions.

Across the room, Melissa watches with great satisfaction.

One of the many reasons the Parker Travel Agency is a success is Luke's willingness to work on Saturdays. The office is in Covina, I live in Bradbury, and Luke lives in Glendale, not far from where Rodney Bernanos lived all those years ago. Lorrie, our senior travel agent, and another important reason for our success, agrees to cover things so Luke can leave early to pick me up by three-thirty. Bradbury is roughly halfway between the office and Rosewood Manor of Altadena, the retirement home where Miss Cherry has been living since being released from the hospital after her stroke. I know the place well.

Before we even make it down the hill from my house to the 210 Freeway, we have a brotherly spat over what music we are going to listen to on the way. I have become a fan of contemporary Christian music with a strong preference for Phil Keaggy's recordings. Luke has yet to discover the incredible new talent emerging in contemporary Christian rock. Lately he's developed a taste for what I regard as ethereal jazz.

I smuggled a Phil Keaggy tape into the van, but he catches me before I can slip it into the player. "Uh, uh. I'm providing the transportation so we listen to *my* music. Here—" he hands me a cassette—"put this in. You might even like it."

"I doubt it."

"Humor me."

I wanly insert the tape in the slot and take a look at the cassette jacket. Andreas Vollenweider, *Down to the Moon.*

"What in the heck is a Vollenweider?"

"Just listen, you big donkey."

The music starts and Luke turns up the volume. The van fills with hip harp music. I give it a fair listen for a few minutes and decide it can't hurt me.

When the first song finishes, Luke asks, "What do you think? Kind of nice, isn't it? Light, unobtrusive, soothing."

"Probably what they play in elevators in heaven."

"Elevators in heaven? I haven't thought about that. I'll take that as a compliment, though." He grins and changes lanes to let some-one in more of a hurry than us pass by.

If my options ever narrow down to living in a rest home, I'd pick Rosewood Manor. At fifteen hundred dollars a month, it is a great deal. Fifty-two very fortunate seniors live in idyllic surroundings under the care of a well-trained and compassionate staff. Family and friends are encouraged to come at mealtimes and are welcome to eat with the residents at no charge. The food is varied and quite good. After a couple of years, I found myself arranging my visits with Miss Cherry to straddle the lunch or dinner hour.

The cook is Marge McZilkie. She likes me and makes a point of saving me servings of her specialty: a raspberry cobbler so good that thoughts of visiting Miss Cherry release a Pavlovian dribble. Miss Cherry and Marge have been at Rosewood Manor longer than any of the current employees and residents. They are the same age and have become best of friends. I can count on Marge to let me know if Miss Cherry is having any problems or if she needs any-thing. Marge knows that Luke and I pay the resident fees in excess of that covered by Miss Cherry's monthly social security payment.

Marge called me the day before to make sure I was coming. She is concerned about Miss Cherry's spirits of late. She believes Miss Cherry is feeling down about something, just what, she really couldn't say for sure. All she knows is, Miss Cherry received a letter recently. The letter came by special courier, which gives me some concern. Marge suspects something in the letter upset Miss Cherry.

I spot Miss Cherry sitting in her wheelchair in the sunny west garden of the rest home. Parked next to her is a tiny black woman who appears to be no less than a hundred years young. They look like salt and pepper figurines, frail breakables cushioned by profuse clusters of jasmine and bougainvillea.

From the distance, I can tell they are engaged in serious dis-course, the old lady seemingly dispensing some worldly advice. Miss Cherry is nodding, one half of her face expressing agreement, or perhaps acceptance, the other half incapable of concurring. She holds her shriveled hand in her good one.

Luke and I make our way across an expansive lawn as green and well-groomed as the grass of Dodger Stadium. As we approach the two women, Miss Cherry notices us and waves. I note it is not her usual happy wave. The tiny black woman stiffly turns her head to see.

I smile and give Miss Cherry my mainstay greeting. "How's my best girl today?" I kiss her cheek and give her a soft hug.

"I'm fine, sweetie." She dabs at the side of her mouth with an embroidered handkerchief, her Satchmo, as she has come to call it in honor of Louis Armstrong's trademark hankie.

"Hi, Miss Cherry." Luke bends down and hugs and kisses her.

"Hello, honey. I'm so glad you came today."

I doubt Luke notices—he's spent one tenth the amount of time with her that I have—but a trace of trepidation in Miss Cherry's voice gives me some concern.

"Boys, this is Emma. She just moved in last week, and we're already good friends."

The old woman smiles and offers her hand to me. I take it, carefully, afraid I might break something. "It's very nice to meet you, ma'am. Any friend of Miss Cherry's is a friend of ours."

"Praise God—well, isn't that special. I feel like I already know you boys." Emma's high-pitched voice is not much more than a parched whisper. "Miss Cherry done told me all 'bout her two best heroes. I'm real proud to mee'cha both. Ya'll go 'head now and have yo'selves a nice visit. Maybe I'll see ya'll at supper."

"Yes, ma'am."

She winks at me. "I hear we're havin' raspberry cobbler for dee-zert." With that she pushes a lever on her wheelchair, and an electric hum carries her off across the lawn.

Luke chuckles. "Emma's got your number, bro."

Miss Cherry rides her wheelchair over to a nearby bench where Luke and I can sit. She looks drained and her eyes are a bit puffy, as though she may have been crying recently. I glance at Luke and see a concurring expression of gravity on his face. Luke and I sit next to each other on the bench while she maneuvers the wheelchair around to face us. I feel strange, as though we're about to be scolded for some wrong we have done, or told that we have to move and change our last name. I don't say anything. It's clear this is to be her show.

It may be my imagination, but I could swear Luke is trying to squeeze himself behind me, like he did that night on Billy Goat Hill when we were awakened by the gang of policemen-bikers.

With effort, Miss Cherry clears her throat and dabs her mouth. Her friend Emma now gone, she makes no effort to mask the pain in her eyes. She takes a deep breath and looks skyward for a moment. "I love you boys more than anything in this world. I hope you know I would never want to do anything to hurt you."

This can't be good.

"We love you, too, Miss Cherry," Luke says.

I nod in agreement, feeling concerned, uncertain.

"I just hope—" she presses her handkerchief at the corner of one eye, but a tear runs down her other cheek—"after what I have to tell you, you'll still love me enough to forgive me."

I look deep into her troubled eyes. I've never seen so much pain. "Why, don't be silly; we'll always love you. What is it? What's wrong?"

She holds my gaze for a long moment and then looks away across to the far side of the lawn toward the spot Emma has just reached. Her forlorn countenance seems to implore the old woman to come back and rescue her. I get up from the bench and kneel beside her wheelchair.

"I am so sorry, boys."

"Whatever it is, there isn't anything that would cause me to stop loving you. I know Luke feels the same. I owe you my life. If you hadn't come and bailed me out of jail that time, I hate to think where I might be now. I doubt I'd be sober. Why, I'd probably be dead. You deserve most of the credit for the happiness in my life."

Her handkerchief falls to the ground as she reaches up and

touches my face. "You were such sweet little boys. I didn't mean for any of it to happen. I should have had the courage to stop it. But I couldn't. I didn't. I wasn't strong enough. I'm so sorry. I'm so very sorry."

"Sorry for what? You don't have anything to be sorry for."

"Yes, I do."

She is weeping now. I put my arms around her and look to Luke for any sign of comprehension, but he just shrugs. He's as baffled as I am. The three of us do nothing until the emotional impasse is finally broken by Miss Cherry.

She exhales a heavy sigh and struggles with her thoughts before finally caving in to her painful purpose. "Lyle Cavendish is dying of cancer, and he wants you both to come and see him in the hospital."

With forced calm, I slowly raise myself upright until, without realizing it, I am looming over her. Suddenly she looks as old as Emma and as vulnerable as young boys prowling the darkness of Billy Goat Hill. "You mean—the Sergeant?"

She tilts her head and looks up at me, shame distorting her face beyond its normal contortion. "Yes, Wade. I've remained in contact with him all these years. I'm sorry I lied to you."

My stomach teetering with restiveness, I place my arms across my midsection. "Why? Why would you keep such a secret?"

She knows how I have longed for years to see him again, how the rawness in my heart has never been able to heal. How could she have lied to me about something as important as all that? Luke gets up from the bench and puts his hand on my shoulder.

She is crying hard now, trembling. She gasps as she speaks. "Mostly I lied to you because I promised Lyle I wouldn't tell. There's much more to it, though. God forgive me!"

I touch her arm. "Calm down now, please don't make yourself sick over this. Just tell us what's going on."

"Parts of the story, the reasons, I don't even know the whole of it."

She tries to reach down to pick up the handkerchief but can't quite reach it. Luke quickly picks it up for her. She dabs her eyes and nose trying to regain some composure.

"I don't understand," Luke says.

Somehow she manages a little smile, half of a smile. "I know you don't, honey."

"Just tell us—what's wrong?" I say.

"We all were part, are part, of something bad—something very, very sad. You boys were, of course, completely innocent. You did nothing wrong. I wish I could say the same for myself, but I guess God found a way to punish me for what I did."

Starting to break down, dizzy, clammy, I hold back against a giant rush of confused emotion. I strain hard and forcibly calm myself. "What do you mean…God found a way to punish you?"

"Look at me, Wade."

"I don't believe God works that way. Your stroke was caused by high blood pressure and a weak artery in your brain, weak from birth, according to your doctor. You know that. I don't think God planned to punish you for something before you were even born."

She looks up at me, her eyes red and weary, pleading for something, what I can't discern. "I deserve what happened to me."

"What's this all about, Miss Cherry?"

"You have to go see Lyle. Please promise me you'll go see him."

"Okay."

"He has to tell you. He needs to tell you, before he dies. Then, if you still want to, come back and we'll talk more."

It is all I can do to keep from screaming out. Luke knows I'm near the brink, and he is patting my back now, desperate in his own way, fearing the situation could easily disintegrate to the level of regret. I am nauseous, my shirt has soaked through, and far back within the forbidden recesses of my mind subliminal suspicions undulate like voracious maggots awakening from a long forced hibernation.

All those years of hard-earned progress, checked fears, subjugated cravings, and buried nightmares come crashing back, demanding reprisal. It is not rational, but primal, the urge that washes over me. For the first time in years I feel a desperate need for a drink. Luke's reassuring hand suddenly feels more like the rabid monkey of addiction sinking its fangs deep into my shoulder.

"Is this about—Three Ponds?" I can't believe I said the words. Luke is shocked but stands firm, his arm now solidly bracing me up.

Her eyes fill with soul-crushing guilt, foreboding of repressed horror clambering to break free of long held silence. "Yes," she confesses in a whisper, "and much, much more."

Outwardly I appear at worst numb. But deep inside me a creepy mouse rides the back of the hawk, its razor sharp talons clawing, its jagged teeth gnawing, floating on a thermal of quivering viscera and quaking bone, my stalled heart laid bare for the feast.

From my pocketed keyring the ball bearing cries out mordantly, mocking me, taunting me, and drilling its message into a thousand holes in my perforated threadbare mind. *Know ye all men by these presents! Victims, perpetrators, accusers all are summoned forth to the judgment ball!*

Luke holds my arm tight as I slump to the ground. The assault on my stomach comes up in one violent contraction, raspberry red with the blood of a decades-old ulcer.

Miss Cherry screams and cries out, "Wade! I'm so sorry, Wade!"

God in heaven, please do not forsake me. I need You, Father! Help me!

fifteen

My Bible never leaves my side, yet I suffer immensely over the next couple of days. God is teaching me. He wants me to be still and listen for His voice. He wants me to trust Him.

We left Miss Cherry whimpering at the gate of her self-imposed drowsy purgatory, her doctor having been called to authorize a strong sedative. Marge McZilkie found me a bottle of Maalox, which I downed in four gulps. She also found the letter in Miss Cherry's closet, neatly folded, tucked in a box filled with keep-sakes, mostly pictures of Luke and me.

Prominent in the stack of snapshots was the photo the Sergeant had taken of Luke and me standing in front of Queenie all those years ago. A magenta lipstick kiss mark adorned the picture, a sadly conflicted woman's seal of authenticity. The picture made me smile for a moment.

Marge had been right about the letter. It was very upsetting…

Dear Cherry,

    I'm sorry it's been so long, and that I have only bad news

to give you. It's been a hard trip through this life, lots of regrets, but none about you. You were my best gal, the only woman I ever loved. I only wish I had listened to you more.

I was a good cop. So were you. I know now that I wasn't good enough. I know now how wrong I was. I know now…

The boys have a right to know, too. I'm at Saint Mary's Hospital in Long Beach…CANCER. Please ask them to come right away. I've had the doctors cut way back on the morphine so I can make some sense when the boys come. I can't hold out for long, though.

Except for seeing them, I've taken care of all my affairs. I've tried to set things right.

After I'm gone, my lawyer, Mr. Ronald Corsetti, will contact you.

I never stopped loving you,

Lyle

As always, Luke is philosophical, stronger than me. On the way to Long Beach, he does his best to mollify my fears, but he too is apprehensive. At one point he looks at me and we exchange nervous grins.

"We're a long way from Billy Goat Hill, aren't we, Wade?"

"Either light years or a week or two, I'm not sure. I'm glad we're doing this together."

"Trish wanted to come. I think she wanted to satisfy her curiosity about the Sergeant."

"So did Melissa. They've probably earned the right to come, the way they've both put up with our stories all these years. But I thought it should be just the two of us."

"I agree. Besides, this outing is too much of a walk into the unknown. Who knows where this is going to take us. We might be sailing right back into a black hole, never to be seen again."

I look at Luke and wonder just how prophetic he might turn out to be.

While riding along on the freeway, listening to harp music, it occurs to me how fortunate Luke and I are to be married to women we trust, that we can talk to. After getting Miss Cherry settled, we had both called our wives. It was what we needed when we were kids, a close trusting relationship with someone who loved us, someone we could talk to no matter what difficulties we encountered. Deprived of that essential thing, when confronted with a very serious problem, we floundered.

We are born into an imperfect world, that's for sure, but kids shouldn't have to deal with stuff like that by themselves. Calling our wives and telling them about the earthshaking news and hearing their compassionate voices—that is about as perfect as the world can get.

Such a wonderful calming thought. *I feel You near me. Thank You, God.*

Luke interrupts my reverie. "Do you think we should talk about it before we see the Sergeant?"

"Talk about what, that he's dying of cancer?"

"No, about what happened all those years ago. That's what he wants to talk about, isn't it?"

"I guess so."

"Wade—it was an accident."

A lump in my throat begins to swell. "Yes, but…"

"There is no *but* about it. It was as much my fault as it was yours. If I hadn't been such a wimp about the mockingbirds, things would have been a lot different, maybe worse, who knows?"

"That's not it. We should have told somebody. I should have told somebody."

"Who could you have told?"

"Lucinda, Pastor Bonner, Jake the barber, maybe?"

Luke pretends to spend a moment in deep thought. "Hmm…you know something. If you really get serious about it, there was only one person who would have truly understood, and might even have known what to do."

"Who?"

"*He, he, he…*Carl the baker, of course."

We laugh for the next ten miles. My little brother has done his duty.

But when we finally leave the freeway and the hospital comes in sight, my stomach begins to twitch. *I can't do this without You, God.*

I don't like hospitals. They make me uncomfortable—the peculiar smells, the maze of unfriendly hallways, not knowing quite how to behave when face-to-face with someone injured or ill. Only once did I enter a hospital for a positive reason, when my daughter, Kate, was born.

How unusual it is that I have never been hospitalized—no diseases, no surgeries, no broken bones. What are the odds? A broken heart and a guilty conscience, my pestilence, never brought me under the purview of modern medicine, or I would have spent most of my childhood in the hospital.

Now, summoned by a ghost from the infinite past, I am about to enter Saint Mary's Hospital in Long Beach. The irony is like a poorly told bad joke. *I know, I know. I am trying, God.*

Luke stands by me in the parking lot as I look up at the sterile hospital structure rising high above us. A man I once knew, the most important earthly man I ever knew, is dying inside this building, and for reasons I do not want to contemplate, he has petitioned me to appear at his deathbed. Nothing and everything fills me with apprehension as I try to brace against the emotional riptide swelling within me like a tsunami approaching landfall.

Entering the building, I am grateful to have Luke pacing alongside me, though his company only carries so much weight. Fear, my old companion, is trying to run me aground, and I feel about as far from my element as a sailor a thousand miles away from the sea. A bizarre, convoluted stream of antiquated images whirls like a dust devil in my head.

We are a solemn pair when a few minutes later we find ourselves standing outside the Sergeant's sixth floor room.

"Look at that." Luke points to the numbers above the door. The Sergeant is in room 6-060. We had lived at 6060 Ruby Place.

"Good sign or bad sign?"

"I don't know. It's kind of weird though, isn't it?"

"Before we go in, I think we should take a moment to pray."

"Good idea."

In the hall outside the Sergeant's hospital room, we bow our heads. "Father in heaven, You are the great Creator of the universe, and we believe all things are possible with You. We ask for Your guidance and protection as we come face-to-face with our old friend, the Sergeant. We ask for Your forgiveness for all of our wrongs, past and present. We ask that You bless the Sergeant in his time of illness. And most of all, Father, we pray that he be comforted in the knowledge that You are his Creator and Your Son Jesus came to the earth and lived among us, died for all of our sins, and rose from the grave to bring us the glorious gift of salvation. We ask that the Sergeant might know You and receive Your gift of salvation by accepting our Lord Jesus as his Savior. Please give us strength and wisdom as we visit our dear old friend. In Jesus' name we pray, amen."

"Amen."

I open my eyes, and a nurse down the hall smiles and nods at me.

I project far more confidence than I feel as together with Luke, I push the heavy hospital door open and step forward into the past.

I am not prepared for what I see—a mere ghost of a fading memory. To be here in his presence, under these circumstances, combines in a single moment the sum total of a lifetime of hope and fear. The mix of emotion is overwhelming.

A voice thick with cobwebs comes weakly from across the room. "I'm glad you came, boys."

The voice leaves no doubt that it's him, or, more accurately, what is left of him. Amplified by my memory, a trace of the sound of Scar still comes through. Staring at a skeleton, I realize his battle with cancer has wound down to the last salvo. A gaunt, yellow, translucent shell of the person I had once revered motions with a twitch of his sunken eyes for us to join him at his bedside. Two chairs have been purposefully positioned for the occasion. My heart pounds as we sit, Luke taking the chair closest to him.

Straight in front of me, a catheter bag hangs from a metal bed rung. It is half-full of urine tinged rust-brown with blood. Scabs that don't look like normal scabs dot his skin like the spots of a leprous leopard. His once thick jet-black hair is gone, except for two strange gray clumps above one ear. The ear looks dry and shriveled, as though it could fall off at any time. I doubt that he weighs a hundred pounds. I wonder if he'll even make it through the night.

His lips are dry and badly cracked, hard looking. They should be bleeding, but they aren't. They part like the bill of a bird when he speaks, his tongue dark and swollen. This is far more upsetting than I had anticipated.

"How is Cherry?"

"She's not doing very well, sir." I do not intend to be morose, but I am determined to make sure only the truth comes from my mouth. I have waited my entire life to tell this man the truth, and I must do my utmost to stay true to that purpose.

He nods, as if the negative report about Miss Cherry was expected. "I have no family. No children. My estate, including a sizeable amount of life insurance, is to be split between you boys and Miss Cherry." It is an abrupt start. He wants that much on the table right up front.

I begin to say, "No, I don't think that would be…" but he flips his hand dissuasively, the sudden movement obviously causing him pain.

"The money is yours to do with as you wish. Give it to charity if you like. No use for money where I'm going."

Where are you going, sir? "Why would you want us…?"

"It's what I want. I know you both have been subsidizing Cherry for quite some time. It's an expensive world we live in. The money is yours."

"Okay—sir."

He nods that it is done. "Luke, I'm dry, would you give me a little squirt?"

A squeeze bottle marked *Water* sits on the bed stand. Luke puts the plastic tip to the Sergeant's mouth and squeezes the bottle. A small amount of water trickles down the Sergeant's chin onto his pale green hospital gown. He nods a thank-you to Luke.

Mesmerized, I watch him.

He looks at me, and his jaundiced eyes seem to sparkle faintly. "We had a great time at Dodger Stadium that day, didn't we, boys?"

I smile. "Yes sir, we sure did." Luke echoes me. "I still have the bat, sir."

"I never could get you to stop calling me 'Sir,' could I?"

"No, sir." I smile again. "It's a matter of respect, I guess. I've always felt that way about you."

His failing, desiccated body appears incapable of producing tears, but his once powerful eyes begin to spill over. He looks away from me, thankfully, for I am very close to losing it. It is killing me to see my former hero in this condition. The love I have always felt for this man rises like a geyser, charging up from the deepest holds of long-imprisoned memory. My emotional balance faltering fast, I glance at Luke, hoping to borrow some of his strength to steady myself, but I see he is already straining under the weight of his own emotion.

The Sergeant gathers himself. "I wanted…I needed you boys to come because I want to apologize to you for the thing I did that I regret more than anything in my life."

I give Luke a confused look. This doesn't feel at all like what I had been expecting. Why would he need to apologize to us? I killed the man, not him. "Apologize, sir?"

"Yes—apologize. This will take a while, so please hear me out. I don't think I have enough left in me to go through it more than once."

I nod tenuously, uncomfortable. Luke plainly would like to leave if it were at all possible. The Sergeant motions for more water. Luke gives him some.

"First, I want you both to know I am very sorry, especially to you, Wade."

Sorry? I'm the one who is sorry. Out of habit from attending to Miss Cherry for so long, I take a tissue and stretch to dab the tears from his face, then catch myself and instead place the tissue in his hand. "Go ahead, sir."

"Please try to bear with me; this isn't going to be easy—for any of us." He clears his throat and looks at the ceiling for a moment.

"Okay."

"In the late 1950s, the Los Angeles Police Department went through a period of heightened paranoia about the increasing presence of east coast organized crime families in Southern California."

What on earth is he talking about? "Organized crime—you mean like the mafia?"

"Yes, the mafia. The O.C.I.U., a small, elite group of prima donna detectives, including Miss Cherry and me, were running too fast and too loose with our tactics. An even smaller group within the O.C.I.U. had begun to carry out covert actions, many of which were never revealed to the mayor or any other elected official, making them extralegal, if not illegal. Most of the cops were good cops doing what they believed to be the right thing."

He pauses to breathe and take another sip of water. I get the feeling he's been working on this speech for a long time. I catch Luke's eye, and he gives me an "I don't have a clue what he's talking about either" look.

"One cop in particular, Lieutenant Theodore Shunkman, took it upon himself to rid the city of all perceived scourges. Ted was a real piece of work. You guys might remember him from that night on Billy Goat Hill."

"I remember him very well," I say from an almost trancelike quarter.

"He tried to punch you that night," Luke says.

The Sergeant might have smiled, perhaps inside, but outside it's a wincing grimace, the cancer taking another bite of something still alive with nerves.

I try to scrounge for levity. "You were supposed to forget about that, Luke."

"I forgot to forget."

The Sergeant stares at us for a moment. "Lieutenant Shunkman was responsible for the murder of four reputed mobsters—all sent one after the other from Miami to set up a West Coast operation. Shunkman was sick, a cunning loose cannon with a conviction that he had been put on this earth to liquidate organized crime. He was assassinating these guys and making the murders look like they were done by a particular local gang of bikers whose death signature was a single bullet between the eyes. The gang was known to fiercely protect their turf, especially from any foreign competition. It took guts for the third and fourth explorers to take up the challenge."

He pauses again to breathe. Speaking is difficult labor, each word like pressing three hundred pounds of dead weight.

Something ticks in the back of my brain, the germination of a vague but very unpleasant thought. I shift in the chair, fidgeting, crossing my legs, then recrossing them. Luke seems fascinated with the story, like when he listened to the Sergeant recite the amazing saga of Jakey Blume.

"Shunkman's first two hits went like clockwork. He had the whole undercover unit crowing over the dumb goons killing each other off. Then he got a little overzealous and ran into some trouble on the third killing. And we caught him in the act of committing the fourth one."

"What trouble did he run into on the third one?" Luke asks.

The Sergeant looks directly at me. "He made the mistake of dumping the body in the wrong place."

Luke stiffens on the edge of his seat, suddenly agitated. "What? Wait a second. Where did he dump the body? You don't mean at Three Ponds?"

"Yes—at Three Ponds."

I nearly choke, feverish realization beading all over my face. Then instantly I get the whole picture.

Luke scrambles out of his chair, rage igniting his firecracker blood. "I don't believe it! You mean you let my brother suffer his whole life thinking *he* killed that man?"

I am up beside him. "Luke! It's okay. Take it easy." I grab him by the shoulders. "It's okay. Calm down."

I haven't seen him this angry since we were kids. I try to ease him back down in the chair, but he pushes me away. "What do you mean, it's okay? It's not okay. This poor excuse for a human being deserves to have cancer! You're a child abuser, for crying out loud!" A fire rages in Luke's eyes, his shock and anger fomenting, seething.

"Luke, stop!"

"The heck I'll stop. Do you have any idea what Wade has been through all these years? Do you? You're scum, Sergeant Cavendish! You hear me? *Scum!*"

A knock sounds at the door. A nurse, the one who smiled at me in the hallway, sheepishly steps into the room. "Just checking, is everything okay in here?"

The Sergeant waves her away.

"I'm sorry, ma'am. Just some understandable emotion is all. We're fine. Aren't we, Luke? We're fine, ma'am. Thank you for checking on us."

The nurse doesn't seem satisfied, but she quietly backs out of the room. She does not close the door all the way, though.

Luke wants to hit something. He takes a deep breath and jams his hands in his pockets. Disgusted, he steps away from the bed and stares out the window at nothing. The Sergeant is no longer fit to look at.

I walk over to the window and stand by Luke. My thought has exploded into a thousand urgent questions, all of which seem inconsequential when compared to the weight of the mystery that has suddenly been lifted from my shoulders. I am in shock, too, my mind racing at the speed of light, struggling to fathom a lifetime of crisscrossed meaning.

I close my eyes and open my heart to the Lord, and God gives me the right words to speak. "Thank you for telling me, sir. My life is already on the right track. Now it's even better."

"There's more to the story, Wade." His voice is now barely above a whisper. "I need to get it all out. I need to tell you everything."

I look at Luke and see his shoulders tighten, but he doesn't turn around. I leave him standing at the window to sort through his thoughts. I return to the bedside and sit where Luke had been, in the chair closest to the Sergeant.

I give him some more water, noting he looks paler, weaker, closer to death. "Go ahead, sir. It's okay—you can tell me everything."

The Sergeant closes his eyes as he speaks, conserving energy. "Shunkman evidently dumped the body at Three Ponds sometime shortly after sunrise, because he met me for breakfast; we were together the rest of the morning and into the afternoon working on paperwork at the Highland Park station. He left the police station in the late afternoon to get ready for a dinner party he and his girl-friend were to attend that evening.

"About fifteen minutes after he left, I got an anonymous phone tip that the body of Johnny "Bloody John" Giacometti could be found near the middle pond of the area unofficially known as Three Ponds."

The face of Bloody John glares at me. I tremble as a chill whip-saws down my spine. Luke comes back to the bed and sits, his anger left to cool somewhere outside the window. I give the Sergeant more water.

"Although I was somewhat skeptical of the phone call, I decided to go out to Three Ponds and take a look by myself. As I made the turn from York Boulevard onto San Pasqual Avenue, I saw Luke, barefoot and hatless, running for home like he was late for dinner. A few minutes later, I found his Dodgers cap floating in the water in the lower pond. I got worried when I heard Mac yowling farther up the draw.

"When I got up to the middle pond…" He opens his eyes and looks at me. "I saw the ball bearings. . ." My heart jumps. ". . .in the mud spelling out the word *Mississippi*."

The ball bearing that has haunted me all my life is in my pocket and now back within two feet of the man who dropped it into my sweaty, trembling, guilty hand. I have never been able to let go of it.

"One ball bearing…was missing from the second *s*," I say, the memory stark, vivid.

Cadaverous eyes, vestiges of his burned-out soul, burrow into me. "Yes—from the second *s*."

Luke huffs and squirms in his chair. "All these years and you…never mind."

The Sergeant's gaze flares then dulls as he works to focus his eyes on Luke. "I followed the sound of Mac and came upon Wade lying unconscious next to Shunkman's third victim. Mac wouldn't let me near your brother at first."

Luke clenches his fists, his eyes watering at the mention of Mac. "Our dog was the best dog that ever lived. I always…" He chokes to a stop, his control poisoned by a flood of emotion. I put my hand on his shoulder and feel him trembling. He sighs deeply and hangs his head down. "I didn't mean to run away. I was scared. I didn't know what to do." He looks up at me, his eyes pooled with long repressed regret.

"I know, I know. It's okay."

His mouth tightens in a pained smile. "That darn Mac didn't run though, did he?"

I pat his shoulder. "No, he didn't, Luke."

The Sergeant, listless, degrading rapidly, focuses on me again. "You had a nasty bump on your forehead, but you were breathing normally. It didn't take long to figure out what had happened—the slingshot floating in the pond, feathers strewn about, the hole in the cardboard, and victim number three leaning back against the rock with a shiny musket ball jammed between his eyes."

My stomach tightens. *Give me strength, Father.*

The Sergeant closes his eyes again. Sorrowfully, he says, "I panicked just like you, Luke. I didn't do the right thing. I didn't think it out."

Speckles of sympathy appear in Luke's eyes, his face drained, haggard.

"I woke up out by San Pasqual Avenue with Mac standing over me, sir. How did I get there?"

"I carried you."

"But why? Why did you leave me there like that?"

He opens his eyes wide and looks at me. The question causes him to rally slightly, fed by a ripple of new energy. "After the murder of the first bad guy from Miami, they sent a replacement, a lowlife by the name of Carlo Puzzi. I had some nagging doubts about Shunkman when he supposedly "discovered" Puzzi's body over by Franklin High School and called it in himself.

"The whole thing was too neat. He overplayed it, crowing on and on about how the stupid gangsters were killing each other off. But I had only a hunch, and no proof to back it up. And part of me felt like if it was Shunkman doing the killings, he was doing us all a big favor. Those were rotten guys he was bumping off."

"Murder is murder, sir."

"Yes it is."

"But why leave me lying in the dirt with a knot on my head?"

"Like I said, I panicked. I just knew at that moment I had to get you away from the crime scene and make it look as if you guys had never been at Three Ponds."

"Why?"

"I wanted to contain and cover up Shunkman's madness, and I couldn't have two young boys caught up in the middle of it all. I had it in my head that I needed to protect the O.C.I.U. You see, there had been rumors that Chief Parker was thinking about shutting the unit down. I didn't want that to happen.

"It was politics pure and simple. We were engaged in some very important work, national security stuff, and some internal matters involving corruption within the Los Angeles Police Department. A scandal involving an O.C.I.U. officer committing vigilante-style murders would have devastated our operation for sure."

"I still don't get the leaving me lying there part. And you talk as if you already knew it was Lieutenant Shunkman. How could you have been so sure it was him?"

"It was him. When I received the phone call at the Highland Park station tipping me to the body at Three Ponds, some things pointed to Shunkman being the caller. The call came from outside to the Highland Park station, through the switchboard, not to the O.C.I.U. at headquarters downtown, where I would normally be reached at that time. I was pretty sure only three people knew I was at the Highland Park station that afternoon—Cherry, Rodney Bernanos, and Shunkman.

"The caller asked for me by name. He also made a mistake. He referred to Johnny Giacometti as "mutt number three," a label a few of us put on Giacometti when he first arrived from Miami. I had spent time in Miami working under cover and knew a little about Giacometti before his bosses picked him for the assignment."

"I remember how tan you were. Your note with the Dodgers tickets mentioned Miami, and I thought that was strange."

His eyelids drift down. "I shouldn't have written that. It was a stupid slip."

Luke has been listening quietly. Now he speaks up. "There's a lot you shouldn't have done, Sergeant."

"And a lot I should have done, too. But there's more to this story, and I want you both to know all of it." He raises his hand to his mouth and coughs.

I cringe when he trails his fingers on the bed sheet leaving a streak of bright red blood. "Do you need the nurse, sir?"

"No. You were out cold, and I couldn't rouse you by the pond. I had to get you away from there, so I carried you out to the road and made sure you were still breathing. I ordered Mac to stay with you. Then I went to a phone booth and made an anonymous call to the police station reporting that someone was lying by the road.

"I quickly drove back to where I left you, arriving just as you and Mac came up onto the road. You looked pretty good, from a distance anyway. I watched you start walking up San Pasqual Road and saw the patrol officer stop and talk to you."

A full-color memory plays in my head as he slowly recounts the most horrifying day of my life. "Yes?"

"Then I called Cherry."

"Are you telling me Miss Cherry knew about the whole thing?"

"No, Wade. Absolutely not. She didn't know about you boys, about you discovering Giacometti's body until much later.

"Luke's Dodgers hat, two pairs of tennis shoes, a slingshot, and the ball bearings were in my car under the seat before she arrived at Three Ponds." He coughs again, grimacing, and wipes more blood on the sheet.

"Let me get the nurse."

"No!"

"Let him talk, Wade."

He looks straight into my eyes. "I got rid of the cardboard, too, and I dug the ball bearing out of Giacometti's head."

Shuddering, I grip the chair arm. In my pocket the ball bearing squirms. "So, Miss Cherry didn't know about us encountering the dead man?"

"No, not then. Cherry and I removed and disposed of the body and set out to trap Shunkman. But even at that point I had badly underestimated just how crazy and dangerous he really was."

"I think you all were crazy," Luke says.

Again, the Sergeant nods. "Cherry and I were in love. But, both of you guys, please believe me—I swear she had nothing what-soever to do with the early decisions. She trusted me as her senior officer in the chain of command. She was an excellent cop, doing her job, following orders.

"Cherry and I thought we had figured out how to nail Shunkman. We took our story to our captain, and he went to the chief. A plan to trap him was quickly put in place."

"So the cover-up went all the way up to the chief of police?"

"I believe so, but I still hadn't told anyone about you boys find-ing the body. I was hoping you were scared enough to keep your mouths shut."

Luke expels a mouth full of invective. "We never told a soul, officer."

"I know you didn't, Luke."

Luke rolls his eyes and shakes his head in disgust.

I don't want to know the answer but can't keep myself from asking. "What would have happened if we had told?"

Luke is heating up again. He slams his hands on his knees. "He had it all figured out, big brother." He glares at the Sergeant. "Didn't you, cop? No one would have believed us, would they? Just two little jerks making up a wild story. Two stupid little fatherless latchkey lunatics starved for attention, isn't that about the way you figured it—Sergeant?"

The Sergeant's eyes flutter weakly. "That's exactly the way I figured it. You are absolutely right."

"So you just left us swinging on our own rope then, didn't you?"

I feel sorry for Luke and wish there was some way to move beyond all this. "You said the whole story, right, sir?" The Sergeant nods. Then it spills out, the one thing I have never told Luke. "I was sure I killed that man. So sure, I almost committed suicide over it."

Luke is aghast. "What!"

"That morning I found you on the bridge by the Rose Bowl?"

"Yes, sir."

New tears spill down the Sergeant's sallow cheeks. "That's when I realized what a terrible mistake I'd made. But I couldn't tell you anything. It was too late to turn back things that had already been put in motion."

"You almost jumped off a bridge?" Luke can't believe it.

I ignore him. "You could have told me anything, sir. I idolized you. I would have believed anything you said. I would have followed any instructions you might have given me."

A pain worse than the ravages of cancer shows in his eyes. "I turned to Rodney for advice." More tears trace down the wet tracks on his face.

Please, God, not Rodney, too. "You mean Rodney knew?"

"I confided many things to Rodney—he was like a father to me. But he did not approve of my activities with the O.C.I.U. He tried to convince me to transfer out of the unit. Rodney wasn't an American citizen. He was French-born and had been a freedom fighter in the First World War. He also returned to France for several years to help the underground resistance against the German occupancy during World War Two. He felt the O.C.I.U. was dark and evil like the Nazi SS. He thought we were a dangerous threat to civil liberty, and he worried that my involvement in the O.C.I.U. would lead to my downfall as a police officer.

"He was right, of course. I knew he would have considered my judgment at the time I found you lying by the body, and my decision to leave things as they were, to let you continue to believe you killed the guy, not only despicable, but Gestapo-like. I only told him you were a troubled kid—like me when I was your age.

"Rodney fell in love with you from the very start, Wade. You reminded him of me when I was a kid, the son he never had. I thought if he took you under his wing, you'd be able to work through your troubles. But I finally broke down and told him the whole story, the truth, just before he died."

I am in tears now, too. "You used Rodney?"

The Sergeant winces. "Yes, in a way I did. I used him to be for you what I didn't have the courage to be."

"Despicable," Luke grumbles.

"Rodney was outraged when I told him the whole story. He was ashamed that I could do such a thing. He even slapped my face, something he never once did when I was growing up."

Yes, the slap...I did see it! "Go on."

"He said he was going to tell you the whole story himself. I was scared, but I thought it was better for you to hear it from him anyway. I was sure he would talk to you about it that day you guys came to visit him at his house, the day he had—the heart attack."

"Geez, sir." More tears come in a rush.

"I think the stress killed him."

Luke shakes his head. "Man, this is only getting worse, Wade."

"The Sergeant saved my life, Luke. I'm pretty sure I would have jumped from the bridge if he hadn't come along."

"It was only luck," the Sergeant counters, refusing undeserved clemency.

"No, sir, I believe it was God reaching down and touching me through you."

The Sergeant looks at me, and I see deep in his eyes a desperate need to believe what I just said is true, that God does reach down to intercede in a life. At this moment, with all of my heart, I want more than anything for my fallen hero to know God's forgiveness.

Luke hisses, "Boy, it turns out Lucinda was right all along. Not letting us see the Sergeant anymore was the best thing she ever did. And poor Miss Cherry, he ruined her life, too."

"Take it easy, Luke."

"You're right about me, Luke—but there's more."

Luke stands up. "Great! What now? Are you going to confess that you were the one who broke into our house and shot Mac?"

The Sergeant closes his eyes. "No, Luke. Lieutenant Shunkman did that."

Luke pales and slumps back down in the chair. I have begun to shake. My head is pounding. *Father, in the name of Jesus, please give me strength.*

"We didn't know Shunkman had found out you guys knew about the body. It wasn't until much later that we were able to piece it together. One of Shunkman's cohorts overheard Cherry's end of an argument she and I had on the telephone. An argument like many we had over whether or not to tell you boys the truth. Part of Cherry's spirit died when she found out she was the source of the leak that almost…"

"Got us killed?"

"Yes. The irony is, Shunkman didn't know you thought *you* killed Giacometti. But it spooked him when the body disappeared from Three Ponds. He became paranoid, obsessed. When he found out you boys knew about the body, I think he convinced himself that you had seen him dump the body there in the first place and had recognized him from that night on Billy Goat Hill. He lost it. Completely snapped.

"And we didn't know he'd started seeing your mom."

I rise out of my seat, my body rigid, my memory on fire, sucking like a vacuum back in time...

She came in late...

Mac awoke with a start...

Laughter...ice tinkling...Fred? Ned? Ted!

She called him Ted!

Good grief, he was the man she brought home with her that night!

"He came to kill—us?"

"We had suspicions he'd recruited a few other officers into his cabal and that they were planning something. We had Shunkman and several others under surveillance and discovered he was dating Lucinda. That's when I suspected he must have found out you knew about the body at Three Ponds. Cherry and I immediately went to your mother and told her everything.

"Your mother was amazing. She could have turned on us, gone to the district attorney, the FBI—but she didn't. She believed in us and backed us all the way. We agreed on a plan to protect you boys, to give us time to discover all of the officers involved with Shunkman, and to keep it all quiet. Cherry and I gave Lucinda seven thousand dollars we had saved for our wedding. Your mother had a lot of emotional and personal problems, but through it all she tried her best to protect you."

"So that's why we moved so suddenly, big brother. Another mystery solved."

"Not suddenly enough."

"Shunkman's luck finally ran out. Your mom had tactfully broken off her relationship with him, and she was helping us by keeping silent, which gave us more time to make sure we roped in all of Shunkman's clan.

"But he'd already been in your house. He knew the layout, which was all he'd wanted in the first place. The night before you were to move to Glendora, he came to your home to shoot all three of you as you slept. He had a silencer. We found it later."

"Maybe God did save us," Luke says.

"I know He did."

"Shunkman came to your house at about three in the morning. He entered the front door with a key we figured he'd stolen from your mom."

"We never locked the doors in those days anyway."

"It was dark, of course, and once inside it would have taken a minute for his eyes to adjust. The inside of the house was in disarray, moving cartons strewn about, furniture shifted around from where he expected it to be; he must have tripped or bumped against something, who knows. The important thing is, the dog heard him. You know the rest."

"I remember, Wade. Mac started out for Billy Goat Hill with us, but he turned around and went back to the house. Maybe he sensed the evil that was coming our way. He probably got back to the house and found Shunkman already inside. He would have gone after him with a vengeance."

"I remember, Luke."

"Only twelve more hours and we would have been gone. Mac would have lived."

"Only twelve more hours."

The room is quiet except for the awful rasp of the Sergeant's erratic gasping for air. He stares at the ceiling, empty, depleted, but looking strangely satisfied and relieved. I know exactly how he feels, burdens lifted, ready to move on.

"What ever happened to Shunkman?" Luke asks.

"He was shot and killed six days later when he and two other renegade cops attempted to kill Giacometti's replacement at a warehouse in North Hollywood. We had them under surveillance, and we were able to interrupt the hit. But Shunkman and his boys refused to surrender, and there was a wild shoot-out. Cherry ended up shooting Shunkman just before he shot me. She probably saved my life.

"Cops killing cops…it really doesn't get any worse than that. So the whole thing was covered up to protect the department. Officially, Shunkman died in the line of duty, shot by a known mafia operative during an attempted arrest. But it ended up costing us our careers.

"For what it's worth, Shunkman had a hunk of meat missing from his neck and shoulder area. It was badly infected and wasn't healing. It must have been terribly painful. Mac got him real good before Shunkman shot him. The injury was severe enough to run him off and foil his plan to kill you."

"Lord have mercy," Luke says.

An incredible peace washes over me as I feel the very presence of God surrounding me with the miracle of the Holy Spirit. For the first time, I truly experience the full and utter wholeness of our Father's deep and abiding love. I understand the depth of His forgiveness for me and for the world. And in this moment of epiphany, I am so overcome by His love that my heart overflows with compassion and understanding for the Sergeant.

"Sir?"

"Yes, Wade?"

"I want you to know something important."

"Yes?"

"I want you to know God loves you. I want you to know I have always loved you, and I still do. I want you to know how much I appreciate knowing the truth. I want you to know you did the right thing in contacting us. And, with all my heart, I want you to know that I forgive you for everything."

His eyes show me such relief I can hardly breathe. "Thank you, son. I just wish Cherry could forgive me, too."

"Have you ever asked her?"

"No. I have no right to ask her."

"Well, if God can forgive you, then so can Miss Cherry."

"That's very kind, but you can't really know that."

"If you believe in God as I do, you *can* know that."

"Believing and knowing are not the same things."

"In my heart, they are the same thing. If you believe, then you will know. The Bible is the record, the rule book, and the manual of life. It's God's holy message to the world. To me, it is the greatest love letter ever written, and it was written to each and every one of us. God loves you very much, sir.

"I know our lives came together for a purpose, a beautiful, incredible, miraculous purpose. I understand now that without you, including everything that has happened, I wouldn't know what I know, and I wouldn't value what I value. I understand now that my suffering was and is for a purpose, and I am filled with such excitement and anticipation that I can hardly wait to see what God has planned next.

"So, as difficult as it may be for you to accept, I can only say that God loves you. He wants you to accept His love as a gift. And there is a Way for you to accept it, and the Way is Jesus Christ."

The Sergeant is completely drained. I lean close to him and take his hand in mine. He squeezes my hand with a last bit of strength and speaks in my ear. "Thank you, Wade. I can't tell you what you've done for me. You have become quite a man. Rodney would be proud."

"Sir, it isn't me doing it. It is God doing it."

"Okay, son."

"Sir, would you like to see Rodney again?"

"If I only could."

"May I come back tomorrow and talk with you some more?"

"I'd like that very much."

Luke says, "Can I come, too?"

"Yes, please do, son."

The Sergeant closes his eyes, and I watch the lids quiver strangely. We sit quietly for a little while, the undertow of emotion releasing us to rise back to the surface. Luke gets up and walks to the window. I follow him with my eyes, half expecting him to turn around and spout a fresh Lukeism to brighten the room. But he doesn't turn around. My little brother is at a loss for words. The window holds him there, perhaps offering him a glimpse into his own past, a view full of ugliness now cleansed and sparkling with the shine of newfound truth.

I get up and walk over next to him.

He turns to me, tears running down his face. "See down there in the parking lot, the blue pickup."

I look and find the truck. In the bed of the pickup are two little boys, one blond and one redhead. They are carbon copies of the man sitting between them. The man has his arms around their shoulders.

Looking out the window, Luke says, "That was amazing, what you said to him. I felt like you were speaking for me *and* to me at the same time."

"It wasn't me—it was God."

We stay by the window for a few minutes while the Sergeant rests. With my arm across Luke's shoulders, my mind floats in a supernatural drift, shifting between images of the past and visions of the future. God shows me Lucinda, and I know loss and courage. Next I see Rodney, and I know caring and humor. Then I see Esther and I know patience and kindness. Last I see Miss Cherry, and I know faith and action.

We, all of us, were in it together, but not together in it. If only there had been more trust, better communication, more love—such is the condition of the world. And I thank God that I finally know who I am and the reason I am here in this world.

From across the room, my gaze still fixed on the parking lot below, I notice the Sergeant's breathing is less labored and more even.

The nurse reappears, her stockings swishing quietly behind us. A long moment passes while she checks over the Sergeant.

Quietly, she says, "I haven't seen him sleep this peacefully in weeks. I was a little worried for a while there, but it seems your visit has done him some good. When I saw you boys praying in the hall, I just knew your visit would be a blessing for that troubled man. I've been praying for him every day. I don't know his personal story, but I do know people. The weight on that man's soul was so heavy. I could feel it."

"Thank you for your prayers, ma'am—and sorry about the ruckus earlier. We'll be back to visit him again tomorrow."

"Praise God, because Mr. Cavendish surely loves you Parker brothers."

"Oh, you know who we are?"

"My Lord, yes, I most certainly do. That man talks about you two all of the time. I heard all about Billy Goat Hill, and I'll tell you this much—God surely must have been watching over you boys."

"Yes, ma'am. He surely was."

"My name is Naomi. Please feel free to ask for me, and I'll be glad to help you in any way I can."

"Thank you, Naomi."

"You're welcome and God bless you boys."

"God bless you too, ma'am."

Out in the hallway, I am suddenly aware of a feeling of unfinished business. And then it hits me, and I am looking forward to tomorrow's visit with more anticipation than a kid slipping out the window for a late-night outing on Billy Goat Hill.

"I haven't seen that look in your eye since Highland Park," Luke says. "Uh oh. What are you thinking?"

"Let's go check on Miss Cherry. I'll tell you on the way, while we listen to some more of your harp music."

It's late afternoon when we arrive at Rosewood Manor. The lobby is filled with the wonderful aroma of raspberry cobbler.

Marge McZilkie calls to us from the adjoining dining room. "Cobbler day. I figured I'd see you right around dinnertime."

I am naturally drawn toward the source of the aroma as we both step into the dining room. "How is she today?"

"Tired, but she's definitely on the upswing. She said she feels like a lifelong fever has finally broken."

"Is she in her room?"

"No, she's with Emma. They're getting some sun on the west patio."

"Thanks, Marge."

"Are you boys staying for dinner, or would you like me to box up some cobbler to go?"

"To go, please."

"You got it."

"Be careful with that stuff," Luke whispers. "You do have addiction tendencies, you know."

Emma notices us as we approach. "Yo angels is here, Miss Cherry."

Miss Cherry has sunglasses on, and her face is framed in a beautiful yellow silk kerchief. She looks like a classy movie star on hiatus at her favorite spa resort.

Luke and I greet her with a hug. "How's our best girl feeling today?"

"Pretty good, I think. I'll know for sure once I hear how things went with Lyle."

"Well, for starters, let me just say God is good."

"Speak it, brother!" Emma chimes. "Dat's what I'm talk'n 'bout!"

"Emma's been giving me quite a pep talk this morning."

Emma grins. "I done told Miss Cherry you boys have nuttin' but the love of Jesus in your hearts."

"Thank you, ma'am."

"No need to thank me. It's a blessin' and a half to know boaf of ya'll. I reckon ya'll got some unfinished bidness. I'll get out the way so's you can tidy things up."

"Thank you, Emma."

"Later, ya'll."

Luke chuckles as Emma rides off into the sunset.

"You were able to see him?"

"Yes, ma'am."

"How is he?"

"He doesn't have much time left, but he's in God's hands now."

"I was thinking about him this morning, how different things might have been if we had gotten married, had children. I still love him."

"He still loves you, too. He said in his letter that he has always loved you."

"I wish we all could go back and rewrite the story. Lord knows I've tried, but I can't seem to forget the past."

"I don't think the past is meant to be forgotten, but there are things that are meant to be forgiven."

"I forgave Lyle a long time ago."

"He doesn't seem to know that."

She looks at me, and then at Luke. We are both smiling. "Luke and I have an idea about something."

"You do?"

"Yes, ma'am. We do."

"Does it involve sliding on cardboard?"

"Funny you should put it that way."

"What?"

"Well, why don't we take a moment to pray together, ask God for His wisdom and guidance, and then we'll see what you think about our idea?"

"Okay," Miss Cherry says, bowing her head.

"Father in heaven, in the spirit of forgiveness…"

A little while later, Luke and I head for home with God's blessing, two raspberry cobblers to go, and some very special arrangements to make.

sixteen

I slept in this morning, no bad dreams. I feel good and refreshed after two emotionally draining days. Melissa and Kate kept me up late with dozens of questions about our visit with the Sergeant. Kate learned more about her father's beginnings than she ever imagined, though certain details and facts were tactfully omitted. God willing, some things she will never know.

This morning, with so much of the story fresh in her mind, she asked if she could come with me today. It was so sweet, her heart so pure, the way she wanted to be with me for moral support. Of course, I had to say no, but it means so much to me that she asked. A part of the father in me will always try to protect her innocence.

I arrive back at Saint Mary's in Long Beach a little after noon, full of hope and promise about day two of my reunion with the Sergeant. Nurse Naomi is in the hall when I exit the elevator.

"Hello, ma'am."

"Oh good—I'm so glad you're here, Mr. Parker."

"Is something wrong?"

"Oh no. Quite to the contrary. In fact, if I didn't know better, I'd say Mr. Cavendish was ready to be discharged from this hospital. The man woke up hungry as a lion, ate a full breakfast, drank a whole pot of coffee, and right now he's sitting up in bed telling the orderly a hilarious story about some kid named Jakey Blume. I've been trying to get Mr. Cavendish to let me take a blood sample all morning, but I can't get a word in edgewise."

"Really?"

"I have three other patients I'd like you and your brother to visit." She grins. "Actually, I don't want to inadvertently raise any hope. We see this sometimes, a sudden but brief euphoric return of faculty and energy as the end draws near."

"Oh."

"Where is your brother, by the way? I thought he was coming back with you today?"

"He'll be here in a little while."

"Good, because Mr. Cavendish has asked me three times already when you guys were coming."

I hear loud laughter coming from the Sergeant's room. The orderly, grinning and shaking his head, fixes the door in the open position. "He wants the door left open."

"Okay," Naomi responds.

"Sheesh! The kid scrambled out through a forest of legs and took off running for home with nothing but his underpants on! Unbelievable story." The orderly walks off chuckling to himself.

Naomi looks at me. "It's a long, but true, story," I say.

"I can only imagine."

"Is that you, Wade?"

"Yes, sir…I'm here. Nice talking with you, Naomi."

The Sergeant is indeed sitting up in bed in the middle of a room bursting with bright Southern California sunshine. I am greeted by a warm grin and a face full of color and joy. His hairless head is crowned with a bright blue Los Angeles Dodgers cap. After the shock of seeing him in such poor condition yesterday, this is like walking into the middle of a miracle.

"Sir, you look…great."

"I feel great!"

"Praise God."

He glances toward the open door. "Isn't Luke with you?"

"No, sir, he had to run an errand, but he'll be here in a little while."

"Good, because this hat is for him, kind of a late replacement for the one he lost way back when."

"That's very thoughtful, sir. He'll be surprised."

"Naomi picked it up for me on her lunch break. If I had a little more mobility, I would have hunted up some bird-patterned gift wrapping."

I laugh out loud. "You remember his issue with mockingbirds?"

"I remember a lot of things. Please, pull up a chair. Maybe it's good that we have a chance to talk just the two of us before your brother arrives."

I take a seat on the window side of the bed. The sun warms my back as blue sky swims in the Sergeant's eyes. "I'm sure glad you're feeling better."

"You have no idea how good I feel. Last night I awoke from a dream, and…well, I don't know how to say it other than I had an…experience."

"Really? What do you mean?"

"Well, kind of like a spiritual thing. I think you…your forgiving me the way that you did, your willingness to overcome all the reasons anyone would need to justify hating my guts forever, has triggered an amazing thing. It has changed me."

"Praise God, sir."

"Yes…praising God! That's part of what I want to talk about!"

"Sure. But maybe you should calm down just a little."

"Okay." He takes a deep breath and exhales with gusto. "If you don't mind my asking, Wade, how did you get religion?"

I chuckle. "I don't know that I have…religion, sir. What happened is I surrendered my life to God, and I accepted Jesus Christ as my Lord and Savior."

"Do you go to church?"

"Oh yes. We are members of a wonderful church."

"Huh. But you don't consider yourself religious?"

"Not really. At least, I don't think of it that way."

"Interesting."

"I'm glad you think so."

The Sergeant effortlessly scoots himself up higher against the headboard. He adjusts his pillows and puts his hand on a Bible that I just now notice is tucked alongside him on the bed. "Naomi gave me this Bible. I did some reading last night. Can you believe it? For the first time in my life, I read part of the Bible.

"Rodney was in my head the whole time. He always tried to share his Christian beliefs with me. I guess he left a strong impression about his faith, because I felt his presence the whole time I was reading."

"I often think of Rodney when I read the Bible. When I do, it's as if he's right there with me, too."

"You know what I remember most about him?"

"What?"

"Rodney had this way about him, a kind of peace that always drew me in close. He would tell me about getting saved, but I never could get my mind around the idea."

"Yes. I experienced the same thing with him."

"Last night, I came to a verse in the book of John where Jesus promises God will send the Holy Spirit as His representative. I marked the verse right here: *I am leaving you with a gift—peace of mind and heart. And the peace I give isn't like the peace the world gives. So don't be troubled or afraid.* That's the message I think Rodney tried so hard to share with me."

"I'd say he succeeded, sir."

The Sergeant looks up at me, his eyes full of joyous comprehension and appreciation. "The way I've felt since you and Luke came to see me yesterday, I believe I've seen a glimpse of that gift, the peace of mind and heart that Rodney had, that you have.

"Last night, after you boys left, I prayed. I thanked God for the chance to tell you guys the truth, and I told Him that I wanted the gift, too. Later, I fell asleep and dreamed about talking with you and explaining more about what went on when you and Luke were on your own. Maybe God wants me to make sure that I have fully cleared my conscience; I don't know."

"Well, all you need to do is acknowledge your past wrongdoings and confess them to Him, who already knows all truth."

"Yes, I understand. But I feel like I need to explain more to you, Wade."

"Well, then…by all means…go ahead and explain."

"That's the strange thing; I don't know what to say, other than I'm open to answer any questions you may have."

I smile. "I guess I am curious about a couple of things."

"Please, ask."

"I understand about what happened at Three Ponds, Shunkman, and the cover-up. But I have always wondered why you were so concerned about me and Luke in the first place. Was it just a coincidence that you showed up on Eagle Rock that day?"

"Cops don't believe in coincidences."

"Neither do champion cardboard sliders."

He grins. "There's your answer. You made a big impression on me that first night we met on Billy Goat Hill."

"I did?"

"More than you realized. I was amazed by your courage, how you showed up to face the challenge to run the Crippler in the dark. Remember, I also grew up in the Highland Park area. I was a Billy Goat Hill regular a generation before you, and I never had the guts to run the Crippler in the daytime, much less in the dark. You were also incredibly courageous when my gang of bikers rode up on you."

"I sure didn't feel courageous."

"You impressed the heck out of me. You were the type of kid I would have liked to have been friends with, when I was your age."

"Really?"

"You were a very special kid, Wade. And Luke was no slouch

either. I was intrigued with you guys, and Cherry's mothering instincts had kicked in, so we decided to do a little follow-up on you."

"I was investigated at the age of eight?"

"Yes, you were, kind of. I made the rounds—Sal's Liquor Store, Kory's Market, Jake's Barbershop, your school—all the places and people I had known since long before you were born. Very basic police work. I was casual about it so as not to worry anyone about you, but I found out a lot."

"Like what?"

He grins. "Sal always knew about your taking soda bottles from the back of his store and bringing them around front for the deposit money."

"Oh."

"And the manager at Kory's suspected you might be responsible for the theft of a comic book or two."

"We never stole any comic books, sir."

"That's half right. Luke did."

"He did? I never knew."

"Jake the barber liked you kids a lot, too, even though you didn't always exactly behave yourselves in his shop."

"You talked to Jake?"

"Are you kidding? Everybody talked to Jake. You couldn't pass by his shop without him dragging you inside to talk."

I laugh. "That was Jake, all right."

"But there was one person who truly cared about you guys and did more to convince me to actively look out for you than anyone else. That's how I found out about the death of your baby brother and your dad taking off."

"Who?"

"Mr. Soldenkov. He felt bad for you guys and was very concerned for your welfare, you and your mom. He told me you were both good boys."

"Who?"

"Mr. Soldenkov."

"Mr. Soldenkov?"

"He worked for Langendorf."

"I've never heard of him."

"Your neighbor, Carl Soldenkov. He was a baker for Lagendorf. He worked nights. Drove a '55 Chevy?"

My chin drops to the floor. "Carl the baker got you to look out for us?"

"Yep. He was quite a character. Did you know he and his wife, I think her name was Esther, helped your mom out after your dad left? They brought over groceries, even bought dog food for Mac. Your mom told us all about it. I think it broke Carl's heart when you moved."

He and his Chevy awakened me nearly every night and rescued me from bad dreams. "I had no idea Carl cared about us that way. I did become good friends with Esther years later, when I went back to the old neighborhood to try to find you. I ended up at Ruby Place that day, and Esther befriended me."

"She did?"

Holding back tears, I say, "Carl had already passed away. Esther gave me Carl's Bible."

"Esther sounds a lot like Naomi."

"I went to the Highland Park police station that day, but I was told you didn't work there anymore."

"I'm sorry."

"Well, since we're on the subject, what happened? I know what you told us yesterday, but did you get fired?"

"I resigned."

"You said there was an investigation?"

"That came after I resigned. I left because my conscience bothered me over what I had done to you boys. I had dishonored the badge and the oath I had sworn to uphold. I didn't live up to my responsibility to Cherry, and I had become something pretty close to what Rodney had warned me about. I also thought if I put myself on the block, things might go better for Cherry, but when it was all said and done, they took her badge, too.

"What got to me more than anything else, though, was the memory of your face as I looked back in the rearview mirror that day I drove off after giving you the ball bearing."

"I still have it."

"I'm sorry, Wade."

"It's okay. Why did you give it to me like that?"

"It was the cruelest thing I ever did. It just shows how far off the track I had fallen. Somehow, I thought it would warn you about what I couldn't talk about. I'm sorry."

I smile. "You know, I have some good things, too, sir. I still have the piece of fake scar you handed to me that first night on Billy Goat Hill. I still have the transistor radio you gave me. I still have the bat Duke Snider gave me for my birthday. And I still have a lot of great memories. All of my life I have believed you cared about me. I think that faith helped get me through to where I am now."

"I always cared about you. But I was weak and not a very good person. Not even half the person Cherry was. I wasn't always in contact with her, but I think she continued to try to keep track of you throughout the years."

"Yes, she did. At one point she showed up to bail me out of jail, and it was she who eventually turned my heart toward God."

"It's been a long time since I've spoken directly to her. When I found out about her stroke…it buried me under a mountain of guilt. I withdrew even more. I guess I've been hiding under that mountain ever since."

"Why don't you ask her to come and see you?"

"I don't have the right to ask her anything."

"You sent her a letter and asked her to pass your message on to us."

"Yes."

"What would you say to her if you could?"

His eyes well up and he looks toward the blue sky framed in the window behind me. He closes his eyes. "With all my heart…I would beg her to please forgive me."

"I forgave you a long time ago, Lyle."

The Sergeant opens his eyes and turns his face toward the door. There in the open doorway is Miss Cherry. Behind her is Luke, his hands on her shoulders offering gentle assistance as she wheels her wheelchair into the room.

The Sergeant looks at me with a look of peace that reminds me a great deal of Rodney. He is speechless.

"You're welcome, sir."

He nods.

"Luke and I will be back later."

"Love your hat, sir," Luke says.

As Luke and I leave, I look back to see Miss Cherry take the Sergeant's hand and place it with hers on the Bible. They begin to pray…

I was able to visit the Sergeant five more times before he passed away. His body was a storm raging with cancer, but his heart and spirit had found peace. His condition seemed to remain on the rebound, and all the way through to the last hour he was lucid and relatively free of pain—another gift from God.

With each visit I learned more about the mystery of my childhood. I learned how omnipresent the Sergeant really was all those years. I learned how complicated and dangerously entwined our lives had become. He insisted he was singularly responsible for shaping my collapsing world. He spoke of the agony of conscience that battled against something deep inside him that would not allow the truth to shine. I am convinced he was a good man who made a bad decision.

He told me he expected me to hold him up as my enemy, and he was truly amazed and grateful for the miracle of our reunion. I explained that if we are pleasing God, He will make our enemies at peace with us. From there he began to see how God's hand is on every moment of our lives, which led to the blessing of lengthy discussions about forgiveness.

I shared with him in great detail how Jesus and the gift of salvation had changed my life, and it was during my second-to-last visit that he told me he was ready to accept Christ. That evening at his bedside, Luke, Miss Cherry, Nurse Naomi, and I prayed over him as he spoke his confession and accepted Jesus as his Lord and Savior. He read from the tattered copy of "The Sinner's Prayer" that Esther gave to me all those years ago.

I believe the Sergeant is in heaven with Matthew, Rodney, Carl, and Esther. Because of Jesus my Redeemer, I believe one day I will be with all of them again. I also maintain hope that my mother may be in heaven, too. Only God knows what she believed, but I pray it may have been the very thing I sensed that she wanted to tell me not long before she died.

The miracle of our reunion with the Sergeant has also given me renewed hope that one day I may even see my earthly father, Earl, again.

seventeen

Seven years have passed since we buried the Sergeant in accordance with his wishes at Forest Lawn, next to Rodney Bernanos.

God, the indefatigable Healer, slowly and steadily sheds His Grace on us. The travel agency has grown, eight offices now, and more profitable than we had ever imagined. The inheritance we received from the Sergeant was put to good use. Luke got his pilot's license and bought an airplane, his final defeat of the mockingbirds, I guess. And after many years of part-time effort, I completed a degree in English literature.

The introspective, well-traveled former champion cardboard rider of Billy Goat Hill is taking a stab at writing a novel. I am also working on a youth counseling certificate, which I pray might come in handy one day soon. God is telling me to get ready for something. I am excited.

Four years ago, Melissa and I bought a cabin on the west shore of Lake Tahoe at Rubicon. Melissa calls it "the project" because we work more than we play when we come to Rubicon. The setting is spectacular—the entire cabin structure projects out over a magnificent grouping of boulders that cling precariously along a thin strip of emerald shoreline.

A short way out from the water's edge, shimmering emerald plunges straight down into an infinite chasm of cobalt blue. Looking down into the waters of Rubicon is like looking up into the twilight sky over Billy Goat Hill. I feel God's presence when I am here. I hear His voice in the sanctity of this breathtaking setting.

We have modified the cabin to be wheelchair friendly for Miss Cherry. She loves coming to the lake and is trying to convince us that she should be a full-time caretaker and year-round resident at Rubicon. Captain Luke regularly flies us up to Tahoe where we celebrate things as a family. The entourage includes Luke's dog, Charlie, a Shepherd-Doberman mix that looks so much like Mac, I have come to call him Charlie Mac so I don't have to constantly correct myself.

Luke and I, with Charlie on point, sometimes make trips to Rubicon alone. Sojourns to talk, just us brothers, still linked sprites. The cabin is a great place to relax, ruminate, and spend time in prayer with the Lord. The pine-scented seclusion offers a kind of spiritual therapy, a natural easing of the soul's troubles, and it is here with Luke that I am most comfortable with thoughts and discussions about our past. I would be less than truthful if I denied that I still think about the troubled times or occasionally have a bad dream. I came from there, it is part of who I am, and it always will be, I guess. But it's this entire life of mine, the total, complete, good and bad reality of me that I have given over to the Lord. I no longer serve the past. I serve the future that is Christ Jesus.

We are here now, brothers Parker, sitting out on the veranda overlooking the splendor and vastness of Lake Tahoe. Enjoying the late afternoon sun, Luke, ever the philosopher, waxes profound as we lounge beneath the heavenly alpine sky.

"Rubicon." Luke gestures to the chilly depths below. Charlie cocks his head to one side and watches Luke intently.

"Rubicon," I answer, wondering if encouraging him is in my best interest.

"It drops off nearly vertical for hundreds of feet. Throw a penny out there, and your wish will come true before it hits bottom."

I gaze upon the rippling veneer lying like a shimmering cloak over the glacial depths. "Tell me more, O great philosopher."

"Now, pay close attention, you big donkey."

"Yes, O younger and smaller donkey."

"Rubicon—it means…"

"Tell me, tell me."

He extends his arm, and with great fervor slices it downward toward the water's surface some fifty odd feet below. Charlie and I look down at the water.

"…to be decisive."

"Ah yes."

"It means to take irrevocable steps…"

"Say it, little donkey."

"…like Caesar did when he crossed the river Rubicon between Cisalpine Gaul and Italy to march against Pompey."

"Did you run into an encyclopedia salesman recently?"

Luke's eyes brighten with passion and bore into me as if making a challenge. "To conquer or perish!" he roars, grinning inscrutably, making Charlie bark and wriggle with excitement.

"To conquer or perish!"

"Something to think about isn't it?"

"Yes. Actually, I've been thinking about a lot of things lately, Luke."

"Me, too. Especially when we are here at the cabin. There is something very special about this location. I read somewhere that the Indians believed Lake Tahoe was a spiritual place."

I muse about the Indians for a moment. "Isn't it remarkable how full the Lake is again, after all these years of drought?"

Luke agrees. "The lake is back up to its natural rim. Its abundance is once again flowing beyond itself, into the Truckee River."

"Kind of amazing, really, if you think about it. After suffering years of deprivation, the lake is full again, even has more than it needs."

"Sounds a lot like us, doesn't it?"

I glance at him. "Hmm. Yes it does, O great philosopher."

He winks.

Sitting here, the lake doing its spiritual number on me, I think about all of them:

Matthew,

Lucinda,

Earl,

Carl,

Rodney,

Esther,

Jake,

Shunkman,

Duke,

Mac,

Miss Cherry,

and especially the Sergeant.

All but Miss Cherry and Duke Snider are fading pictures, images and sounds floating in a river of memories. Now and then I hear Mac barking, though faint, far away.

To the west behind me, the sun is fast slipping down into the cradle of evening; a waning sliver of fire sets ablaze the windows of cabins far across the lake along the Nevada shoreline. As I look up, the orange flares of mirrored light seem to douse all at once, as if, at long last, the flaming quintessence of the past has been extinguished. I close my eyes, and except for missing Melissa and Kate, stillness and quiet dwell within me.

Charlie curls himself up in a furry circle at my feet.

Luke gets up and stretches and goes into the cabin. He reappears with two glasses of iced tea and settles into the deeply cushioned chaise lounge next to me.

He raises his glass, signaling a toast. "I want to say something I've never said before, big brother."

"What's that?" I raise my glass to meet his.

"Thank you for watching out for me when we were kids. You had to take on the responsibility for just about everything, and I know it wasn't easy." He gazes at me, his bright eyes serene, glimmering.

He's always been able to sneak up on me like this. I never see it coming. My chest warms. "I couldn't have made it without you, brother."

As we sit here enjoying the unwinding mood of dusk, a gray dove glides down and alights on the deck in front of us. Charlie opens one eye and gives the dove his permission to stay.

"Some bird dog," Luke mutters.

"Not a mockingbird," I say.

Luke grins and coos at the dove. "Mockingbirds are for kids, big brother."

I nod speculatively as my mind drifts back to the beginning, to a time and place where grand adventures filled our indulgent hearts and courage coursed through our veins with the merciful blue blood of innocence; to a micro-world full of excitement and risk where even the smallest occurrence was important, serious, and equally free of lasting consequence. Something indefinable, deep inside me, cherishes those days. That short-lived period of family life that existed before Matthew died, before Earl ran off to Barstow, leaving us ill-prepared to deal with most things, much less the worst of things. Before the Sergeant and Miss Cherry came along and the world tilted off its axis.

The hole in me has been mended. I have a Friend now who will never let me down, who will always be here for me and upon whom I can always trust. *Thank You, Jesus.*

"Wade?"

"Yes, O great philosopher?"

"If they made a movie about us, about our lives, what would they call it?"

"How about *Billy Goat Hill?*"

Luke unleashes a hearty laugh. "That's a good one. Like who's ever heard of Billy Goat Hill?"

"God has."

We both sit for a few more minutes, being together, thinking our own thoughts.

The dove hops up on the lounge near Luke's feet, fluffs out its feathers, and lowers its body comfortably down over its legs, as though it plans to spend the night right there. I feel that secure with Luke, too. The dove sleepily closes its eyes.

The lake works on me some more, brings up thoughts of Duke Snider, opening day at Dodger Stadium, my daydream about going down into the clubhouse with him, then him giving me the bat for real. In my heart, I feel Duke really might have said something like what I had imagined he said that day.

"We must find a way to forgive, or we only end up blaming ourselves."

"Jesus is the way, the truth, and the light," I say out loud without realizing it.

"Amen," Luke replies.

I go inside the cabin and return with the bat that Duke Snider gave to me.

"Oh no, not the bat," Luke teases.

"You've never even touched this thing, have you?"

"Are you kidding—you never let me. You used to threaten me with death if I got anywhere near it."

"Here." I hold it out to him. Older brothers have to be magnanimous once in a while.

Luke gets up without disturbing the dove. He takes the bat and raises it over his shoulder. Beaming just like the freckle-faced kid he was long ago, he takes a warm-up swing toward Nevada. "Wow! It gives you chills doesn't it?"

"I still get chills just looking at it."

For a moment we are boys again, best pals, kindred spirits transcending the purlieus of time, joined together by the lasting magnificence of good childhood memories.

Luke swings the bat again, this time with much more vitality. "It kind of makes you feel powerful, too."

In a flash of clarity I know what needs to be done. I take the keyring out of my pocket and remove the ball bearing.

Luke smiles knowingly and hands me the bat. "To conquer or perish," he proclaims, and squares up his shoulders as though preparing to advance on Pompey.

I step to the lake-most point of the veranda and gaze out over the Rubicon. My heart is filled with the spirit of the Lord as Lake Tahoe shimmers under the vestiges of a warm cinnamon sunset. With closed eyes, I visualize little Wade Parker and Luke. I say a silent prayer for all children who need someone to trust, someone to care enough to understand. I pray that they might come to know God as I have. I pray that the Lord in His holy wisdom might one day use me to reach lost and troubled kids for His purposes.

Father, I want to be like Your Son Jesus. As He suffered for me, let me suffer for Him. Use me God, I am Yours.

Then I do what I believe Duke Snider would do. I toss the ball bearing up in the pine-scented air, swing the bat with my arms fully extended, and cream that sucker on the sweet spot with everything I have.

"Your will be done on earth as it is in heaven!" Luke shouts victoriously.

The dove takes flight into the twinkling heavens, Charlie barks, and in my head I hear the Sergeant whisper one last time…*"Never look back, Wade."*

For the first time in my life, I feel like everything is right.

I leave the bat with Luke and go inside the cabin to call Melissa. I want to tell her about an idea I have to start a foundation to help troubled kids, maybe build a shelter for runaways in Los Angeles. She'll think it's a crazy, wonderful idea, and she'll help me with everything she has to give. I know she will.

Maybe Luke will sign on as my partner.

I praise You, Father. With You—I know all things are possible.

AUTHOR'S NOTE:
THE STORY BEHIND THE STORY

Dear Reader,

I have been asked many times how much of this story really happened. I frequently hear comments and questions like, "This feels too real to be a novel," or "Did this or that actually happen?" So here's a brief synopsis of the story behind the story.

The character of Wade Parker is imbued with the true feeling and emotion of my early youth, and the relationship between Wade and Luke is loosely based on my recollections of my relationship with my brother Paul. We did suffer the death of our younger brother, John; our family did fall apart; we did have a dog named Mac; and Billy Goat Hill, Eagle Rock, Three Ponds, and Cavendish Caverns all were real places.

Drawing from the pathos and drama of my personal history, I constructed a fictional world set within and without the boundaries of my real-life childhood experience. This methodology is not unusual. Some of the best novels ever written have been biographically inspired. What is important, and what I would like most to share with you, is how God worked a miracle in my life and continues to work miracles through the writing and publication of this book.

I wrote the first passages of *Billy Goat Hill* in the summer of 1992. Though writing has always provided an artistic release, breathing life into the character of Wade Parker began a kind of catharsis I had not previously experienced as a writer. I am a novelist, one who imagines a story and then tells it, but this time something compelled me to dig inward and dare to reveal a good deal of truth about my own life. I did not yet know God as my Creator or Jesus Christ as my Lord and Savior, nor was I aware of the existence of the Holy Spirit. I now know how omnipresent the mysterious Holy Triune is.

As the manuscript progressed, my soul whirled and stirred with a passion of Spirit that was so freeing it amazed me. Wade Parker emerged with a powerful purpose, challenging me, often goading me to acknowledge what was missing in my own life...the ability to forgive. In many ways this is a very personal book as my heart is laid bare through the voice of Wade Parker. Forgiveness, which is the essence of Christ, has become elemental to my faith, and it is my fervent hope that my readers be impacted by this essential message.

I self-published the original version, titled *The King of Billy Goat Hill*, under the pen name Mark Stanleigh, in 1996. The secular version was something of a success, but more important, the release of the book began part two of an incredible journey. For sixteen months I traveled the country doing personal appearances, meeting people, and thinking, thinking, thinking. Wade Parker took me on a sojourn into the wilderness culminating with a spiritual epiphany that changed my life forever. At the age of forty-eight, I came to understand that God was real and He had a plan for my life.

I soon found myself in God's boot camp learning about His will and His Word, and not, to my surprise and disappointment, doing much writing. For the next five years, He saw fit to engage me in many things, but not writing. Then, when He knew I was ready, and when I least expected it, he worked another incredible miracle. He arranged for me to meet and become friends with David Van Diest, who is now my agent.

By then I had adjusted to the idea that God's plan for me apparently did not include writing, so it took a while for me and David, two new friends getting to know each other, to come around to the subject. Eventually we did, and the long version of what ultimately transpired will be saved for forums other than this short letter. A summary of the amazing events that led to the publication of this book reads as follows: A novel written by a secular writer is published in 1996. Writing the book is a life-changing experience that leads the writer toward God. Nine years later, five years after the writer has given his heart to the Lord (and has done very little writing in between), and without pursuing it, he is offered a contract to rewrite and publish a novel about forgiveness, the writing of which led the writer to know the Lord in the first place.

I share this with you, dear reader, because I'd like you to be in on God's miracle. You see, only God could make this happen. I can't tell you how rare it is for a previously published secular novel to be rewritten and published by a Christian book publisher. (Francine Rivers' *Redeeming Love* is the only one that comes to mind, which I highly recommend, by the way.)

I praise God that you have had the opportunity to read this book and welcome your comments and questions.

Blessings,

Mark Stanleigh Morris

DISCUSSION GUIDE

1. Part of the story in *Billy Goat Hill* derives from the death of baby Matthew, the subsequent disintegration of the Parker family, and how these circumstances affect the surviving brothers, Wade and Luke. The Parker family didn't seem to have much of a spiritual foundation. How do you think this fact affected their responses to Matthew's death? How has tragedy impacted your life? In what ways did your spiritual foundation or lack of one make a difference?

2. Told from Wade's point of view, the story delves into his perception of his responsibility as the older brother. Where are you in the birth order in your family? If you were (are) the oldest, how do you identify with Wade? If you are not the oldest, did the story cause you to think about your relationship with an older sibling? How so?

3. About the only constant throughout their entire childhood was the brotherly love shared by Wade and Luke. What role do you think that played in their survival? Do you think Matthew's death strengthened the love between Wade and Luke? Why or why not?

4. By the end of the book, how did you feel toward the Sergeant? Were you able to see him with sympathy as Wade did, as a good man who made a terrible decision? Were you able to forgive the Sergeant as Wade did? If not, why not? What about Miss Cherry's role in the cover-up? How do you feel about her? Perhaps you have also made bad choices in your life. How has forgiveness made a difference?

5. Do you see the characters of Rodney and Esther as heroes in *Billy Goat Hill*? How so? If you have been blessed with a Rodney or an Esther in your life, how was your life impacted as a result? How might you be a Rodney or an Esther for someone lost or hurting?

6. The Lord works in mysterious ways, and so often His mystery is beautiful, magnificent, and awe inspiring. Wade had no one to teach him how to be a man, yet he ultimately became a man of God. What do you think may have been God's purpose in designing such a mysterious path for Wade? What mysteries have you encountered on your path? What do you think might be God's plan for your future?

7. Billy Goat Hill, Eagle Rock, Three Ponds, Cavendish Caverns...what sort of places did you escape to when you were a kid? How did they affect you?

8. Often we fail to realize how perceptive children are. The old saying, "Kids are resilient and have a way of bouncing back," may have some truth to it. On the other hand, some scars can last a lifetime. What childhood scars do you bear? What has helped you to heal or to overcome those scars?

9. Did you have a loving pet when you were a child? How did you relate to the relationship between the boys and Mac? How were you affected when you learned of Mac's heroic death?

10. Have you ever known someone like Lucinda, a person unable to cope with a tragic loss? Were you able to identify with her? How so?

11. What do you think happened to Earl? How important might it be to Wade and Luke if Earl reappeared one day? Has anything similar ever happened in your life or to someone you know?

12. What did you think of Wade's imaginary friendship with baseball legend Duke Snider? Could you relate? What relationships resided in your imagination as a child?

13. You could say the beginning of Wade's lifelong dilemma goes all the way back to an innocent schoolyard dare. Were you ever part of a dare or challenge that got out of hand?

14. Alcoholism, divorce, child abandonment—such patterns of abuse in families are often perpetuated from generation to generation. *Billy Goat Hill* presents a kind of "how to" message of hope: that by embracing forgiveness, which is the promise of Christ, cycles of abuse can be broken. Has forgiveness played a role in changing your life? How so?

15. Sadly, so many marriages today do not prevail. Though faced with some very dark times, Melissa never gave up on Wade, and their marriage was sustained. Has faith played a role in overcoming difficulties in your marriage? How so?

The irrepressible Parker brothers return in the exciting sequel to MARK STANLEIGH MORRIS'S endearing debut novel, *Billy Goat Hill!*

Now in their midforties, Wade and Luke sell their thriving travel agency and plunge in to helping lost and hurting teens in Northeastern Los Angeles. Together with Jose Reyes, a former gang member turned youth pastor, the brothers establish the Rodney L. Bernanos Center near the site of their childhood home. A colorful cast of street-hardened characters conspire to test the brothers' faith as they walk the walk and talk the talk of *forgiveness* in this now spiritually dark quadrant of the city. Progress is hard-earned, but the youth center thrives…enraging a formidable enemy and igniting a battle for the very soul of the community.

COMING FALL 2006!

C'mon and say, "G'day!"

and join two Sisterchicks on their adventure to the land of kangaroos and koalas in...

Now Available!

When Kathleen and her husband, Tony, pack up and fly off to New Zealand for Tony's three-month film job, Kathleen discovers more than her geography has flip-flopped. In the land down under, comfort food comes in a jar labeled "Vegemite," gardens sprout hobbit statues, and if you're not careful, you just might venture into the Chocolate Fish café with feathers in your hair.

Of course, the feathers could open up a conversation with fellow diner Jill, also a California girl and an instant Sisterchick. Together they take in a performance at the Sydney Opera House in Australia; hold "hands" with a mama kangaroo and greet her in-pocket joey; watch dolphins surf the New Zealand waves; and discover that one's heart is likely to fall head over heels into a deeper sense of God's love.

ISBN 1-59052-411-X

A long-buried nightmare is unearthed when a paroled killer shows up in Detective John Russell's driveway

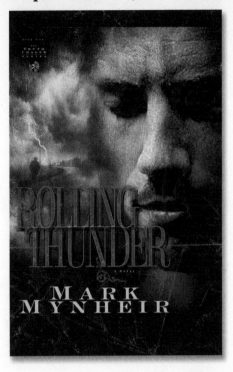

"A remarkable first novel, with strong action and a solid moral. Readers will eagerly await the next installment from Mark Mynheir."
—T. DAVIS BUNN, BESTSELLING AUTHOR

Rolling Thunder by MARK MYNHEIR

Ten-year-old Dylan Jacobs is missing from state care. John Russell is the team leader of the Florida Department of Law Enforcement task force trying to find him. Although the governor has declared this a top priority, all the team is turning up are corruption and crime. Meanwhile, John's own long-buried nightmare is unearthed when a paroled killer shows up in his driveway. He struggles to leave old horrors where they belong—in the past. Determined to protect her children and help her husband, his wife, Marie, does some investigating of her own. Because she soon realizes, what you don't know *can* hurt you.

ISBN 1-59052-376-8

COMING JUNE 2005!

Hotter than the eyes of hell...

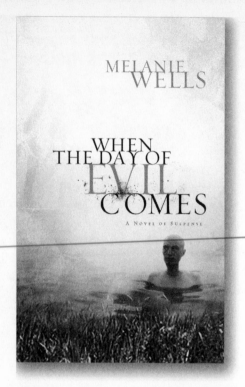

"*I saw the first fly alight on the edge of my plate during supper. This was no ordinary fly. It was huge. The size of a small Volkswagen. I could have painted daisies on it and sold rides to small children.*"

When the Day of Evil Comes by MELANIE WELLS

School is back in session, but for psychology professor Dylan Foster, the promise of a new semester is dying in the heat of the late Texas summer. First, there is the bizarre encounter with a ghastly pale stranger. Then her mother's engagement ring turns up—the same ring that was buried with her mother two years before. Soon, Dylan's carefully ordered world is unraveling, one thread at a time. She is about to get a crash course in spiritual warfare—and a glimpse of her own small but significant role in a vast eternal conflict. But when the dust settles, will anything be left of her life as she knows it?

ISBN 1-59052-426-8

Shocking Murder Destroys Deputy's Sense of Justice

Shattered Justice by bestselling author KAREN BALL

When Sheriff's deputy Dan Justice is called to the scene of a shooting, he feels like he's in a nightmare. He turns over the bodies and discovers a horrifying truth: two of the victims are those dearest to him. Dan's world falls apart. How can God be just in light of this crime? Can his sisters and small-town community—especially one woman who loves him—help Dan overcome this tragedy? Or will bitterness and anger shatter his entire soul?

ISBN 1-59052-413-6

COMING JULY 2005!

Can Money, Fame, and Power Buy Happiness?

Dark Star: Confessions of a Rock Idol
by CRESTON MAPES

Everett Lester and his band, DeathStroke, ride the crest of a wave that has catapulted them to superstardom. But the longer they're immersed in fame, wealth, and power, the more that drugs, alcohol, and loose discontentment threaten to swallow Everett whole. He's headed down a perilous road of no apparent return when he's charged with the murder of his personal psychic. The only hope he can cling to, his only reason for living, comes from Kansas. The compelling letters from a Christian woman cut straight to Everett's empty heart and threaten a fulfillment he's never known. But what if he's found guilty of murder? Will he recognize the spiritual battle that's raging for his soul?
ISBN 1-59052-472-1

COMING JULY 2005!